To Jessica
Dreams can come true!
Best Wishes

Darmi Mickel

Denise Chartier Bobola

Misplaced Magic

Misplaced Magic

Dormi Meckel &
Denise Chartier Bobola

Library of Congress Control Number: 2008907243
ISBN: Hardcover   978-1-4363-6348-8
               Softcover   978-1-4363-6347-1

This book was printed in the United States of America.

To order additional copies of this book, contact:
Xlibris Corporation
1-888-795-4274
www.Xlibris.com
Orders@Xlibris.com
51479

This book is dedicated to our families who endured our preoccupation with tolerance, support, and encouragement. And especially to our science advisor, Edward (Mr. Ed) Workman.

Author Biography

Denise Bobola and Dormi Meckel are alumnae of Madonna College and Transylvania University respectively.

The authors work fulltime jobs while caring for their families and various pets (familiars?) in an area of Pedestria southwest of Detroit, Michigan.

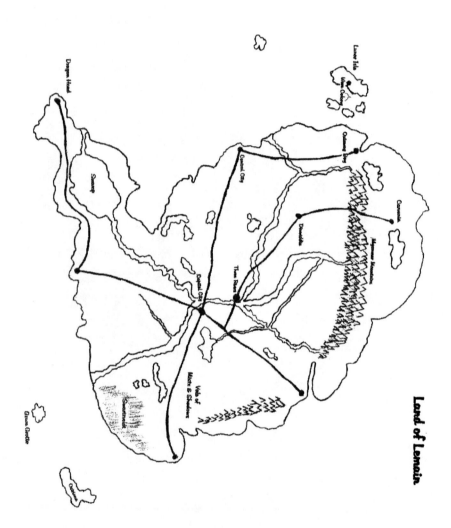

Land of Lenain

Hazelnut Cottage at Sunny Acres School

Woods

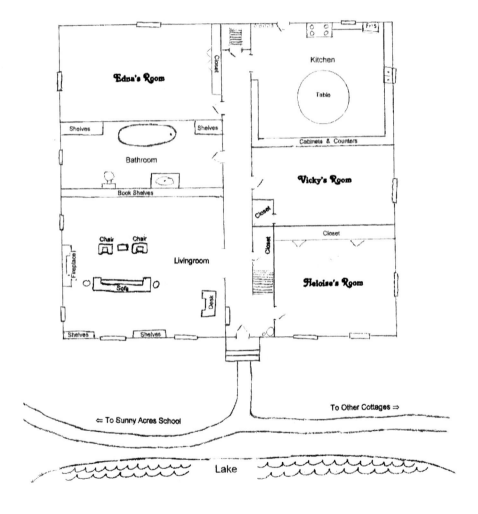

Edna's Room

Closet

Kitchen

Table

Shelves

Shelves

Cabinets & Counters

Bathroom

Vicky's Room

Book Shelves

Closet

Closet

Closet

Chair Chair

Livingroom

Heloise's Room

Fireplace

Sofa

Desk

Shelves

Shelves

⇐ To Sunny Acres School

To Other Cottages ⇒

Lake

Prologue

"Oof!" Edna Fitzsimmons grunted as she tumbled out of the mass transitor with a thud. No matter how clean and neat she was when she first entered a mass transitor, by the time she arrived at her destination, her hair would be tangled, her blouse would be spotted, and her skirt would be a wrinkled mess. This time, she had a skinned knee to add to the list. *Why didn't anyone else have these problems when transiting?* she wondered.

Mrs. Tenant called for their attention as she gave the class their last-minute instructions. "Remember that you are representing the Academy of Magic. This field trip is a treat, and if you expect to continue to receive them, you will behave responsibly. There will be no shenanigans."

The teacher frowned directly at Edna as the door of the building opened, and a young man wearing a brilliant white lab coat joined them. "Thank you for waiting, Mrs. Tenant. If you will follow me, we can begin the tour."

As the students lined up to follow their guide, Mrs. Tenant glanced over each one.

"Edna Fitzsimmons, straighten your vest," she chastised the pretty auburn-haired girl in the second row.

"Only you could get so wrinkled between the school and here," another girl with stringy blond hair snickered. Edna pulled at her green vest and smoothed her plaid skirt.

"Well, at least I can brush out the wrinkles, Hattie. You can't change your looks." Hattie stared venomously at Edna before turning to enter the laboratory. Inside, the class was split into two groups. To her dismay, Edna found herself in the same group as Hattie. Mrs. Tenant joined the other half of the class.

Their tour guide led them into a room lined with cages. "This is where we keep experimental animals," he began.

"What kind of experiments do you do on them?" Edna asked.

The guide looked startled. "There are many different experiments performed on the animals. It depends on the type of animal being used and what information we need at the time. You really need to step away from the cages," he snapped.

Edna looked more closely at the cage next to her. The occupant was a half-grown wolf. She saw the dimness in his eyes and the way his ribs were clearly outlined under his dull, tangled coat. "What information are you getting from starving this poor wolf half to death?" she asked in an accusing tone.

"We're not starving him," the man denied testily. "We've been feeding him twice a day since he was brought in. He just refuses to eat."

"The poor thing," Edna said again as the class group was led out of the room.

Hattie glared at her through thick glasses. "Don't be such a bleeding heart, Fitzsimmons," she sneered at Edna. "My grandmother runs this laboratory, and she has the Council's approval. The experiments are important to all of us, and after all, they're only animals."

"If the Council approves of this, then they're the animals. Maybe they should be kept locked up in cages," Edna hissed. "This is wrong, Hattie Homborg, and you know it. Someone needs to stop this mistreatment of defenseless animals."

"Well, it won't be you. You wouldn't have the nerve," Hattie taunted.

"You just wait and see, Hattie," Edna replied.

"Enough bickering, girls," Mrs. Tenant interrupted as she joined the group. "You're not giving a good impression of the Academy of Magic. It's time to return to school now. We're joining the rest of the class outside."

When they returned to the Academy of Magic, Edna did not even protest the extra work she was given in punishment for unbecoming conduct. She spent the rest of the afternoon brooding about what she had seen at the laboratory. The empty expression of the young wolf's eyes haunted her. "I will get him out of there," she told herself firmly. "They aren't taking proper care of him. I'm going back tonight, and I'll release all of them."

That night, Edna waited impatiently for her family to go to bed. Their farm was a little way outside of town, and she couldn't use a transitor without it being noticed, so it would take a while to reach the laboratory. She didn't dare ride one of the horses; it would make too much noise. When the house quieted down, Edna crept out of her bedroom window and started the journey into town.

It took over an hour to reach the Capital City Experimental Research Laboratory on foot. She circled the building, searching for a likely way in. "Well, look at that," she whispered in surprise upon seeing a doorway propped open. "Lucky for me this is a warm night. It's also good that these people are overconfident."

Slipping through the doorway, she started down the hallway, trying the doors as she went. Some of them were locked, but others turned out to be offices. Edna continued on until she found her way back to the room where the animals were kept.

She went first to the cage containing the malnourished wolf. The wolf opened his eyes and gazed at her apathetically before closing them again. "I'm getting you out of here," she told him, opening the cage door. "Come on, don't just lie there. You can't stay here, or you'll die." The wolf lay there quietly, only moving when she reached into the cage and pulled on his ruff. "Let's go," she urged. "I'm going to release the others too. None of you should have to stay here."

One by one, she opened the cages. The other animals didn't hesitate before jumping to the floor. The cats landed noiselessly, unlike the large bears, which lumbered down and moved toward the doorway. It took more time than she liked to head them all to the exit, especially because she had to make sure the poor starving wolf didn't fall behind. At the door, she waved them outside. "Run, all of you. You have to run fast and far. Don't let them catch you."

"What are you doing, girl?" a gruff voice demanded from behind her. "Stop them! You can't let them out!"

"Too late," Edna insisted defiantly. "I already did."

The security guard rushed over to the crystal screen. "Alert!" he said urgently. "There's been an escape! The experimental animals have been released. Send immediate assistance!"

"The Search and Recovery Squad has been deployed. Post a list with images if possible," answered a sharp female voice before disconnecting.

The guard turned back to Edna and told her sternly, "You have no idea what you've done. I'll have to notify the Council. You'll have a hearing for this, make no mistake about it."

Edna was held until morning in a small office in the Council building. From there, she was escorted in front of the Council Panel as the first on the agenda. As she was led to the front of the large dark-paneled chamber, Edna searched anxiously for her parents. She was saddened but not surprised to find them absent from this gathering since her family had never shown any affection toward her. She felt quite small and afraid as she looked up at the high bench dominating one side of the chamber and encountered the piercing stare of five sets of eyes belonging to the members of the Judicial Panel of the Lemain Magic Council. As tears welled in her eyes, she could almost hear Grandpa Vernon's voice in her ears. *Buck up, girl. Always remember, the only one you can truly depend on in this life is you! Don't waste your efforts blaming others for letting you down. Just make sure you don't let yourself down. You, and you alone, are responsible for your own fate.*

"This is a most severe offense. The animals in that laboratory were part of a crucial study," the chief arbiter spoke harshly.

"It's not right to cage them and then—"

The arbiter cut Edna off in midsentence. "You have no idea what was being done or how it will affect our lives. Not to mention the fact that there were creatures there that could seriously endanger people. If they aren't recovered, it could be a disaster."

"I didn't know, Your Honor," Edna said, hanging her head.

"That cannot be an excuse," the arbiter answered. "It's just fortunate that a message arrived alerting the guards to the break-in."

"Who sent the message?" Edna ventured tenuously.

"We haven't traced the message yet, but that is beside the point. Due to the serious nature of the offense, we find that we must send you to Aunt Mildred's Home for Wayward and Orphaned Witches. You will finish your schooling there."

"Wait! What about my parents?"

The arbiter consulted his notes. "Your parents have received the proper notification. Case concluded." He reached over and tapped the chime next to his left elbow with a small silver hammer, ending all further argument.

A stern witch stepped forward and tapped Edna's arm. "Come with me, girl. I'm to transport you to the school."

Edna dispiritedly accompanied her through a small door to one side of the bench. The guard escorted them to one of the small horseless black carriages used for transporting prisoners.

The trip to Aunt Mildred's was accomplished in silence. Edna stared out the small window with a mixture of curiosity and apprehension as they traveled through Capital City. Except for school and the occasional visit to the market, Edna hadn't been off the family farm since she was born.

As they approached the outskirts of the city, the carriage turned down a short lane lined with small neat houses. At the end of the lane was a large rambling Victorian-style house encircled with a wide veranda. The yellow house with peach—colored trim looked nothing at all like the dour prison Edna had imagined. When they arrived, the stern witch paused in the entrance hall. She scanned the area then called to a tall girl with wire-rimmed glasses and a long braid of light golden brown hair who was crossing the hallway. "Heloise, I need you to run an errand for me."

"Yes, Dame Beatrice," Heloise answered, "but Mrs. Thistlewaite is expecting me back in the kitchen."

"I'll inform her that you'll be along shortly. This is Edna Fitzsimmons. She will be in your section. Please show her to her quarters, and then you can take her with you to the kitchen. Aunt Mildred will be meeting with her tomorrow morning before class."

Heloise pointed Edna toward the stairway, and they started upstairs. The small sparsely furnished room was cheerfully decorated with pale yellow walls and floral window boxes. There were two school uniforms folded neatly on the end of one of the beds, as well as a box on the floor. "It looks like they were expecting me," Edna said wryly.

"Yes, probably," Heloise was matter-of-fact. "You should change into your uniform before we go down. The rest of your things can wait until later."

Edna changed into the dark gray skirt and sweater with a white blouse underneath. She smoothed the plain black stockings up her legs and tied the black oxfords.

"You had better take off the earrings," Heloise advised.

When Edna was ready, they started back toward the kitchen. "What's it like here?" Edna asked a little nervously.

"It's all right, I guess. We have classes every day, and we also have assigned tasks. I'm assigned to help Mrs. Thistlewaite in the kitchen. That's where we're going now. I usually work on dinner preparation. I'm in class before lunch of course, but I help prepare that on the weekends. Maybe you'll be assigned there too," she added.

"I wouldn't mind that. Is Mrs. Thistlewaite nice?"

"I think so. Her daughter, Agnes, works in the kitchen too. She's in our section though it's just because her mother works here. She's apprenticing in between classes. Here we are now."

Heloise opened the door and let Edna enter first. "Sorry I took so long," she said to a plump little witch. "This is Edna. She just got here."

"That's all right, Heloise," Mrs. Thistlewaite answered. "Dame Beatrice told me she sent you to get Edna settled. You can help Agnes with the potatoes, and Edna can start on the green beans." She flashed a warm smile at Edna.

They moved over to the table where a short thin girl with wild wisps of blond hair framing a face remarkably similar to Mrs. Thistlewaite's was standing. Edna watched with fascination as the girl peeled each potato with a deft wave of her wand. Heloise introduced Edna and Agnes then pulled a wand from her pocket, which she used on a knife that started chopping the peeled potatoes. Edna stared in dismay at the huge bowl of fresh green beans.

"Oh no," Edna moaned, "they took away my wand last night. How am I supposed to prepare these beans?"

Heloise looked from the bowl to Edna before replying, "Well, if you don't have your wand, I guess you'll just have to do it the Pedestrian way—by hand." She turned back to her chopping then continued, "We'll have time to get to know each other after dinner. You were coming up with us, weren't you, Agnes?"

"Sure. We still have homework to finish," Agnes reminded her. "We can help Edna get started on the lessons. It will be better if she already knows where we are in the books when she gets in to class tomorrow."

When their jobs were finished in the kitchen, Heloise showed Edna to the dining hall. Edna felt overwhelmed upon seeing the crowded tables. Even though there weren't as many students here as there were at her old school, she didn't know anyone here. Heloise introduced her to Amelia, the other girl in their section. Amelia was a small sharp-faced girl with mud brown hair, the ugliest glasses she'd ever seen, and a wine-stain birthmark on the side of her face. She glanced at Edna then turned back to the book she had propped against the milk pitcher. Heloise rolled her eyes and then grinned. They ate quickly and carried their plates over to the collection bin. Then they stopped in the kitchen to let Agnes know they were going upstairs to start their homework.

"Okay, I'll be right up. I just have to finish filing these recipe cards." She turned and picked up the lacquered black box where the recipe cards were stored.

"How pretty that is," Edna said, admiring the brightly colored stones on the lid.

"Thanks." Agnes smiled. "I'll tell you about it after our homework is finished."

When they reached their section's study room, Heloise spread her books and papers out on a table. Edna joined her and began looking at the books while they waited for Agnes. She was pleased to find that the lessons at Aunt Mildred's were pretty much equal to her classes at the Academy of Magic. As long as Heloise and Agnes were willing to help her with some of the minor discrepancies, she should do well in class.

Twenty minutes later, Agnes hurried in, and they started on their next day's assignments. When their homework was finished, they put the books away and started to talk. Agnes had brought up some snacks to share.

"I guess you've both heard why I'm here," Edna began.

Agnes glanced over at Heloise before answering. "We . . . It would be kind of hard to have missed it. There were alerts out everywhere."

"And even with a Council conviction, you're still willing to speak to me?"

Heloise smiled. "Of course we are. It's not like you did anything wrong. It sounded like those poor animals were suffering. You were only trying to help them. You just went about it the wrong way."

"You should have planned better so you wouldn't get caught," Agnes added.

"Thanks." Edna grimaced. "I'll remember that for next time. But then I wouldn't have gotten caught if someone hadn't turned me in."

"Who turned you in?" Agnes asked, wide-eyed.

"They said they didn't know, but it could only have been one person." Edna's eyes narrowed. "You wait, though. I'll find some way to get even."

"Just be careful," Heloise warned. "It's bad enough getting sent here. I don't think we want to know where they would put us next."

"They would probably put me in that filthy lab and do experiments on me," Edna grumbled. "But since you both know all about me, why don't you tell me how you got here."

Heloise's expression saddened. "I've been here five months," she began. "I lived over in Dinwiddie." She paused. "Do you know where that is?" When Edna nodded, she continued, "My parents owned the town bookstore, and we lived over the store. They heard about an estate auction on the other side of the mountains. There were some very rare books about vampires available, and they went to bid on them. The auction ran late, and they didn't start home until after dark. The mountain trolls killed them," she finished, her voice breaking.

"Why did you get sent here?" Edna pressed.

"I don't have any other relatives," Heloise told her. "Since there was no one else to take me, I was sent here."

There was a moment of awkward silence before Edna turned to Agnes. "How about you?" she asked.

"Well, my mother is the cook here. The women in our family have been cooks for generations. We always store our family recipes in that black box you were asking about. It's been passed down from mother to daughter almost forever. My mother got it from my great aunt Enid. Grandma died when Mom was a little girl, but when she was old enough, Great Aunt Enid gave it to her. It's the only thing we have from Grandma," Agnes finished.

"What about your father?" Edna asked.

"He went on an archeological dig in Osiriana right after I was born. The reports my mother got said he left to retrieve some equipment and never returned, so I never really knew him."

"Oh, I'm so sorry," Edna gasped.

"It's all right." Agnes shrugged her shoulders. "I think it's part of a family curse or something. Shortly after a female child is born, the father dies or disappears. It happens to all the women in my family."

"So you're going to be a cook?" Edna continued after a brief silence.

"Yes, that's why I'm learning how to cook for large gatherings."

"Maybe since we're helping, we could learn too," Edna suggested. "Then we could all work together."

"That sounds like a great idea," Heloise decided.

"I think so too," agreed Agnes. "I think it would be perfect."

"Great, then we have a plan." Edna smiled. "We'll start learning more tomorrow."

"Okay then, I'll see you in the morning," Agnes said, gathering her things and starting back to her mother's quarters.

"Good night," chorused Heloise and Edna.

Chapter 1

"Everything's looking good so far," whispered Edna as she glided next to Heloise who was levitating a pan of dirty dishes out of the banquet hall. Both witches were dressed in the regulation mauve-and-teal uniform jumpsuits of food service workers in Lemain. Heloise had to agree with her friend and business partner as she gazed around the glowing gold and white marble hall filled with five hundred of the most important witches and wizards in Capital City. No expense had been spared.

The immense crystal chandeliers bathed the hall with brilliant, sparkling, refracted rainbows of light. The long oak tables were beautiful in their own right, having been extensively polished with rose oil by hundreds of gnome slaves for centuries. They were further enhanced with delicate lace table clothes from the elf kingdom of Shahara. This unstated support of the nonhumanoid creatures of Lemain didn't sit too well with the old hidebound members of the current political party in power. This celebration feast marked the culmination of the most successful year they'd had since starting their catering business, Enchanting Edibles, after leaving Aunt Mildred's. They had eked out a meager existence catering private birthday parties and the occasional office Christmas party for the first couple of years. So they were surprised and thrilled when Oswald Thurgood had hired them to cater one of his campaign dinners. Then Thurgood's wife, Cordelia, began hiring them for her frequent and lavish tea parties. After that, they found themselves in great demand throughout Capital City.

The only dark spot was the animosity they experienced from some of the tradespeople and other catering companies whose businesses were suffering due to their fame and good fortune. There had even been a few instances of attempted sabotage by their rivals, but today everything seemed to be going perfectly.

All the celebrants seemed to be having a good time, a very good time—too good in fact.

"Edna, what did you do to the punch?" hissed Heloise.

"I just added a little Enhancement Elixir to liven things up," replied Edna with a smug smile.

"Oh dear," groaned Heloise, "well, you'd better keep an eye on the guests. Secretary Brooks of Health and Welfare is beginning to float out of his chair."

"Oops, sorry," muttered Edna. "By the way, is Agnes ready for President Thurgood's inaugural speech?"

"I believe so," answered Heloise as they craned their necks to peer around the hall. "Oh yes, there she is by the large cauldron in the corner behind the podium."

They concentrated their gaze on the witch and the cauldron in the far corner. Even though Agnes was the undisputed master chef of their catering business, she was also the best at creating whatever special effects the customer wanted. As Edna and Heloise watched, Agnes added a pinch of powder to the cauldron, causing it to hiss and sputter and boil even more furiously than before.

Edna turned toward Heloise. "I have no idea what she is doing, but from the looks of that cauldron, I think the grand finale is ready."

"Either that, or we're about to witness the greatest explosion since Mount Venusia," muttered Heloise.

Just then, a loud trumpet fanfare was heard throughout the hall; and the newly elected president of the Magic Council, Oswald Thurgood, ascended to the podium. Thurgood was a tall thin man with aquiline features and silver hair. Dressed in the dark purple robes of his new office, he looked as regal as the ancient kings as he stood on the podium waiting for the applause to subside.

"Thank you, everyone, for joining me to celebrate our grand victory in the recent election," began President Thurgood. Thunderous applause, cheers, and a few whistles were heard from every table. "Since this is a party, I won't bore you with a long speech, not today anyway," continued Thurgood with a chuckle. "As I'm sure you remember from the campaign, one of the last things my esteemed rival for this office said to me was, 'You'll get the president's chair when pigs fly!' Well, this is my response!" With a flourish, Thurgood pointed to Agnes, who finished her incantation with a flick of her wand at the large black cauldron in front of her. Immediately, bright pink pigs with white feathery wings came pouring out of the cauldron to fly around the hall.

The guests' shrieks of delight soon turned to shrieks of terror as the pigs began attacking the food still on the tables and even some of the guests. Soon, the entire hall was hysterical mayhem as guests scrambled for cover under the tables or raced for the doors.

"What did you do?" shouted Edna and Heloise as they rushed to Agnes.

"President Thurgood asked for flying pigs, so I gave him flying pigs," replied Agnes calmly as she surveyed the surrounding chaos.

"This is a disaster. We're ruined," moaned Heloise as she left to help President Thurgood pull a grunting pig off his wife's ample lap.

Edna whirled on Agnes. "Agnes, you nitwit, he meant the illusion of flying pigs, not actual pigs! Now get rid of them!"

"Oh very well," sniffed Agnes as she began the spell to remove the ravening pigs from the hall. "But people really should be more explicit when requesting special effects. Otherwise there's no telling what they might get."

After the pigs had been disposed of and all evidence of their disastrous attack removed, the guests settled down to await the finishing touch to the banquet: dessert. In the kitchen area just off the banquet hall, President Thurgood addressed the caterers.

"If you mess up one more thing during this banquet, just one more, I personally will make you pay dearly for your error!" growled Thurgood. After a meaningful glare at the three witches, he returned to the hall.

"All right then, not too bad, huh?" asked Edna with a bright smile. "Let's get the cake ready." Heloise and Agnes looked at each other and, with an anxious shake of their heads, turned to follow Edna over to the cake. The cake was a five-tiered creation roughly the size of a farm wagon and gaudily decorated with icing in the official Magic Council colors of scarlet, violet, and gold. As they approached the cake, Heloise brought them to a halt.

"Wait! Is there anything that could possibly be wrong with this cake?"

Frowning thoughtfully, Agnes answered slowly, "I followed the usual recipe and used all the regular ingredients."

"And it's been sitting right here all during the banquet," Edna added helpfully.

They turned at the slamming of the door to face the irate secretary of the treasury, Hattie Homborg. "What are you waiting for?" screeched Secretary Homborg, her hooked-nosed, pockmarked face red with rage. "Bring out that damn cake—now!"

Sharing the briefest of glances, the three caterers sprang into action. Agnes and Heloise hurriedly started pushing the wheeled platform the cake rested on while Edna held the door to the hall open.

The cake entered the banquet hall to appreciative oohs and aahs as President Thurgood stepped forward with a knife the size of a broadsword to cut the first piece. The moment the knife pierced the first tier of the cake, there was a deafening explosion followed by chunks of cake with gooey multicolored frosting flying across the hall.

Over the screams of the guests could be heard President Thurgood, shouting, "That's the last straw! Get the caterers! I want them out of Lemain within the hour!"

Chapter 2

"How much longer, Heloise?" growled Edna as she stormed into the tiny wood-paneled office.

Glancing over her tortoiseshell half-glasses, Heloise rebuked, "Really, Edna, I do wish you would be quieter. This is a library after all."

"Yeah, okay, whatever," Edna grumbled as she flopped into a faded green armchair. She gazed through the door opening into the main library. Rows upon rows of floor-to-ceiling bookshelves were the only things she saw. There was nary a person in sight.

Heaving a sigh, Heloise replied, "Forty-five years, two months, and six hours, give or take."

"This is totally outrageous. It's completely unfair," Edna ranted as Heloise resumed her seat behind the massive battered wooden desk.

Heloise was silent for a moment as she studied her old friend. The past five years had been hard on all of them, but Edna's overly emotional temperament seemed to make their punishment more difficult for her to bear. Heloise had helped her friend through many rough spots over the years, but not since their days at Aunt Mildred's Home for Wayward and Orphaned Witches had she seen her friend and companion this upset. Putting as much compassion as she could into her voice, she asked, "What's wrong, Edna? What's happened to upset you so?"

"What's . . . wrong?" Edna stammered, turning angry, flashing wild-green eyes at Heloise. "I'll tell you what's wrong," she continued. "The Council should never have sent us here in the first place! That's what's wrong! This punishment is supremely unjust!"

"Well, we did rather make a mess of things at the Council president's inauguration banquet," observed Heloise.

"That was an accident!" Edna cried vehemently as she shot out of the chair and began pacing, her long auburn hair swinging with a life of its own. "It wasn't our fault," she continued, beginning to tick items off with her fingers. "First, they insisted that we do our civic duty by rendering free service to the local community to promote favorable publicity for the Unified Witchcraft and Wizardry Council. Then they give out all the plum assignments and stick us with that foul-smelling toad farmer. Then at the last moment, we get hired to cater the banquet." Edna abruptly stopped pacing and glared down at Heloise. "Under those circumstances, anyone could be expected to make a few minor mistakes."

Heloise took a sip of her tea and coughed, trying to hide a smile as she remembered the scene so long ago of staid, officious witches and wizards scrambling under tables and racing for the doors to avoid flying chunks of cake. Having gotten her mirth under control momentarily, she replied, "Well, I guess the Council just failed to see the humor in the situation."

"That's my point exactly!" raged Edna. "Why should we have to pay the price simply because the Council lacks a sense of humor?"

Pushing her chair back from the desk, Heloise started, "First off, we got a very good deal with our attorney's plea bargain. Fifty years exile with the stipulation of no witchcraft is a lot better than what President Thurgood wanted to do with us." Then she shivered, remembering. "Second, at least some of the Council members have a sense of humor. Have you seen any of the illustrated children's books lately?"

"You don't mean," Edna gasped, wide-eyed. Heloise nodded. "I always thought that picture of the witch in Hansel and Gretel looked a lot like Hattie Homborg from the treasury department," Edna laughed. "Wonder who sent that picture to the Pedestrians," she chuckled.

"Okay," Edna grudgingly agreed. "Maybe we did get what we deserved, but even the Pedestrians have a system of early parole for good behavior. Why don't we have a system like that? And of all places, how on earth did we wind up in a remote mountain range at Sunny Acres School for the Gifted?"

After many years in this friendship, Heloise realized that they were now getting close to the real cause of her friend's current problem, so she said, "Well, Sunny Acres seemed like the place we could all use our abilities the best. You in the administrative office, me with my books in the library, and Agnes in the kitchen. Now,what is really bothering you?"

Sitting back in the green armchair, Edna let her shoulders droop. "It's that Wilkins boy," she muttered.

Heloise looked at her inquisitively. "Jason or Jeremy?" she asked.

"What?" exclaimed Edna. "There are two of them?"

"Of course," replied Heloise, "they're twins."

"Oh great," groaned Edna. "So one or the other or both is making my life a living nightmare. Every time something goes wrong, I look around and see . . . ," she paused, "well . . . a Wilkins boy."

She continued, "Remember when I stayed up for forty-eight hours straight typing the school's annual fiscal report? The next morning, when I entered my office, I found the report solidified into an eight-and-a-half-by-eleven-inch polymer briquette because it had been soaked in superglue. Two weeks ago, I found ink spilled in the office aquarium. And since tropical fish are finicky about their living conditions to begin with, the ink was the last straw for most of them. I spent most of the day holding services for the dearly departed over the faculty toilet and requisitioning replacements. Last week, in search of a stapler for the one hundred copies of the school's academic accreditation report that I'd spent three days copying and collating, Wilkins tripped me in the hall. And I had to start the collating process all over again. After each of these incidences, I would look around and find one of the Wilkins boys nearby. But before I could say anything, the class bell would ring, and he'd be gone. Oooh, it's so frustrating, I could scream!"

Ever the diplomat, Heloise bit her tongue to refrain from reminding her friend that she had already done that not fifteen minutes earlier in this very office. Instead, she tried consoling Edna by reminding her, "After all, these are just boys. They're only fourteen years old, and all fourteen-year-olds will play pranks."

Slowly an evil gleam crept into Edna's eye. "Pranks, is it? They want to play pranks with me, do they? They haven't seen pranks the likes of what I'll show them."

Suddenly worried, Heloise snapped, "Edna, you wouldn't!"

With her most coy and innocent look, Edna replied, "Nothing serious, I was just thinking that a good case of boils on the backside would serve them right."

"Boils!" Heloise exclaimed. "Edna, you didn't!"

"Didn't what?" Edna asked.

"There have been three cases of infectious boils reported in the infirmary this week," Heloise explained. "Oh, Edna," she breathed, "please tell me this wasn't your doing?"

"Me!" exclaimed Edna. "Of course it wasn't me! I would like nothing better than to give some of the students at the illustrious Sunny Acres School for the Gifted a good case of boils, but it's just a pleasant daydream. If there really is an outbreak of backside boils, maybe housekeeping isn't disinfecting the toilet seats well enough."

Heloise looked at her curiously. "There's one thing I don't understand. You're the school administrator. How did you miss the fact that there are two boys?"

"Well, it shouldn't be that difficult to understand," Edna said defensively. "All I ever see are the reports. When I got a report for either Jeremy Wilkins or Jason Wilkins, I just assumed that someone spelled the name wrong. Really, people should show more imagination when naming their children."

At that moment, a black-and-silver ring-tailed ball of fur streaked over the desk, up Edna's arm, and wrapped itself tightly around her neck. Immediately, upon its heels appeared a short figure wearing a chef's uniform with frizzled blond hair sticking out from under the cap and brandishing a large wooden spoon. "Edna," shrieked the face under the chef's cap, "keep that obnoxious varmint out of my kitchen, or I swear it will end up in next week's surprise stew!"

"Agnes, please keep your voice down," Heloise hissed vehemently at the white-clad figure. "Remember, this—"

"Is a library, and we must be quiet at all times," chimed in Edna and Agnes.

"Well," sniffed Heloise, "if you know the rules so well, I don't see why you can't obey them."

"Oh, chill out, Heloise," chided Edna as she stroked the soft fur of her raccoon familiar, Rapscallion. Turning to Agnes, she sighed and asked, "Okay, what did Rap do this time?"

Before Agnes could respond, a small husky voice murmured in Edna's ear. "I did nothing objectionable. I was merely practicing quality control to ensure that the dinner was fit for both humans and raccoons."

"It Wasn't That Simple!" Agnes began, then blushed, and glanced at Heloise. "Sorry," she whispered. "That mangy furball ran through my kitchen sticking his paws in everything from the soup to the custard and, aside from upsetting all the kitchen staff, contaminated the entire dinner."

"Humph!" snorted Rap in Agnes's direction. "Humans always overreact to the most insignificant things."

"Okay okay," Edna stage-whispered. "Let's not make a Council case out of a molehill. Agnes, can you still serve the dinner if you cast a decontaminant spell over the food?"

"Well, I suppose that would work if I was allowed to cast a spell," replied Agnes reluctantly. "But you know what will happen if I'm caught using magic. Really, Edna, you should have more control over that animal."

Just then, a glowing orb appeared in front of them with a man's head inside. In a deep bass voice that always reminded Edna of hot fudge being slowly poured over a mountain of ice cream, Rory Van der Haven asked, "Did I just hear someone suggesting the forbidden use of magic?"

Blushing furiously, Edna stammered, "Of course not, Rory. We know better than . . . to do anything . . . like that."

Rory smiled a smile that set off his sleek black hair and brilliant blue eyes to perfection. His brilliant smile also created a faint feeling of fluttering butterflies in the stomach for Edna though she'd never admit it.

"Oh good," he replied, "because I'd hate to include such an offense in my report. Actually, I didn't come to spy on you." He continued in a more serious tone, "I wanted to give you a warning. I've been hearing some strange rumors around the Department of

Magical Justice that I think you should know. It seems someone wants your sentence to be permanent."

"What?" cried Edna, Heloise, and Agnes in unison. "Who?" "How?" "Why?" Each of the witches fired at the wizard in the orb.

"Just calm down," Rory said in his most soothing voice. "All I know is that someone has been spreading rumors that you were getting your catering supplies from the swamp trolls."

Heloise gasped, "That's absolutely not true!"

Agnes simply stood there with her wooden spoon drooping at her side and her mouth and eyes as wide as they could possibly be. All the color had drained from Edna's face, and her hands were clenched at her sides.

"When I find out who started that rumor, they're dead meat!" she growled.

"Hmmmm, I rather thought that would be your reaction," murmured Rory. "So far, whoever it is hasn't convinced the Council to make your banishment permanent, but I worry that they may take drastic and more direct action to prevent you from returning to Lemain. So please be careful, and watch your backs. Oh, and by the way," he whispered to Agnes, "I agree that the decontaminant spell should save your dinner." Rory smiled once more and winked at Edna, and the orb disappeared.

Heloise and Agnes stared in astonishment at Edna for a moment while Edna gazed smiling at the spot where the orb had been. "Okay," said Agnes, "what was that all about?"

"Yes," added Heloise, "Edna dear, is there something you haven't told us?"

Edna blushed and dropped her eyes. "It's nothing really," she replied. "When we got into all that trouble with President Thurgood, I thought it would be a good idea to cultivate a friendship with someone in the Department of Justice."

"Um, of course," Heloise muttered as she slowly shifted her attention to Agnes, who was still staring at Edna with a stunned look of total disbelief. "Agnes dear," Heloise continued, "don't you have a dinner to repair?"

Agnes started as though waking from a trance.

"Oh yes," chimed in Edna, "what are you serving this evening?"

Smiling brightly, Agnes replied, "We'll begin the meal with frog leg soup and cricket salad."

"Are you out of your mind?" shouted Edna and Heloise together. Heloise sank into the armchair with her head in her hands as Edna tried to reason with Agnes.

"Don't you realize that you'll be tossed out on your ear if the parents ever find out you're feeding that kind of food to their little darlings? Not that I wouldn't mind slipping them a couple of nightshade cocktails myself," she muttered. "Why don't you feed them the regular Pedestrian food?" As a frown began to form on Agnes's brow, Edna quickly added, "You know, macaroni and cheese or something with marshmallows—all kids like marshmallows."

Looking up from where she sat, Heloise said, "Whatever made you decide to serve such archaic Lemain foods all of a sudden?"

"I was looking through my closet today when a package fell off the top shelf. Lo and behold, it was my mother's recipe box. I hadn't even realized I had packed it in our hurry to leave Lemain," Agnes said excitedly.

"Well, whatever you're serving, you'd better get busy. It's almost dinnertime now!"

"Oh dear," squeaked Agnes as she ran from the room.

Edna smirked at Heloise, "This should be a very interesting dinner. Shall we get ready?"

A tiny spot of crimson appeared on each of Heloise's cheeks as she got to her feet and smoothed her skirt. "Actually, I have other plans for the evening," she said with a slight smile.

Now it was Edna's turn to look astonished since they had always attended the school meals together. "And just what might those plans be?" she inquired.

"If you must know, I have a date with Leonard Marshall," Heloise replied.

"Ooh, goody!" Edna exclaimed as she perched on the edge of the desk with Rapscallion in her lap. "Come on, give me the juicy details," she demanded of her friend.

Heloise began her explanation as she paced around her office. "As you know, I've been helping Leonard do research for his medieval history study, and he wanted to repay me by taking me into Laurelwood for dinner and a concert in the park."

Just then, there came a soft knocking at the office doorjamb, which Agnes hadn't closed in her haste to return to the kitchen; and the women looked up to see a tall man with wavy chestnut hair, soft brown eyes, and a pleasant, if somewhat nervous, smile standing there.

"Oh, hello, Leonard," Heloise said breathlessly. "Have you met my friend Edna Fitzsimmons?"

"Yes, indeed, you work in the admissions office, I believe," Leonard Marshall answered as he strode forward to shake Edna's hand. "How pleasant to see you again, Ms. Fitzsimmons."

Edna hopped down from her perch on Heloise's desk, dumping Rap unceremoniously on the floor to shake Leonard Marshall's hand. "Nice to see you, Mr. Marshall." Edna smiled, noting his tweed jacket with leather elbow patches and his comical green plaid bow tie. "I've got to be going. You two have a nice evening," Edna said cheerfully. Turning to Heloise with a wicked grin, she whispered, "I expect a complete report when you get back." With that, she whirled out of the office.

Heloise smiled shyly at Leonard. Normally a confident, take-charge sort of person, she suddenly felt very nervous about going on a date with a man. She'd spent most of her life with her books and in the company of her friends Edna and Agnes. Except for the occasional dance she was forced into with one of the students who came to Aunt Mildred's from Brother Timothy's School for Boys during holiday balls, she'd never had any social interaction with members of the opposite sex.

"Um . . . I'll get my shawl," Heloise stammered. Leonard just stood by the door, smiling. Heloise went to the closet behind her desk. *Why oh why did I ever think keeping this date a secret was a good idea? I have no clue how to act on a date! I should have asked Edna for advice. She'd know what to do.*

She took the pale gray angora shawl from the hook on the inside of the closet door and wrapped it around her shoulders. She closed the closet door and stared at Leonard's smiling face. Taking a deep breath, she returned his smile. *Oh well, he's always been a perfect gentleman while we were doing research. I just hope he doesn't turn out to be a wolf in sheep's clothing.*

Following Rap down the bright spacious corridor, Edna pondered her choices for the evening. Usually, she and Heloise would enjoy Agnes's dinner in the main dining room with the rest of the faculty, staff, and students; however, with the advent of Heloise's date with

Leonard Marshall and the chaos in the kitchen, dining at the school didn't hold much appeal.

Stopping at the large mullioned window of the corridor's southeast corner, Edna gazed over the tops of vividly colored trees to the cottage nestled in the valley on the shore of the lake. Hazelnut cottage had been "home" for Edna and Heloise since they first arrived in the Pedestrian world. The late-afternoon autumn sunlight sparkled like diamonds on the surface of the remote mountain lake and bathed their quaint cottage with an inviting rosy glow. Suddenly, Edna could think of nothing she would like better than a hyacinth-scented bubble bath followed by a glass of crisp white Rhine wine and a peanut butter and dill pickle sandwich.

Scooping Rap up in her arms, Edna hurried down the steep stairs from the library wing. "Excuse me," Rap mumbled. "Is there a fire in the building of which I am unaware? Because that is the only reason I can conceive of for such unseemly haste."

"Do you want a nice can of tuna for dinner, or would you rather see what you can snag out of the lake?" snarled Edna.

"Uh . . . er . . . I . . . well tuna would be preferable," stammered Rap.

"Then shush!" Edna continued her rapid descent of the five flights of stairs as Rap wrapped his paws around her neck.

"But where are we to have this wonderful repast?" Rap asked as they passed the floor for the dining hall, from which they could already hear the scuffing of chairs and the clink of utensils.

"We're going home, of course," replied Edna with exasperation.

"Home?" squeaked Rap. "Did the Council rescind their verdict?"

"Of course not, you nitwit, home to the cottage."

Rap's only answer was a dejected "Oh" as he slumped against her shoulder. Never slowing, Edna tried to smile pleasantly at passing students and faculty as she made her way, hair and skirt flying, down the main hall to the front doors of the school.

Once outside the front doors, Edna set Rap down and took a deep breath of the crisp autumn air. *This would be a wonderful place to live if only the circumstances were different. As far as punishments went, banishment to this place wasn't bad at all,* Edna thought as she turned to admire the school. The five-story edifice with its square corner towers, made entirely with pale gray granite blocks quarried from the local mountains, was a beautiful and impressive sight bathed in the rays of the setting sun.

She thoroughly enjoyed the mountain environment with its changing seasons—the renewal of life in spring with flowering buds on the trees and soft green shoots of grass, the warm breezes and vibrant colors of summer, the thrilling contrast of the cool and crisp air wafting through fiery leaves in the fall, and even the frozen white silence of winter—as long as she could enjoy it from the comfort of an armchair beside the fireplace. She'd also enjoyed becoming acquainted with the deer, foxes, rabbits, squirrels, woodchucks, and, of course, raccoons living in the forest.

Edna smiled serenely as she and her familiar crossed the sloping lawn toward the path leading through the trees. After only a few steps into the dense shadows, Edna and Rap stopped short. Where most people considered the woods to be quiet, Edna was familiar with all the sounds that nature usually contained—the whirring of bird's wings, the rustle of undergrowth from small animals, the cracking of twigs from larger animals, and the chirring of insects. But now the forest was absolutely silent.

"What's wrong?" whispered Edna to Rap.

"I'm not sure," Rap whispered back. "Let me reconnoiter." As Edna stealthily followed Rap into the deeper gloom of the path, her unease grew.

When Rap had advanced about twenty yards, the area erupted in the chitinous, scrabbling sound of hundreds of thousands of insect legs. The attackers were six-inch-long pale gray creatures with hundreds of tiny legs, a two-pronged stinger tail, horns, and razor-sharp teeth.

The creatures advanced quickly toward Rap. Fueled by fear and adrenaline, Edna frantically searched the ground for a weapon. Grabbing a three-foot section of a tree limb, she started swinging at the wicked-looking things attacking her familiar.

She spent several panicked minutes ferociously bashing the creatures, trying to reach Rap. No matter how many of them she killed, more came swarming out of the woods.

Rap shot her a frantic look and screamed, "Run, mistress! I will hold them off!" Then he was overcome. Edna stared in shock for the briefest of moments, but when they turned toward her, she dropped her crude club and ran.

Chapter 3

"Oh my, Leonard, I wasn't expecting all this!" Heloise exclaimed.

"Is anything wrong?" he asked, eyeing her warily.

"Not at all," she answered in surprise. "I just didn't think you'd go to this much trouble."

"It's not any trouble," Leonard answered, looking around the room. They were in a homey Italian restaurant with friendly service and excellent food. It also had the perfect Italian ambiance, with red-and-white checked tablecloths topped by empty Chianti bottles serving as makeshift candleholders. "I wanted to take you somewhere nice, and I remembered that you said you enjoy classical music. You were so much help on that project. It would have taken me much longer to do all that research, and it's likely I would have missed a lot of those references you showed me." Leonard smiled shyly.

"I'm sure you would have found everything you needed," Heloise laughed. "You were doing your own research before I met you."

"I would have found it eventually," Leonard agreed. "But it would have taken longer. Also, it was interesting working with someone else. I haven't done that often."

When they finished their meal, they left for the bandstand in the park. Some people had spread blankets out and were having a picnic. There were also chairs set up on one side of the park. Leonard guided her over to the chairs, and they sat just as the small orchestra filed on stage. Heloise quickly fell under the spell of the music; however, Leonard found his attention wandering. *Meeting Heloise's friend . . . What is her name again? Oh yes, Edna.* She was very much on his mind. *Something about her is familiar if I could just put my claw—no, finger—on it.* He pondered throughout the concert, worrying at it like a dog with a bone.

> The young wolf skulked into the dark alley to avoid the Search and Recovery Squad. He nosed his way under a large empty carton as the alleyway was flooded with light. He needed to escape the city and return home, but the squad was making that difficult. He knew there had been several recoveries made. He had seen Leander taken just that morning.
>
> He whimpered softly from under the carton. The most serious hindrance to his escape was not the squad, but his weakness. He had to find something to eat. They had no idea how to care for him or what he needed to eat. The girl who released them should have made better plans. Chasing them out of the building and telling them not to get caught was not really very helpful.

Leonard's eyes snapped open. That was who Heloise's friend reminded him of. She looked like the girl who released him from the laboratory. *But it couldn't be . . . could it?* He had a feeling he would be keeping a closer eye on Edna Fitzsimmons than he had previously. He was grateful that Heloise hadn't noticed his distraction.

"The forest is full of quatos!" shrieked Edna. Agnes turned from the coatrack where she had just hung up her pristine white chef's jacket to reveal a dingy gray Witches and Wizards University (WWU) tee shirt. Agnes carefully studied her friend for any evidence of wounds while recalling what she knew of quatos. Quatos are evil magical beasts with a hundred legs, the tail of a scorpion, horns on the head, dozens of razor-sharp teeth, and possessed of extremely potent venom.

"Do they have them here?" Agnes asked with astonishment.

"If they didn't, I guess they do now!" shouted Edna.

"No no no," answered Agnes. "I mean are quatos supposed to be in the Pedestrian world?"

Pausing for a deep breath, Edna thought a moment. "I don't remember ever hearing them mentioned in our Pedestrian studies class, do you? The only place I know that they can be found, until now, is in the Schwartzvelt back home. Oh, I wish Heloise were here. She'd know what to do."

"Heloise isn't here? Where has she gone?" queried Agnes anxiously.

"She had a date with Leonard Marshall for dinner and a concert in Laurelwood."

"Where is Rap?" asked Agnes.

With a moan, Edna slid to the floor. "He stayed behind to distract them so I could escape," she answered.

"Oh my goodness!" Agnes exclaimed, her hands flying to her mouth. "Are his shielding spells strong enough to ward them off this long?"

"I'm not sure," sobbed Edna, dropping her head into her hands. Just then, the office door creaked open, and a very bedraggled and ragged-looking raccoon entered. "Rap!" Edna cried as she ran across the floor to her injured familiar.

Rap looked bad. Several patches of fur were missing from his back, and his tail could no longer be described as bushy. His left ear looked as though it had been put through a single-cut paper shredder, and blood dripped from three deep scratches on his nose.

"I eluded the monsters, mistress," Rap said weakly. "I'm so glad you were able to escape." At that, his eyes rolled up in his head, and he fell on his side.

Agnes was the first to speak. "He's obviously been poisoned. What are we going to do?"

"We've got to get him to a qualified veterinarian. These Pedestrian animal doctors would have no idea how to treat this," Edna insisted. "I'm going to have to contact the Department of Magical Justice. Just pray that Rory is on duty."

"Do you really think that's the best thing to do?" queried Agnes.

"That's the Only thing to do!" shouted Edna, cradling Rap's body in her arms.

"If he doesn't get the proper treatment immediately, he'll die!"

Agnes stepped back as Edna invoked the spell for communicating with the Department of Magical Justice. In a few moments, a glowing orb appeared suspended in midair with the bespectacled face of a frizzy red-haired witch unknown to either of them. "What is the nature of the call?" the witch in the orb asked in clipped tones.

"Is Rory Van der Haven there?" asked Edna frantically.

"I'll check. Please hold," replied the witch who then disappeared from the orb. During what seemed an interminable length of time, actually about thirty seconds, Edna and Agnes exchanged fearful looks. Finally, Rory's handsome face appeared in the orb.

"What seems to be the problem?" he asked calmly. As Edna tearfully explained what had happened, his face took on a menacing frown.

"Stand back," he said sternly. "I'm opening an interdimensional portal."

An eight-foot shimmering oval suddenly appeared in the middle of Agnes's small office. Rory stepped through the oval and immediately went to Edna and scooped Rap out of her arms. As Rory examined the limp raccoon, Edna tremulously asked, "Will he be all right?"

Rory raised a worried face to her and smiled. "His heartbeat and aura are still strong. We have an emergency veterinarian on call. I think he'll make it."

"Oh, thank you," Edna cried as she hugged Rory and seriously squeezed Rap between them.

"Don't go anywhere. I'll have to get a full report of what happened," Rory ordered Agnes and Edna and disappeared.

Agnes and Edna gazed at each other for a moment after Rory's departure then cried, "Heloise!"

"She's out on a date. She'll be going home to the cottage, and we've got to warn her!" Edna looked imploringly at Agnes. "We've got to use Coco to send her a message."

"But"—Agnes looked protectively at her cockatoo familiar on a perch in the corner of her office—"she's not familiar with this geography. She could get lost!"

Edna couldn't believe what she was hearing. "I was attacked in the forest by quatos. Rap is almost dead, and Heloise is out on a date from which she will probably be returning straight to the cottage—the last place any of us should be—and you're worried about your stupid bird getting lost?"

"Oh, very well," responded Agnes. "You write the note while I get Coco."

As Edna quickly scribbled a note telling Heloise to return to the school kitchen and not to go near the forest or their cottage, Agnes coaxed the cockatoo off her perch. After tying the note to Coco's leg and explaining what she was to do, Agnes released her into the night sky from the kitchen's back door.

"Would you like to stop for coffee before I take you back to school?" Leonard asked as the concert ended.

"Thank you, I'd like that," Heloise answered.

They went to a small café where they could have their coffee on an outdoor patio. Owing to the coolness of the evening, they had the patio to themselves.

Heloise sat at the small wrought iron table and gazed at the tiny white lights decorating the trees that surrounded the patio while she waited for Leonard to return with their coffee.

"You don't live at the school, do you?" Heloise questioned Leonard as he set a steaming mug topped with a generous dollop of whipped cream before her.

"No, I don't. I live here in town," he explained before smiling disparagingly. "Well, it's just barely in town. It's right on the edge of the forest. It's just a small place. We don't need much."

"Oh, I thought you lived alone," Heloise said, confused and a little disappointed.

"I live with my mother. I told her how much you've helped me with my research. You can probably expect her thanks in the form of some baked goods sometime soon."

"Oh, that's really not necessary, Leonard," Heloise said, flustered.

She attempted to change the subject and was asking about Leonard's next research project when a beautiful white cockatoo landed on the table and hopped over to her. She began to detach the note from the bird's leg when she noticed Leonard's startled expression.

"Don't be so surprised, Leonard," she laughed lightly. "I thought you would have noticed I have some rather . . . unique friends. They never manage to follow the conventional path."

"I understand," Leonard assured her hesitantly. "Academia is full of people who are true individuals."

"It certainly is," she agreed while scanning the note.

Heloise,
Do not return to the cottage.
We will be waiting for you in the school kitchen.
Edna

"Is it something important?" Leonard asked curiously.

"I'm not sure," she said slowly. "I'm just supposed to return to the school instead of going home."

"Then we should probably start back," Leonard suggested.

"I believe that would be a good idea."

Leonard took a moment to drain his coffee cup before standing and leading Heloise away from the café. He drove back to the school and walked with her to the kitchen entrance. Heloise paused before going in. "Thank you, Leonard. I enjoyed this evening immensely."

"I'm very glad because I did too," he replied with a smile. "I'll stop by the library tomorrow."

"I'll see you then," she said before turning and going into the kitchen.

Chapter 4

When Agnes returned to the kitchen office, she found Rory Van der Haven attempting to calm Edna. "Ahem." Agnes cleared her throat loudly as she entered the office.

"So glad you could join us, Ms. Thistlewaite." Rory smiled. "I'll need to get a thorough report of everything that occurred today since I saw you last. Do you mind if I record your statements?" When they shook their heads, he pulled an object from the pocket of the double-breasted black pinstriped suit that he wore for Pedestrian world assignments. He placed the large orange-and-brown cat's-eye marble on Agnes's desk where it looked at each of them and blinked.

As Edna described her harrowing experience with the quatos in the forest, Rory nodded encouragingly. With only an occasional question from the Department of Magical Justice investigator to interrupt her, Edna wracked her mind to recall every minute detail as she continued her narrative. When she had finished and Agnes insisted that she had no more information to add, she offered them both a cup of tea.

"Actually, I still need to speak to Ms. Amburgy," Rory said, returning the marble to his pocket.

Before anyone could reply, the main door to the kitchen opened; and as they watched, Heloise gracefully floated across the floor to the kitchen office. Even with all the trauma and heartache of the evening, Edna couldn't repress a smile.

"Had a good evening then, did you?" she asked Heloise.

Blushing faintly, Heloise answered, "Yes, it was quite nice. I'd forgotten how pleasant an evening on the town could be."

"Sorry to burst your bubble, dear, but we've got major problems," stated Agnes.

Listening with mounting horror, Heloise sat as Agnes and Edna recounted what had happened during the evening since she had left the school grounds for her date with Leonard Marshall.

"Ms. Amburgy, where were you when the attack took place?" Rory asked politely.

"I was in town at a concert with Leonard Marshall," Heloise replied.

"Did you say Leonard Marshall?" asked Rory.

"Yes," Heloise answered, "why do you ask?"

"I'm not sure," muttered Rory. Shaking himself as though waking from a dream, Rory apologized, "I'm sorry, the name Leonard Marshall seemed to ring a bell with me, but I can't figure out why. Okay, I will report this incident to the Council. In the meantime, the Committee of Dangerous Magical Beasts will take care of the quatos." As Edna began to protest, Rory smiled gently at her. "Don't worry, I'll notify you when it is safe for you to return to your cottage." With that, he created an interdimensional portal, said "Good evening" to Agnes and Heloise, and disappeared.

"Since it seems we shall have to wait here for the all-clear signal, why don't we have some tea? Agnes, weren't you telling me the other day about receiving an exotic blend from Jakarta?" Heloise asked with as much enthusiasm as she could muster.

"Oh yes, just the thing. I haven't had a chance to try it myself," Agnes replied breathlessly as she bustled from the office.

Heloise turned to regard Edna, sitting with her shoulders slumped, staring morosely at the floor. "Edna," Heloise spoke softly, "what is Rap's condition?"

Edna looked up at Heloise with red-rimmed eyes. "Rory took him to a wizard veterinarian, and he's going to be okay, but he has to stay in the veterinary hospital in Capital City for at least two weeks. I know how troublesome he can be and what a scamp he is, but he almost died to save me, and I miss him so much," Edna wept quietly.

"It's all right, dear," Heloise consoled Edna as she put an arm around her shoulders. "Our familiars enhance our magical powers and thereby become extensions of ourselves, so we keenly grieve their absence."

"I should have been stronger. I should have used my magic to fry those lousy quatos!" Edna growled through clenched teeth. Then her shoulders sagged again. "But I remembered the sanctions of the Magic Council and knew that using any magic, above the most basic disguise or communications spells, would get us banished forever. I would have done it to save Rap, but I couldn't do that to you and Agnes."

As if summoned by the sound of her name, Agnes appeared in the doorway with a tray bearing a simple tea service. As she set out cups and began pouring the fragrant, spicy tea, Agnes asked, "Heloise, after delivering the message, do you know if Coco returned to the school?"

Heloise looked startled. "After Coco arrived and I removed the note, I let her go, and I didn't notice what direction she went after that. I was reading the note and trying to convince Leonard that I have quirky friends that like to send messages via birds to allay his suspicions. After all, it's not really that uncommon. Hasn't she returned?"

"No, she hasn't," Agnes answered with worry in her voice. "And it's not like her."

Noting the look of concern on Agnes's face seemed to snap Edna out of her gloom and self-pity. "Wait," Edna said sternly. "Before we panic and assume the worst, let's check out a couple of things first. Heloise, where is Beowulf?"

Heloise put her hand in the deep pocket of her twill skirt and encountered the sleeping form of a brown-and-silver velvet-haired chinchilla. "He's right here," she announced.

With raised eyebrows, Edna inquired, "You took him on your date?"

Somewhat defiantly, Heloise replied, "Well, it seemed like a good idea at the time. Besides, I didn't have an opportunity to get him home before my date since there were people in my office when Leonard came to pick me up if you recall."

"Oh yeah, right," Edna mumbled. "I'll try to find Coco." Edna placed the index fingers of each hand against her temples.

"Wait!" shouted Agnes, afraid that Edna was about to perform a major spell.

"Chill out, Agnes. Animal telepathy and animal empathy are so far below the Council's magic radar, they'll never know as long as no one squeals," Edna said with a knowing look at Agnes.

Heloise and Agnes waited anxiously while Edna used her special affinity with the animal world to locate Agnes's missing cockatoo. After several minutes, Edna opened her eyes and grinned mischievously at Agnes. "Do you know that really huge barn owl who lives in the school stables? Well, his name is Nathan, and it appears that Heloise wasn't the only one who had a date for tonight."

Edna and Heloise burst into uncontrollable giggles at the look of disgust on Agnes's face, and she couldn't help but succumb to the infectious laughter. The brief laugh produced the positive effect of relieving the stress and tension caused by the frantic events of the evening. After they had regained their composure and drunk most of the tea, they received the all-clear signal to return to the cottage from the Department of Magical Justice. Much to Edna's disappointment, the notification was given by the frizzy red-haired witch instead of being delivered personally by Rory Van der Haven.

Since it was well past eleven in the evening and they had to be up early, especially Agnes, they quickly said good night and went to their waiting beds. As Heloise and Edna navigated the path through the woods in the cool moonlit night, Edna observed, "This is looking to be a most interesting school term, and I don't mean that in a good way."

Chapter 5

Beep beep beep beep. Agnes stared blearily at the digital clock beside her bed as she fumbled for the switch to silence the obnoxious alarm. The digits on the clock face read 5:00 a.m. Agnes groaned as she pulled herself from the soft, warm bed.

Maybe if I just set the snooze alarm for fifteen more minutes, she thought; but even as the thought occurred to her, she knew it wouldn't work. She knew if she gave in to the temptation to crawl back under her fluffy down comforter, she wouldn't wake again until well after lunch, and the residents of Sunny Acres were counting on her for their breakfast.

She stumbled into the ancient bathroom with the modern fixtures thinking how much easier it was back home. Back in Lemain, the water was instantly the proper temperature. With the wave of a wand, her hair was perfectly groomed, and her clothing was cleaned and pressed.

One good thing about this world's technology was the pulsating shower, which helped bring Agnes to complete wakefulness. As she toweled off after her shower, she examined her face and body in the bathroom's full-length mirror. The reflection staring back at her wasn't of fashion model or movie star caliber, but it wasn't bad. The body was fit and athletic; the facial features were attractive enough with a slightly rounded chin, full lips, a nose that some would call pert, wide blue eyes, and slightly arched brows. *So why,* she wondered, *were men attracted to Heloise and Edna while I haven't noticed any romantic interest from any male in my entire life? It just doesn't seem fair.*

She'd often heard her mother and grandmother repeat the adage, "The way to a man's heart is through his stomach." She'd cooked lots of meals for lots of men and received numerous compliments on her cooking from those men, but not one single invitation for a date. What was wrong with her?

Not only was she feeling romantically bereft, but she also loved children. She desperately wanted a daughter she could teach to cook and to whom she could pass the ancient family recipes, and her biological clock was ticking louder every day. She knew there were several ways that she could arrange to have a daughter, through magic or with the scientific technology of this world; but she was old-fashioned enough to believe in love, marriage, and the nuclear family. *Oh well,* Agnes thought, *this is a totally nonproductive train of thought, and it certainly isn't getting breakfast ready.*

She quickly dressed in old faded green hospital scrubs, which she usually wore for comfort and which she knew would be hidden by her chef's jacket.

As Agnes hurried down the silent, cold stone corridor to the kitchen, she thought of her two friends who were probably at that moment sleeping peacefully in their warm beds in their cute little cottage by the lake. She supposed she wasn't being very charitable toward her friends. After all, their jobs were completely different from hers. They probably had difficult duties associated with their jobs that she knew nothing about. And if Edna and Heloise were more popular with the men, it was probably because they were more outgoing and not afraid to talk to men.

As Agnes opened the door to the kitchen, she surveyed the room, looking for anything that might be out of place. She almost dropped her lacquered recipe box when she saw a young girl bent over looking under the massive kitchen ovens. "Excuse me," Agnes announced to the vast almost-empty kitchen.

"Ms. Thistlewaite," the child proclaimed as she straightened and stood at attention. The child stared in awe at Agnes as she advanced across the kitchen floor.

Oh my goodness, this must be an angel, Agnes thought as she studied the small person before her. *The child could only be about eight or nine years old,* Agnes judged. She had golden ringlets flowing from her head, robin's egg blue eyes, and a cherubic face that would have made Michelangelo weep. Agnes thought she had never seen a more perfect child.

"Okay, who are you, and what are you doing in my kitchen?"

The girl took a step back and stammered, "I . . . I . . . was assigned to . . . to kitchen detail this month, Ms. Thistlewaite."

Agnes checked her watch. "You're not due to report for duty for another hour and a half."

"I . . . I . . . I know, Ms. Thistlewaite. I couldn't sleep, and I just couldn't wait."

Agnes was stunned. Most students treated being assigned to kitchen duty as a punishment. This was the first student she'd encountered who seemed eager to work in the kitchen.

"I'm sorry . . . if I . . . I . . . did something wrong," the child replied with trembling lips and a quivering chin.

Oh heavens, thought Agnes, *I didn't mean to frighten the child.*

When she neared the girl, Agnes dropped to her knees in the middle of the kitchen floor. "I'm sorry, sweetheart. I didn't mean to frighten you. What is your name?"

Sniffing back sobs, the child answered, "My name is Valerie Valentine."

"Valerie, how old are you?"

"I'm nine years old," the girl replied.

"Okay, Valerie, why are you so excited to be here?"

"I've always wanted to learn how to cook, but they wouldn't let me at the foster home. They kept saying that I was too little and too young."

"Oh, so how long did you live in the foster home?"

Valerie frowned in concentration. "I think I was there for five years. I went there right after my parents died."

"You poor child, I'm so sorry," Agnes replied compassionately. She got to her feet and took Valerie by the hand. "Since you're already here, why don't you help me get the kitchen ready so we can begin preparing breakfast?"

The beaming smile on Valerie's face was all the answer she needed.

When Edna stumbled into the tiny kitchen in the cottage the next morning, Heloise was already making coffee. "Oh my goodness, Edna, you look terrible."

"Gee, thanks a lot, and a good morning to you too," Edna grumbled.

"I'm sorry, dear. But seriously, did you sleep at all last night?"

"Not much," Edna admitted. "How about some of that coffee?" As Heloise opened the cabinet, Edna remarked, "Don't bother with a cup. Just hook up a line so the caffeine can get directly into my bloodstream." Heloise clucked sympathetically and poured the coffee.

They sat quietly at the large round maple table in the cozy kitchen and sipped the aromatic brew. After a few minutes, Edna glanced at Heloise over the rim of her cup and noticed the rosy glow in her friend's cheeks. "You certainly seem chipper this morning," she observed.

Heloise lifted bright eyes to Edna's face. "I really don't understand it after all the excitement, but I slept wonderfully last night."

"Uh-huh." Edna's eyes narrowed suspiciously. "I seem to remember that you were supposed to give complete details of your date with Leonard, and just because we didn't have time last night doesn't mean you're off the hook."

"Oh my, look at the time!" exclaimed Heloise. "We'll have to hurry if we're to have breakfast with Agnes."

"Cute, real cute, Heloise. You can run, but you can't hide. I know where you live!" Edna called as Heloise hurried from the kitchen to her bedroom.

"Let's review the clues, Sherlock Fitzsimmons," Edna said to herself as she entered her bedroom and began to dress. "First, Heloise tries to keep the date a secret. Then she returns from the date floating three inches off the floor—literally! Also, she is probably the only one of us who slept well last night. And this morning, she is avoiding discussing her date. Given these facts, the only possible conclusion, . . ." Edna made a large flourish and turned to the padded basket in the corner where Rap usually slept. There was a sharp pain in her heart when Edna realized the basket was unoccupied. "Well, anyway, " Edna continued, "it must have been one heck of a date, and I think our Heloise is more than a little infatuated."

"Are you ready?" called Heloise from the front door.

"Coming!" answered Edna as she smoothed her thick brown turtleneck sweater over the rust-colored suede skirt. Her outfit, combined with her auburn hair and green eyes, made her look like autumn personified. As she neared the front door of the cottage, she stopped dead in awe. Heloise's light honey brown hair, which she usually wore pinned up on top of her head, was cascading in waves to her waist. And the peach-colored mohair dress with the fitted bodice, long tapered sleeves, and flared skirt enhanced her rosy complexion and added a spark of color to her gray eyes.

"Excuse me, but where are your glasses?" asked Edna as they started up the path to the school.

"I'm wearing those plastic lenses that fit right on top of the eyeball. I think they're called compacts or contracts."

"Thank goodness you didn't use a spell," Edna replied. "And why the new hairstyle? Is there something special going on today?"

"I just thought a change would be nice," responded Heloise with feigned nonchalance as she continued her rapid pace up the path.

Oh, how the plot thickens, thought Edna, following Heloise through the front doors of the school.

After the drama of the previous night, the normalcy of the morning routine at the school was very reassuring. *Oh no,* thought Edna, *if this is beginning to seem normal to me, I've definitely been here too long!* Edna and Heloise joined the throng of students and staff traversing the east corridor toward the dining room. As they entered and took their places at the table reserved for faculty and staff against the north wall, Edna observed, "Can you imagine the reaction of these people if they knew there were quatos in the forest last night?"

"I imagine they would be just as panicked as you were," Heloise replied smugly.

Edna stared at Heloise with her mouth opened in astonishment. Then understanding dawned, and she asked, "Agnes?"

Heloise smiled. "She may have mentioned that you were not your usual calm, cool, collected self when you arrived at her office last night."

Fuming, Edna muttered, "I'll get even!"

After the student waiter took Heloise's order for jasmine tea and Edna's order for "the strongest coffee available," they joined the breakfast buffet line. They passed by the usual offerings of scrambled eggs, pancakes, and waffles. When they came to the hot cereals, between the oatmeal and the cream of wheat were the scant remains of a pale green substance with a consistency that was neither as creamy as the cream of wheat nor as course as the oatmeal. Edna and Heloise exchanged questioning glances. At that moment, Agnes entered from the kitchen with a large steaming pan of the green cereal. As Agnes replaced the almost-empty pan with the full one, Edna leaned forward and hissed, "What is that?"

"It's mashed tent caterpillars with maple syrup. It's one of my great-grandmother's favorite recipes," whispered Agnes.

"Agnes, that sounds more like a spell ingredient than a breakfast food," Heloise admonished.

"But the Pedestrians like it," Agnes answered. "This is the fifth pan I've had to put out."

"Where did you get the tent caterpillars?" Edna asked with an arched eyebrow.

"Have you noticed any tent caterpillars in the woods lately?" Agnes grinned.

"Well," Edna began, "now that you mention it."

"Agnes, you didn't . . . ," Heloise hissed.

"Yep, I cleaned up the forest, saved a few trees, and created a tasty breakfast all at the same time. Cream of wheat and oatmeal can't make that claim," Agnes stated proudly.

Edna sneaked a peek at the viscous substance and quickly looked away as her stomach threatened to hurl its contents. "Hey, what's the holdup?" came a voice from down the line.

Heloise leaned forward and whispered to Agnes, "We need to talk—ASAP."

As Edna and Heloise made their way back to the table with their portions of fresh fruit, eggs, and toast, Edna whispered, "What is she thinking, digging out those archaic recipes? Our people quit eating most of that stuff a hundred years ago. The only ones I can think of who might be interested are members of the Methuselah Club."

"You're right, and I can't imagine why she would jeopardize our situation by using those recipes. I shudder to think what the Magic Council would do if they found out about this," replaced Heloise.

"Okay, maybe I've missed something, but how are we in danger just because Agnes is serving green slime? I can see the local health department shutting down the school's kitchen and Agnes getting canned, but we can hide her in the closet of the cottage for the next forty-five-plus years. What am I saying? Agnes locked in our closet for forth-five years, yakking her head off! Please forgive me. It's the stress. I wasn't thinking. I need more coffee," Edna murmured as she dropped her head to the cup of sweet, creamy brown liquid that would clear her head and revitalize her senses.

Agnes arrived at the table about twenty minutes later, sweating and panting from the exertion of feeding 350 students, twenty faculty, and seventeen staff members. Since there were several faculty and staff members still eating, Heloise suggested they move to the relative privacy at the end of the table.

"Agnes, what were you thinking?" began Heloise in a very disapproving voice.

With an air of absolute innocence, Agnes replied, "Whatever do you mean?"

"During the time we've been in the Pedestrian world you haven't even mentioned your heirloom recipe box. Now that you've found it, why would you decide to use one of the most obscure recipes?"

"Yeah, you're right, it is kind of weird. I can't explain it, but this morning, I just felt like I had to make one of the recipes in the back of box." Agnes looked at Heloise and held up her hand palm outward. "Don't start with me! I know that mashed tent worms with maple syrup isn't a staple of the Pedestrian diet. But this dish is high in protein, high in fiber, has several trace vitamins. And besides, they like it! Where's the harm?"

"Somehow, I find it hard to believe that the quatos' attack last night and your irresistible urge to serve a Lemain dish to Pedestrians that would surely be seen as a violation of the Lemain Secrecy Act is completely coincidental. I believe we may have an enemy who doesn't want us to return to Lemain," answered Heloise.

"Is someone really after us?" Agnes whispered to Heloise.

"Don't tell me you think all that's been happening is accidental?" Edna replied in exasperation.

Agnes sighed, "I guess not, but it's easier to believe in accidents than malice. Why would someone want to hurt us? We're no threat to anyone."

They sat quietly for a few minutes trying to think of a motive behind the odd occurrences of the past twenty-four hours. Suddenly, Agnes looked up. "I just remembered I have a new helper in the kitchen. Edna, could you check her admission papers and let me know what you find out?"

"I suppose I can. Why do you want to know her background?"

"She just seems like such a special child. Her name is Valerie Valentine, and she's nine years old. Her parents are dead, and she's been living in a foster home for the past five years."

Noting the look of excited anticipation on Agnes's face, Edna agreed to find out what she could about the little girl.

Late that afternoon, Leonard decided that it was past time to ask Heloise some questions. He started to go to the library, stopping just long enough to pick up some research material that he needed to return. That would be a good excuse to be there, and hopefully, he could think of a way to phrase his inquires without offending her. "Exactly how well do you know Edna?" would not be a good start. "What kind of people use birds as messengers?" wasn't an improvement. He was afraid that no matter what he said, it would sound like an accusation. Maybe he would just see how the conversation would go.

The library door was propped open, and before entering, he paused to gather his courage. He heard Edna's voice and hesitated, not wanting to interrupt.

"Really, Heloise, I still want to know how the quatos got here. You know that they must have been deliberately brought over in order to . . ."

At the mention of quatos, Leonard dropped the books and papers he was holding.

"Did you hear someone?" Heloise asked. She hurried over to the doorway. "Leonard, I wasn't expecting you. How long have you been standing out here?"

"I just arrived. I was planning on returning these to you, but they just slipped out of my hands. I'm so sorry," he answered, his nostrils flaring slightly with his shallow breaths.

"It's all right," Heloise assured him. "Come in and talk with us. Edna's here too."

"No, I really can't," Leonard said distractedly, avoiding her gaze. "I just remembered that I need to get home. There's something I need to check on."

"Oh, I see," Heloise said in confusion. "Well, I don't want to detain you."

Leonard stepped back several steps before turning and walking away. Heloise watched his retreat before returning to Edna. "I wonder what has him acting so strangely," she mused.

"Maybe it has something to do with your date," Edna speculated.

"I thought he enjoyed himself," Heloise said, looking crestfallen. "He said he had a good time."

"Well then, you shouldn't worry about it. What I want to know is where the quatos came from."

"Edna, we've been talking about that all day. There's really no way we can figure it out from here. When Rory is able to update you on Rap's condition, you can see if he found anything. Until then, as much as patience is not your strong suit, we'll just have to wait."

Leonard drove home as quickly as he dared on the steep and winding roads. He wished yet again that he could live close enough to the school that he could walk every day; he knew, however, that the risks were too high. Being too different called attention to oneself. Right now, he needed to get home and tell his mother what he had heard at the library. It wasn't bad enough that there were quatos here. The thing that really frightened him was that Heloise and her friend knew what they were.

He pulled the car up in front of the small house and sat for a moment, gathering his thoughts before entering his home. His mother was standing in front of the stove, adding herbs to a simmering pot. "Leonard, I didn't expect you home this early," she said in surprise. Seeing his distress, she moved closer to him. "What happened?" she asked in a flat tone.

"I overheard something at school," he answered, shivering slightly. "Heloise and her friend Edna saw some quatos."

"Quatos! I wonder what they are doing in the Pedestrian world. Did you tell them what they are and where they come from?" she questioned sharply.

"There was no need. They knew what they were, but they were trying to discover how they got here," he said, sounding strained.

"That doesn't make sense. To recognize quatos for what they are, they must be familiar with our world," Mrs. Marshall speculated.

"Do you think they could be here looking for me?" Leonard asked.

Mrs. Marshall looked at her son and recognized the empty expression he had worn when he returned to her after his escape from the laboratory back in Lemain. "If they are here for you, they will be disappointed. I won't allow them to take you back there again."

"How will we stop them?" he asked in a defeated voice.

"We've had to move before," she reminded him. "I know you like it here, but if need be, we'll find another place that suits us."

Leonard sighed, "This house has been perfect for us, and I do like my job. But I really thought I could trust Heloise. That's what is most disappointing."

"I'm going to contact your aunt Lucinda," she spoke decisively. "She can do some research at home. She'll let us know who those women are answering to and if they might be a threat."

Chapter 6

Edna arrived at the admissions office bright and early the next morning. She greeted Janet, the receptionist, with a smile. "What's on the agenda for this morning?"

"You're starting out the day with a new admission. They're due at nine o'clock," Janet answered, picking up a folder and passing it to Edna. "Here's the file."

Edna glanced at the preadmission form and frowned. "Is this some kind of joke?"

"What do you mean?" Janet asked.

"You're telling me that this child's name is actually John Smith?" Edna replied, raising an eyebrow.

Janet smiled and shrugged. "It could happen."

At precisely nine o'clock, Janet knocked at Edna's office doorway. She poked her head in and announced, "John Smith and his mother are here."

Edna peered over the edge of the Weekly Disciplinary Reports folder she was reading. "Thank you, Janet. Send them in, please."

Janet withdrew, and a few moments later, Mrs. Smith and John entered. Edna directed them to the chairs in front of her desk. Studying them, Edna observed that Mrs. Smith was shorter than average, with a stocky build and unusually broad shoulders. Both mother and son had stiff, wiry black hair and a greenish tinge to their skin, and their facial features seemed a little squashed. John, who appeared to be approximately ten years old, also had rather pointed ears.

Edna didn't want to seem rude, but she couldn't help staring at them. Fortunately, they didn't appear to notice her lapse in manners. Clearing her throat, Edna began, "So, Mrs. Smith, why do you want John to attend Sunny Acres School?"

In a harsh, guttural voice, Mrs. Smith replied, "John special boy, needs special school."

Fighting to keep a smile on her face, Edna turned her attention to the boy. "How about you, John, are you looking forward to coming here to school?" There were a few moments of strained silence. During this time, John simply frowned and stared at her. Edna struggled to keep herself from squirming in discomfort. "Well then," she finally blurted, "why don't we get you started on your admission test. After you've finished that, we can have a quick tour of the school."

Edna set John up at a small table and started timing his test. She gave Mrs. Smith some booklets about the school's history and an outline of the curriculum. Returning to the papers she had been reviewing, she split her attention between John, who was writing rapidly although holding the pen clumsily, and Mrs. Smith, who was staring blankly into space.

John finished with his paper in a remarkably short amount of time. Edna placed it in the folder along with his admission form.

"Wonderful," Edna said with forced cheerfulness. "Now I can take you on a little tour."

She began on the ground floor with the dining hall, grateful that it was nowhere near mealtime and therefore empty. Pointing out classrooms along the way, she said, "It's unfortunate that classes are in session at the moment, so I can't show you inside." Edna continued chatting merrily as she always did when showing the school to prospective students and their parents. If she was hoping to establish a line of communication, she was doomed to disappointment. John and his mother maintained an eerie silence that Edna found unnerving. Even more strangely, both mother and son seemed to be mentally mapping the rooms and corridors as they went along.

Moving down the fifth-floor hallway, Edna saw Heloise straightening some shelves in the library. She was relieved to note the absence of any students. "Let's just go into the library for a moment,"

Edna suggested in a strained voice. "I'm sure you'll be impressed with our study resource section."

The Smiths followed Edna through the heavy double doors into the quiet sanctuary. "Heloise," Edna spoke in slightly quieter tones than usual. "I hoped you wouldn't mind giving a small tour of the library to a new prospective student."

"Of course, I'd be happy to," Heloise answered.

John trailed silently after Heloise while his mother remained by the doors. While she pointed out the various sections of the library, the boy stared around apathetically. Returning to where Edna was waiting, Heloise gave her a curious look.

"All righty then," Edna said somewhat nervously. "I think that completes our tour. I'll just make sure you find the exit."

Outside the massive front doors, Edna bid them a thankful good-bye. "You'll be receiving a letter shortly with your test scores," she assured them. She watched as the visitors descended the front steps where an ancient black limousine awaited them. Edna felt a shiver ripple through her and sincerely hoped that would be the last she saw of them. They had given her a thoroughly creepy feeling, not the least due to the fact they seemed strangely familiar, somehow.

Over the next couple of weeks, Edna was to have several more strange interviews with similarly unusual prospective students. She became more uneasy with each incident. Never one to conceal her opinions, Edna voiced her reservations about these students at the next admissions committee meeting. The board took her comments under advisement; however, they pointed out that all of their transcripts, test scores, and references were impeccable. The board invariably granted them all enrollment.

Every one of the new students made Edna feel creepy. As the number of new students continued to increase, her suspicions grew proportionately. She remembered her conversation with Heloise the night after the Smiths first visited Sunny Acres.

"Heloise, what did you think of those two today?"

"Well, really, Edna, they were hardly in the library for more than ten minutes. You can't expect me to form an opinion in that length of time." Heloise stopped for a moment, crinkling her brow. "It was strange, though," she continued. "Something about them seemed oddly familiar."

"That's exactly what I thought!" Edna exclaimed, slapping her hand down on the table. "I just can't put my finger on it."

In the meantime, Agnes was delighted with Valerie's intelligence and enthusiasm as she learned to cook. Valerie had continued showing up at the kitchen early in the morning, arriving after Agnes but before any of the other kitchen staff. One morning, while Valerie was mixing the dough for the biscuits under Agnes's watchful eye, she turned and asked, "Ms. Thistlewaite, why do you glow?"

With a startled look, Agnes asked, "What do you mean, dear?"

Valerie returned to the dough. "Nothing, you just have a real pretty purplish glow."

Agnes frowned. "Have you seen anyone else who glows?"

"Well, some of the students glow."

"Anyone else?"

Valerie stopped kneading the dough and frowned in concentration. "The librarian, Ms. Amburgy; the admissions lady with the long hair; and the history teacher, Mr. Marshall. But his glow is more reddish. Oh, and the new students, but they all have a muddy brown glow. Yuck!"

Agnes was so flabbergasted she almost dropped the rolling pin she was holding. *Could this child be talking about auras?* she wondered. *But if she can see auras and distinguish specific colors, she must have magic!*

"Are you okay?" Valerie asked as she turned to take the rolling pin from Agnes's limp hand.

"Yes, dear, I'm fine," Agnes replied, but her mind was racing. *I've got to talk to Edna and Heloise—today!* Agnes excused herself while she went to her office and fired off e-mails to her friends.

E. & H.

Meet me in the dining hall for dinner. I have something of utmost importance to tell you.

A.

Edna met Heloise in the library at six o'clock that evening. When they got to the dining hall, it was fairly full, but they managed to find three seats at the end of the staff table. Agnes must have been watching because she quickly joined them. She excitedly whispered, "We've got to talk. I've learned something amazing!"

"Do we have to do it right this minute, or can we eat first? I'm starving," Edna retorted sharply.

"No need to be snappish, Edna," Heloise admonished. To Agnes, she said,

"Perhaps we should get our food first. It will look less suspicious if we talk over dinner."

As they joined the buffet line, Edna shot Agnes a fearful look. "You haven't used any of those ancient recipes from that box, have you?"

"Of course not," Agnes replied with a hurt look. To Edna's great relief, the choices were rib roast, beef stew, or chicken caesar salad. There was also a choice of potatoes, green beans, and Yorkshire pudding. They filled their plates and returned to the head table. After they had resumed their seats, Agnes asked in a low voice, "Did you check Valerie's admission record?"

"Yes, I did," replied Edna, lifting a generous forkful of salad to her mouth.

"What did you find out?" hissed Agnes.

"Valerie's parents were Michael and Gloria Valentine. They owned a combination book-and-music store in Pittsburgh and died in a single car accident when their car went out of control on an icy street coming down from Mount Washington one night. There were no known living relatives, so Valerie became a ward of the state and wound up in a foster home." Edna took a large swig of iced tea.

Agnes looked disappointed. "That's all? There's no information about their lives before the accident?"

Edna slammed her glass on the table. "Look, we're not some clandestine government agency! We don't do high-level security checks on our students and their families!" Agnes pulled back and looked as though she'd been slapped in the face.

Heloise put her hand on Edna's arm. "Edna, please calm down." Turning to Agnes, she said, "Please forgive her. Rap still hasn't returned, and she's having problems with the admissions committee."

"I'm sorry, Edna, I never stopped to think about what you're going through. What problem are you having with the committee?"

Edna pointed to the left and said, "Them."

Heloise and Agnes turned to look at the group of students Edna indicated. They were looking at a group of approximately a dozen students, all dressed in black. They all had black hair, squashed faces, and an unhealthy greenish pallor to their skin. They were sitting at one end of the third long table in the hall. In spite of the fact that the hall was crowded at this time of night, there were several empty seats all around them.

"See, even the other students don't want to be near them," Edna observed.

"Who are they?" Agnes asked.

"Supposedly they are all incredibly intelligent students from impeccable families and impeccable communities with impeccable references. Bull!" snorted Edna.

"Remember that day a couple of weeks ago when I brought that first one into the library?" she asked Heloise. "We both thought then that they looked familiar. Well, I think I've figured it out. Take a really good look at them." She paused, looking at Heloise and Agnes. "Don't you think they look like human-goblin hybrids?" For a few moments, they studied Sunny Acres newest students.

"Oh my goodness, you're right!" gasped Agnes. "It's beginning to make sense. I think it all ties in. Listen, I have some information that I need to share with you, but this is not the time or place. Can we all meet at the cottage in about an hour?"

Edna and Heloise exchanged a curious look. "Sure," they answered in unison.

Chapter 7

Leonard paced nervously behind his cottage. It had been two weeks since he had overheard Heloise and Edna talking about the quatos in the school library. His mother sent a message to Aunt Lucinda right after he had spoken to her. There had been no contact from her yet, and Leonard was unsettled. He had been avoiding Heloise, hoping to have more information before he spoke to her again.

"Leonard," his mother called from the house. "Come inside. I need to talk to you." He stiffened, then turned, and started back inside. In the kitchen, she waved him to sit at the table. "Here, you can eat as we talk. You haven't been eating properly again." She set a dish of savory stew down for him along with a steaming cup of tea.

Leonard sniffed appreciatively and licked his lips. "I haven't been very hungry, or maybe it's been hard to concentrate on food with everything so up in the air."

"Well, you can relax, then. Lucinda just answered my message."

Leonard froze in midbite with his fork still in his mouth. Swallowing carefully, he returned his fork to his plate and visibly braced himself for the news.

"I said to relax, Leonard. Lucinda spoke to a friend of hers who works for *Magic Moments* magazine. She remembered the entire story. Heloise is from Lemain. She was banished five years ago when she ruined President Thurgood's inauguration banquet," his mother informed him.

"How did she manage that?" Leonard asked.

"She owned a catering company with her friends Edna Fitzsimmons and Agnes Thistlewaite."

"They're both here too," Leonard confirmed.

"Well, it apparently involved flying pigs and an exploding cake. Although what they thought they were doing—bringing flying pigs to a banquet—I certainly do not understand. And as for an exploding cake, well, that's just silly! Anyway, they were banished to this world for fifty years. So it had almost nothing to do with you," his mother finished.

"What do you mean, 'almost nothing'?" Leonard asked suspiciously.

Mrs. Marshall smiled slightly. "They met at Aunt Mildred's School for Wayward and Orphaned Witches. I don't know about the other two, but Edna was there as punishment."

"You're having too much fun with this!" Leonard growled. "Tell me the rest of the story."

"You still need to work on patience," his mother chided. "You've been impatient since you were a little boy. All right, Ms. Fitzsimmons sneaked into the Capital City Research Laboratory and released all the experimental animals when she was a young girl." She stared at him expectantly.

"Including one half-starved wolf," he said, wide-eyed. "I thought she looked familiar, but I just wasn't sure."

"I think that if she rescued you, then you don't need to worry about her turning you in now," Mrs. Marshall reassured him.

"I'm not so sure," Leonard said, his brow furrowing. "As far as she knew, she was setting a poor scared animal free. She might feel differently if she knew that animal was a werewolf. Not very many people are sympathetic to that condition," he finished bitterly.

"Does that mean you're not going to even give them a chance? It seems to me that makes you as intolerant as you believe they might be," his mother commented.

"I'll think about it," Leonard promised. "We're taking the children on a picnic tomorrow. There might be a chance to talk to Heloise then." He pushed the food away and went back outside to resume prowling the edge of the forest.

On their way back to the cottage after dinner, Edna couldn't repress a small shudder of fear as they entered the ancient forest path. Ever since the attack of the quatos, Edna had been forced to give up the idea that this was a benign world in which they had been forced to live. It was turning out to be a world with big nasty and deadly teeth. Although she was reluctantly willing to acknowledge the existence and power of those teeth, she was more determined than ever to pull them. Edna had been called a lot of names in her life, but she wasn't about to be called a *victim*.

There was a surprise waiting for them when they reached the cottage. Once they got inside and locked the door, Heloise and Edna went to their bedrooms to change into nightgowns and robes. When Edna opened her door and flung her sweater into the corner, she was rewarded by the sound of a familiar voice. "Excuse me," came Rap's disgruntled voice, "I just happen to be sleeping."

"Rap!" Edna squealed as she scooped him in her arms and twirled around the room.

"Yes, mistress, it's very good to see you too. But if you continue to swing me around, I fear I may be ill."

"Oh, sorry," Edna said, setting Rap gently on her bed. "How are you? When did you get back?"

"Obviously, I was cured, and I returned approximately two hours ago," replied Rap as he used his front paws to smooth back the ruffled fur on his face. "Did you wish for a minute-by-minute account of my last two weeks?" Rap inquired.

"Rap, don't you start with me," Edna began furiously. Then she noticed the twitching whiskers and the gleam in his eye that indicated that Rap was teasing her. "Oh, Rap, you are such a stinker!" exclaimed Edna as she fell on the bed and hugged her favorite raccoon.

"Easy, I'm still recuperating," Rap complained. Just then, Heloise appeared in the doorway.

"What's going on?" Then she spied the two on the bed. "Oh, Rap, I'm so glad you're back. You can't imagine how impossible Edna's been since you've been gone."

"What is this, 'pick on Edna' night?" Edna retorted. Rap continued grooming his fur, and Heloise just smiled. "Okay, everybody, out! I have to change."

Having already changed into her nightclothes, which consisted of a neatly pressed pale green pajama set with a matching fleece robe, Heloise looked at Rap. "Why don't we see if there's any tuna fish in the kitchen?"

After they left, Edna hurriedly stripped off her business suit, flinging articles of clothing helter-skelter about the room. Digging through her overstuffed and disorganized dresser drawers, she eventually found a pair of lightweight lavender sweatpants and a white tee shirt. The tee shirt had a red arrow on the front, pointing to her left side, and lettering proclaiming "I'm with Stupid." She topped off the ensemble with a thick royal blue terry cloth robe.

When Agnes arrived at the cottage, she found Edna and Heloise drinking hot chocolate in the kitchen and Rap having a late-night snack on the counter. "What . . . ?" Edna began as Agnes entered the kitchen carrying her recipe box.

"Just a minute please," panted Agnes as she set the box on the table and gratefully wrapped her chilled hands around the cup of cocoa Heloise set before her. Everyone sat quietly for a few minutes while Agnes regained her breath and sipped from her mug. Finally, Agnes raised her head and blurted, "I think Valerie has magic abilities!"

Edna's eyes bulged, and her mouth fell open. Heloise's cup slipped from her nerveless fingers and slopped chocolate across the table. Agnes jumped up to get a towel and clean up the spill while she waited for the questions her friends were sure to have.

"What makes you think Valerie has magic?" Heloise croaked in a whisper.

Agnes hastily resumed her seat and leaned across the table. "She sees auras and can distinguish specific colors for different groups. She doesn't know they are auras. She just says we have a purplish glow, and she sees a muddy brown glow around the new students," she replied.

"Don't you see?" continued Agnes excitedly. "It all makes sense. If Valerie sees us with purplish auras, which would be correct for magic users, and the new students whom we suspect to be goblin-human hybrids with dull brown auras, which would be right for semievil creatures, she must have the magical talent of aura detection!"

"This is very hard to believe. After all, aura detection is a fairly rare talent," Heloise stated.

"Hard to believe, nothing! This is flat-out impossible," interjected Edna. "Valerie is a Pedestrian, her parents were Pedestrians, and the last known case of spontaneous magical ability manifesting in a child without at least one magical parent was over nine hundred years ago."

"Edna's got a point," Heloise agreed.

"But how else can we explain it?" asked Agnes.

Heloise turned to Edna. "What did the records say Valerie's parents' names were?"

"Um . . ." Edna thought for a moment. "Michael and Gloria Valentine."

Heloise dashed out of the kitchen. In a moment, she returned with a huge stack of magazines.

Edna gasped as she realized she was looking at current issues of the magic world's leading weekly newsmagazine, *Magic Moments.* "Where did you get these?" she demanded of Heloise.

"I've had a subscription to this magazine since I was nine years old."

"But why are you receiving it in the Pedestrian world?"

"Well, I wanted to keep up with what was going on at home. And since their motto is that they 'deliver anywhere,' I didn't see any point in canceling my subscription just because we were banished."

Edna grinned and clapped her hands in glee. "This is wonderful. Heloise, I never suspected that you could be so sneaky and devious."

Heloise leaned close to Edna and murmured, "I try not to let it show. It's more effective that way, you know."

As far as Edna was concerned, this was the second highlight to an otherwise disappointing day. First, of course, was Rap's return; and now (after all these years), she'd discovered that Heloise was not only not the Goody Two-shoes she'd suspected her of being ever since they met at Aunt Mildred's, but she could also be even more devious than Edna herself.

"How are these magazines going to help us?" Agnes asked.

All serious once again, Heloise replied, "The name Michael Valentine rang a bell in my memory. I seem to remember reading about a Michael Valentine running for Council representative and then not finishing the election."

"Okay, obviously, we have to look through these magazines for something. But what exactly are we looking for?" Edna asked.

"We have to look for any mention of Michael or Gloria Valentine, why he dropped out of the Council race, and any mention of where they are now," Heloise answered.

"Heloise, you do realize that the *Magic Moments* magazine articles aren't in any existing database in the Pedestrian world?"

"Yes, so?"

"So that means we have to manually read each and every one of these magazines to find the information that we want!"

"Excuse me, Edna, but I think you've been spoiled by the technology of this world."

"Maybe the magical world could do with a little of the Pedestrian world's technology," Edna retorted. "Think about it. In the Pedestrian world, they have information systems where all you have to do is type a name onto the glowing screen of a computer and a zillion Web sites appear concerning that name. You can even access all information available on a single person if you know their social security number."

"I don't disagree with you about the advantages of the Pedestrian technology, but that doesn't help us at this moment. Right now, we have to find out what we can by reading every article manually. I would suggest we get started."

Sometime around three in the morning, Edna rubbed her bloodshot eyes, stretched, and yawned. "So far, I've found one article where they mention that a young sociology professor from Capital City University, Michael Valentine, is entering the political race for a seat on the Magic Council, and another one a little later where he is quoted as saying that if he is elected, he will head up an investigation into 'illegal, immoral, and unethical experimentation being done upon innocent victims by the Capital City Research Laboratories.' Bet he really tweaked somebody's nose with that statement."

"Hmm," mused Heloise. "That could tie in with the articles I've found. About two weeks before the election was to take place, someone made an allegation that Michael Valentine was accepting illegal and unreported campaign contributions from organized crime. When the authorities arrived at his home in Hopkinsville with a search warrant, no trace of either Mr. or Mrs. Valentine could be found although the house appeared to have been ransacked, and foul play was suspected. Unfortunately, they didn't give any details as to why foul play was suspected. Another article a week later states that the whereabouts and condition of the Valentines is still unknown, but investigation of bank records shows large sums of money being transferred to Michael's bank account from the account of Vinny Sarducci, a suspected crime boss. It also states that Vinny Sarducci was unavailable for comment."

Edna and Heloise both looked at Agnes who was still reading intently. "Well, what did you find?" Edna asked impatiently.

"Huh, what? Oh," Agnes mumbled as she raised her bleary eyes from the magazine. "I didn't really find any mention of Valerie's parents, but did you notice all the disappearances from Lemain in the past few years?"

"What disappearances?" Edna and Heloise asked in unison.

"There have been more than a dozen disappearances just in the past three years," Agnes said. "Most of them were just minor-level government employees, but a couple were pretty important. Look," said Agnes, shuffling through a pile of magazines by her left elbow. "Here's an article about William Brockhurst, the CEO of Grand Odessa National Bank who disappeared almost three years ago. And there's another one here somewhere about Julius Ravenmore, the spokesman for the Witches and Wizards Antidefamation League, who disappeared just a month ago."

The three friends stared at one another in dazed silence. Finally, Edna whispered, "Do you think there's a connection?"

"Hush, I'm thinking," Heloise replied as she went to the stove and began fixing what had to be her fifth cup of tea since they began their marathon reading session. "It's beginning to make some sense, but I still can't see the whole picture," Heloise said as she returned to the table. "If something shady was going on at the research labs and the person behind it didn't want anyone to find out, it would make sense to get rid of anyone who might find out and blow the whistle."

"Wow, it must be something pretty awful for someone to go to such extreme measures!" Edna exclaimed. "But what could it be, and how are we going to find out? I mean, we can't do much investigating from here."

A slow smile crept across Heloise's lips. "Edna dear, do you think you could persuade Rory Van der Haven to do you a favor?" Heloise asked in her sweetest voice.

Edna looked at Heloise in alarm. "What, so we can pick up next week's *Magic Moments* and read an article about an officer from the Department of Magical Justice disappearing? No way!" Edna said vehemently.

"Of course you're right, but we could see what he knows about what's going on at the research labs and with all these disappearances, couldn't we?"

"Yeah, I suppose you're right. He's our best contact with Lemain. What am I saying? He's our only *friendly* contact with Lemain. Before we start asking Rory questions, we have to get our ducks in a row."

Heloise and Agnes looked at each other in bewilderment then turned to stare at Edna. When Edna looked at them and noticed their odd stares, she realized that some explanation was needed. "In the Pedestrian vernacular, 'ducks in a row' means to have all your facts straight. Before we call in anyone, I think we should have everything completely thought out," Edna said. "We've got to create a timeline of events, or else we'll all get as thoroughly confused as I am right now."

Heloise frowned thoughtfully and nodded. "You have a very good point, Edna. How do we go about it?"

"Both of you, look away from me," Edna advised. Then Edna looked toward the southeast wall of the kitchen, waved her arm, and incanted, "Scriptumcalxbord." Standing on the floor next to the wall was a large chalkboard complete with chalk and eraser. "Let's list what we know so far," Edna said as she began writing.

Approximately twenty-eight years ago, the animals were rescued from the experimental lab in Capital City.

Twelve years later, we get banished after the inauguration banquet.

Nine years after that, Michael and Gloria Valentine disappear under suspicious circumstances during a Council election campaign.

In the past three years, Brockhurst and Ravenmore both disappear.

Five weeks ago, quatos show up in the forest.

Edna turned from the board and gazed at her friends. "Does anybody see a connection?" Agnes silently shook her head.

"Um," Heloise said, "it looks like someone was trying to eliminate strong voices in business and government. As for the rest of it, well, there's just not enough information to form an opinion."

"Great, there's something majorly sinister going on in Lemain, and we can't find out what because we're stuck here!" Edna said. "This sucks swamp water," she lamented as she sank into a chair.

"What in heaven's name is going on?" boomed a deep voice from the southwest corner of the kitchen.

Edna jumped up from the table with an astonished squeak. "Rory Van der Haven, what are you doing in our kitchen at this hour of the morning?"

Rory glowered at Edna. "Our tracking board at the department just lit up with the indication of nonauthorized magical use, and I was sent to investigate."

Edna blushed with embarrassment. "That was probably the chalkboard," she explained. "I thought it was such a small thing that you wouldn't notice. Besides, we had to have it," she continued in a rush. "Oh, Rory, you wouldn't believe what has been going on," she said excitedly as she pointed to the board.

Rory approached and studied the chalkboard. "Hmm, very interesting," he murmured. He turned to face them. "How did you come by this information?"

"Well, of course, we had firsthand knowledge of the quatos and the new students. And we found other resources for information of the disappearances from Lemain." Edna's gaze turned to the magazines strewn across the table.

Rory raised a quizzical eyebrow as he studied the magazines. He looked at the three women and sank into a chair. "I know I'm not going to like the answer, but I have to ask, where did these come from?"

Heloise cleared her throat. "I've had a subscription to *Magic Moments* for years."

Rory's eyes narrowed. "And when was the last time you renewed your subscription? Because if you have solicited the delivery of this magazine since your banishment, it's a direct violation of your sentence."

Drawing herself up to her full height of five feet and seven inches, Heloise replied, "My parents purchased a *lifetime* subscription for me before they died. As soon as we were informed of the location of our banishment, I simply submitted a change of address form."

Rory thought for a few moments. "Very clever, Heloise. Technically, you haven't violated any of the restrictions. But I would advise you not to let anyone, present company excluded, know that you are still receiving these."

"Rory, do you have any idea what is going on?" Edna asked, gesturing to the chalkboard.

"The department has an ongoing investigation into the disappearances," Rory began. "I would guess that the quatos were an attempt on your lives, but we haven't yet been able to find out who sent them. As for the goblins in your school, I'm not sure. They might be part of the recapture team from the Capital City Experimental Laboratory. Hattie Homborg has been hiring some strange characters lately. I must admit, I'm rather mystified as to why they would have been sent to the Pedestrian world and especially to this school."

Edna looked sharply at Rory. "What is this about a recapture team, and what does Hattie Homborg have to do with it?"

"You may recall that a while back, a young girl"—Rory smirked at Edna—"set loose all of the animals at the lab. Unfortunately, not all of the animals were recovered, and they are still searching for them. And our illustrious secretary of the treasury took special interest in the recovery of the animals since the chief magical director of Capital City labs is her grandmother."

"I forgot that Hattie told me that," Edna spat. "No wonder those poor animals were so horribly mistreated."

"Now, Edna," Rory began.

"Don't 'now, Edna' me," Edna responded. "You weren't there. It was so bad. There was one poor wolf who was so starved, I had to help him get out of his cage. I wish I could lock Hattie in a cage and starve her. It would serve her right. I'll tell you right now, Rory Van der Haven, if those goblins are here to recapture some poor animal that escaped from the lab, I certainly won't help them!"

"And neither will we," spoke up Heloise and Agnes.

Rory looked at the three defiant witches; then he closed his eyes as he rubbed his forehead with one hand. "Ladies, please don't cause any more trouble," he pleaded. "I can't keep bailing you out. I'm up to my neck investigating a running street battle and explosions allegedly being perpetrated by a well-known crime lord in Capital City."

"Would you be referring to Vinny Sarducci?" asked Heloise.

Rory shot her a penetrating look. "How did . . . ? Oh right, the magazines. Well, Sarducci is pretty steamed up and is telling anyone who will listen that the Council and the banks are conspiring to frame him for the disappearance of several important Lemain citizens. All of the attacks so far have been against Council members and bank officials, but innocent bystanders are beginning to be injured."

"Why would anyone become a crime lord?" came the soft-spoken question from the end of the table. Edna, Heloise, and Rory all stared dumbfounded at Agnes. "I mean, if it's all about having money, why don't they just create some with a spell?" Agnes continued.

Heloise was the first to respond. "Agnes, don't you remember at Aunt Mildred's when we learned about the physical properties of bespelled items?" Agnes furrowed her brow and shook her head. "Money that is created by magic only retains its form for about an hour."

"Oh, sorry, I must have forgotten," said Agnes.

Edna turned to Rory. "Speaking of funny money, have you seen the money they use in this world? Most of it is made of paper, and they don't use gold or silver in the coins. Well, there is a little bit of silver in a couple of the coins, but most of the coins are made with common minerals. Can you believe that?" Rory looked skeptical.

"Yes, it's true," added Heloise. "Any alchemist worth his compounds could be quite wealthy in the Pedestrian world."

"Ahem." Rory cleared his throat. "To return to your original question, Agnes, being a crime lord isn't just about amassing money. Some people get a thrill from the power they feel by intimidating others."

"That sounds like they are just a bunch of bullies," Agnes said.

"Yeah, that pretty much describes them. They're bullies, just more dangerous than most and on a broader scale," agreed Rory.

"Oh my goodness, look!" squealed Agnes, pointing to the kitchen window that faced east. As they looked out the window, they observed the pearly gray of predawn gradually being replaced by the rosy glow of sunrise.

"Oh, puss buckets!" exclaimed Edna.

Heloise shot Edna a disapproving look. "Edna, please, your language," she hissed.

Edna looked at her in surprise. "Don't you realize what today is?"

"Of course I do. It's Saturday. No classes, no duties—a day off."

"No, actually, it's the day that we agreed to take the first-, second-, and third-year classes on their annual Fall Foliage Picnic," Edna replied.

"And I agreed to make the box lunches," Agnes squeaked as she scurried for the door.

"Oh, Edna, I'm so sorry. I forgot all about it," Heloise apologized.

"Well, you can make up for it by figuring out how we're going to survive the day. We've been up all night, and we'll be dead on our feet . . . unless . . ." Edna turned to Rory with a gleam in her eye.

"Oh no, don't look at me like that, Edna," Rory said as he began backing toward the corner of the kitchen.

"But, Rory, all we need is just the teensiest bit of Energy Elixir," Edna wheedled.

"Absolutely not," Rory said vehemently, opening an interdimensional portal. "You're in enough trouble already, and if you didn't sleep last night, you have only yourselves to blame," he added as he stepped through the portal and disappeared.

"Fat lot of help he is," said Edna, stomping her foot.

"Huh? What, where? Are we under attack?" Rap mumbled sleepily from his cushion in the corner.

"Hush, Rap, go back to sleep," murmured Heloise.

"Very well, if you insist," Rap replied and curled once more into a sleeping ball.

Edna glared at Heloise. "Great, what do we do now? You had to keep us up all night reading your stupid magazines, didn't you? How could you? You know how cranky I get when I don't sleep."

Heloise had a fleeting mental picture of using a ball-peen hammer to deliver her friend to the sleeping state she so obviously desired. With a valiant effort of will, she barely managed to banish the image from her mind. Finally, she said, "Look, Edna, we have a couple of hours before the picnic. We'll sleep for a while. Then I'll make some of my special triple-strength tea, which should keep us on our feet until after the outing."

"Oh well, I suppose that's all we can do at this point," Edna grumbled as she stalked toward her bedroom. Heloise sighed as she looked around the tiny kitchen. Usually one of the tidiest rooms in the cottage, it was now littered with strewn magazines, scattered coffee cups, and an absurdly large chalkboard. She briefly thought of removing the chalkboard but quickly dismissed the idea at the thought of another visit from the justice department, and the officer this time might be someone less friendly than Rory Van der Haven. *Oh well,* Heloise thought, *we'll just have to do the best we can.* She turned off the kitchen light and proceeded gratefully toward the comfort of her own room.

Chapter 8

After Edna had been asleep for three hours, Rap quietly entered her bedroom. *Oh, I daresay this is going to be unpleasant,* Rap thought as he crept toward Edna's bed. Edna lay with her arms raised over her head and her legs spread across the bed as though she were caught in the midstride of a full run. *Humans are so funny. I wonder what they dream about to contort their bodies into such strange shapes when they sleep?* Just then, Edna gave a snort and flipped her body 180 degrees to land facedown on the bed. As soft snorts and grunts emanated from the vicinity of Edna's head, Rap mused, *I wonder if I can escape her wrath by blackmailing her with the fact that she snores?*

Rap climbed to the top of her pillow and stretched out one tiny forepaw to begin tickling Edna's ear. Fortunately, Rap was an old hand at waking Edna and managed to avoid Edna's slap as she raised her shoulders from the bed. "Go 'way," Edna mumbled sleepily as she buried her head back in the pillow.

Rap grabbed a few strands of Edna's hair in his paw and tugged gently. "Mistress, wake up, mistress," Rap said softly.

"Mmmmph," was Edna's only reply.

"Please, mistress, Heloise says you must wake up now." Edna grabbed the pillow and pulled it over her head, flipping Rap to the bottom of the bed. Rap crawled up Edna's body and wormed his nose between the pillow and her ear. He whispered in her ear, "If you don't get up right now, a lot of children will be very disappointed."

Hearing a catch in her breath, Rap continued, "And I'll tell the entire school—no, wait—I'll tell Rory Van der Haven that you snore!"

That did the trick. Edna sat bolt up in the bed and glared at Rap. "It's a lie, and don't you dare tell anyone!" Rap smiled as he made his way to his bed in the corner of Edna's room. *That's what I call a great start,* he thought. *A good day's work and all accomplished in ten minutes.* "Of all the animals in the world, how did I wind up with such a sneaking, conniving, disloyal varmint as you?" Edna asked.

"I attribute it to your exceptional good luck," came the low-pitched reply as Rap rolled over, turning his back to Edna.

Edna stomped into the kitchen where Heloise was already brewing her special tea. The aroma was enough to at least open Edna's eyes although it didn't do much to improve her mood.

"Did Rap survive waking you?" Heloise asked with a smile.

"Yeah, now the rat fink is sleeping soundly in his bed," Edna grudgingly admitted. "I don't believe it," she continued. "I feel worse now than I did before I went to bed." Edna studied Heloise's face. "Why do you look so bright-eyed and chipper?" she asked.

"While you were snoring"—Edna shot her a dirty look, but she went on—"I meditated, did some yoga, and took a cold-water herbal bath."

"Sounds terrible," Edna muttered as she gratefully accepted the large mug of black tea Heloise offered.

"Actually, it is quite invigorating. You should try it sometime," Heloise responded perkily.

Edna stared at Heloise with bloodshot eyes as a frown crept across her brow. Setting the mug down carefully on the table, Edna spoke with carefully modulated tones. "Heloise, first off, I want you to know that I love you like a sister . . . No, scratch that. I had a sister once, and I didn't like her a whole lot. Okay, I love you better than a sister. You are the best friend I've ever had in my life, but if you don't stop being so irritatingly cheerful, I'm going to have to hurt you—severely. Do you understand me?"

Heloise smiled. "Yes, of course, dear. Just drink your tea."

Still glowering, Edna raised the mug to her lips and took a healthy swig. Edna's eyes popped open, and she turned an astonished face to Heloise. "Wow, what's in this tea?" she asked.

"I would prefer to keep the ingredients secret for the moment, but I will explain," Heloise said. "Do you remember how I excelled in chemistry and elixir formulation in school?"

"I should," Edna said. "I copied your notes often enough."

"Well, I created this tea from the chemical ingredients in the Energy Elixir. It took quite a bit of experimentation, but I believe the formula is pretty close now."

"I would say so," agreed Edna cheerfully. "I feel great! We'd better get ready. We're supposed to meet the children in the dining hall in less than an hour," said Edna.

"Exactly how many children are we taking?" asked Heloise.

Edna looked at Heloise, perplexed. "There are thirty students in each class. We're taking the first three classes. Gee . . . I guess that would be about ninety children. Why?"

"I just hope we can handle that many," said Heloise.

"Unless they stage a well-planned mutiny, I should hope that the three of us can handle them. Leonard is coming, isn't he?" asked Edna.

Heloise turned to the sink and began washing cups. "I'm not sure if he'll remember."

"Didn't you remind him when you had your heads together in the library?" Edna asked.

"Leonard hasn't come by the library for quite a while. In fact, I've seen so little of him lately that if I didn't know better, I'd swear he's been avoiding me."

"Oh, Heloise, I'm so sorry," Edna said softly.

"Sorry for what?" Heloise asked. "We are colleagues who went out to dinner once. It's not as though we were engaged in a romance," Heloise said with a catch in her voice.

"But I know you were beginning to have romantic feelings toward Leonard," protested Edna.

"Perhaps that was just wishful thinking on my part," Heloise observed. "Besides, maybe Leonard has a perfectly good reason for not visiting the library lately."

"He'd better, or he'll be answering to me," Edna muttered under her breath. Edna would never tell Heloise or Agnes, but they were closer and dearer to her than anyone she had ever known. She was apt to respond negatively to any perceived insult to them as though she was the intended target.

Heloise and Agnes had both been close to her, supportive of her, and seemed to sincerely care about her ever since she first met them at Aunt Mildred's. That was a lot more than she could say of her own family. Edna had never had a close relationship with anyone in her family. It hurt as much as a knife to the gut to have her family disown her. As her father had put it so eloquently, "She's not worth what it costs to feed her. Take her out of our lives, and be done with her."

As she looked back on her life, Edna thought that being sent to Aunt Mildred's School was probably the best thing that could have happened to her. Because of a quirky chance of fate, Edna wound up in a place where she would meet the two most important people in her life: Heloise and Agnes.

There was no way she would ever let anyone hurt Heloise, even if only with a broken heart, without a really fantastically good reason. At the first opportunity, she and Leonard Marshall would be having an in-depth discussion. She sincerely hoped that Leonard had a good reason for not seeing Heloise lately. Aside from Heloise's feelings toward him, he seemed like the perfect match for her. They were both brainiacs who loved books, research, art, and classical music. They also made a really cute couple and would probably have adorable babies. Babies that she could play Aunt Edna to and spoil outrageously. That thought brought a smile to her lips and a warm comfortable feeling to the rest of her.

"Edna? *Edna? EDNA!*" Heloise shouted while shaking Edna's shoulder. "Are you all right?" she asked.

"Sure, of course," Edna replied with a slightly dazed expression.

"If we don't get moving right now, we're going to be late," Heloise said.

"Oh, right," Edna jumped up from the table, knocking Agnes's recipe box to the floor. "Oh, for pity's sake! Agnes must have forgotten this when she ran out of here this morning. I guess we'd better return it before she misses it and goes ballistic." Edna stuffed the recipe cards back into the box and headed for her bedroom. Heloise shook her head and followed her friend down the hall to get ready for the day's activities.

When Edna and Heloise were ready, they met at the front door of the cottage. Heloise was suitably attired for a day in the woods. She wore a bright orange fleece-lined nylon jacket over a flannel shirt, heavy beige twill slacks, heavy cotton socks, and leather hiking boots. Edna was dressed much more casually. She wore a brown suede cowboy hat, a brown suede-fringed jacket over a thin cotton tee shirt, tight blue jeans, and brown suede moccasins with no socks.

"Edna, are you sure—" Heloise began.

"Don't start," Edna responded defensively. "My clothes are just fine for a picnic. Don't be a mother hen."

"Very well," Heloise said. "Let's go."

Edna led the way up the path toward the school with a brisk and jaunty step. As they passed through the wooded portion of the path, Edna determinedly focused her gaze in front of her, refusing to look into the woods on either side of the path. When they arrived at the dining hall, they were pleased to see the room filled with eager smiling faces. Most of the children were dressed in sneakers, blue jeans, and nylon, denim, corduroy, or flannel jackets, although one boy was also wearing a long hooded yellow rain slicker. As they drew closer, they could hear the boy in the slicker telling other children, "According to my calculations, there is an 85 percent chance of heavy rainstorms this afternoon."

Leonard was already there speaking quietly with some of the students. Their eyes met, and Heloise's smile faded quickly as Leonard immediately turned away from her to speak to another student. "How about I give him a sharp kick where it will do the most good?" whispered Edna.

"You'll do no such thing," hissed Heloise. "At least until he's had a chance to explain his behavior. Then we'll see." Edna's face split with a malicious grin as she thought about the pleasure she would derive inflicting pain on the rotten scoundrel that was causing her friend such misery. "Let's check on the box lunches," Heloise suggested.

When they got to the back of the dining hall, they found Agnes and Valerie stacking white boxes on the cafeteria line. "Is everything ready?" asked Heloise.

Agnes looked up and mopped the sweat from her forehead with her apron. "Yes, we just finished, and I would never have been done on time without the assistance of the best helper in the school." Agnes smiled and affectionately ruffled Valerie's blond curls.

"Geez, Agnes, you look terrible," remarked Edna.

"Thanks a lot," retorted Agnes.

Heloise pulled a small thermos from the inside pocket of her jacket and handed it to Agnes. Agnes took the thermos and looked at Heloise with raised eyebrows. "It's my own special blend of tea. I think you'll find it refreshing," explained Heloise.

"Hey, Agnes, there isn't anything weird in these lunches, is there?" Edna asked.

"Not unless you consider peanut butter and jelly sandwiches, an apple, two chocolate chip cookies, and a grape juice box *weird*," sniffed Agnes.

"No, that sounds bland enough to suit anyone," sighed Edna.

Heloise and Edna made sure that each child put a box lunch in his or her backpack and, with Leonard's help, herded the juvenile mob toward the front doors of the school. Just before they could escape into the bright autumn day, Pamela Sanderson, the school nurse, came running down the hall carrying what appeared to be a small white suitcase. "Wait, take this," Ms. Sanderson panted as she thrust the case at Leonard. Leonard looked puzzled until he turned the case over and noticed the large red cross on the side.

"Thank you so much, Pamela," Heloise said. "I had completely forgotten about first aid. Let's just hope we don't need to use it."

"Well, better safe than sorry, I always say," the nurse replied. "Have fun, and don't get lost." She smiled and waved to the children before turning to make her way back up the corridor.

Heloise and Leonard held the massive oak double doors open while Edna led the group across the school's immaculate front lawn. Once everyone was regrouped on the lawn, they formed a double line with Edna and Valerie leading, Heloise and Bobby Gallagher in the middle, and Marcia Turner and Leonard, with the first aid kit's shoulder strap across his chest, bringing up the rear.

Boisterously singing one of the school's more popular and sillier hiking songs, they headed southeast into the dense forest.

For an hour and a half, the children and their three chaperones marveled at the beauty and majestic wonder of the forest. They were entertained by the play of sunlight on the vibrant red leaves of the sugar maple, the yellow and burnt orange of oak leaves, and the occasional silver and white sparkle of beech leaves. They were scolded by territorial squirrels and teased by playful chipmunks. The children got to observe a black diamondback rattlesnake sunning itself stretched across the path and to learn one of the most important facts about the interaction between people and snakes: leave them alone, and they'll leave you alone.

They saw lots of woolly caterpillars, and Edna explained that according to folklore, the color and thickness of the bands on their bodies foretells the weather conditions for the coming winter. All of the caterpillars they saw that day indicated that the coming winter would be extremely cold with large amounts of snow.

There were sightings of deer, rabbits, and pheasants; and Charles Langhorne II, the undisputed science nerd of the school, insisted he heard the unmistakable scurrying of shrews in the leaf mold on the forest floor.

Edna sidled up to Heloise on the outer edge of the children, listening to Charles Langhorne II. Edna leaned over to Heloise and whispered, "I know this kid is supposed to be a shoo-in for the next Nobel Prize in science, but does he really know what he's talking about?"

Heloise smiled. "Considering he has established an IQ rating of 235, well over genius level, and he posted perfect scores on both the ACT and SAT tests by the age of twelve, I would say he probably does know all the scientific facts."

"I've been wondering about something," Edna continued. "Why is his name Charles Langhorne II instead of Charles Langhorne Jr.? I mean, in Lemain, a child named after his or her parent is known as Junior. Numerals are only used after the same name has been passed down three or more times in a row."

"I wondered about that too and did some research," Heloise said. "Evidently, in Pedestria, the decision to use Junior or numerals for names passed from one generation to another is completely up to the discretion of the parents."

"That's just plain silly," Edna objected. She shot a disgusted look at Heloise and walked away, shaking her head and muttering, "Silly Pedestrians, illogical world. To live here is to go stark raving bonkers!"

Eventually, they reached a large clearing that was known to the locals as the Theater. In the middle of the clearing was a huge granite slab, and around the perimeter were smaller protrusions of granite. Edna turned and shouted to the group, "Here we are! It's picnic time!" There was a flurry of activity as the children scrambled to remove their lunches from their backpacks and join their friends.

Leonard and Heloise suddenly realized that the buffer of children they'd so carefully kept between them had disappeared. They looked at each other for a moment; then Heloise blushed and looked around the clearing for a group that she could easily join without looking like she was running away from Leonard.

"Um"—Leonard cleared his throat—"this looks as good a place as any. Shall we?"

Heloise gave Leonard a brief smile and sat on the sun-warmed rock. As they ate their gummy peanut butter and jelly sandwiches, Heloise was pleased to note that Agnes had thoughtfully put a bottle of springwater instead of a juice box in her lunch. Leonard and Heloise ate their meal in silence until they began on their apples.

"Heloise," Leonard began tentatively, "I think we need to talk."

"Okay, Leonard, what would you like to talk about?"

Before he could answer, they were interrupted by shouts from the far side of the clearing. "Help! Somebody help! Bobby fell in a hole!" Leonard and Heloise dropped their apples and started running.

"Show us!" Leonard shouted at the boy who had sounded the alarm. They ran down the path until they came to a large rock outcropping slick with moisture and mossy growths. The rock sloped off to the right side of the path and ended in a sharp cliff edge.

Johnny Thompson was in tears. "We didn't mean for anything to happen. We just dared him to go to the edge of the cliff 'cause we know he's scared of heights."

Leonard grabbed Johnny by the shoulders. "Where is he?"

Johnny pointed toward the steepest sloping portion of the rock. "He fell into a hole down there," he sobbed.

Leonard narrowed his eyes and scanned the expanse of rock. He began to run down the rock, slipping in places but managing to stay on his feet. Suddenly, he threw himself forward as though he was a racing swimmer making a shallow dive and slid down the rock on his belly. When Leonard reached Bobby's struggling form, he grasped the collar of his jacket with his teeth and began a four-footed backward crawl toward safety.

When they had regained the forest path, Heloise rushed forward to check Bobby's injuries. "That was absolutely amazing, Leonard," Heloise said in a low voice.

"Yeah, Leonard, I never knew you had such strong teeth," Edna whispered in awe. Leonard was sitting on the path taking deep breaths, trying to counteract the effects of his recent adrenaline rush. Suddenly, it dawned on him what Edna had said and how he had exposed his deepest secret just moments before. He glanced fearfully at Heloise and Edna, wondering if they realized the significance of what he had done.

Heloise and Edna checked Bobby to determine how serious his injuries were. "Wasn't it wild how Leonard grabbed Bobby and pulled him out of that hole?" Edna asked Heloise excitedly. "Have you ever seen anything like it?"

"Actually, I think maybe I have," Heloise whispered, darting a suspicious look at Leonard.

"When? Where?" Edna insisted.

"Not now. We need to check something in the library when we get back to school," Heloise answered. She looked up at the crowd surrounding them and announced, "Nothing seems to be broken, just some scrapes and bruises. Leonard, would you please get the first aid kit?" Heloise smiled down at the still-trembling pale boy on the ground. "Well, Mr. Explorer, have you had enough excitement for one day?" Bobby nodded mutely. "Then I think we'll get you patched up, and all head back to the school."

Leonard returned with the kit and watched while Edna and Heloise cleaned Bobby's scrapes and bandaged the worst ones with antibiotic ointment and gauze pads. They helped a wobbly Bobby to his feet, and his buddies supported him up the path to the idyllic clearing where they had so recently been enjoying a pleasant picnic. By the time they had finished gathering the picnic debris, Bobby was entertaining anyone who would listen by recounting his life-threatening experience and his bravery.

Edna whispered to Heloise as they were bagging the last of the empty juice boxes, "To hear him tell the story, you'd think he was that Pedestrian folk hero, Davey Boone. Or was it Daniel Crockett? You know whom I'm talking about—the one who went into the woods at the age of six with only a sharp stick and killed six bears before lunchtime. Bobby's rendition of the event is just *slightly* more credible than that."

Instead of joining her chuckle, Edna was surprised to see a frown crease Heloise's brow. "We'll be incredibly fortunate if Bobby manages to convince the rest of the students that he rescued himself from that hole." Heloise looked at Edna intensely. "Trust me, Edna, if I'm correct, we absolutely do not want anyone to know how Leonard rescued Bobby."

The group slowly traversed the path back to the school as dark gray clouds began to slowly roll across the sky. The children were a little quieter than they had been, but they seemed to be in amazingly high spirits and possessed an uncommon energy considering all the exercise and the excitement of the afternoon. As Heloise watched, she noticed that Edna was acting very peculiar. Edna was scratching and fidgeting, pulling at her clothing; and finally, she began limping. When they arrived at the front doors of the school, Edna held one door open while shifting her weight gingerly from foot to foot. After the last child passed through the large front doors, Edna sank down on the stone portico with her back against the wall.

"Stay here. I'll be right back," Heloise said softly. Edna just groaned and removed her sweat-stained suede hat.

Heloise returned twenty minutes later and knelt down beside Edna. "All the students have been sent to their rooms to bathe. Bobby has gone to the infirmary to be checked out by Pamela Sanderson, and Leonard ran out the back door to the staff parking lot as though all the hounds in hell were at his heels. Now what is wrong with you?"

Edna turned tear-filled eyes to her friend. "Oh, Heloise, I hurt!"

"Where?" Heloise asked.

"Everywhere," Edna moaned.

"Oh, Edna, you silly thing! Is it the clothing?"

"Yes, I've never been so miserable!" whimpered Edna.

"Let's go up to the library. I kept the first aid kit. We'll fix you up in no time," Heloise said.

"Not up five floors to the library!" exclaimed Edna. "I can't walk."

"You'll walk, crawl, or dance a jig if you expect any help from me, Edna Fitzsimmons! I'm sorry you are in pain, but you brought it on yourself. Now move before we have to add a major pain in the rear to your list of ailments!" Heloise stood with the first aid kit over her shoulder and held the massive door open for Edna.

"Did anyone ever tell you that you have a serious mean streak?" Edna grumbled as she limped through the door past Heloise.

"No, but thank you for your observation," Heloise replied.

Leonard realized as soon as he looked at Heloise that he had made a serious error. The suspicion on her face was plain. Edna appeared to be more amazed than accusing, but surely, Heloise would clue her in as to exactly how unusual his actions really were. *Why did this have to happen now when he had just decided to tell Heloise everything?* "I know that life isn't fair, but shouldn't things even out sometimes?" he muttered. "And we still have to get everyone back to the school."

When Heloise asked him for the first aid kit, Leonard brought it over to her. He did notice, however, that she avoided meeting his eyes. Trapped in an emotional and mental quagmire, he assisted in the cleanup of the picnic area while his mind darted about looking for a solution to the problem he had created.

Bobby's voice broke through Leonard's musings. "It was really cool. I could feel myself starting to fall. That was kind of scary," he admitted. "Then I slid straight into the hole."

"What happened then?" asked Jimmy Llewellyn eagerly.

"I was able to stick my foot out, so I didn't fall all the way down," Bobby answered. "Then I started to pull myself up again," he glanced down at his skinny arms. "I'm really strong, a lot stronger than I look. Anyway, that's when Mr. Marshall and Ms. Amburgy got there."

Johnny Thompson looked excited. "Is that when Mr. Marshall rescued you? I couldn't see what happened because Ms. Amburgy stepped in front of me."

"Well, I was almost out of the hole anyway," Bobby bragged inaccurately. "Mr. Marshall just pulled me the rest of the way and then helped me up the rocks."

As the other boys were gazing at Bobby in admiration, Leonard gave a small sigh of relief. If the children believed Bobby's story, and it appeared that they did, it was one less threat he had to deal with.

On the way back to the school, Leonard stayed at the back of the group with the excuse of making sure that no one wandered away looking for further adventures. This was partially true. He was keeping an eye on the children, but his other eye was fixed firmly on Heloise and Edna. He noticed when Edna began exhibiting signs of discomfort. It appeared that the fashion-conscious woman was starting to recognize her poor choice in clothing. He was amazed that such an apparently intelligent woman could be so impractical. *Come to think of it, Edna had been leading the group and explaining all the flora and fauna they encountered during their hike. And hadn't Heloise once mentioned that Edna grew up on a farm?* Leonard mused. *It stands to reason that of us all, Edna would best know how to dress for a hike in the woods, yet she dressed in a manner more suited for a stroll in the town park. What on earth was she thinking?*

After reaching the school without further incident, Leonard waited as the students went upstairs. He saw the speculation in Heloise's eyes and felt panic set in. He knew he had to leave immediately before Heloise could corner him with her questions. Moving quickly, he exited through the rear door to the staff parking lot. He drove down the steep winding road much faster than safety allowed.

Upon reaching his house, Leonard rushed into his room. Fueled by panic, he pulled a large suitcase and a duffel bag out onto his bed and began to hastily stuff his possessions in helter-skelter. He barely glanced up as his mother entered the room. "Leonard, what are you doing?" she asked in confusion.

"I need to leave," he said, gathering up an armful of shirts and cramming them into his case.

"What happened?" Mrs. Marshall questioned.

"I can't believe I did it," Leonard groaned, sinking down on the edge of his bed. "I just wasn't thinking. One of the boys slid down the cliff and got trapped in a hole. I scrambled down after him and pulled him back up the path."

"Why would that be a problem?" his mother asked blankly.

"I went down on all fours and pulled him up with my teeth."

Mrs. Marshall was silent for a minute. "Yes, that does put a different light on things," she allowed.

"I don't think Edna caught what I did, but Heloise knew it was unusual. She kept watching me suspiciously," Leonard said, panic creeping back into his voice. "I'll go on ahead and find another place to settle. You can follow me when everything's ready."

Eleanor watched Leonard's frantic movements. He seemed to be overreacting again. He had done this ever since he was a little boy. Fortunately, she knew how to deal with this situation. "Will you be leaving tonight, Leonard?" she asked.

"I'll have to," he looked around the comfortable room that had been his sanctuary for so many pleasant years. "I don't want to leave. I have really enjoyed teaching at Sunny Acres, and I've been more comfortable in this house than any other place I can remember. This house has been perfect for us, located on the edge of the forest the way it is. I thought I'd found somewhere safe to live out my life."

"It certainly has seemed ideal for us. It will be difficult to find another location this convenient," Mrs. Marshall agreed.

Leonard stared thoughtfully at his suitcase for several minutes. "I really don't want to start over again. I like it here, and I like my job. I haven't broken any laws, and I haven't ever hurt anyone." His voice was rising with anger. "Why should I have to uproot my life when I haven't done anything wrong?" He glared at his mother. "I rescued that boy. He could have been badly injured or worse if I hadn't done what I did. I don't deserve to be punished for saving him even if the method was a trifle unorthodox. We're not going anywhere!" he snarled. "And Heloise will just have to accept me for who and what I am." Leonard stomped out of his room and slammed the kitchen door as he headed into the forest.

Mrs. Marshall smiled slyly. Humming under her breath, she unpacked Leonard's suitcase, returning the case and the duffel bag to the closet. As she walked into the cozy living room, she looked over at the calico cat that had pushed aside the blue chintz curtain to doze in a patch of sunlight. "It works every time, Cookie. If I let him talk it out long enough, he works himself up with righteous indignation and proves he does have a backbone." She crossed the room to her rocking chair and, still smiling, resumed her knitting.

Chapter 9

Back in Lemain, Rory Van der Haven was trying, with little success, to concentrate on writing up the report on his investigation of Vinny Sarducci's bank records. Although the investigation had revealed some very interesting anomalies in transferred funds, his mind kept returning to Edna's problems in the Pedestrian world. Snapping yet another well-chewed pencil in two, he disgustedly flung the pieces at the wastebasket across the room. The two other officers in the room looked up from their desks in surprise. Rory Van der Haven had a reputation for being the calmest member of the force. Rory glowered at the officers as he rose from his desk. "I'm taking a break. Anybody got a problem with that?" The officers quickly looked back at their paperwork.

Rory strode out of the room and down the main corridor to the department's solitary coffeemaker. He gave an angry jab of his wand to start the decrepit machine brewing coffee to fill the pot that some inconsiderate person had left empty. While he waited, he gazed out the small grimy window and thought. He remembered when he had first met Edna Fitzsimmons, right after the banquet disaster. She'd asked about obtaining legal counsel, court procedures, and what type of sentence they might expect. He was immediately impressed with her passion and sincerity and thought of her as a most interesting woman. He had spent a great deal of time helping her with her case.

After Edna and her friends were sentenced with banishment, he tried to put her out of his mind. This was difficult since he was frequently the officer assigned to the random checks the court required. As time wore on, he became increasingly interested in the plight of the banished witches and even began to question the fairness of their sentence.

Now it appeared as though their very lives were in danger, and he was stuck in Lemain investigating bank records. Rory viciously grabbed the pot and poured coffee into his cup, splashing scalding liquid over his hand.

"Rajjelfragitts!" he exclaimed as he replaced the pot and headed to the washroom to run cold water over his rapidly reddening hand.

Rory had long suspected that the witches "crime" had been arranged by someone who harbored ill will toward them. He really wanted to investigate their arrest and conviction, but he'd already roused the suspicions of his superiors with all the visits he'd made to the Pedestrian world recently. He couldn't chance any more overt action on his part. A thought suddenly came to him as the stream of cold water eased his scalded hand. The captain had forced his partner, Vic, to take an accumulated six months of vacation time beginning just last week. Maybe he could call in a favor and get Vic to take that vacation time at Sunny Acres School. Rory couldn't think of anyone he would trust more than Vic to handle whatever was threatening the three witches and hopefully to keep them out of trouble with the Department of Justice at the same time.

Rory and Vic had been partners ever since they had joined law enforcement. They had risen through the ranks together until they finally attained their gold investigator's stars. Along with a master's skill with any weapon, Vic was the undisputed best in the department at hand-to-hand combat. Rory smiled thinking about a recent raid they had conducted on an illegal alchemy lab. Vic incapacitated two of the three wizards in a whirling blur of martial arts moves before they could even reach for their wands. Afterward, Rory jokingly thanked Vic for leaving the third wizard for him to subdue. Vic had replied that Rory needed something to occupy his time during the raid.

Feeling more confident than he had in several weeks, Rory retrieved his coffee and hurried off to call Vic.

When Rory input Vic's personal code and activated the crystal screen, he was greeted with a gruff, "Whadda you want?"

"Whoa, partner," Rory said soothingly, "if this is what you're like after only a week, how are you going to survive six months?"

"Sorry, pal," answered Vic, "I thought maybe it was the captain calling to tell me this miserable 'vacation' was being made permanent."

Rory smiled. "Aren't you getting lots of rest and relaxation?"

"I'll get all the rest and relaxation I need when I'm dead!" growled Vic.

"What have you been doing with all your free time?" Rory asked.

"Watching the grass grow, what do you think?" Vic answered.

"What would you say to doing a little bodyguard duty?"

Vic's expression immediately perked up. "Am I being recalled to duty?"

"Uh, not exactly," Rory said. "It's more along the line of a personal favor and not something I want the department to know about."

"Ooh, that does sound interesting. Tell me more."

Rory took a large swig of his lukewarm coffee before continuing. "Do you remember Edna Fitzsimmons?" Rory asked his partner.

"Was that the witch with all that auburn hair and those amazing green eyes?"

"That's the one," Rory agreed. "Well, she has a bit of a problem."

"A bit of a problem," choked Vic. "That's a pretty mild way of referring to banishment from Lemain."

"No no, this has nothing to do with the banishment, or at least I don't think it does," Rory responded with a thoughtful frown. After a brief pause, Rory continued, "Edna and her friends have noticed some peculiar things happening in the Pedestrian world. Approximately six weeks ago, Edna was attacked by quatos in a forest near where they are living. Then several new students bearing a strong resemblance to goblins enrolled in the school where they're working. Becoming suspicious, Edna and her friends did some research through issues of *Magic Moments* and discovered reports of some unusual disappearances of important figures from Lemain.

"There have also been some nasty rumors about their business practices before they were banished. Now all this can be chalked up to coincidence or something much more sinister, and you know what I think about coincidence."

"Yeah, I don't believe in it either," said Vic. "Okay, this all sounds much too interesting to pass up. I just have one question—will I get to kick some butt?"

Chapter 10

After a torturous climb, Edna finally arrived on the fifth floor, the floor of the library. Leaning against the wall, Edna pulled herself down the hall toward the head librarian's office door where Heloise stood waiting. "Edna, get your fat fanny down here!"

Edna stood still and looked at Heloise with her eyes and mouth round with astonishment. "My what?"

"It's just an expression, and you know it. Now get in here before someone sees you," Heloise said in exasperation.

Edna finally made it to Heloise's office and immediately fell into the overstuffed green armchair. Heloise looked at her with disgust. "Strip." Edna's eyebrows shot up.

"I can't treat what I can't see, at least not with this," Heloise gestured to the kit.

Edna disrobed, and Heloise surveyed the damage. Edna's normally creamy skin now bore a bright red rash everywhere the clothing had touched her body. She had angry welts between her legs where the tight, stiff fabric had chafed her skin. Worst of all were her feet. The inadequate protection of the moccasins caused blisters on her feet, which ruptured then bled. No wonder she rebelled against making the climb to the fifth-floor library.

Heloise opened the kit and handed Edna a tube of ointment. "Rub that onto the rash and the welts while I take care of your poor feet," Heloise said. Heloise washed Edna's feet with an antiseptic solution, gently rubbed on a cream that contained antibiotics and painkillers, then swathed her feet with several layers of gauze bandages.

"Oh, thank you, Heloise. I feel so much better," Edna sighed as she was about to sit back down in the armchair.

"Stop!" Edna paused in midsquat. "You're covered in greasy ointment. Don't sit in my chair," Heloise said. She scavenged in the coat closet at the back of her office and returned with an old brown hooded robe and a pair of rubber galoshes. "Wear these," she said.

Edna donned the robe and the boots. "Won't I look ridiculous crossing the school grounds wearing these?" Edna asked.

"I doubt that anyone will be looking," said Heloise. "Check it out." She pointed at the window. The gray clouds that began rolling over the sky on their way back to the school had now turned black, and fat wet drops were falling. As they watched, lightning flickered in the distance and was followed several seconds later by the ominous rumble of thunder.

Heloise smiled at Edna, and Edna laughed. "All right, all right already. I'm convinced. The next time I want to know what the weather is going to be instead of checking out the TV weathermen, I'll ask Charles Langhorne II."

Heloise's expression became serious. "I've got some research to do."

Edna stood at the window watching the storm roll in as Heloise searched through the computer files of past periodicals. Shortly, Edna was distracted by Heloise's cry, "Got it!" Edna rushed to Heloise's side. On the screen was a picture of German shepherd dogs rescuing ice fishermen by grasping the collars of their jackets and pulling them backward across the ice.

"Oh, Heloise," gasped Edna, "what does this mean?"

"I'm still not entirely certain," Heloise said thoughtfully. "It could be something simple and completely innocent."

"What, like he was raised by wolves or something?" Edna asked.

"Or he could be a lycanthrope with the ability to change at will," Heloise replied.

"That's not an improvement," observed Edna.

"Or he could be a werewolf," Heloise said dejectedly.

They were silent for several minutes. Finally, Edna looked at Heloise. "You know him a lot better than I do. What do you think is the most likely answer?"

Heloise covered her eyes and shook her head. "I'm not sure. There's just not enough information. I know he lives with his mother, so I doubt that he was raised by wolves. As for him being a self-choice lycanthrope or a werewolf . . . They don't seem to fit since Leonard is a vegetarian. I just don't know."

There was a short rap on Heloise's door, and a moment later, a short man with a ruddy complexion and white mutton-chop sideburns stuck his head inside the door. "Ms. Amburgy, Ms. Fitzsimmons, so glad I found you here," said Walter Higgins, owner and headmaster of Sunny Acres School. "I wanted to introduce you to our new martial arts teacher, Ms. Victoria Lake." He extended his arm, and on cue, Ms. Lake entered the room. Edna and Heloise stared aghast at the person who stood smiling before them. She had to be at least five feet and nine inches tall (most of which were legs), slender with an hourglass figure encased in a tailored bright red pantsuit. Her hair wasn't so much gold as it was brilliant daffodil yellow, falling in alternating waves and ringlets to her waist. Her smile revealed perfectly straight, sparkling white teeth, and her eyes were the most brilliant shade of deep violet they had ever seen.

They awkwardly exchanged greetings, and Victoria Lake insisted they call her Vicky. Then Heloise addressed Mr. Higgins, "I wasn't aware that Sunny Acres had included a course of martial arts in the curriculum."

"It recently came to my attention that all of the best private schools have begun offering martial arts. There wasn't time to get the course added to the school catalog for this fall. Besides, I wasn't sure just when Ms. Lake would be available to begin teaching. By the way, ladies, since you have a three-bedroom cottage, I've made arrangements for Ms. Lake to room with you."

"Oh, Mr. Higgins, I don't think that will work," Heloise said hurriedly. "We've turned the third bedroom into an office and use it to store all of our books."

"I'm sorry, there really isn't any other option," said Mr. Higgins sympathetically.

"What about our pets?" interjected Edna. "Perhaps Ms. Lake is allergic to animals."

"Oh, I love animals. In fact, I have a cat," Vicky responded.

"Good, then it's all settled." Mr. Higgins clapped his hands. "I've taken the liberty of having the handyman, Carl, take Ms. Lake's luggage to the cottage. I'll leave you to get acquainted, and Ms. Lake can get unpacked. See you at dinner." Walter Higgins waved cheerfully and left.

Heloise and Edna frowned at each other and then turned their gaze to Vicky Lake. They were surprised to see that her smile had been replaced with an expression of intense seriousness. "Ladies, we have a lot to discuss, and I think the cottage would be the best place for our conversation. Shall we go?" She turned and strode briskly out of the library.

Edna looked questioningly at Heloise. "What is going on?"

"I suspect we'll discover that when we get to the cottage," Heloise replied.

Edna gathered her clothing and followed Heloise to the school's entrance.

As Vicky, Heloise, and Edna looked across the rain-swept lawn of the school, they were astounded with the ferocity of the thunderstorm. The blinding flashes of lightning and crashes of thunder were almost simultaneous. "We can't cross that field in this! We'll get fried!" shouted Edna above the noise of the wind and thunder.

"Hmm . . ." Vicky glanced at her watch and appeared to come to a decision. She looked around at the windows of the school. Not seeing any observers, she produced a slender willow wand from inside her suit, waved it over their heads, and whispered, "Sceldhydar." Immediately, the three were encased in an invisible but impervious shield. "Okay, let's go," she said. As the three ran across the lawn to the woods under the invisibility shield spell, Heloise couldn't help but wonder just who this woman was and what she was doing at Sunny Acres School.

At the same time, Edna was evaluating the situation a little differently. *I don't like this female. I'm not sure who she is or what she's up to. But I don't know her, I don't trust her, and I definitely don't like her.*

When they reached the cottage, Rap was waiting for them at the door. Rap stood up on his hind legs and crossed his furry little paws in front of him. "Would anyone care to explain the meaning of this intrusion to our abode?" he demanded.

Several cases were stacked against the walls of the cottage entrance, including an animal carrier. "Oh, Suzy," cried Vicky as she hastily opened the animal carrier. She removed a fairly large blue-eyed Siamese cat from the carrier and cradled it to her chest. Vicky nuzzled the cat and turned to introduce her familiar to the others.

"This is my Suzy," Vicky Lake announced fondly.

Rap leapt to Edna's shoulder, almost knocking her over. "A cat! You don't seriously expect me to share my home with a cat, do you? Especially a Siamese cat?" Suzy hissed and slashed a paw full of fully extended razor-sharp claws in the direction of Rap's nose.

Vicky's eyes narrowed menacingly. "This isn't going to be a problem, is it?"

Edna grabbed Rap before he could attack the cat. "Rap, you're the host. Mind your manners."

"We'll discuss this later," Heloise snapped at the raccoon. She smiled at Vicky. "I'm sure everything will work out all right. Rap just reacts poorly to changes or surprises. Would you like us to help you get settled?"

Vicky's expression smoothed, and she replied, "That won't be necessary. Just show me to my room, please." Keeping a tight hold on her Siamese cat, Vicky followed Heloise down the hall to the third bedroom. After she had inspected the room and found that it wasn't nearly so cluttered as Heloise and Edna had professed to Mr. Higgins, she stated that it would be perfect and that she could get it set up by herself.

Edna, Heloise, and Rap retreated to the kitchen. "What are we going to do about her?" Edna demanded.

Heloise filled the kettle and set it on the stove. She then went to the cabinet to bring out the box of tea and two cups. It took her a little longer than usual since she was working with one hand. The other hand was in her pocket, stroking Beowulf.

"Heloise, are you going to answer me?" Edna insisted.

Heloise massaged the frown creases between her brows with one hand before replying, "Please, Edna, for once in your life, be quiet and exhibit some patience."

Edna fell into a chair at the table with Rap firmly grasped in her lap, an expression of shock on her face. Heloise rarely ever talked to her like this, and she'd done it twice in one day.

"Please, not so tight, mistress," rasped Rap, barely breathing.

Edna was surprised to realize she had her familiar in a stranglehold. "Oh, sorry, Rap," she apologized.

The kitchen remained quiet until the whistle of the teakettle broke the silence. Heloise filled two mugs with her special brew and brought them to the table. "I don't like using the *special* tea this often, but it doesn't look like we're going to have a chance to sleep at least until after dinner tonight." Her feelings still smarting from Heloise's remark about her patience, Edna refused to say anything and sipped the invigorating brew. "Okay, what do you think is going on?" Heloise finally asked.

Seizing the opportunity to speak, Edna replied, "I have no frickin' frackin' idea! But I'll tell you one thing, I don't trust this Vicky Lake! Have you noticed how much she resembles that doll all the girls at school are crazy about? You know, the one with the convertible and the palatial condominium? No one could be that beautiful and be real."

"Is someone talking about me?" Vicky asked as she entered the kitchen. "Um, that tea smells wonderful. May I have a cup?" She sat at the table and smiled expectantly at Heloise.

"Of course," Heloise returned the smile and poured a cup of tea for Vicky.

After taking a sip of the tea, Vicky gave a huge sigh. "I realize that I wasn't expected and am not exactly welcome here, but I came as a favor to Rory Van der Haven. He seemed to think that you had a problem you couldn't handle without violating your sentence restrictions."

"How do we know you're telling the truth and Rory actually sent you?" Edna asked.

"Well, there is this," Vicky replied, handing over an envelope addressed to Edna. Edna ripped the envelope from Vicky's hand and tore it open.

Dear Edna,

First, I want you to know that if there were any way possible, I would personally be there to guarantee your safety. Unfortunately, I can't be there. But my partner, Vic, has some free time and is willing to do me the favor of watching out for you.

Vic and I have watched each other's backs for many years, and I trust her with my life and with yours. Please cooperate with her and help her. She's the best officer in the department, except for me, of course. She'll do everything in her power to ensure your safety.

I'll check in with you as often as I can. Take care.

Sincerely,
Rory

Edna finished reading and looked at Vicky. "Well, you certainly come highly recommended," Edna admitted, disgruntled.

"Oh, thank goodness," sighed Heloise. "I was afraid the justice department had sent you to spy on us."

"Technically, the justice department doesn't know I'm here, and I'd be just as happy if they didn't find out," Vicky said. "Since we have a little time before dinner, why don't you ladies tell me what has been happening here in the wonderful world of Pedestrians?"

"Oh, you mean your 'partner' didn't fill you in when you agreed to do this favor for him?" Edna asked venomously.

With a glacial stare, Vicky responded, "Actually, he did, but I was hoping to get more details from your accounts of the situation."

"Edna, behave yourself," Heloise admonished. "I don't know why you have to be so cranky. Ms. Lake is here to help us. Do you want to refuse her help?"

Edna thought for a moment and, frowning, finally grumbled, "Of course not. I may be cranky, but I'm not stupid."

Heloise and Edna spent the better part of the next hour explaining in great detail everything that had been happening at Sunny Acres School for the past six weeks. Edna was telling about Bobby's rescue during the picnic when she felt a sharp kick to her right shin. Her mouth snapped shut, and she stared at Heloise in shock. Heloise had her finger to her lips and was shaking her head. Vicky looked up from her notepad where she had been diligently recording their story.

She looked at Edna in concern. "Are you all right?"

"I'm fine. It's just a leg cramp," Edna replied.

"Oh, I see, please continue. What did Leonard Marshall do then?"

Before Edna could say anything, Heloise answered, "Since Bobby had fallen into a hole, Mr. Marshall pulled him out. Then we cleaned up the picnic area and returned to the school."

"It certainly is puzzling," Vicky admitted, closing her notepad. "I'll be interested in seeing these new students. Could you point them out to me at dinner?"

"Don't worry, you can't miss them. I'm surprised the Pedestrians don't notice how strange they are," Edna said.

"Well, if I'm to be introduced to the school tonight, I suppose we had better dress for dinner," Vicky said, rising from the table. At that moment, Vicky's Siamese cat, Suzy, entered the kitchen and began sniffing at the luxuriously cushioned pet bed, which was currently unoccupied, with Rap having maintained his position on Edna's lap during the witches' conversation. Rap immediately raced to the corner and stood his ground in the middle of the bed.

"Surely you are not planning to allow this *feline* the run of the cottage while we attend dinner?" Rap asked, with a contemptuous look at Suzy.

In her sweetest tone of voice, Vicky replied, "Under the circumstances, I believe it would be best if all of us, witches and familiars, attend the dinner together. Come, Suzy." With that, Vicky swept out of the kitchen, closely followed by her cat.

"Did you see that?" sputtered Rap. "That horrid creature flicked her tail in my face!"

"Oh, come off it. You've had worse things in your face than her tail. Whose nose was buried in the garbage cans behind the kitchen last week?" Edna asked.

"Well, if someone would remember to feed me occasionally, I wouldn't be forced to forage for my meals," Rap rejoined.

"I'm sorry," Edna said contritely. "Look, I'm not any happier about them being here than you are, but we need their help. Just try to stay out of their way for the time being."

"Yes, please try to be agreeable, Rap," Heloise implored. "It won't be forever, just until we can figure out what is going on. Besides, I'm sure Agnes will give you a very nice dinner in the kitchen tonight." That perked up Rap's spirits.

"I wonder if she has any of that fresh salmon left," Rap mused as he followed Heloise and Edna out of the kitchen.

While the three witches were talking in the kitchen, the rain stopped, and the temperature dropped drastically. Anticipating the change in the weather, Heloise had dressed appropriately for the walk to the school and the upcoming dinner. She was wearing a voluminous navy blue wool skirt with a beige angora turtleneck sweater. She finished off her ensemble with short fleece-lined dress boots and a navy blue hooded cape. When Vicky joined them by the front door, Edna and Heloise both gasped when they saw what she was wearing. Vicky had on a shocking-pink body stocking with ruffles around the neckline and cuffs and purple crushed-velvet hot pants with silver studs. She was also wearing purple suede boots with four-inch heels and carrying a fringed purple suede jacket.

Heloise was the first to recover. "What in heaven's name do you think you are wearing?" she demanded.

Vicky looked down at herself and asked, "What's wrong with what I'm wearing?"

Edna choked back a laugh and said, "Nothing, except you're apt to start a riot in the school. And of course, every male over the age of twelve will be following you around and drooling on your heels."

"Oh, perhaps this attire is a little too provocative for Pedestrians. Excuse me a moment." Vicky hastily retreated to her room.

While Vicky was changing into more subdued clothing, Heloise examined Edna's choice of attire for the evening. Edna was wearing a long black evening gown with a low-cut back and a sequined belt. "Aren't you a bit overdressed for dinner at the school?" Heloise asked.

Blushing slightly, Edna replied, "Well, it is customary to dress for dinner, and we are introducing a new faculty member tonight. Okay, it's the only thing I have that doesn't chafe my sore spots."

Glancing down at her feet, Heloise was horrified to see fuzzy pink slippers! "Edna, what do you have on your feet?" she exclaimed.

"My feet hurt, and these are comfortable," Edna said defiantly. Just then, Vicky's door opened.

"Oh well, there's nothing we can do about it now. We're going to be late as it is," Heloise muttered in exasperation. "Just keep those slippers out of sight," she admonished Edna. Vicky's clothing change was a definite improvement to Heloise's way of thinking. She was wearing a cream-colored peasant blouse, a knee-length brown suede skirt, low-heeled brown suede boots, a matching jacket, and a cowboy hat.

"How many cows gave their all for that outfit?" Edna quipped.

Vicky ignored the remark. "Shall we go?" Vicky asked as she turned and opened the door. "Come, Suzy."

"I guess Her Highness has spoken. Let's go," said Edna as she scooped up Rap and headed out the door. Heloise sighed as she closed the cottage door and followed her companions along the path through the forest.

Suzy and Rap led the way through the trees, each stalking a separate side of the path. Every so often, Suzy would drift over to Rap's side of the trail and brush against him, causing him to jump. The third time this happened, Rap stopped and glared at Suzy. "If it wouldn't be too much of an inconvenience, would you mind staying on your side of the path?" he asked the cat. Suzy just purred and rubbed her whiskers against Rap's nose. He immediately lost all pretense of urbanity. "Get off, you stupid feline!" he shrieked, jumping backward. Unfortunately, Rap didn't realize a large log was right behind him. As he fell over backward with all four paws scrabbling wildly for something to grab on to, Suzy haughtily raised her tail and continued up the path.

"That's enough, you two," Vicky said. "You can play later. We don't have time now."

Rap picked himself up and went to walk beside Edna. "Play indeed," Rap said huffily. "Did you see what that cat did? That animal is absolutely insufferable!"

"Hush," Edna advised her familiar. "We still need their help. You can get even with the cat when this is over."

"Ah yes, sweet revenge." Rap smiled.

When they reached the school, they found Walter Higgins waiting for them at the front door. "Welcome, ladies, we were beginning to worry about you," he said as he held the door open for them. "Everyone is already assembled in the dining hall. Interesting footwear, Ms. Fitzsimmons," he whispered in an aside to Edna. Edna blushed and adjusted her dress to better cover the offending slippers.

As they hurried down the brightly lit corridor, they could hear the babble of voices coming from the dining hall.

Entering the hall, they noticed that seats had been saved for them at the head table right beside Walter Higgins. After they had hung up their jackets and taken their places at the table, Mr. Higgins stood and cleared his throat. An immediate hush fell over the room as everyone stared at the head table.

"Students and faculty members," Mr. Higgins began, "I would like to introduce to you our newest faculty member, Ms. Lake." Putting a hand under her elbow, he helped Vicky to stand beside him. When the thunderous applause died down, he continued, "Ms. Lake will be teaching a new elective course in martial arts starting tomorrow. Anyone whose class schedule is not already overburdened can sign up for one of the classes being offered on the sheet at the door of the dining hall. Wait, wait!" Mr. Higgins shouted over the uproar as most of the male students and some of the faculty began a mass exodus toward the door. "Excuse me, I should have said, you may sign up *after dinner.*" Mr. Higgins chuckled softly and sat down.

There was a collective groan of disappointment from those who had rushed toward the door as they regained their seats. "Predictable. Disgusting but predictable," Edna muttered as she grabbed her salad fork and stabbed a cherry tomato.

"Look at the table in the far corner," Heloise whispered urgently. Edna looked at the table indicated and noticed that the suspected half goblins were talking furiously among themselves and all wearing extremely ugly expressions, even uglier than usual for them.

"Aha, it seems that not all of our students are thrilled with the addition of Vicky to the faculty staff. I wonder if they recognize her," Edna smirked.

Heloise leaned over and whispered to Vicky, "Do you recognize any of the students sitting at the table in the far left corner?

Vicky smiled at some comment of Mr. Higgins then turned her gaze to the table of half goblins. "Aside from the fact that they all obviously have goblin blood in their ancestry, I don't recognize any of them. However, the fourth boy from the right on the far side of the table bears a striking resemblance to Smrrg, the leader of the Eastern Mountain Clan."

"What should we do?" asked Heloise anxiously.

"Unless they attack here and now, we do nothing. Just wait and watch," Vicky answered.

For the remainder of the meal, Edna practiced people watching. The goblins continued to be agitated and ate little. Most of the boys were also eating little, spending most of their energy staring at Vicky Lake, except for Charles Langhorne II who was expounding upon the merits of martial arts to anyone who would listen. The girls were either arguing with the boys or actively ignoring them.

At one point during the dinner, the music teacher, Edward Bigelow, passed a note to Heloise. Opening the tightly folded slip of paper, Heloise read, "We must talk. Meet me after dinner in the staff parking lot. Leonard." Heloise crumpled the note and jammed it into her pocket. Beowulf's angry squeal made Heloise rapidly move the crumpled note to her other pocket.

"We need to talk to Agnes after dinner. Tell Vicky," Edna murmured to Heloise.

A soft sheen of perspiration broke out on Heloise's brow. How could she be in the kitchen with Agnes and in the parking lot with Leonard at the same time? She looked at Leonard at the end of the table. He certainly appeared stressed out as he raised his water glass and slopped half the contents onto the table. Even his bow tie was askew. She felt a sharp pang of remorse. Regardless of who or what Leonard was, he had always behaved like a kind, considerate gentleman to her. She felt she owed it to him to hear his side of the story before she wrote him out of her life forever.

"You and Vicky explain everything to Agnes. I have something to do after dinner. I'll meet you at home."

"What?" Edna exclaimed, drawing looks from those around them. Heloise gave Edna her sternest librarian "you're making too much noise" look.

Heloise smiled sweetly and said, "Excuse us please." Grabbing Edna's arm, she walked them out of the dining hall and into the closest ladies' room. After checking to make sure they were alone, Heloise sank down on a red velvet settee. She began, "I can't go with you to talk to Agnes because I have to meet Leonard after dinner."

"Are you completely nuts?" Edna asked. "We discussed Leonard this afternoon. What if he is a werewolf?"

Heloise looked up at Edna and spread her hands. "We have to find out one way or another, don't we? I've given this a lot of thought, and I just don't believe that Leonard Marshall has an evil atom in his body."

"Oh, for Callisto's sake, Heloise, did it ever occur to you that he may be acting this way just to lull you into a false sense of security?"

"I don't believe that, and my mind is made up," Heloise said. "I will meet with Leonard."

Noting the determined look on Heloise's face, Edna gave up. "Okay, it's your funeral, but I don't like the idea of you walking home alone in the dark. Meet us in the kitchen after you finish with

Leonard. Now can we get back to dinner? Agnes prepared fudge swirl cheesecake for dessert, and I definitely don't want to miss that."

On the way back to the dining hall, Edna and Heloise passed two boys with their heads together, whispering intently. Edna stopped and stared at the boys as they continued down the corridor. "Wasn't that Jason and Jeremy Wilkins?" she asked.

"Yes, I believe it was," answered Heloise.

"You know, they haven't bothered me for quite a while," Edna said wistfully. "Pretty sad when I find myself missing constant torment by a couple of adolescent boys. I wonder what they're up to."

Back inside the dining hall, they found that all of the fudge swirl cheesecake was gone. The only dessert left was a cloudy green gelatin with a faintly unpleasant odor. Edna snatched up the cup of offensive gelatin at her plate and stalked toward the kitchen.

In the meantime, students were filing out of the hall, with most of the males stopping to sign the martial arts class schedule posted at the door. Heloise took this opportunity to slip out the side door and make her way to the staff parking lot.

"Agnes!" Edna shouted as she slammed through the double swinging doors into the kitchen. The dozen or more kitchen helpers who were scurrying around and cleaning up the dinner debris glanced over at Edna then returned to their work. Edna frowned and stalked toward Agnes's office. Agnes jumped up from her seat behind the desk as Edna burst through the door. "What do you call this?" Edna asked, thrusting the cup in front of Agnes's face.

Agnes examined the bowl and said, "It looks like green gelatin."

"Okay, but what is it made of?" Edna demanded.

"Well, I guess it's made of what all green gelatin is made of," Agnes answered, beginning to back away from Edna. Edna's gaze landed on a recipe card on Agnes's desk. Reading upside down, Edna read Frog Toe-Jam Gelatin at the top of the card.

Edna glared ferociously at Agnes and set the cup on the desk. In an ominously quiet voice, Edna said, "I can't believe you did this. We talked about this, and you did it anyway." Agnes shrank back further. "I've had it! Where is that box?"

Speechless, Agnes could only point. Edna followed the direction of her finger to a bookshelf on the wall next to the door. Sitting prominently in the middle of the third shelf was the black lacquered box, which held the recipes that represented Agnes's family heritage. Panting heavily, Edna viciously grabbed the box. She then snatched the gelatin recipe from Agnes's desk and shoved it into the box.

Passing a hand over her tired, burning eyes, Edna said, "I'm sorry, Agnes, but are you aware that you've only been bringing out these obscure and arcane recipes since the weird things have been happening around here?"

Agnes tentatively moved toward Edna. "Do you really think there is a connection?" Agnes asked.

"Well, I'm not sure, but it's the only connection I can see at the moment," Edna replied, replacing the recipe box on the shelf. "If you have another explanation, I'd love to hear it." Trying to ignore Agnes's crestfallen expression, Edna continued, "I don't pretend to know what is going on, but at least some of it seems to be connected to this box. Come on, Agnes, you've cooked for at least twenty-three years without ever feeling the need to resort to your old family recipes—especially the oldest and most bizarre recipes."

"I'm sorry, Edna, I don't know what comes over me. I just can't seem to keep myself from using those recipes." Agnes sank down in her chair and dropped her head to her hands. "I think I must be going crazy."

"Don't be silly, Agnes, you're not crazy," Edna said. "At least not any more than usual." Agnes raised her head and gave Edna a reproachful look. "Well, you must admit, you've always been slightly left-of-center."

"Ah, there you are, Ms. Thistlewaite," Walter Higgins boomed in a jovial tone of voice as he escorted Vicky Lake into the office. "I wanted to introduce you to our newest faculty member, Ms. Victoria Lake." As Vicky and Agnes exchanged handshakes, Mr. Higgins noticed Edna standing off to the side of the room. "Ms. Fitzsimmons, have you met Ms. Lake? Oh, of course you have. She's staying at your cottage," he chuckled. "How silly of me. I'm afraid the older I get, the more forgetful I become."

Vicky spoke up, "Thank you so much for introducing me to everyone, but if you don't mind, I'd like to stay and chat with Edna and Agnes for a bit." Vicky flashed a brilliant smile at Walter Higgins.

"Of course, my dear. Don't keep Ms. Lake up too late," he advised Agnes and Edna. "She has her first class early in the morning, and from the looks of the sign-up sheet, it's going to be a very full class."

I'll bet it's full—full of boys, thought Edna.

Walter Higgins wished them all a good night and left. The three witches stood looking at one another for a few minutes. Edna finally broke the silence. "Agnes, why don't you get a couple more chairs and a pot of tea? We may be here a while."

"Yes yes. So sorry, please excuse me," Agnes mumbled as she bustled out into the main kitchen.

"So where is Heloise?" Vicky asked Edna.

"She had to go talk to someone. She'll meet us here when she's finished," Edna answered. Looking around the office, Vicky's gaze fell upon the dish of gelatin.

Wrinkling her nose, Vicky asked, "What's this?"

"You don't want to know," Edna answered as she quickly moved the dish to the top of the filing cabinet.

Agnes returned with two straight-backed chairs and placed them in front of her desk. "Please have a seat. The tea will be here in a few minutes."

They all took seats; then Agnes said, "What brings you to Sunny Acres School, Ms. Lake?"

Vicky raised an eyebrow and looked at Edna. "Do you want to explain the situation, or shall I?"

Edna quickly filled Agnes in on Rory's requesting Vicky's help on their behalf. By the time she finished, Valerie was entering the office with a tea service including a plate of crisp, delightfully aromatic cookies.

Valerie placed the tray on Agnes's desk and looked up at Vicky. "Oh, you're one of them," she said. "Are you from the same place as Ms. Thistlewaite?" Vicky looked startled and momentarily speechless.

"Valerie, this is Ms. Lake. She's the new martial arts teacher. Ms. Lake, this is Valerie Valentine, one of the students and my best kitchen helper," Agnes said by way of introduction.

Vicky looked inquiringly at Valerie. "What did you mean when you said, 'You're one of them'? And why did you ask if I'm from the same place as Ms. Thistlewaite?"

"Well," Valerie responded, "you have the same purplish glow that Ms. Thistlewaite and Ms. Fitzsimmons have, so I thought maybe you were from that other world, Lemain." Edna groaned and covered her eyes with one hand.

Still smiling at the child, Vicky said, "Thank you, Valerie, you can go now. I need to talk to Ms. Thistlewaite and Ms. Fitzsimmons alone."

As soon as Valerie closed the door, Vicky turned a frosty glare on Agnes. "Just what *exactly* have you told that child?"

Flustered, Agnes tried to explain. "First, I discovered that Valerie could see auras. Then I found out that her parents were Gloria and Michael Valentine. Well, she was confused, and I had to give her some sort of explanation, didn't I? But don't worry, she promised to keep it a secret."

Still glaring, Vicky said, "You know what they say about secrets, don't you? Only two can keep a secret, and then only if one of them is dead." Vicky raised her eyes to the ceiling. "Oh, Rory, what have you gotten me into?" she muttered.

Vicky picked up a cup and stared into the steaming brown liquid as Edna and Agnes quietly sipped their tea. "Have you got anything to put in this?" Vicky asked.

"Of course," replied Agnes, "there's sugar, lemon, or milk. What would you like?"

"I think she means something just a little stronger," Edna suggested.

"Oh, right," Agnes said. She turned to the bottom drawer of the filing cabinet and produced a half-full bottle of fourteen-year-old brandy. Vicky poured a generous dollop of brandy into her tea and took a sip. She sighed, closed her eyes, and sat back in her chair. Agnes looked at Edna, but Edna just shrugged and took a cookie from the plate, inspecting it suspiciously.

When Vicky finally opened her eyes, she asked, "Have you three always been like this, or has this just happened since you were banished?" Agnes blushed and silently dropped her eyes to her now-empty cup.

Edna shrugged and replied, "This is pretty much the way we've always been. It's done all right for us so far."

Vicky gave her an incredulous look. "Oh yes, you three have done soooo well," she said sarcastically. "Blowing up President Thurgood's inauguration cake, getting banished to the Pedestrian world, being attacked by quatos, and now spreading knowledge of

Lemain to Pedestrians! It's absolutely amazing that you've survived this long. The three of you shouldn't be allowed out in public without a keeper."

"Wait just a minute." Edna bristled. "Those things weren't our fault, except for Agnes spilling the beans. Things just happen to us."

"Great," Vicky said, grabbing the brandy. "So you're not criminally stupid. You're just magnets for trouble."

"Whatever," Edna replied as she gave Vicky a scathing look and added brandy to her cup.

"Speaking of trouble magnets," Vicky began, "where is Heloise, and who was she meeting?"

"If you must know, she was meeting with Leonard Marshall, the history teacher," Edna said.

"Was he that nervous-looking guy with the ugly bow tie at the end of the table?"

"Yeah, that was him," Edna agreed.

"For someone who had rescued a boy just this afternoon, he didn't look too happy," Vicky observed.

"I think he may have some other things on his mind," Edna replied warily, remembering that they had not mentioned their suspicions of Leonard's unusual attributes or Heloise's feelings to Vicky.

They sat in silence, each deep in their own thoughts, sipping from their cups for several minutes. The silence was broken by Agnes. "Oh dear, we're out of tea," she giggled. "I'll get us another pot."

Edna stared at her in shock as Agnes stumbled to the door. Edna's and Vicky's gaze went to the brandy bottle simultaneously. The bottle was now empty.

Vicky turned to Edna. "Does Agnes have a problem that I should know about?"

"No," Edna answered slowly. "She's just a bit stressed out at the moment." *Great,* thought Edna, *we're making such a wonderful first impression on this woman. Not that I really care what Ms. Perfect thinks, but what is she going to tell Rory? I must have been born under a black moon. Just when I think things are as bad as they can possibly be, they get worse.*

Chapter 11

It's much easier, mused Leonard to himself, *to decide upon a course of action than it is to actually carry it out. Righteous indignation only goes so far.*

It had been over an hour since Leonard had stormed into the forest, determined to confront Heloise at the earliest opportunity. If he had been able to locate her at that time, all these issues would have been resolved. Unfortunately, he wasn't that lucky.

First of all, there was a storm on his way back to the school. He sheltered under the trees during the worst of it; however, he was still uncomfortably wet when he reached the school. Naturally, he made the library his first stop in his search, only to find it dark and deserted. The evidence of first aid being administered caused him to wince. He then continued on to the administration office to see if Heloise was with Edna. Finding the office closed also, he finally thought to check the time.

"How did it get this late?" Leonard asked himself, astounded. "Dinner is in less than an hour. I'll have to talk to Heloise later."

He knew that he needed to be presentable both for dinner and also to, hopefully, impress Heloise. He looked down at his uncomfortable damp shirt and jeans and groaned. Then he remembered leaving his battered old car at home and running through the woods to the school. There was no time to run back home to change and make it back in time. He wasn't sure he had the stamina to do so in any case after such an eventful day. He always kept a clean shirt in his office in case of accidents, but what about the rest of his clothes? *Accidents*—that was it! A month previously, he had run into the Wilkins boys in the hall—literally. They had been carrying a container of some sticky substance, which ended up all over his clothes. The clothes had been hanging behind his office door since he picked them up from the dry cleaners. *There are times,* he thought with a small smile, *that being absentminded works in one's favor.*

When he entered the dining hall, Leonard glanced around quickly, hoping to locate Heloise. Things would be so much easier if he could speak to her before everyone sat down to dinner. He was disappointed to discover that Heloise hadn't arrived yet, nor had her friend Edna. He thought about his options. He could wait for her at the front entrance, but that might annoy her, and he was already chilled. Waiting at the staff table was probably his best choice. The far end was always slow to fill up, and it was also protected from drafts. Hopefully, Heloise would join him when she arrived.

There were beverages on the sideboard, so Leonard helped himself to a cup of hot tea before claiming the end seat at the table. Staff members began to fill the empty seats. Leonard's hopes were dashed when Heloise and Edna entered the hall, flanked by Walter Higgins and a tall blond woman. Leonard studied her for a moment and perceived a dangerous air but didn't feel any personal threat from her. They all took the empty seats at the center of the table. Leonard heard Higgins speaking; however, he was concentrating on how best to approach Heloise and didn't pay attention to what was being said.

Ed Bigelow slid into the seat next to him, interrupting his train of thought. "Hey, Len." Ed smiled cheerily and draped his napkin over his lap. "I was afraid I was going to miss dinner. I had the Wilkins twins busy straightening up the shelves in the music room. I can't believe how little these kids care about their instruments."

"What were you reprimanding them for?" Leonard asked.

"They were passing notes in class again." Ed grinned. "It's not a major transgression, but at least it got my classroom cleaned."

Leonard stared for a moment before smiling. "Of course, note passing is a time-honored tradition." He scrabbled in his jacket pocket and pulled out a ragged notepad and a pencil stub. After scribbling for a moment, he ripped off the sheet and folded it into a compact square. At that point, it was only a matter of waiting for his chance to pass the note to Heloise.

His contemplative mood was interrupted as a large percentage of the male students, and even some of the faculty, began an exodus from the dining hall. Mr. Higgins made a small joke, and everyone returned to his or her seat. Leonard glanced about guardedly, wondering if anyone had noticed his distraction. He had missed Mr. Higgins's entire speech. He hoped it wouldn't come back to haunt him.

"Why aren't you eating, Len?" Ed asked. "I thought this mushroom casserole was your favorite? You usually can't get enough of it."

It was a good thing that Edward didn't mind carrying the conversation. Leonard hoped that Ed's natural jocularity would conceal his own lack of attention. Ed finished eating hurriedly and moved to stand.

"I believe this would be a good opportunity to introduce myself to the new martial arts instructor," Ed said, standing.

Leonard reached into his pocket and held out his note. "As long as you're going that way, would you mind handing this to Heloise?" he requested, tugging nervously at his tie.

"Passing notes at dinner, are you?" Ed smiled slyly. "Well, at least it won't earn you a detention." He moved down the row of teachers toward Vicky, pausing behind Heloise just long enough to slip Leonard's note into her hand.

Leonard watched anxiously as Heloise opened the scrap of paper and read the words he had scribbled. *I should have phrased it more eloquently,* he mentally scolded himself. He reached for his water glass just as Heloise's eyes met his, causing his hand to tremble. The water slopped over the side and soaked the cuff of his shirtsleeve.

Heloise smiled sympathetically at him and gave an almost-imperceptible nod. Leonard's breath huffed out; Heloise would meet him after dinner. Now all he had to do was come up with an acceptable explanation for his unacceptable behavior.

Heloise stepped out of the side door and looked intently around the parking lot.

She hated how hard it was to see during the dark of the moon. A startled gasp escaped her when Leonard slipped out of the shadows and moved closer to her.

"Oh, Leonard, I didn't see you there. How do you manage to blend in so well with your surroundings?" she asked breathlessly.

"I've had to learn to adapt, or as you say 'blend in,' since I was just a boy," Leonard answered quietly. "Heloise, I really need to talk to you."

"I think that would be a good idea, Leonard. I can't understand or accept things of which I'm unaware."

"Are you so sure that you can accept what I have to tell you?" he asked uncertainly.

"There's only one way to find out, isn't there?" Heloise answered.

"It's still rather difficult to talk about. The only other person I've discussed it with is my mother." Leonard hesitated and found that he needed to look away before he was able to continue. "When I was fourteen years old, I was kidnapped and held for several weeks."

"Leonard, how awful!" Heloise gasped. "What happened? Who kidnapped you? Were they ever caught?"

Leonard gave a wry grin. "It would sound much too melodramatic to describe them as evil scientists. However, I was held in a laboratory, and they did perform experiments on me and several others."

"What kind of experiments?" Heloise asked in a stunned voice.

"I really didn't understand much of it. I was young, and they kept me pretty much out of it while I was there," Leonard answered evasively.

"What made them finally release you?" Heloise asked curiously.

"We weren't really released. It was only a fluke that enabled us to escape. I've never been sure how long it took me to get home. We lived out in the country, and I was fairly weak. I told Mother what had happened, and she and my aunt Lucinda arranged for us to disappear," Leonard said, deciding that was as much as he dared to tell her. "Unfortunately, sometimes, it still affects my behavior."

"I can understand how it would," Heloise said, laying a reassuring hand on his arm. "After something that traumatic, that would have to be the case."

"I just wanted to let you know that if you choose not to see me anymore . . ." His voice faded.

"Oh heavens! Leonard, how could you possibly think that?" Heloise sputtered. "You're a charming man, and I enjoy your company."

Leonard smiled shyly. "I'm glad it's mutual. Now however, I think it's time that you rejoined your friends." Leonard's eyes widened as Heloise took a step to close the distance between them. She placed a hand on his shoulder and rose on tiptoe to gently kiss him before moving away. He watched as she went inside and then began his long walk back home with a lighter heart.

Chapter 12

When Agnes returned to her office, she was followed by Heloise, carrying the tea tray. "Really, Heloise, I could have carried the teapot," Agnes protested.

"I know, dear," answered Heloise. "I just wanted to help out. Hello, Vicky, Edna, have you brought Agnes up to speed about what's happening?"

"Yes, we have," said Vicky. "Although whether she'll remember it is doubtful." Vicky stared disapprovingly as Agnes fished another bottle of brandy out of the filing cabinet.

Heloise took the bottle as Agnes flopped ungracefully into her chair. "Thank you, dear, but I think we've all had enough brandy for tonight," Heloise said gently, returning the bottle to the file drawer.

"Okay." Agnes hiccupped then giggled. "Don't want anyone to think I'm not a gracious host." Agnes then laid her head on the desk and began to snore softly.

"Unbelievable," muttered Vicky as she stared at Agnes.

Heloise looked at Edna, and Edna waggled her eyebrows in silent question. Heloise smiled serenely and mouthed "Later." Ignoring Agnes, Vicky turned her attention to Heloise. "How was your meeting with Leonard Marshall?" Heloise took a moment to pour herself a cup of tea and take a seat.

"It went very well. We managed to clear up some misunderstandings and answer some questions we both had," Heloise answered, still wearing that serene smile.

Vicky frowned. "What misunderstandings? What questions?"

Still smiling, Heloise replied, "Nothing that would interest you. It's just between Leonard and myself. You shouldn't frown like that, my dear. You'll wrinkle that beautiful face."

Vicky frowned even harder. "What is wrong with you witches? I came here as a favor to Rory Van der Haven because he seems to think that you are in danger from evil forces, and you all want to keep secrets from me."

"I can't believe that private communications between Leonard Marshall and myself can have any bearing on the 'evil forces' plotting against us. Rest assured, any information I have that relates to the dangerous and peculiar activities that are threatening us, I will relay it to you immediately."

"But until we get to the bottom of this situation, you can't know what is relevant and what isn't," Vicky insisted vehemently. Now Heloise began to frown.

"Whoa, girls," Edna interjected. "Look, it's getting late. And obviously, we need to get some sleep." She pointed at Agnes who was still snoring with a slack-jawed smile on her face. "Let's put Agnes to bed and go home." Vicky and Heloise nodded in grudging agreement and put their cups on the desk.

"Hey, Vicky, why don't you round up the critters while Heloise and I put Agnes to bed? We can meet at the front door," Edna suggested. Vicky nodded and left the office while Edna and Heloise struggled to get Agnes out of her chair.

They had Agnes almost to the door when Edna remembered the recipe box. Leaning Agnes against the doorjamb, Edna ran back and scooped the box under her arm. When they got Agnes to her room, they decided to let her sleep in her clothes. Heloise raised a questioning eyebrow when Edna insisted on leaving four aspirin and a large glass of ice water beside the bed. "Trust me, she'll want this when she wakes up," Edna said. Then they retrieved their jackets from outside the dining hall and went to meet Vicky.

At the front door, they found Vicky impatiently tapping her booted foot and holding Rap against her shoulder while her cat, Suzy, paced back and forth in front of her, twitching her tail angrily. "It's about time," she said heatedly. "Take him." She thrust Rap at Edna. Edna barely managed to grasp Rap as Vicky spun on her heel and flung open the door.

"What's been going on?" Edna whispered to Rap as she followed Vicky into the frosty night. Rap raised eyes bloodshot with fatigue to Edna's face.

"She wouldn't leave me alone. Everywhere I went, she followed. She kept rubbing up against me. It was horrible. This has got to be one on the worst nights of my life." Rap moaned and buried his face in her shoulder. Realization slowly dawned on Edna as she followed Vicky who was angrily stalking down the forest path. She looked down and, by the light of the moon, could see the Siamese cat weaving intricate patterns around her feet.

"Hey, Vicky, could you corral your cat before I trip over her?" Edna called.

Vicky stopped abruptly and turned. "Suzy, come here!" she demanded. Suzy, of course, ignored her mistress. After a couple more tries at calling her, Vicky stomped back to Edna's position on the path and scooped up the cat. "You're a bad influence on my familiar," Vicky hissed at Edna and turned away.

Edna barely stifled a laugh. *Ms. Perfect doesn't even know what's going on with her own cat. Maybe I can enjoy a little revenge before we thwart the "evil forces." I just hope Rap can hold up.*

As they continued down the path, a thought suddenly occurred to Edna. *Old man Higgins must really be losing it. Today is Saturday, and he said Vicky has a martial arts class early tomorrow.* "Hey Vicky, tomorrow is Sunday and we don't have classes on Sunday".

"There is a class in the morning," Vicky responded. "Mr. Higgins thought it would be a good idea to have one introductory class so that if it seemed too strenuous, enrollees could back out without being embarrassed."

When they arrived at the cottage, Vicky immediately stormed into her room with Suzy in her arms and slammed the door. "Kitchen," Heloise whispered and continued down the hall.

In the kitchen, Rap revived enough to look at Edna pitifully and ask, "Tuna fish?"

Edna laughed, feeling in better spirits than she had all evening. She put Rap on the floor and went to the cabinet where the cans of tuna were kept. As Edna prepared the tuna for Rap, Heloise surprised her by pulling a bottle of wine from the refrigerator. "What, no tea or hot cocoa?" Edna asked.

"Actually, I'm in a mood to celebrate," Heloise informed her.

"Ooh, that must have been an exceptionally good conversation with Leonard. Just how much *talking* did you do?" Edna inquired.

Heloise gave her a reproachful look. "If you can refrain from being vulgar, I'll tell you all about it."

Heloise told Edna all that had transpired between her and Leonard. They talked and laughed while Rap ate his tuna and curled up in his cushioned bed in the corner but not without complaining about a "cat scent" on the cushions. Beowulf also made a rare foray from Heloise's pocket to sit on the table and nibble on fresh greens. Just before midnight, Edna gave a huge yawn and said, "Just remember, I'm to be called Aunt Edna, and I expect to be godmother to at least one of the rug rats."

Heloise smiled and asked, "And what do you plan on having your children call me?"

Edna frowned and said, "It's not very likely that I'll have any children. I'll probably just be a maiden aunt."

Heloise looked surprised. "But what about Rory?"

Edna gave her a penetrating look. "What chance have I got with Rory? I'm stuck here in Pedestria for another forty-five years. Besides, look at Vicky. She's been his partner for several years. I know I'm not ugly, but I can't compete with that kind of beauty. Aside from beauty, she's smart and strong. And compared to her, I'm swamp muck. After being with her all these years, I'm sure Rory has higher standards for whatever woman he plans to get involved with.

"Don't get me wrong, there's no problem with my self-esteem. But I know when I'm outclassed, and I just can't compete. Don't know why I ever thought I had a chance with Rory," she murmured under her breath with a tear in her eye. "I'm beat. I'm going to bed," Edna said, averting her face as she left the kitchen.

Chapter 13

Over the next two weeks, everyone was much too busy for any in-depth conversations. Vicky was kept busy with full-to-bursting classes, mostly comprised of boys although a few of the girls seemed to idolize her and were studying hard to do well in the physical exercises she set for them. Heloise seemed to be smiling constantly, which Edna found to be extremely irritating, and Leonard resumed his research studies.

Agnes was very twitchy and started at any noise. Whenever Edna or Heloise talked to Agnes, the conversation always came around to her recipe box and why she would feel compelled to use the archaic recipes. It seemed to Edna that Agnes's preoccupation with her recipe box was similar to a junkie looking for his next fix. It definitely worried her. The familiars had their own concerns. Rap was continually seeking out new hiding places while Suzy was hunting out those same hiding places. Beowulf had taken to squeaking so much that Heloise had to put him in his cage while she was fulfilling her duties as head librarian. Even Coco, Agnes's cockatoo, had stopped visiting Nathan, the barn owl, and became vicious if anyone tried to take her from her perch in Agnes's office.

The three women were sitting in front of the fire on a crisp fall evening. Edna and Heloise were talking while Agnes read.

"What's going on with the critters?" Edna complained. "They're driving me crazy."

"You're the one they usually talk to. Why don't you ask them?" Heloise suggested.

"They're not talking to me. Even Rap doesn't want to tell me anything."

Agnes looked up from the new issue of *Magic Moments*. "They're probably just excited about Halloween."

Edna shot her an exasperated look. "They've never been so excited about it before. Why should this year be any different?"

"Perhaps they're just tuning in to our emotions," Heloise suggested. "They may not even realize what's bothering them."

"Could be," Edna said, losing interest. "We'll find out sometime."

Meanwhile, Sunny Acres School was being decorated to the hilt. Skeletons and ghosts were seen in every hallway, spiderwebs with nasty-looking spiders adorned every light fixture, and green slimy goo was found in many unlikely places. Edna was always suspicious when she encountered the green goo, thanks to Agnes's recipe box. Nothing out of the ordinary occurred during those two weeks, with the exception of a minor explosion in the chemistry laboratory.

Finally, it was Halloween. After the Halloween banquet where the students were stuffed full of candy and carbonated drinks, the children all piled into faculty cars to descend upon the town of Laurelwood for some trick-or-treating.

Edna, Heloise, Vicky, and Agnes retreated to the cottage with their familiars for a quiet evening. Since it was a Saturday night and none of them had to get up early the next morning, they decided to at least partially pay tribute to All Hallows Eve in the traditional sense.

Gathering in the small kitchen of the cottage, they brought pictures of deceased loved ones and ancestors. Agnes also brought her recipe box, for what reasons only she knew. After lighting candles and saying prayers for the continued peace and protection of the souls of their ancestors and deceased loved ones, they brought out pictures of currently living loved ones. As they laid the pictures on the table, Edna was dismayed to see that along with pictures of her mother, father, and a handsome young man in a military uniform, Vicky also had a picture of Rory. Edna hadn't had any opportunity to get Rory's picture, and since her dufus family had disowned her, the only people whose pictures she cared to pray for were Heloise and Agnes. After they preformed the ritual prayer of protection from evil spirits for their living loved ones, Edna silently sent her own personal prayer of protection for Rory.

As everyone cleared their pictures from the table, Heloise announced, "I believe it's time for hot cocoa and marshmallows!" Heloise turned toward the pot on the stove where she'd been simmering sweetened milk. Beowulf began frantically scrabbling, trying to climb out of her pocket.

Sleeping quietly on his cushioned bed in the corner, Rap suddenly opened his eyes and sprang out of bed. Suzy was similarly agitated, and Coco was beating her head against the door of her cage.

Stunned, the witches looked at their familiars. "Mistress, let us out now if you value your life," Rap implored Edna. Not stopping to question, Edna released the latch on Coco's cage and ran down the hall to open the front door.

"What's going on?" Heloise asked as Beowulf ran after the other fleeing familiars.

"I'm not sure, but it seems important, at least to them," Edna replied as they watched their familiars rush into the darkness. "They must know something we don't. You know, how they have different senses than we do."

"Well, don't just stand there. Let's go!" shouted Vicky as she ran into the night after the animals. Edna, Heloise, and Agnes looked at one another then ran after Vicky without a word.

As they ran, they heard shouts, growls, grunts, and curses. The moon was full, but it wasn't providing much light in the dense foliage of the forest. They'd already lost track of Vicky and were just following the noise of the conflict ahead of them. As they ran through the underbrush, they tried to understand why their familiars would desert them and go running off into the night.

As Edna began to develop a stitch in her side, she realized that they were nearing the Theater and that the sounds of combat were fading. When they broke into the area called the Theater, they were astonished to see a gray wolf with a wounded paw lying across one of the enormous granite boulders. Heloise had a sudden feeling about the wolf and waved them away. "Go on, I'll take care of him," she told the others. Edna and Agnes continued running across the clearing.

Heloise turned her attention to the wolf. Its eyes were closed, and its sides heaved with heavy breathing. Heloise tore a strip of cloth from her skirt and used it to bind the wolf's left front paw. As she checked the wolf for any more injuries, he whimpered when she ran her hands over his left side but still didn't open his eyes.

Meanwhile, Edna and Agnes arrived at the far end of the clearing to find Vicky and the familiars in a chaotic battle. They were fighting with eight dark beings between three and four feet in height. The animals were biting, clawing, and pecking their attackers.

Vicky was a whirling ball of energy, punching and kicking with such speed and ferocity that Edna was amazed. Coco had her talons hooked on to the ears of her opponent while she viciously pecked the top of his head. Suzy was jumping and slashing at the attackers' faces with her razor-sharp claws. Beowulf and Rap had teamed up against one of the attackers. Beowulf was biting the back of the attacker's neck while Rap ran around on the ground darting in to bite feet, ankles, and the backs of the knees.

Since Vicky seemed to be holding her own with her opponents, Edna and Agnes jumped in to help the animals. Agnes began kicking and hitting the one whose head was being pecked by Coco. Edna found a stout stick and began swinging it like a club. She started with the attacker that Beowulf and Rap were fighting. Raising the stick high over her head, Edna brought it down on the attacker's head with all her strength. The attacker's eyes rolled back in his head, and he started to slump to the ground. There was a flash of electric blue, and the attacker vanished. Edna was so astonished she almost dropped the stick. Fortunately, Rap was quick enough to maneuver so that he could break Beowulf's fall.

Looking around, Edna could see that Vicky had dispatched two of her opponents, Coco and Agnes were fighting one, and Suzy was struggling with one. "Go help Suzy!" Edna shouted to Rap and Beowulf as she ran to where Vicky continued to spin, kick, and punch. With their combined efforts, Edna and Vicky quickly defeated their attackers. As they turned to check on the others, there were two simultaneous blue flashes, and they realized the battle was over.

Edna leaned on her makeshift club panting while she and Vicky waited for the others to join them. "Who were they?" Edna gasped between breaths.

Vicky looked at Edna with surprise. "You have been here too long if you can't even recognize goblins."

"Of course I recognize goblins. I meant, what were they doing here?"

"We don't have any way of knowing that. But my guess would be that someone sent them," Vicky said thoughtfully.

Looking up, Edna watched the others coming toward them. Agnes and Rap were limping, Beowulf was still riding on Rap's back, and Suzy was walking haughtily with her tail held high.

"What happened to you?" Edna asked Rap with great concern.

"I broke a claw. It's nothing serious," Rap replied wearily.

"How about you?" Edna turned to Agnes.

"I think I broke my foot," she answered, flopping ungracefully to the ground.

"What did you do to break your foot?" Edna asked as Vicky knelt to examine the injury.

"Well, I kicked the stupid thing!"

"You should have kicked it in a soft spot."

"I thought where I was kicking was a soft spot," Agnes replied with exasperation.

"Goblins don't have many soft spots on their bodies," Vicky interjected. "And the ones they have, you probably couldn't have reached with a kick anyway. Yep, it sure is broken," she said, finished with her assessment of the injured foot. "Let's get you back to the cottage. Edna, give me a hand."

Edna and Vicky each grabbed an arm and helped Agnes up onto her one good foot. As they helped support Agnes across the clearing toward where Heloise waited with the wolf, Edna noticed that even after frantic battle and all of her wild exertions, Vicky was calm, cool, and collected. Not even a single strand of her hair was out of place. By contrast, Edna also noticed that she and Agnes were dirty and sweaty, with grass stains on their clothing and bits of leaves stuck in their wildly disarrayed hair. *How does she do it?* Edna wondered. *It's just not fair. She must have a weakness somewhere, and I'm going to find it if it's the last thing I do.*

When they returned to the boulder, they found Heloise sitting with the wolf's head in her lap. Heloise looked at them anxiously. "His injuries don't appear that severe, but I can't get him to wake up."

Vicky inspected the wolf briefly. "I believe they used some sort of a tranquilizer on him. We better get him up to the cottage too."

"And just how do you propose we do that?" Edna asked sarcastically from where she stood supporting Agnes.

Vicky reached behind her head and pulled her wand from the sheath strapped between her shoulder blades. "You had your wand all along?" sputtered Edna in disbelief. "Why didn't you use it on the goblins?"

A mischievous smile played at the corners of Vicky's mouth. "I thought we didn't want to attract attention. Besides, I needed the exercise. I haven't had a good workout in a month." While Edna stood gaping at her, Vicky used her wand to slightly levitate the wolf and began slowly moving through the forest toward the cottage.

Once they were back at the well-lit cottage, they were better able to assess the damage each of them had sustained. Heloise discovered that Beowulf had a small cut in one of his long ears. She quickly swabbed the cut with antiseptic before dabbing ointment on it. Suzy appeared to be as unscathed as her mistress.

The worst injuries seemed to be Agnes's broken foot and the deep gash in the wolf's paw. They laid the wolf on the cushions of Rap's bed in the corner of the kitchen. When Rap started to protest, Edna gave him a blistering look and made him curl up in the equally comfortable basket in the bedroom. While Heloise wrapped a loose bandage around the wolf's paw, Edna and Vicky made Agnes as comfortable as possible on the sofa in the living room.

"I guess I'd better go get Pamela Sanderson," Edna sighed tiredly.

"Edna, do you really think it's a good idea to bring the school nurse down here?" Agnes wailed.

"Gee, Agnes, you're right. Let's think about the situation for a minute. You're down here in the cottage with a broken foot. The closest trained medical professional is up at the school, not to mention the medical equipment and supplies that are also up at the school. Add to that the fact that you are the school's head cook and your kitchen is at the school. On top of which, there's the fact that your room with all of your clothing is at the school.

"I suppose we could let the students prepare their own meals while you lie on our sofa and hope that your foot heals properly, but frankly, I don't think I could stand the stench you'll be exuding if you don't change your clothes for eight weeks!"

"All right, all right, you've made your point," grumbled Agnes.

"May I make a suggestion?" Vicky spoke up. "You might want to clean up a bit before you go. No need to frighten the poor nurse."

Edna checked her reflection in the mirror over the mantle, cast a withering glance at Vicky, and stomped out of the room. In a few seconds, they heard the bathroom door slam. Then minutes later, they heard the slamming of the front door.

A half hour later, Edna returned with Pamela Sanderson on the school's utility cart. After some careful maneuvering, Agnes was on the cart and headed back to the school with the nurse. Edna went to the kitchen where she found Heloise sipping at a steaming cup of hot cocoa. Heloise looked up and noticed Edna staring enviously at the frothy mug.

"Can I get you some?" Heloise asked.

"Oh yes, please," Edna answered as she sank into the closest chair. "Heavy on the marshmallows," Edna requested. Edna couldn't believe how utterly wretched she felt. Her entire body ached. Even her hair hurt. She had a feeling that this was one Halloween she would remember for a long, long time.

When Heloise gave her the mug of cocoa, she held it with both hands, closed her eyes, and deeply breathed in the aroma before taking a sip. Opening her eyes, she looked around and saw that Heloise had covered the wolf with a soft brown blanket. "How is he?" Edna asked, nodding toward the wolf.

Heloise looked at the sleeping wolf. "I've cleaned and dressed his paw as well as I can. Now it's up to Mother Nature."

As they drank the cocoa and discussed the events of the evening, Edna continued to steal glances at the wolf. "I know you're going to think I've gone completely bonkers, but I have the strangest feeling that I've seen that wolf before," Edna said.

Heloise choked on her cocoa. When she'd regained her composure, she said, "All wolves look fairly similar. Maybe you've just seen one that looks like him."

"Maybe," Edna admitted, "but I don't know. I just have the strangest feeling when I look at him."

"I know what you mean," Heloise murmured into her mug.

"What?" Edna asked.

"I just said, 'It remains to be seen,'" replied Heloise.

Edna licked the frothy mustache off her upper lip. "So why don't you tell me why we're keeping a strange wolf in our kitchen for the night."

"He was hurt and needed to be taken care of." Heloise avoided meeting her gaze. "We couldn't just leave him there."

"Heloise, this is a wolf we're talking about. What if he wakes up hungry during the night?"

"I'll be sure to keep my door latched," Heloise said reassuringly.

"And what are we going to do with him in the morning?" Edna insisted.

"We'll worry about that in the morning."

"Speaking of strange feelings, where is Vicky?" Edna inquired. She stared intently at Heloise, waiting for an answer.

Heloise hesitated, looking extremely uncomfortable. "She had to go somewhere. She said she needed to talk to someone."

"Where and who?" Edna wanted to know.

"If you must know, she went to Lemain to tell Rory about the goblin attack," Heloise finally admitted.

"That makes sense," Edna remarked calmly. Heloise was surprised. Knowing Edna's quick temper and her poorly disguised dislike of Vicky, this was not the reaction she expected. She watched suspiciously as Edna drained her mug. "Well, I'd better be going," Edna said as she rose from the table.

"Now, Edna, don't do anything foolish," Heloise admonished. Edna looked at her in surprise.

"Heloise, I've heard 'going to bed' called many things but 'foolish' wasn't one of them. Get a grip. Good night."

Heloise sat contemplating the current situation. Suddenly, there was a bloodcurdling scream and the sound of shattering glass from Edna's bedroom. Heloise smiled as she began cleaning the kitchen and washing the cocoa mugs.

"Thank goodness, and to think, I was worried that something was wrong with Edna," Heloise chuckled softly.

Chapter 14

Edna slept fitfully that night. She alternated between staring at the dark ceiling and having disturbing dreams of Vicky being held in Rory's warm embrace. By the time the pearly gray dawn finally peeked through her bedroom window, Edna decided that sleep was no longer an option. Yawning, she pulled a heavy red fleece robe on over her typical sleepwear of sweatpants and tee shirt.

She stumbled wearily down the hall to the kitchen in search of the marvelous brown beverage that she hoped would rejuvenate her and bring all of her dilemmas into perspective so that she could figure out a way to deal with them—in other words, coffee.

When she entered the kitchen, she had to clap a hand over her mouth to keep from gasping out loud. Instead of a gray wolf lying on the cushions in the corner of the kitchen, there was now a man. The man appeared to be naked, with the exception of the blanket skewed across the most delicate parts of his body. As she looked at the man on the cushions, it occurred to Edna that she recognized him. *Oh great heavenly goddess,* she thought, *it's Leonard Marshall!* She backed silently out of the kitchen, then spun around, and raced down the hall to Heloise's room.

"Heloise, get up! Get up right now!"

Heloise sat bolt upright, smacking her head with a resounding thunk on the protruding ornamental scrollwork of her headboard.

"Edna, what are you yelling about?" Heloise asked, rubbing her head. She groggily sat up and swung her legs over the edge of the bed. Rubbing her sleep encrusted eyes, she tried to pay attention to Edna's excited babbling. Looking at the less-than-bright light outside her window, Heloise wondered what could have agitated Edna so early in the morning. For that matter, whatever could have gotten Edna out of bed at this hour? She quickly donned the pink-and-green floral print robe that matched her pajamas and relented to Edna's insistent tugging on her arm.

"You won't believe it! I don't believe it! Guess who is in the kitchen? Never mind, you'll never guess."

"Is it possibly Leonard Marshall?" Heloise asked.

Edna came to a dead stop in the middle of the hall. "You knew?" she asked. She stared at Heloise with a shocked expression as she waited for an answer. Just then, Rap emerged from Edna's bedroom.

Rubbing his red-rimmed eyes with his furry paws, he asked, "Is there an emergency? What is going on?"

"Shhh! Just be quiet, and follow us," Edna said. They continued down the hall toward the kitchen.

When they entered the kitchen, they stopped and stared at the figure lying on the cushions in the corner. Heloise wore a slight smile, enjoying the muscular, slightly furred form of Leonard sleeping peacefully.

"What is this man doing on our kitchen floor?" Rap asked indignantly.

"Can you please be silent?" Edna asked Rap as she scooped him up and began backing down the hall. Edna had noticed the expression on Heloise's face when they entered the kitchen and correctly assumed that Heloise would be the best one, by herself, to wake her sleeping friend.

As Edna and Rap retreated down the hall, Heloise moved toward Leonard. *I could get used to seeing this image when I wake each morning,* thought Heloise as she neared Leonard.

Heloise stopped and studied Leonard as he slept. She noted his smooth forehead, not furrowed with concentration or worry. She also observed the relaxed set of his jaw. It didn't exhibit the stiff, grim expression he had been wearing lately. While examining his injuries, she noticed an ugly bruise along the left side of his rib cage in addition to his snugly bandaged hand. *Oh goddess, please let everything work out all right,* thought Heloise. *Because I don't think I could bear the thought of not having him around. In fact, I think I may be falling in love with him.*

Heloise reached out and gently shook Leonard's shoulder. Leonard slowly stretched and murmured, "Ummm." Heloise adjusted the blanket to cover Leonard more thoroughly.

Once again, she shook his shoulder and softly insisted, "Leonard, Leonard, you need to wake up. Leonard, you need to wake up, now!"

Leonard blearily opened his eyes as Heloise sat back on her heels on the floor. "What happened? Where am I?" Leonard asked sleepily.

"You're in my cottage, and you saved us from an attack by goblins last night," Heloise answered. Leonard's brown eyes met Heloise's hazel eyes with a mixed expression of shock and fear. "Oh, Leonard, I know you're a werewolf. I've suspected it for a few months. I don't care. You proved last night that you are a wonderful, caring person. That's all that is important to me. Edna, Agnes, and I will all protect your secret."

Meanwhile, back in Lemain, the secretary of the treasury, Hattie Homborg, was listening to a report by twelve battered and bruised goblins. She didn't like what she was hearing.

Anyone entering Hattie Homburg's office was immediately impressed with its size. Judging from the size of the building or from the distance between the doors of the offices in the corridor, most people would expect an office twelve feet by fourteen feet; however, Hattie Homborg's office measured thirty feet by seventy feet. Obviously, the interior dimensions of her office had been enhanced magically.

The entrance door to Hattie's office was at the farthest end of the room from the desk. The short wall immediately inside the door was covered with gilt-framed mirrors. Along the interior wall hung original masterpieces by the great artists of Lemain. These artists included Grimbold, Uruk, Camponella, and Vortz. The long wall on the opposite side was filled with stained glass windows showing various magical creatures native to Lemain. The images included unicorns, pixies, goblins, fairies, ogres, dragons, and many others. The gold-inlaid white marble floor was almost completely covered with an intricately woven, plush carpet whose scene depicted the splitting of the races—magical and nonmagical.

Hattie's enormous desk was made of the blackest ebony. It had many drawers, all with intricately carved ivory handles. The high-backed chair behind the desk was upholstered with bloodred damask.

The wall behind the desk was covered, floor to ceiling, with crystal screens, each showing a different picture that changed every minute or so. Although the ostentatious opulence of the room made the first-time visitor wonder just what the taxpayer's money was paying for, their attention was quickly grasped by the rapidly changing crystal-screen display.

Most of the scenes displayed were of high-level officials in their offices, but some of the pictures portrayed the high-level officials in what could only be described as "private moments." Some of the displays showed high-level officials engaging in blatantly illegal activities. At this particular moment, the screens were being totally ignored by Hattie and her visitors.

"What do you mean you were unable to complete the mission, Grrmulsh?" Hattie screeched. "Since when can't a dozen goblins kill three unempowered witches?"

Grrmulsh, who was Smrrg's great-grandson and great-grandnephew—goblins not having any laws against interfamilial marriages—tried to explain. "Oh, most wonderful and evil mistress, they were warned," Grrmulsh began. "And they had help. They had these furry and feathered creatures who attacked first. And then when the witches showed up, there were four, not three."

Hattie glared venomously at Grrmulsh. "Everyone knows that goblins aren't noted for their mathematical skills, but surely, you can count to three. There were three witches you were supposed to kill, and you failed!"

"Please, evil mistress, there was another one," Grrmulsh pleaded. "She was like a force of nature, constantly spinning while kicking and punching. We couldn't find an opening in which to attack her. And of course, with the recall spell, which brought us back to Lemain whenever we were rendered unconscious, we didn't get a chance to reattack as we would in a goblin battle."

Hattie glared at Grrmulsh for a moment, then turned with a flurry of her robe, and stalked to her massive desk to study the crystal screens on the wall. "Aaaaarrrgggghhh!" Hattie's scream of rage could be heard throughout the floor. "Incompetents, incompetents! I'm surrounded by incompetents!" raged Hattie.

"We also found the werewolf," continued Grrmulsh.

"But you didn't bring him back, did you?" Hattie turned to look at the goblins. "Out! Get out of my office, you miserable slugs!"

"But, most evil mistress, the grand goblin Smrrg said we were to be paid for this assignment," Grrmulsh said. "We have to return with payment."

"Payment, payment?" Hattie laughed. "Let me tell you something, pip-squeak: I pay for results, nothing less. You can go back and tell all the goblins of the Eastern Mountain Range that Hattie Homborg only pays for results. If you goblins can't deliver, I don't pay! Got it?" Noting the hesitant look on the faces of the goblins, Hattie added, "If you don't like it, you can always take it up with your union representative. Now get out of my office!"

As Hattie stalked back and forth in front of the crystal screens used for spying on her adversaries, she was extremely upset that her plan hadn't worked. She remembered Edna Fitzsimmons from their days in school together before Edna was sent to Aunt Mildred's. As far as Hattie was concerned, Edna Fitzsimmons was one of those radical, left-winged animal rights reactionaries. These reactionaries were always having bake sales, elixir sales, and wand washes to raise money for their own little personal charities.

Bunch of wimps, Hattie thought. *Everyone knows you don't get rich supporting charities. There has got to be a way to get the artifact and get rid of those obnoxious witches. Even if I can't find the artifact, which I know they have, I will eliminate Edna Fitzsimmons and her friends. I need intelligence. I need to know what those witches are doing.*

"Willis," Hattie snapped at her assistant cowering in the corner. "Find out who in the justice department is keeping an eye on the three banished witches, and get him in my office, pronto!"

"Yes, mistress. Of course, mistress. Right away, mistress," Willis responded tremulously as he hurried from the room. Once outside Hattie's office, Willis finally felt safe enough to take a deep breath. As he hurried down the hall, he thought, *The only good thing about being assistant to the secretary of the treasury is being sent on errands. I don't know how I got so unlucky as to be picked to be her assistant. I used to be so happy working in the Council Government's General Aide Pool. I'd type some reports, deliver some messages, and occasionally escort a visiting dignitary. I never asked for this job! If I didn't have a wife and five kids, I'd quit right now. But of course, I do have a family, and I need this job.*

Willis continued toward the Department of Justice building as he berated the shortsightedness that caused him to be in his current miserable situation. When he arrived at the Department of Justice, he asked for the office or person in charge of banished witches and was directed to the Investigators of Special Affairs office.

In the office, he saw two officers. One was a frizzy red-haired witch wearing square black glasses and shuffling papers on her desk. The other was a large broad-shouldered man with an extremely short haircut, pacing the far end of the room.

Willis approached the red-haired witch and explained what he needed.

"Oh yeah, I remember that case. I'm not sure that any one of our officers was assigned to watch them, but I believe I know of an officer who has been involved since the case began. Hold on a minute, and let me check my records. All right, here it is." She pulled a card from the file box on her desk. "You need to see Investigator Rory Van der Haven. He should be back any minute. Have a seat over there." She pointed to a wooden bench against the wall. Heaving a sigh, Willis went to the bench and sat.

In less than five minutes, Rory came down the hall carrying a steaming mug of coffee. Willis jumped up and approached him. "Investigator Van der Haven?" Willis asked.

"Can I help you?" Rory replied, looking inquiringly at the slightly built younger man.

"Secretary of the Treasury Hattie Homborg sent me to summon you to her office," Willis said in a rush.

Rory frowned. "I'm kind of busy right now. How about I stop by her office tomorrow?"

"Oh no, that won't do!" Willis exclaimed. "This is most important. You must come right now." Willis stood wringing his hands.

"Okay, okay. Just let me get rid of this," Rory said in a placating tone of voice as he gestured with his coffee mug. *Nervous little guy,* Rory thought as he carried his mug to his desk. *I wonder what's put a bee in Homborg's bonnet this time.* When he returned to Willis, all he said was, "Lead on."

When they arrived at Hattie's office, Rory was astounded with the interior dimensions of the room. He was further amazed by the room's decorations, but what intrigued him the most was the wall of crystal screens. As he watched from the open door, he noted the screens showing various people, some important political and business figures. When Hattie heard their footsteps on the marble floor, she turned from the wall of screens and pushed a button. The screens immediately switched to a mural of a snowcapped mountain.

Aha, thought Rory. *So our secretary of the treasury is keeping closer tabs on her adversaries than anyone suspected.* His mind suddenly flashed to a screen he glimpsed just before Hattie switched to the mural. The screen showed the investigator's office in the Department of Justice. *Oh, for Callisto's sake, she's screening all the government offices too!* When his mind escaped from the hold of the crystal screens, he noticed a faint, slightly unpleasant odor.

The beaming smile on Hattie's yellow-skinned, pockmarked face was less than inviting. "This is Investigator Rory Van der Haven," Willis announced to Hattie as they approached the desk.

"Welcome, Investigator Van der Haven," Hattie said in the most pleasant voice she could muster. "It was so nice of you to agree to meet with me."

"I wasn't aware that I had a choice," Rory answered guardedly. Hattie frowned at Willis, who appeared to shrink a couple of inches under her gaze.

"Please forgive my assistant. He's not terribly bright, and he sometimes misunderstands my instructions. Willis, get in your corner," Hattie hissed as her hapless assistant slouched toward the corner like a whipped cur. When Hattie returned her attention to Rory, her smile was back in place. "I have some questions about the three witches that were banished five years ago."

"Yes, Ms. Secretary, and which witches would that be?" Rory asked.

Hattie's smile slipped slightly. "I'm referring to the witches who exploded the cake at President Thurgood's inauguration banquet. I'm talking about two-time offender Edna Fitzsimmons and her cohorts Heloise Amburgy and Agnes Thistlewaite. You are familiar with these names, aren't you, Investigator Van der Haven?"

Rory began to feel uncomfortable under Hattie's predatory stare. "Yes, I'm familiar with that case."

"Good," Hattie said. "I was wondering how the banishment is progressing. Are the witches behaving? Have there been any infractions of the banishment restrictions?"

Rory was getting a familiar prickling feeling at the base of his neck. This sensation had always warned him of imminent danger, and he had no reason not to trust it now. "As far as I know, the witches in question are abiding by the terms of the sentence passed on them by the Council," Rory answered cautiously.

Hattie frowned and leaned on her desk. "Do you really expect me to believe that those three haven't disobeyed a single restriction?"

The prickling of his neck had increased to the point that Rory had to exert extreme willpower to resist rubbing the afflicted area. "The only infractions that I am aware of are the minor ones we expect from banished offenders while they adjust to their new environment," Rory answered formally.

"Very well," Hattie said. She stood and paced toward the windows with her hands clasped behind her back. After an uncomfortable silence of several minutes, during which time Rory rubbed vigorously at the irritated spot on his neck, Hattie turned once again toward Rory.

"Another matter has come to the Council's attention. We have reason to believe that one or all of these three witches have stolen a rare magical artifact and removed it to the Pedestrian world. As I'm sure you are aware, theft of such an artifact is a national offense, punishable by extinction."

"I believe that extinction is more harsh than the offense requires. They would be more likely to be sentenced to a lifetime of indentured servitude, but I've observed no evidence that they have any such artifact in their possession," Rory responded with equal parts of anger and nervousness.

"Investigator Van der Haven, I want you to conduct intense surveillance of these three witches and attempt to locate this artifact," Hattie continued with a slim shadow of her previous smile. "I have already prepared the papers for you to be assigned to this project, and you are to report only to me. You are to watch the witches and report any infractions of their banishment restrictions. You will also take every opportunity to search their living quarters and belongings for the artifact. If you find the artifact, you will deliver it to me at once. Do you understand these orders?"

"Yes, Ms. Secretary. Can you tell me what this artifact looks like? It would make my job easier if I knew what to look for," Rory replied stoically.

Hattie focused her most malevolent glare upon Rory. "Understand this, Investigator, it is not my job to make yours easier." She hesitated. "However, in the interest of efficiency, I will tell you that the size, shape, and color of the item are unknown. But it is definitely magical."

Rory was flabbergasted. Before he could raise any objections or ask any more questions, Hattie was dismissing him. "You have your orders, Investigator. Now carry them out. Just remember, you are to discuss these orders with no one, and you are to report only to me. Now go."

Feeling slightly dazed, Rory left Hattie Homborg's office. Before he had gotten halfway to his office, he encountered Vic. She looked grave.

"We need to talk," she told him.

Remembering the crystal screen display in Hattie's office, he said, "Okay, but not here." Taking her arm, Rory guided Vic toward the nearest exit. "Let's take a walk in the park," he suggested.

Although his partner appeared anxious to talk, Rory insisted they remain silent until they arrived at the park. They strolled the paths among mothers with small children, businessmen taking a leisurely lunch, and students reading and enjoying the warm sunshine. When they reached a remote bench on the far side of the park, Rory carefully scanned the area, then sat with a deep sigh, and put his head in his hands.

"Rory, what's wrong?" Vic asked as she sat beside him.

"I've got the worst headache of my life," Rory answered. "Got any elixirs with you?"

Pulling a small vial from her pocket, Vic said, "Here you go, pard. Doesn't seem like your day is going any better than mine. Want to bring me up to speed?"

Rory swallowed the contents of the vial and waited a few moments for the elixir to take effect. "First, tell me, how are they?"

Vic told him about the goblin attack. "The most serious injury seems to be Agnes's broken foot."

"How did she break her foot?" Rory asked.

Vic smiled. "She kicked a goblin between the legs, thinking that would be a 'soft spot.' Pedestrian defensive training doesn't take into account goblin physique."

Rory laughed so hard, he had to hold his head as the pain briefly returned. "Are Edna and Heloise okay?"

"Yeah, they're fine, but I don't think your girlfriend likes me too much."

Rory glanced sharply at Vic. "She's not my girlfriend," he retorted.

"Well, you might want to inform her of that fact. She's exhibiting all the signs of a jealous girlfriend," Vic said, watching her partner closely. Rory was wearing a slightly stupefied smile. *Gotcha*, Vic thought. *You've been acting strange ever since the first day she walked into our office. You may not be as unsusceptible to feminine charms as you think.* "Okay, it's your turn. Why were you coming from the Council building?"

Rory's smile faded. He told Vic about his summons to Hattie Homborg's office, the wall of crystal screens, and his new assignment as Hattie's personal snoop. "I just can't believe that they have deliberately taken a magical artifact from Lemain. It seems more like someone is setting them up—like it's a personal vendetta."

"Son, you haven't been doing your homework," Vic said, slinging an arm around Rory's shoulders. "I would be very surprised if a personal vendetta wasn't involved."

Rory gave her a perplexed look. "Who could they have ticked off that badly?"

"You really don't know, do you?" Vic responded in surprise. "Hattie Homborg and Edna Fitzsimmons were in school together before Edna's animal heist. In fact, Hattie was the one that alerted the laboratory security staff that there would be a break-in that night. If anyone has a motive for revenge, Edna does."

"How did you find all that out?" Rory asked.

"Duh, when you asked me to bodyguard Edna, Heloise, and Agnes, I did extensive background checks on each of them. Come on, you don't think I just stumbled on this information by sheer dumb luck, do you?"

Rory smiled ruefully. "I should know better than to underestimate you. A few things are beginning to make sense. When I was in Hattie's office, I noticed a peculiar odor. I think our secretary of the treasury instigated the goblin attack."

"Rory, that's just plain crazy," Vic said just a bit too loudly. She looked around quickly to make sure no one had overheard her. "I know we've had a truce with the goblins since the end of the Goblin Wars, but no one would be stupid enough to risk working with them again. It would be safer to frolic with manticores. Even her evil grandfather Vincent Homborg had sense enough not to enlist goblin aid."

"Okay," Rory said angrily, "how do you explain goblins being sent to attack Edna, Heloise, and Agnes? You know they had to have been sent since the goblins don't have access to the Pedestrian world. And what other explanation can there be for the smell of goblins in Hattie's office? Come on, Vic, you seem to have all the answers. Answer this puzzle!"

Vic's violet eyes sparked, and she answered in a dangerously quiet voice, "Consider carefully, do you really want to take that tone with me? We've been partners and friends for many years, but if you continue, I'll take you on right here and now.

Regardless of who wins, we'll both be on report. Then who will protect your precious little witch and her friends?"

Still fuming, Rory glowered at Vic in silence. Even though he still believed she was wrong, he had to agree with her reasoning. After a few more tense minutes, Rory broke the silence. "Hell's bells, Vic, I'm not angry with you. The whole situation is just so confusing and frustrating."

Vic's expression softened. "Yeah, I know, pard," she said, playfully punching his shoulder. "But we can't go around accusing the secretary of the treasury with evidence tampering, attempted murder, and consorting with goblins without hard evidence. If we approached the Council with nothing but our theories, the least of our worries would be getting chucked into the Lemain Mental Institution."

"Point taken. What should we do next?" Rory asked.

"Well, if Hattie wants you to investigate the banished witches, let's go to the cottage and brainstorm with Edna and Heloise to see if we can figure out what's really going on." Rory looked at her with surprise. Blushing faintly, Vic said, "Don't look at me like that. I still think Edna's a bit of a flake, but she's not stupid, and Heloise is not only smart—she's intuitive. Besides, if two heads are better than one, just imagine how good four heads should be."

Chapter 15

Vicky and Rory encountered an unexpected scene when they stepped through the interdimensional portal into the cottage kitchen. Heloise was sitting on the tile floor face-to-face with a man wrapped in a blanket, on cushions that Rory thought he remembered as being Rap's bed.

When they heard the pop of the collapsing portal, Heloise and Leonard turned to stare at Vicky and Rory. Heloise was the first to recover. She stood and faced them, placing herself between them and Leonard. "Vicky, do you really think it was necessary to bring Rory back with you?"

"Actually, circumstances have changed. Rory wasn't so much brought as sent. We need to discuss the situation with you and Edna. By the way, who is your visitor?"

Vicky smiled at Heloise's obvious discomfort.

Rory gently pushed Heloise aside and offered a hand to pull Leonard to a standing position. "Do you come here often?" Rory asked Leonard.

"No, this is my first time," Leonard answered as he drew the blanket closer around him, cringing slightly as he jarred his injured hand. "You?"

"Oh, I drop by from time to time," Rory replied, desperately trying to maintain a serious expression.

"Rory!" came a squeal from the doorway. Rory barely had time to turn around before Edna flung herself into his arms. "Oh, I'm so glad you're here! You can't imagine what's been happening! I've been so scared!"

"Edna, Edna, let go. You're choking me," Rory rasped. Edna eased her death grip on Rory's neck but wouldn't release him. "Vicky told me about the goblin attack, and I came as soon as I could to make sure that you were safe."

"Why don't we sit down, and I'll make us some breakfast," Heloise suggested. "Vicky, would you please make the introductions?" As Leonard, Vicky, and Rory took seats at the table, Heloise pulled Edna away from Rory. "I'm going to need help with breakfast." Edna reluctantly joined Heloise in the meal preparations.

As Heloise and Edna began toasting bread and scrambling eggs, Rap entered the kitchen closely followed by Suzy. "Oh, how nice, we have company."

"Suzy, Suzy, come here!" Vicky demanded. Suzy ignored her. Vicky marched over and grabbed Suzy. Suzy struggled and squirmed in Vicky's grasp until Vicky explained, nose to nose, that if she didn't behave, she would be locked in the travel carrier. Vicky returned to her seat with Suzy unenthusiastically crouched on her lap.

Feeling very satisfied with himself, Rap jumped on the counter next to the stove. When he tried to snatch some eggs from the pan, Edna swatted his paw with the wooden spoon she'd been using to stir the eggs. "Keep it up, and you'll be fishing your breakfast from the lake!" Edna snarled. Rap favored her with his best hurt expression, then jumped to the floor, and curled up on his bed.

Meanwhile, Vicky introduced Rory to Leonard. "Mr. Marshall, Leonard, this is my . . . uh . . . cousin Rory Van der Haven," Vicky began. "Rory, this is Leonard Marshall, the history teacher at Sunny Acres School."

"Pleased to meet you, Mr. Van der Haven." Leonard fumbled to hold the blanket around him with his bandaged left hand as he extended his right hand to Rory.

"Likewise, but under the circumstances, I don't think we need to be so formal. Call me Rory, and I'll call you Leonard, okay?" Rory shook Leonard's hand. Leonard smiled and agreed. "So, Leonard, how long have you been teaching at the school?"

Leonard paused to think for a moment. "I believe it's been about seventeen years. I answered an ad shortly after receiving my masters degree from the University of Pittsburgh."

"That's in Oakland, isn't it?" Rory asked.

"Why, yes, it is. Have you been there?"

"I've visited a couple of times. Was Dr. Edelweiss still teaching philosophy when you were there?"

Leonard suddenly remembered the eccentric elderly professor with shoulder-length white hair. "Yes, he was. I only managed to get into one of his courses. He had a strange way of arriving at the lecture hall, as I remember. No one ever saw him enter the hall, but right after the bell rang, he would pop up from behind the podium. The class made a game of determining how Dr. Edelweiss got into the hall. We all contributed for a six-pack of Iron City beer to the person who discovered his secret. At the end of the semester, we gave up and presented the beer to Dr. Edelweiss. He seemed to really get a kick out of beating our game."

Rory chuckled softly. "He would. He always liked his little pranks."

"You knew Dr. Edelweiss?" Leonard asked.

"You could say that—he was my grandfather," Rory replied.

"Edna, the potatoes!" Heloise said sharply. Edna had been listening in on the conversation at the table and was staring dumbfounded at Rory's revelation. Completely forgotten, the hash browns had begun to smoke.

"Oops, sorry," Edna said as she quickly began flipping the patties. "I hope someone likes their hash browns extracrispy," she said with mock cheerfulness.

Vicky had to hold a hand over her mouth to hide her smile. *This is more entertaining than being in Grand Square for the Restoration Day Festival. I think I'll let Rory dangle the bait a little longer. Then I'll reel them all in.*

"Where did you live while you were attending Pitt?" Rory continued.

"We rented a small house across the street from Schenley Park, near the botanical gardens. The park and the gardens were great places to study," Leonard replied.

"Let me ask you a question, Rory." Leonard's gut instinct made him want to believe that all the people in this kitchen were trustworthy and could safely be brought into his confidence. However, he was reluctant to divulge any secrets without assurances of his personal safety, and Rory's questions had raised his suspicions. "What do you do for a living?"

Without batting an eye, Rory responded, "I work in Information Retrieval and Processing for a major organization."

"That organization wouldn't happen to be the Lemain Department of Justice, would it?

For a few moments, the little kitchen in the cottage by the lake was absolutely silent. The silence was broken at last by a loud, deep belly laugh coming from Vicky. Vicky's explosion of laughter scared Rap and Suzy so badly that they jumped to the counter and cowered together under the cabinet in the farthest corner from the table.

"This is great! This is frickin' fantastic!" Vicky yelled exuberantly. "The rest of you are all pussyfooting around, and Leonard just lays it all out on the table. He trumped all of you."

Edna and Heloise looked at Rory who had his head in his hand, with his elbow propped on the table. When he lifted his head, he ignored everyone but Leonard. Looking Leonard straight in the eye, he asked, "How long have you known?"

"I knew you were from Lemain the minute you entered the kitchen."

Rory looked astounded. "How?"

"Because I recognized the scent of sparrow lilies. You'd been close to them just before arriving here, hadn't you?" Rory nodded agreement. "I knew about Heloise and Edna when I overheard them talking the day after the quatos attack."

"What about Vicky?" Rory asked.

"Actually, until just now, I would never have suspected Ms. Lake."

"Bullyah!" shouted Vicky and pumped her arm in victory. "My record is intact! No one has ever penetrated my disguise!"

Edna was standing stock-still, glaring at Vicky's amazing display. Heloise leaned across the table. "Is she usually like this?" she whispered to Rory.

"No, usually, she's a lot more subdued. The last time I can remember her being this loud was when we celebrated getting our gold investigator's shields. We closed down the bar." He looked at Heloise. "No, I mean we literally closed down the bar. Even though everyone involved paid restitution, the bar never reopened."

"My goodness, Rory," Heloise said, looking at him appreciatively. "You've obviously led a much more exciting life than I had imagined. Why don't we all sit down and have some breakfast? I don't know about the rest of you, but I think I'll be better able to make sense of all this after I've had something to eat."

Vicky and Rory gave each other sheepish looks and nodded their agreement. Edna and Heloise brought plates of hash browns, eggs, and toast to the table. Heloise personally served Leonard a large bowl of steaming oatmeal, fragrant with cinnamon and brown sugar. A large pitcher of orange juice and a pot of coffee completed the breakfast feast.

Heloise left briefly to fetch a large brass safety pin, which she used to pin Leonard's blanket together so he would have free use of his hands for eating. Meanwhile, Edna brought her chair around to sit on the opposite side of Rory, forcing Rory and Vicky to move their chairs to allow Edna access to the table.

Leaning toward Rory, Edna murmured, "You never mentioned you had a grandfather who was a professor in the Pedestrian world or that you had visited here before. Gee, Rory, there's a lot I don't know about you." Edna dropped her eyes demurely and peered up at him through her dark eyelashes. "But I'd be willing to learn."

Unfortunately, Rory was trying to swallow a piece of toast just then and began to choke. Horrified, Edna began to slap Rory between his shoulder blades.

Vicky jumped up. "Out of the way! Get back!" Vicky snapped at Edna. Vicky pulled Rory out of his chair as his face was changing from red to blue. Standing behind him, Vicky wrapped her arms around him, clasped her hands together, and pulled Rory sharply toward her. Rory coughed a toast projectile across the kitchen, hitting the counter just as Rap and Suzy were venturing out from their hiding place under the cabinet. Cat and raccoon retreated in a flash.

Edna gazed at Vicky in awe as she helped Rory sit down. "That was amazing. How did you do that?"

"Everyone in the justice department learns that during first aid training. It's called the Koldar maneuver."

Leonard cleared his throat. "Don't you mean the Heimlich maneuver?"

"Heimlich?" Vicky frowned. "Oh yeah, that was the name he used when he traveled. In Lemain, the maneuver was discovered by Ishtavar Koldar. He is head shaman for the Plegarian Plains tribes. Leonard, you've been away from Lemain too long."

"Ah, excuse me," Leonard tentatively ventured. "This is all very interesting, but I'm getting rather uncomfortably cold. Could we continue this discussion after I've found some clothes?"

"Yeah, speaking of that . . . Why is he wearing a blanket, Edna?" Rory questioned. "I mean, I don't want to pry, but do you usually have men running around here without their clothes?"

"He's not mine." Edna grinned roguishly. "You'll have to take that up with Heloise."

Heloise met Rory's challenging stare. "I suppose that would depend on what you consider often," she teased.

Leonard sputtered into his cup, "Heloise!"

Vicky snickered under her breath. "It looks like Heloise is not as meek as she appears at first. I think that the better question would be, Leonard, how long have you been a werewolf?"

"That would be since I was nine," Leonard admitted.

"What do you normally do about clothing at this time of the month?" Heloise asked Leonard, deftly redirecting the conversation away from explanations that Leonard might not wish to give.

"Usually, I'm home. And when the transformation begins, I remove my clothing. Then when it's time to transform back, I make sure I'm close to home. Obviously, that wasn't possible this time. So now I'm asking if I can retrieve my clothing before this brainstorming session continues?"

"Oh, Leonard, of course we'll get your clothes!" Heloise exclaimed. She gave everyone at the table her well-practiced no-nonsense glare, which always demanded immediate compliance.

"Sure, we'll get Leonard's clothes," Rory agreed. "How do we get to your house?"

"Well, we could take my car if it were here."

"Where is your car?"

"It's at my house."

"And your clothes?"

"They're at my house also."

"I have an idea," Heloise said. "Rory, you and Leonard are of similar height and build. Why don't you let Leonard borrow your clothes while we retrieve his clothes?"

"Oh, I don't know about that," Rory began to object.

"I'm sorry, Rory, did you have a better idea?" Heloise said in a dangerously sweet voice.

"Why can't we go get Leonard's clothes while he waits here?"

"Mainly because my mother won't give you the time of day, let alone my clothing, without my being there," Leonard replied rather smugly.

Rory frowned and looked around the table. Leonard stared back expressionlessly. Heloise smiled encouragingly. Edna gazed at him with excited anticipation. Finally, he looked at Vicky.

Vicky raised her eyebrows and shrugged her shoulders. "It's your call, pard. Looks like a stalemate to me. Either let Leonard retrieve his clothes, or we can sit around staring at each other for who knows how long."

With a clenched jaw, Rory stood and gestured to Leonard. "Come on, let's change." Rory left the kitchen with Leonard following.

The women left in the kitchen and looked at one another. "Heloise, I've got a great idea," Edna began. "I know you're going to want to go with Leonard, and you should take Vicky along in case there are more goblins or quatos around. So why don't I stay here and keep Rory company?"

Heloise frowned. "Edna, that is one of the worst ideas I've heard. I agree that I should accompany Leonard, and it would be wise to have Vicky with us, but there is no way that you are staying in the cottage alone with Rory."

"Why not?" Edna demanded.

"It simply wouldn't be proper for you to be alone in the cottage with a man who is wearing only a blanket," Heloise stated righteously.

"But you were in the kitchen alone with Leonard when he was wearing just a blanket!" Edna snapped indignantly.

"That was different," Heloise murmured.

"What?" squawked Edna.

Vicky left the table to refill her coffee cup. As she crossed the kitchen to the stove, she noticed Rap and Suzy slinking around the edge of the room toward the door.

"I think it would be in our best interest to vacate the premises at this time. I've found that it's not wise to be in the same room when those two are arguing. Why don't we go down to the lake? I can teach you how to catch fish. Have you ever had fresh mountain trout?" Rap asked in a low voice. Suzy just purred and wrapped her tail around Rap's as they strode from the kitchen.

Edna and Heloise sat glaring at each other in silence for a few more minutes, and then Leonard and Rory returned.

The exchange of apparel made an amazing transformation in the appearance of the men. Dressed in Rory's double-breasted charcoal gray pinstriped suit, Leonard bore little resemblance to the shy, conservative, scholarly persona that he usually exhibited. Even though the jacket was a bit tight across the shoulders, and the pants were a couple of inches too short, the suit fit well enough to make Leonard appear suave, sophisticated, and confident.

Rory had fashioned the brown blanket into a toga with the use of the brass safety pin. The blanket toga exposed his slim yet muscular tanned arms and legs.

Edna, Heloise, and Vicky gazed appreciatively at the men. "Oh my, Leonard, I guess the clothes do make the man," Heloise commented. "You certainly do dress up well."

Leonard blushed. "This isn't exactly my style."

Heloise smiled. *Perhaps it's not your style now, my dear, but styles can change—or be changed.*

Edna had moved over to rub her shoulder against Rory's bare arm. "And you certainly do dress down well," she purred with an arched eyebrow and a mischievous gleam in her eye.

Rory cleared his throat loudly. "Okay, folks, the sooner you leave, the sooner you can get back."

Edna cast a pleading glance that melted before Heloise's unrelenting frown. She sighed, "We'll be ready to go as soon as we get dressed."

Chapter 16

After Edna and Heloise dressed, they left the cottage with Leonard and Vicky. Since Leonard was the only one of them with a car and his car was at his house, they were going to have to walk through the forest to Leonard's house.

"Where are the kids?" asked Edna. Vicky cocked an eyebrow at her. "You know, Rap, Suzy, and Beowulf?"

Vicky smirked, "The last I saw of Rap and Suzy, they were headed to the lake so Rap could teach Suzy how to fish. I wouldn't be surprised if Rap learns a thing or two before they get back."

Edna looked slightly bewildered. "Well, what about Beowulf?"

Heloise, walking hand in hand with Leonard in the lead, turned and said over her shoulder, "Don't worry, Beowulf is right where he belongs—in my pocket."

"Good grief, Heloise, do you take that chinchilla in the shower with you?" Edna demanded. Heloise ignored the question and continued walking.

As they maintained the pace set by Leonard through the forest, Edna studied her old friend. Edna and Vicky were dressed simply in blue jeans, sweaters, hiking boots, and heavy weatherproof jackets. Heloise, on the other hand, had dressed in a forest green velour pantsuit, an apricot turtleneck jersey, a matching green corduroy jacket, and soft green miniboots. It dawned on Edna that Heloise must have dressed with the thought of meeting Leonard's mother in mind. *Oh well,* she thought, *at least she dressed more sensibly than I did for the picnic. I still can't understand why I suddenly went brain-dead when I dressed for that outing.*

As they walked, Edna couldn't help but enjoy her surroundings. She loved nothing more than being in the woods on a crisp, cool, sunny morning like this one. She noticed all the frenetic activity of the smaller forest dwellers and went over to a tree to talk to one of them. "Good morning, Mr. Squirrel," she called. "How are you this fine morning?"

The squirrel looked around, twitching his bushy brown tail. Looking straight at Edna, he asked, "Was that you speaking to me?"

"Yes, it was," Edna replied with a smile.

"Oh, good grief!" the squirrel chattered in exasperation. "As if I didn't have enough to do getting my family ready for the coming winter, now I'm going to be bothered by a silly human who happens to speak 'squirrel.' I haven't time to talk to any silly humans. Now go away!" With that remark, he turned and scampered up and around the trunk of the tree.

Edna stood looking at the place where the squirrel had disappeared. Usually, the creatures she initiated conversations with were polite and happy to talk to her. She had never before encountered a creature with more than two legs who was so rude. She felt a tap on her shoulder.

"Look, Edna, I already know you're a nutcase. You don't have to convince me by talking to squirrels. Shall we catch up to Heloise and Leonard?" Vicky chided.

Edna gave Vicky an evil look and flounced away, at least as well as anyone can flounce wearing hiking boots.

Edna tried to maintain an angry silence, but her gregarious nature got the better of her, and soon, she was asking Vicky about her life in Lemain.

Vicky told about being raised by her father in the town of Windersham after her mother was killed by an exploding cauldron in a freak accident when Vicky was very young. Her father raised her as the son he'd always wanted, and since he was in the military during the Goblin Wars, that included a great deal of physical training. "With that upbringing, it seemed only natural for me to join the Lemain Department of Justice when I finished school," Vicky concluded.

"What kind of upbringing did Rory have?" Edna asked nonchalantly.

Vicky looked at her with a small quirk of a smile. "If you're wondering if I knew Rory during childhood, the answer is no. And if you want any details about Rory's life, you're going to have to ask him."

Blushing furiously, Edna walked on in silence.

After approximately an hour, they reached the edge of the forest and were crossing a well-manicured lawn with a small vegetable garden in one corner. They approached the back porch of a small neat white house with green trim and Victorian scrollwork around the eaves. If it hadn't obviously been large enough for human habitation, Edna would have thought it was a dollhouse.

When they reached the steps, the door flew open, and a small woman with graying hair and snapping brown eyes stepped onto the porch. "Leonard, where have you been? I've been worried sick. Where did you get those clothes? Oh my heavens, what's happened to your hand?" Mrs. Marshall said all in a rush.

"Mom, relax, everything's okay," Leonard assured her. "There was a small fracas on the school grounds last night, so I stayed over. A friend loaned the clothes to me so that I could come home and change. And my hand is just fine. It's been bandaged by the best field medic around." Leonard smiled at Heloise and squeezed her hand.

Mrs. Marshall cocked her eyebrow at her son. "Who are your friends, dear?"

"Huh . . . what?" Leonard turned his startled expression back to his mother. "Oh, sorry, Mom. This is Heloise Amburgy, the school librarian, who has been helping me with my research. This is Edna Fitzsimmons, the school's admissions counselor. And this is Vicky Lake, the new martial arts instructor. Ladies, this is my mother, Eleanor."

The women all exchanged greetings. "Come on, let's all go inside before the neighbors start gawking," Mrs. Marshall suggested, holding the door open.

They passed from the back porch into an immaculate kitchen. Oak cabinets with glass doors covered the top half of two walls. The counters were made of intricately patterned blue-and-white ceramic tiles, which beautifully matched the blue-and-white checked curtains on the windows. Hanging from a ceiling rack was a set of brilliantly polished copper pans. Looking from left to right around the room from the back door was a double stainless steel sink with a garbage disposal and an industrial-sized dishwasher. Over the sink was a bay window with shelves holding several pots of growing herbs. On the next wall was a double door, restaurant-style refrigerator, and a door that they assumed opened to the pantry. On the next wall was the door to the hallway; then a double-oven stove with a built-in overhead microwave.

"Boy, am I glad Agnes isn't here," Edna said. "She'd stroke out if she could see this kitchen! Mrs. Marshall, Leonard never told us you're a gourmet chef."

"Oh my, I don't think I'm quite the caliber of a gourmet chef, and please call me Eleanor." Turning to her son, Eleanor Marshall admonished Leonard, "Shouldn't you shower and change, dear?"

Looking extremely uncomfortable, Leonard stammered, "Yes, of course . . . You're right . . . I should shower and dress." Casting a pleading glance at Heloise, Leonard excused himself. "Excuse me, ladies, I'll just be a moment. Please . . . um . . . Make yourselves at home." With that, Leonard exited the kitchen at top speed, worrying all the while what course the conversation between Heloise and his mother would take.

Eleanor Marshall watched her son exit the room. With a sigh, she turned to Heloise, Edna, and Vicky. "Men can be so silly sometimes. Shall we have some tea?"

The women had a merry time preparing the tea and talking about the foibles of men. Edna and Vicky were impressed with the quality of the china they took from the cabinets for the tea service.

"Can you believe this?" Edna whispered to Vicky. "This is vintage Olivia china. This china hasn't been made in three hundred years!"

The china had a distinctive pattern of yellow flowers against green leaves with a rim of real gold around the edge of each piece. Although the china was extraordinarily beautiful, its primary value was due to magical properties. Olivia china was noted for its ability to retain the temperature of the food placed on it. If hot food was put on the china, it stayed hot. If cold food was put on the china, it stayed cold.

"You're right, and look at the amount of Olivia china they have!" Vicky whispered back. "You could buy the firstborn child of every member of the Council with a set of china like this. My mother saved two place settings for me if I ever got married, and it took her three years to pay for it."

"It is nice, isn't it?" Mrs. Marshall commented as she crossed the kitchen toward Edna and Vicky. Surprised, Edna and Vicky fumbled the teacup they were admiring and barely managed to place it safely on the tray. "My family had been collecting Olivia china for generations," Mrs. Marshall continued. "They acquired it a piece at a time over many years, and the collection is always added to and passed on to the firstborn female. Unfortunately, all of my sisters and I have had only male children, so now we wait for the first female grandchild to be born. Shall we have our tea in the parlor?"

As they took the tea service to the parlor, they could hear the sound of a shower running and a melodious baritone voice singing "Raindrops Keep Falling on My Head."

With a slightly embarrassed smile, Mrs. Marshall explained, "Leonard has always sung while showering."

The parlor was furnished with comfortably overstuffed chairs and a sofa. There was a small piano in the corner under a bay window and a floor-to-ceiling mahogany bookcase on one wall filled with leather-bound volumes and framed photographs.

While Mrs. Marshall poured the tea and made idle chitchat with Heloise and Vicky, Edna examined the photos on the bookcase. There were several photos of what appeared to be family gatherings. One photo showed three women and two men who were so obviously related that Edna would have bet her eyeteeth they were Eleanor's brothers and sisters. A half-dozen photos depicted Mrs. Marshall with a man and a child at various stages of the child's development. Edna could only assume that the child was Leonard and the man, Leonard's father. But there was one photo in particular that caught Edna's attention. It was a photo of the man she assumed was Mr. Marshall dressed in a white lab coat next to a young woman in a lab coat standing in front of the main building of Capital City Laboratories.

Edna turned to Mrs. Marshall. "Excuse me, Eleanor, where is Mr. Marshall?"

The conversation abruptly ended as they all turned to stare at Edna. Mrs. Marshall slowly lowered her teacup to her lap. With a pained expression, she replied, "John was lost many years ago."

Edna rejoined the group and took a seat on the sofa. Picking up a cup, she asked, "How was he lost?" Heloise delivered a sharp kick to Edna's ankle. Edna frowned at Heloise and continued. "I mean no disrespect, but did he die or just wander off or what?"

Mrs. Marshall sighed, "It's a rather complicated story, and for you to understand, I'll have to give you some background. John was a biochemical botanist working on a compound that would produce hardier crops and increase their yield of viable food materials. He had a young assistant, Barbara Spencer, who had just received her PhD from Lemain University, South Campus. Barbara spent a great deal of time at our house, especially during holidays, since she had no family of her own."

Eleanor took a sip of tea. "John began coming home talking about strange and what he suspected were unethical experiments being performed in another department of the laboratory. One day, John went into the lab vowing to get some answers, and he never returned home."

"Oh, Eleanor, I'm so sorry!" Heloise exclaimed as she went to put an arm around the older woman's shoulders.

Sympathetic but undaunted, Edna proceeded, "What explanation did the officials at Capital City Laboratories give you?"

Eleanor's expression grew angry. "They proposed the theory that John had run off with his assistant, Barbara, since she disappeared the same night. They spread the rumor that John was having a love affair with Barbara. Absolute nonsense! Barbara was like a niece to us. We befriended her since she had no relatives and hadn't been in Capital City long enough to make any friends. She spent all the holidays with us, and once she became aware of Leonard's condition, she spent her weekends with us as well."

Eleanor's hand shook as she took a sip of tea. "Barbara was working so hard trying to find a cure for Leonard's condition on her own time." Eleanor's voice cracked slightly as she forced back tears in an effort to remain strong. "Several days before she and John disappeared, she seemed to be making some progress." She turned beseeching eyes on her guests. "Can you imagine what it's like after living for so many years with a 'special needs' child to finally have some small glimmer of hope and then to have that hope totally destroyed just a few days later? To make matters worse, Leonard was abducted the next day when he went to search for his father. It was four weeks before I knew what had happened to him."

"Mom, no! Don't do this!" Leonard cried as he hurried to her chair and gathered her in his arms. He was now casually dressed in a heather brown cable-knit sweater, blue jeans, and running shoes.

"I'm sorry, sweetheart," Eleanor sobbed into his shoulder as she patted his back. "Sometimes the frustration just overwhelms me." She pulled back from his embrace and gave him a wan smile. She noted the pained expression on Leonard's face. "Don't worry, dear, it's a girl thing. Sometimes we just have to release our pent-up emotions, or we'll burst. I'll be fine." She patted his arm one more time and turned to their guests. "Please pardon me, ladies. It's obviously still a stressful topic for me."

"Think nothing of it, Eleanor." Vicky smiled brightly. "That was nothing. You should see me when I'm PMS'ing. I cry buckets when I get a run in my hose."

Heloise had moved to join Edna at the bookcase when Leonard entered the room. Heloise was distressed because although Vicky was trying to make Eleanor's outburst seem trivial, she could still palpably feel the older woman's anguish.

"Heloise, Heloise, look at this," Edna hissed, pointing to the photograph of John Marshall and Barbara Spencer in front of Capital City Laboratories.

"What?" Heloise snapped irritably.

"Look at the woman. Doesn't she look familiar?" Edna asked.

"Oh, for heaven's sake, Edna, I don't . . . Wait, she does look familiar. Where have we seen her before?"

"Remember that bus tour we took two summers ago?"

"You mean when we visited the major attractions of the central Pedestrian world?" Heloise replied.

"That's right. Do you remember that place we stopped at with all the horses?" Edna whispered excitedly.

"The Equestrian Village?" Heloise suggested.

"Yeah, that's the one. Ring any bells?" Edna asked.

"Oh my goodness, was she the horse trainer that guided our tour?" Heloise uttered in a shocked whisper.

"Don't you think we should be getting back to the cottage?" Leonard had walked up quietly behind them and touched Heloise gently on the shoulder.

"Leonard!" Heloise jumped. "You startled me."

"Sorry about that," Leonard responded. "But we really should be going. I'm sure Rory would like his clothes back."

"Besides, we still have a great deal to discuss," Vicky added as she joined them by the bookcase.

"Would you young people care to join me for lunch?" Eleanor called from the kitchen doorway. "I've got a great big pot of vegetable soup and fresh baked bread."

Leonard raised his eyebrows in silent appeal, knowing his mother baked the best bread in at least two dimensions, but Vicky frowned and shook her head. With a sigh of regret, Leonard called back to his mother, "Thanks anyway, Mom, but we've got to be going."

"Oh, that's a shame." Mrs. Marshall seemed genuinely disappointed as she hurried from the kitchen to escort them to the front door. "It's been very nice meeting you," she said to Vicky and Edna. "Please do visit again sometime." Turning, she clasped both Heloise's hands in hers. "Heloise, please come to dinner with Leonard and me real soon."

"Thank you, I'd like that very much," Heloise warmly returned Eleanor's smile.

Carrying Rory's neatly hung clothing, Leonard led the way down the front walk to a boxy dull green four-door sedan parked at the curb. "Don't wait dinner for me. I'm not sure how long I'll be gone!" he called to his mother while holding the passenger door open for Heloise.

Chapter 17

The car started after the third try, and Leonard slowly began driving back toward Sunny Acres School.

"Okay, Edna, Heloise, would you care to explain what you found so fascinating about those pictures?" Vicky asked.

Heloise turned to look at Edna. Edna gave her a quizzical look and shrugged her shoulders.

"While I was examining the photographs, I thought I recognized one of the people, and I asked Heloise for confirmation," Edna answered Vicky's question.

Vicky waited expectantly for Edna to continue. Finally, she said, "I'm here on my vacation time, I might add, to help you. If you are going to force me to drag every tiny bit of information from you, my time here will be over, Hattie Homborg will have been elected Council president, and we will be no closer to knowing what is going on than we are now! Will you please cooperate with Rory and me so that we can help you?" Vicky was almost shouting in exasperation.

Heloise looked horrified. "I'm so sorry, Vicky, we really didn't mean to make this difficult for you."

"Oh never mind," Edna said with obvious annoyance. "I'll tell you everything we know up to this point. When I was looking at the pictures, I thought I recognized one of the people. And when I asked Heloise, she agreed that a horse trainer we met during our vacation a couple of years ago looked exactly like Barbara Spencer."

"What?" Leonard yelled.

Edna and Vicky picked themselves up off the floor of the backseat where they had been hurled painfully when the car came to a screeching halt in the middle of the road. Vicky lurched forward and grabbed Leonard's neck with one hand while pointing her wand at his temple with the other hand. "Leonard, if you ever do anything like that again, I'll numb your brain so bad you won't remember your own name," she hissed through clenched teeth.

The four of them sat in a silent tableau of shock for a few moments until they were roused by the blare of a car horn behind them. Vicky let go and sat back but kept her wand pointed at Leonard's head. Leonard restarted the car, which had stalled, and continued their trip.

"I . . . I'm sorry," Leonard began in a somewhat shaky voice. "I was startled. Did you actually meet Barbara?"

"We think so," Heloise answered tentatively. "Please keep your eyes on the road. We also think that Barbara and your father may have been made to disappear the same way several others in Lemain have in the past several years."

"Hey, Vicky, tell me about that mind-numbing thing you threatened Leonard with," Edna insisted. "I never heard about any spell like that when I was in school."

"Sorry, that's classified information," Vicky said sternly.

"Oh, I don't think so, sweetheart," Edna said venomously. "This information highway you want us to travel is a two-way street. If you expect us to share information with you, you've got to be willing to share information with us. Fair is fair, after all."

Now Vicky was in a quandary. She hadn't expected so much resistance from these banished witches. Seldom in her career had she met subjects so difficult to intimidate. "Let me talk it over with Rory, okay? We've got to practice some CYA before breaking department regulations."

"Okay, whatever," Edna responded as she turned and gazed out the car window. Edna suspiciously peered over Leonard's shoulder at the speedometer—the gauge read 30 mph. That would have been acceptable to Edna except that the speed limit signs spaced sporadically along the side of the road all read 50 mph. "Leonard, why are we going so slow? Didn't you feed the gerbils this morning? Let's pick up the pace. I'd like to get home before supper."

The animosity in Leonard's little green car was thick by the time they reached the parking lot at the Sunny Acres School. The four of them remained silent as they walked the path to the cottage although Leonard and Heloise did hold hands. When they approached the front steps to the cottage, they were surprised to find Rory on his hands and knees, still in his blanket toga, vigorously scrubbing the stoop.

"Rory, what are you doing?" Edna shouted as she pushed Heloise and Leonard aside and ran toward him. Rory was panting and was bathed in sweat as he turned a dazed expression toward Edna. Edna took the boar bristle scrub brush from Rory's hand and helped him to his feet.

"You certainly got back quickly. Did you bring my clothes?" Rory asked groggily.

"Don't worry, I've got your clothes." Leonard strode forward. "Let's all go inside." Leonard took Rory's arm and led him gently into the cottage. Edna cast an anxious glance back at Heloise and Vicky, then followed the men inside.

When the group rejoined in the entrance of the cottage, Rory was leaning against the stair railing and shaking his head.

"I really don't know what came over me. It was as though I was outside my body, watching myself do all this cleaning and straightening, and I just couldn't stop myself," Rory moaned.

"Sounds like a compulsion spell to me," Vicky said, frowning thoughtfully.

The scene in the cottage entrance presented an interesting vignette momentarily. Rory looked shaken, Edna worried, Heloise perplexed, Leonard confused, and Vicky indifferent. For the fourth time that day, Leonard surprised them by suddenly snapping to his full height and taking charge of the situation.

"Ladies, would you please prepare lunch while I help Rory get cleaned up and properly attired? I'm sure that we're all very hungry after the energetic morning we've had. Heloise, may we use your room?"

Too astonished to speak, Heloise merely nodded. Leonard smiled briefly, and the men left. Leonard's air of authority was so unexpected, even Edna didn't raise any objections.

Vicky calmly removed her jacket and turned to hang it on one of the hooks just inside the door. "Edna, Heloise, take a look around. Do you notice anything different about the cottage?" Vicky asked. As Edna and Heloise looked around, they were astonished at the transformation. Aside from the almost-overwhelming odor of pine oil, all the surfaces around them were shining brilliantly.

"Heloise, look at the chandelier," Edna insisted.

"Oh my goodness, that's brass, isn't it? I always thought it was wrought iron! We'd better check on the rest of the cottage," Heloise urged.

As they roamed the ground-floor rooms of the cottage, they were continually amazed. Wood that was once assumed to be dark-stained pine or walnut now looked like birch or ash. Metal that had once been the black of wrought iron now was revealed as brass, copper, or pewter. All the counters and tabletops were clutter free, everything having been neatly put away.

Edna and Heloise looked at each other flabbergasted. How had this happened? They had done their best to keep the cottage clean during their stay, but it had never looked this good. When Edna and Heloise moved into the cottage, it had looked like an old quaint cottage that had been modernized for twentieth-century usage. But it hadn't looked anything like this. Now it looked like a country manor home on a somewhat smaller scale.

"How did Rory do all this in four and a half hours?" Edna asked in disbelief.

"It's amazing what one can accomplish when under a compulsion spell," Vicky replied.

"What makes you think Rory was affected by a compulsion spell?" Edna snapped.

"Well, let's examine the facts. We leave, and the subject appears okay. We return in four and a half hours to find the subject vigorously scrubbing the front steps. I've been to Rory's apartment, and I can swear that he is not a neatnik. His style is more laid-back, cluttered, bachelor. Therefore, the only reason I can think of for his sudden burst of domesticity is a compulsion spell. Got any better theories?"

"Okay!" Edna snapped. "I'll agree that he was under a compulsion spell if you can tell me how the spell was cast! He was here alone. There was no one around to cast any kind of spell. He is one of the justice department's top investigators. Aren't you folks trained to defend yourselves against spell casters?"

"Yes, we are," Vicky responded defiantly. "But if you had paid attention during your classes at Aunt Mildred's, you would know that objects, as well as people, can initiate a compulsion spell!"

Hoping to diffuse a potentially volatile situation, Heloise interjected a question, "Vicky, our basic magic classes were a long time ago, and we haven't been able to practice for quite a while. Could you please refresh my memory as to what objects can be enchanted to pass along spells?"

Vicky gave an exasperated sigh. "Just about anything that is of nature can do the job, anything that is—or was—plant, animal, or mineral. We need to see if Rory can remember what he was touching when the cleaning compulsion came over him."

"Well, we'd better get busy making lunch," Heloise said as she started for the kitchen. "I can't offer everyone vegetable soup and fresh baked bread on such short notice, but I can throw together a decent quiche while the two of you make a tossed salad."

As the three women prepared the meal in an uneasy silence, Rap and Suzy sauntered into the kitchen.

By the time Leonard and Rory joined them, the table had been set with plates holding steaming wedges of quiche, a large bowl of crisp green salad, and a large pot of orange spice tea. Dressed in his suit once more, Rory had lost his previous dazed expression and regained his usual composed attitude.

As they ate, Vicky asked Rory to explain in detail what he had been doing just prior to experiencing the compulsion to clean the cottage with such enthusiasm. Rory told them about searching the cottage for something a bit stronger than coffee to drink; then the next thing he knew, Edna was helping him up from the front stoop.

"I think it's pretty obvious there is something in this cottage that doesn't belong here." Vicky's eyes narrowed suspiciously. "Edna, Heloise, is there anything in the cottage that you would like to tell us about?"

"What do you mean?" Heloise asked.

Edna's eyes flashed angrily. "What are you implying?"

"Vic, let me take it from here," Rory said quietly. "Hattie Homborg has made the allegation that one of you illegally removed a rare magical artifact from Lemain when you were banished. Please wait, let me finish." Rory held up his hand as Edna's eyes grew wide, and she opened her mouth. "I've been commanded by Secretary Homborg to investigate and try to locate the artifact."

"Oooh, that vindictive w-w-witch!" Edna rose and began to pace the kitchen in agitation. "You would think that getting us banished would satisfy the mean, ugly sow. But oh no, that's not good enough for her! Now when we haven't a prayer of fighting back, she's got to invent imaginary violations to keep us here forever! Why Won't She Leave Us Alone?" Edna screamed to the ceiling in frustration. She whirled and leaned on the table, nose to nose with Rory. "You don't really believe that we deliberately took a rare magic artifact from Lemain, do you?"

"Of course I don't," Rory said soothingly. "Although you three seem to attract trouble like . . . like honey attracts bees, I don't believe any of you would deliberately break the law nor do anything to jeopardize your chances to return to Lemain. I can't even begin to guess what Homborg's agenda is, but she certainly has it in for you. What did you do to antagonize her to the point that she would want you permanently banished?"

"It's me," Edna sank back down in her chair. "Hattie has hated me since we were in school together. I don't know why. Hattie was the spoiled rich kid with powerful parents, and she was just plain mean from day one. Most of the class tried to make friends with her, but with her overbearing arrogance and her snide remarks, she pretty much shut herself off from the rest of us. For some unknown reason, she took a particular dislike to me. So basically, Hattie Homborg has been making my life as miserable as possible for as long as I've known her."

"Considering my recent experience, I would venture to guess that there is an object in this cottage with magical properties of which you are unaware. It could be something you brought with you when you were banished, or it could have been planted here. Either way, we need to find it. Before we do that, however, there are a couple of things we need to discuss. To begin with, I would like to hear Leonard's story. Then we need to come up with a cover story to explain my presence if I'm to stick around and continue to investigate." Rory looked pointedly at Leonard.

"First off, Leonard, how did you become a werewolf? Were you born with the condition, or were you cursed, or were you bitten?"

Before answering, Leonard looked at Heloise as though begging forgiveness with his eyes. Turning back toward Rory, he began, "It all started one summer night when I was nine years old. We were having our annual family barbeque, and when it began to get dark, my cousin Leander and I started catching fireflies. Actually, we did more chasing than catching. I was only nine. Leander was seven, and most of the fireflies were quicker than we were. Anyway, the night got darker. But there was a bright full moon, so we pursued the fireflies into the woods. We weren't really paying attention to anything but the fireflies, and the next thing I knew, I was staring into a pair of large luminous yellow eyes. I yelled for Leander to run. He was behind me, and he started running for the house and screaming like a banshee. I turned to run and tripped over a tree root. Before I could get up, I felt a crushing, burning pain in my left leg. I screamed and tried to crawl away from whatever gripped my leg. I was so scared, I never looked to see what had bitten me. I just knew I was going to be eaten.

"Fortunately, my parents and aunts and uncles had become concerned by our absence and came looking for us, so they were close by and came rushing in like the cavalry when they heard Leander screaming. They beat off the wolf and treated the bite on my leg. At first, everyone thought it was just an unfortunate encounter with a normal forest wolf. But when the next full moon came around, we learned the truth. My life has been anything but normal since that time."

"So your lycanthropy stems from a bite, and it's governed by the lunar cycle?" Rory asked.

"That's about it," agreed Leonard.

"I have to believe that you've searched for a remedy for your infection," Rory speculated.

"Of course I have. My father was a scientist, and he was searching for a cure when he disappeared."

"Have you ever tried hunting for the alpha wolf?" Rory continued.

Leonard gave Rory a look of extreme disbelief. "Do you have any idea how many wolves and werewolves there are in Lemain? It could take hundreds of years to find the alpha wolf! Besides which, I've never deliberately hurt any being since my first transformation, and I don't want to start now. Anyway, I don't know about you, but I can think of much better ways to spend my next hundred years." He glanced slyly at Heloise, who blushed like a demure adolescent.

"All right, all right," Rory said hastily. "Don't get your knickers in a twist. As an investigator, I have to ask these questions. Okay, so instead of offing the alpha wolf, you decided to explore other means of reversing the condition? Tell me what your father was researching."

"When my father hired a biogeneticist, Barbara Spencer, it seemed like the perfect way to solve my problem without endangering anyone's life. Barbara had recently graduated from the university. She applied for an apprenticeship at the laboratory. My father came home that night and told Mother all about her. None of the other departments had an opening at that time, but Dad said that for her, he would make an opening. He was very impressed by her credentials, and I believe that even then he was hoping to work on my condition."

"You said that you had never hurt anyone since your first transformation," Vicky interrupted. She observed him sternly. "Does that mean you injured someone that first time?"

Leonard closed his eyes as he recalled his first transformation when he was only a child. "Remember that no one knew that the wolf that attacked me was a werecreature, so they took no special precautions. I was already in bed when the moon rose, and all I remember is a white-hot pain as if I was being torn apart.

"My parents came when they heard me yelling, but they told me later that they saw a wolf jumping out of the open window. They thought that a wolf had entered and dragged me off. They spent the entire night searching for me.

"I don't remember anything that happened that night any more than I remember any of my transformations. All I know is that I came to in a nearby park. And when I looked around, trying to remember what happened, I saw a rabbit lying near me. It had been ripped apart, and I had blood on my hands."

Leonard met Vicky's eyes and heaved a shuddering breath. "I couldn't believe that I had killed the rabbit, and I vowed that I'd never let it happen again. I haven't eaten meat since that day."

"Well, that explains how a werewolf could be a vegetarian. I've never heard of it before." Vicky shrugged. "It must have been a shock for a kid to see the results of that kind of violence."

Just then, Rap spoke from his cushioned bed in the corner, which he was currently sharing with Suzy. "Pardon me, kind people, but could one of you please open the window before that great stupid bird knocks itself silly?"

Everyone's attention immediately turned to the window over the kitchen sink. There was Coco rapping her beak against the windowpane with the rhythmic quality of a metronome. "Oh my!" Heloise exclaimed as she scurried over to open the window.

Coco glided gracefully to land in the center of the table, overturning the salad bowl. Vicky rapidly reached for the piece of rolled paper attached to Coco's leg, only to encounter the sharp point of the bird's beak on the back of her hand.

"Get back, Vicky, Coco doesn't know you yet. Let me," Edna said as she deftly grabbed the cockatoo's leg and removed the message. With an indignant squawk, Coco spread her wings and swooped across the kitchen and out the window.

Edna unrolled the scrap of paper and read aloud as the others peered over her shoulder.

Edna, Heloise,

Come quick. I just woke up, and I'm stuck in my room on the third floor. Silly building doesn't have any elevators apparently. My assistant cook quit and walked out, and the student helpers don't know what to do. Dinner must be ready in less than two hours, and as of right now, there's no one to prepare it!

I know you have a lot going on right now, but I really need your help. Please come to the school and fix dinner this evening. We can relay messages, and I'll guide you through the entire procedure. I think I left my recipe box at the cottage last night. You can bring it with you. Just come, please. Now!

Agnes

Edna glanced at the kitchen wall clock and gasped. "Oh my goodness, it's already 4:30! We'll never get a meal prepared for that many in an hour and a half. Heloise, what are we going to do?"

When Heloise didn't immediately respond, Edna looked at her friend intently. The skin around Heloise's eyes was a pearly gray, and she appeared to be a bit shaken. Finally, Heloise heaved a great shuddering sigh. "We'll just have to see what Agnes has on hand that we can prepare in the time we have."

"Oh, but, Heloise, wouldn't it be so much simpler to go to the Chicken Palace and order several hundred Special Meal Deals to go?" Edna pleaded.

"Don't be ridiculous!" Heloise frowned. "We would have no way of paying for that much food, let alone transporting it back to the school!"

"It was just a suggestion," Edna sulked.

Heloise turned to the others, her composure restored once again. "Leonard, why don't you take Rory back to your house and try to think up a story to cover his presence at the school? Vicky, you're with us." Without waiting for a reply, she swept out of the kitchen, rapidly followed by the others.

Suzy yawned and stretched her body in an undulating wave that began at the tip of her nose and ended at the tip of her seal-point tail. As she began to saunter toward the kitchen door, obviously intending to accompany her mistress, Rap lifted his head.

"Wait a moment, surely you're not planning to go with them? They don't need our help. Besides, it would be worth our hides if that witch catches us in her kitchen."

Suzy looked over her shoulder and trilled at him. Then she was out the door and down the hall.

"Oh, bother," Rap muttered in annoyance. "I suppose I had better go with them. No telling what sort of trouble they might get themselves into if I'm not along." Suddenly, a thought occurred to him, and his expression brightened. "That's right. Agnes has a broken foot and can't get to the kitchen. She'll have no way of knowing if I've been in her kitchen or not. Oh, this opportunity is much too good to pass up." Rap scrambled to his feet and hurried to the front door.

The others had already donned their jackets and were rapidly leaving the cottage. Rap just barely managed to slip out the door before Rory slammed it shut. He scampered to catch up with Suzy who was leading the procession up the path.

"Did you see that?" Rap panted, slightly breathless. "That big galoot nearly slammed my tail in the door!" Suzy gave Rap a sideways glance with an expression on her face that could only be described as a cat smirk. "Think it's funny, do you?" Rap bristled. "Have you ever seen a raccoon without a tail? Well, let me assure you, it's not a pretty sight. My uncle Salvador lost his tail in an accident and couldn't keep his balance afterward. He was the laughingstock of the family, always staggering around and falling over. He couldn't even catch his own fish anymore. Pitiful, absolutely pitiful."

Rap maintained a running commentary of his uncle's misfortunes as he and Suzy led the way toward the school. Right behind them came Heloise and Leonard hand in hand, followed by Vicky and Rory with their heads together, whispering furiously. Edna brought up the rear of the little procession, looking very disgruntled and staring daggers at Vicky and Rory.

When they reached the juncture where another path split off, leading to the parking area behind the school, Leonard and Rory left to get Leonard's car. Edna caught up to walk beside Vicky. "What were you and Rory talking about so intently?" she demanded.

"Just discussing strategy," Vicky replied nonchalantly. No matter how hard she tried, Edna couldn't get Vicky to divulge any more information.

When they reached the school, they smiled and nodded to a few students and Ed Bigelow but didn't stop to talk as they hurried down the north corridor toward the kitchen.

Chapter 18

"I can't believe I let her talk me into this," Leonard grumbled as he guided the car down the road to his house. "It's not that I mind helping or that I don't want you around—"

"Look, I know it's difficult for you," Rory interrupted. "If there was any other way, believe me, I'd take it in a heartbeat."

"It's not that I'm averse to doing this. I guess it worries me that I don't know what to expect."

"Come on, Leonard. You should be accustomed to playing an undercover role by now." Rory grinned at him. "You've been doing it since you were nine years old."

"That's true," Leonard said ruefully. "But just because it's been necessary, doesn't mean that I've enjoyed doing it." He pulled into his yard and parked the car. "Let's go in and get you settled. Then we'll talk about how we're going to handle everything."

Rory followed Leonard into the house. Eleanor looked up as they entered. Seeing that Leonard had brought a friend with him, she smiled and stood to greet him.

"Mother, this is Rory Van der Haven. He's from the Department of Magical Justice," Leonard began. Eleanor's shoulders stiffened, and her eyes narrowed. Leonard scented the danger and quickly continued. "Rory is a friend of Edna's. He's here to help them and needs a place to stay."

"I see," she said coolly. "And would you remind me again why we should be helping anyone from the Department of Magical Justice even if he is a friend of Edna's?"

"Mrs. Marshall," said Rory, stepping forward, "no one understands better than I how trying Edna can be. I also know that she's a good person who is always willing to help other people. Right now, she's the one who needs help through no fault of her own."

"You misunderstand me. I don't have any problems with Edna. I've met her, and she was a friendly and charming young woman. She would be welcome here anytime. On the other hand, I do have problems with the Department of Magical Justice or any other department affiliated with the current administration of Lemain. Your task would be to convince me why I should feel the need to assist you in your representation of the Lemain government," Eleanor replied tartly.

"Edna has a very powerful enemy in Lemain government who was able to get her and her friends unjustly banished. Now this woman is endangering them here in Pedestria," Rory explained. "My partner and I are two of the very few people who are both willing to help them and also in a position where we are able to help them effectively."

"Who is this powerful enemy, and why is she out to get Edna?" Eleanor persisted.

"Edna and her friends are in trouble with the Council secretary of the treasury. The grudge between them goes back to when they were still in school, and it hasn't gotten any better over the years. Hattie Homborg is a very powerful and dangerous enemy. She is the one responsible for getting Edna and her friends unjustly banished. Now she is endangering them here in Pedestria," Rory explained. "Unfortunately, although we know where the danger is coming from, we don't know where or how she will strike next."

"Remember I told you about the quatos attack in the woods," Leonard said. "Not to mention those students that had goblin blood," he shuddered. "They smelled awful."

"You knew about them?" Rory questioned sharply. "Why didn't you report it?"

"As if anyone would accept the word of a werewolf," Eleanor scoffed.

"There is that," Rory admitted. "Plus, I'm guessing you wouldn't want to draw the attention to yourself."

"Why do you think we moved to Pedestria?" Leonard asked dryly.

"We've forgotten the entire point of this discussion," Eleanor interrupted. "Which is how you plan on helping Edna."

Leonard's posture relaxed slightly. He was always relieved when he succeeded in distracting his mother so that she forgot she didn't approve of what he was doing. "I guess you need access to the school," he said to Rory. "It wouldn't be much help if you couldn't get in there when Edna's working."

"I'll need to be able to move around freely," Rory agreed. "I need to do some investigating, and that means I'll need to be able to get in everywhere."

"Maybe you could pose as a teacher," Eleanor suggested.

"Vicky is already doing that. We shouldn't bring in too many new teachers midyear," Rory disagreed. "Maybe I could go in as a public health inspector."

"I don't believe that would give you as much access as you're probably going to want," Leonard mused. "I was thinking you could go in with some kind of official title." He stopped to think for a moment. "What do you think of coming in as a state licensing inspector? You would be able to poke into every nook and cranny, and no one would raise an eyebrow."

"That sounds like what I'm looking for," Rory said thoughtfully.

"No, wait a minute," Leonard sighed in disappointment. "We're forgetting about Walter Higgins."

"What about him?" Rory grinned.

"We can't possibly do this without him catching on to something. He watches over the school like a hawk," Leonard answered.

"And why should that be a problem?" Rory's grin widened. "Do you mean to tell me that you don't know about Walter Higgins?" When Leonard just looked blankly at him, he continued, "Walter Higgins is from Lemain. He's very rich, very philanthropic, and has connections so far up the administrative ladder that no one knows where they stop."

"Are you sure it's the same Higgins?"

"The very same. He's helped us out before when we've needed to place people somewhere safe," Rory informed him.

"Would that include three banished witches who need watching over?" Eleanor asked.

"Indeed it would, Mrs. Marshall."

"Well, if you're going to be staying here, you had better bring in your things," she said briskly.

"Actually, when I left home this morning, I wasn't expecting to stay. I'll pop back and grab a few things, and then we should get over to the school and save Edna and Heloise from Vicky," Rory suggested.

"I would think it's more likely that Vicky is the one who needs saving from them," Eleanor said drolly.

Rory glanced over at Leonard. "It's obvious she doesn't know Vicky," he smirked. Rory took out his wand, opened an interdimensional portal, and stepped back into Lemain.

Eleanor turned to face her son. "Just for the record, Leonard, your distraction didn't work. I didn't forget my objections to getting involved in this mess."

Leonard looked at her, shamefaced. "I never have been able to fool you," he sighed. "So why did you go along with it?"

"I like the idea of someone being here for a while," she said. "I want to go back to Lemain for a visit. I haven't seen your aunt Lucinda for a long time. If there's someone here who knows about you, I'll feel better than if you were alone."

"I can take care of myself, Mom. I'm not that nine-year-old boy anymore."

"I know you aren't, but I still worry. It's what mothers do."

"When are you going to leave?" Leonard asked.

"I'll pack tonight while you're at the school. Then I can leave in the morning."

They both turned as the interdimensional portal opened, and Rory stepped through. Leonard showed him to the room he would be using during his stay. After he put his belongings away, they returned to the sitting room.

"We'll be going back to the school now, Mother," Leonard informed her. "I don't expect that we'll be late getting back tonight."

"That's all right. I'll be busy getting my things together. I'll need to screen Lucinda too and let her know to expect me."

"We'll see you later, then," Leonard stooped to kiss her cheek before going out the door.

Chapter 19

When the three witches and their familiars burst through the door between the serving area and the kitchen, they were suddenly struck with the glaring pristine whiteness of Sunny Acres School kitchen. The shining whiteness of the walls, tile floor, and marble countertops was almost blinding.

The kitchen encompassed a large area with work counters around the walls and several stainless steel worktables placed strategically throughout the room. Standing next to one worktable at the far end of the kitchen were two seventh-grade girls and one ninth-grade boy. Edna opened her mouth to call to the students, but before she could speak, Valerie came running out of Agnes's office.

"Ms. Amburgy, Ms. Fitzsimmons, Ms. Thistlewaite said you'd come. You've got to help! Nothing's ready, and there aren't any cooks!" Valerie stopped to catch her breath.

Heloise placed a reassuring hand on Valerie's shoulder. "Don't worry, dear, your new cooks have arrived. Now we need to see Ms. Thistlewaite's menu plan so we know what we're supposed to be preparing for dinner tonight. Can you get that for us?"

"Oh, sure. Here it is." Valerie pulled a much-creased piece of paper from her jumper pocket and handed it to Heloise. Heloise unfolded the paper, read for a moment, then closed her eyes, and groaned.

"What is it? What's wrong?" Edna insisted, grabbing the paper from Heloise's hand. She read,

DINNER MENU
Rolled Meatloaf with Broccoli and Cheese
Baked Chicken
Potatoes Au Gratin
Asparagus Vinaigrette
Watercress Salad
Raspberry Mousse
Ice Cream

Edna cleared her throat. "Okay, I can see where this menu is a little too ambitious for tonight, but it's not a problem. We'll just make a few adjustments. Let's see what's in the cooler." She smiled smugly and started toward the large walk-in cooler.

Sunny Acres School's walk-in cooler was famous in the local community. With dimensions equivalent to a small house, the school's cooler could easily hold enough food to supply a moderate-sized army for at least a week. A local rumor has it that an army battalion on maneuvers accidentally entered the cooler; and after eating their way out, six months later, the soldiers were all given medical discharges for exceeding the army's weight requirements.

On the left-hand shelves, immediately inside the cooler door, they discovered several ten-pound plastic containers filled with a ground-beef mixture. Edna stuck her head out the door of the cooler and called to the student helpers, "Wash your hands! Get your aprons on! And somebody please find the automatic hamburger patty press!"

As the students scurried to obey, Edna, Heloise, and Vicky set the containers of ground meat on the nearest counter space. Heloise showed the ninth grader how to operate the patty press, and Vicky got the girls to start tearing greens for the salad. Meanwhile, Edna bustled about the kitchen, turning on the enormous ovens and all the deep fat fryers. Despite her earlier reluctance, it seemed obvious that Edna had decided to take charge of the dinner preparations.

Soon, everyone in the kitchen was busy with his or her individual tasks. Huge trays of hamburgers were broiling in one oven, and pans of cooked french fries were keeping warm in another oven. Heloise and Vicky were slicing tomatoes and cucumbers to add to the salad, and Edna was on her hands and knees rummaging in the cabinets under the counter.

Vicky endured several minutes of loud banging and clattering issuing from the cabinet before she yelled, "Hey, keep it down over there! Do you have to make so much noise?"

Edna withdrew her head and shoulders from the cabinet and fixed Vicky with a steely gaze. "Actually, yes, I do. I can do many things quietly, but cooking isn't one of them."

Vicky turned to Heloise in exasperation, but Heloise just shrugged her shoulders and nodded her head. "In my line of work, I've met some pretty strange characters. But I swear, you three take the cauldron," Vicky muttered.

By the time the first diners arrived, everything was ready. The chalk menu board at the front of the serving line now read,

Gourmet Hamburgers
Fried Chicken
French Fries
Tossed Salad
Ice Cream

The three witches were helping on the serving line when they were startled to see Walter Higgins in line with Rory and Leonard. Walter Higgins stopped in front of Vicky. "Well well, Ms. Lake, are you auditioning for another job?" He smiled jovially.

"Uh, no, sir. Just lending a helping hand." Vicky grimaced.

Rory stopped next with a hamburger on his tray. "Boy oh boy!" he exclaimed with a mischievous smile and a twinkle in his eye. "I wish the rest of the squad could see this—Vic Lake in an apron!"

Vicky gave him the most sickeningly sweet smile she could muster. "Would you like fries with that?" she asked as she completely covered his burger with the golden brown spuds.

Heloise was dismayed when she saw Leonard in line. "Oh, Leonard, I didn't expect you to be having dinner here tonight. I thought you'd be eating at your house. We didn't fix any vegetarian dishes."

"Mother is packing to visit Aunt Lucinda, so we decided to eat here. Besides, we need to talk to you after dinner. Don't worry about the food. I'll just fill up on salad. I need to maintain my boyish figure," Leonard replied with a wink and a grin.

"We were planning on visiting Agnes after dinner, but it shouldn't take long," Heloise mused. "Why don't you and Rory wait for us in the dining room?"

"Sounds like a date to me," Leonard said cheerfully. Then he leaned close and gave Heloise a quick peck on the cheek.

Blushing faintly, Heloise began backing away from Leonard and headed toward the kitchen door. "Leonard, what's gotten into you?" she hissed. "You really shouldn't do things like that in front of the students." With that, she spun on her heel and disappeared into the kitchen.

When dinner was over and the kitchen restored to its former immaculate condition, Edna and Heloise joined Vicky in Agnes's office. When they entered the office, they found Vicky sitting with a mug of coffee in her hand and her feet propped up on the desk.

Edna plopped in a chair, grabbed the mug from Vicky's hand, and took a swig.

Heloise looked from Vicky to Edna with an expression of mild exasperation.

"Look, ladies, I know we're all tired and it's been a long day. But before we relax, we need to check on Agnes," Heloise insisted.

"You two go right ahead," Vicky said. She removed her shoes and began rubbing her feet. "These poor aching puppies aren't going anywhere for at least thirty minutes."

"Ah, what's the matter?" Edna began in a sarcastic, babyish tone. "Does the big bad martial arts teacher's tootsies hurt?"

Vicky glared at Edna with a lethal look. She growled in a menacing low voice, "I can hike for miles, run marathons, and kickbox for hours. But I'm not used to standing in one spot for over two hours. So yeah, my feet hurt, all right? Now back off!"

Before Edna could reply and set off World War III, Heloise gently, but firmly, pulled her from the chair and steered her toward the door. "Edna and I will go visit Agnes while you rest your feet. We'll be back shortly," Heloise called over her shoulder.

Heloise kept a firm grip on Edna's arm all the way to the narrow stone stairs at the back of the kitchen. "Agnes had better not give me a hard time," Edna fumed as they climbed the stairs to Agnes's room on the third floor. "I'm not in the mood to listen to her whine about how we messed up her precious menu plan."

"Let me explain to Agnes about the changes we had to make to the dinner," Heloise sighed tiredly. "I honestly don't understand why you two bicker all the time."

Edna stopped short in the middle of a flight of stairs. "We do, don't we? I never really thought about it before. I guess we just have a knack for pushing each other's buttons." She shrugged.

When they reached Agnes's room, they found Agnes sitting up in bed with her foot encased in a thick fluorescent green cast and propped up on pillows. There were books, magazines, and crossword puzzles scattered over the surface of her bed; and her thirteen-inch color television was playing quietly in the corner, tuned to the local PBS station.

After a quick visual search of the room for some sort of conversational catalyst, Edna focused on Agnes as she lay on her bed. "Yo, Agnes, so how's it hanging?"

"What have you done to my kitchen?" was Agnes's response.

"I can explain," Heloise interjected. "By the time we received your message and got to the kitchen, there simply wasn't time to prepare the menu you had planned. We had to improvise." Heloise looked to Edna for confirmation, but she had determinedly focused her attention on the TV program, which was currently requesting donations to support the local opera company.

"Everyone seemed to enjoy the hamburgers and fried chicken," Heloise finished lamely.

"Oh well, just as long as everyone was happy with the meal, I guess it's okay," Agnes said as she leaned back against the pillows and stared dreamily at the ceiling. "Please follow the menu plan on the clipboard next to my desk in the future." Agnes's eyes slowly closed, and soft snoring sounds began issuing from her mouth.

Heloise turned her shocked gaze on Edna who shook her head. "Let's tuck her in and go meet the guys."

"But is Agnes all right? Why did she just fall asleep in the middle of a conversation?"

Edna looked at Heloise in mild disgust. "Did you check out the pill bottle on her night table? She's obviously had at least two superstrength painkillers tonight. That's enough to knock anyone out."

Edna's tone softened, "Come on, Heloise. Agnes isn't becoming a drug addict. She had a really nasty injury, and she needs the painkillers so she can rest and heal."

"Yes, of course, you're right. However, I think we should keep an eye on Agnes's behavior in the future."

"Heloise, hadn't we better go and meet the guys in the dining room? They're waiting for us," Edna said rather impatiently.

"Yes, of course, but shouldn't we at least put Agnes in her pajamas before we go?" Heloise queried.

Edna inhaled deeply and muttered under her breath for a few seconds before answering, "Tell you what, Heloise, I'll turn off her lights and TV and cover her with a blanket. But I draw the line at changing Agnes into her jammies. Trust me, with these drugs in her system, she'll never notice."

Edna and Heloise hastily prepared Agnes for bed, turned off the TV and lights, and softly left her room.

Outside Agnes's room, they both heaved a sigh of relief. Heloise looked at the ornate broach watch that she wore just above her left breast. "Oh my heavens, they're still waiting!"

Chapter 20

E dna and Heloise ran pell-mell down three flights of stone stairs through the now-empty kitchen and slid around the well-polished tile floor of the serving counter into the dining room.

When they entered, they saw Rory, Leonard, and Walter Higgins sitting at the head table. The three men had their heads close together, and they watched closely as Rory drew on a napkin. They looked up as Edna and Heloise approached. Rory looked serious, Leonard looked worried, and Walter Higgins beamed.

"Welcome, ladies!" Walter Higgins exclaimed as they drew near. "We were just drawing up our battle plans as it were. Well, I guess 'battle plans' isn't exactly the correct terminology, but we are devising a strategy. We would certainly welcome your input since you are directly concerned." He then dropped his head to study Rory's diagram.

Edna took a seat beside Rory while Heloise slid in beside Leonard and squeezed his arm. Leonard gave Heloise a brief smile without losing any of his worried expression.

Still smiling, Walter Higgins said, "We've decided that the best way for Mr. Van der Haven to fulfill his task is to tell the school that he is a member of the State Accreditation Board, thereby giving him access to every area of the school." A slight frown creased his brow as he continued, "I must say I'm a bit concerned about the fact that you ladies neglected to inform me of the recent attacks you have experienced. I had rather hoped that you trusted me enough to come straight to me with any problems you encountered." He sighed and shook his head. "Oh well, water under the bridge. Now that I'm aware of what has been happening, I'll be keeping an eye on all of you." He gave Edna and Heloise a stern look. "In the meantime, I'll make some discreet inquiries of my contacts in Lemain."

"You have contacts in Lemain?" Heloise's look of chagrin rapidly changed to one of surprise.

"Yes, of course, I have loads of contacts in Lemain. After all, I'm from Lemain. How do you suppose these jobs were arranged for you after your banishment, my dear?"

After several moments of stunned silence from Edna and Heloise, Rory leaned over and whispered in Edna's ear, "If you're not trying to catch flies, please close your mouth. You look like a widemouthed bass."

Edna promptly closed her mouth with a resounding snap that nearly took off the tip of her tongue.

"Why did no one tell us?" Heloise asked.

"The Council ordered that that particular information was to be revealed on a 'need to know' basis, and they determined you didn't need to know," Rory explained.

"Of all the arrogant—" Edna's eyes flashed green fire.

"Uh, Mr. Van der Haven," Walter Higgins interrupted, "I believe under the circumstances that these ladies have earned the right to know."

As the two men stared at each other, Edna noticed something inside the oversized breast pocket of Higgins jacket begin to move. Slowly, two long furry white ears emerged from the pocket followed by a pair of tiny bright pink eyes.

"Mr. Higgins!" Edna squeaked, her eyes round as saucers. She blinked her eyes and cleared her throat. "What is that thing in your pocket?"

Breaking off his staring contest with Rory, Higgins looked first at Edna then down at his pocket. A gentle smile broke across his face as he removed the creature from his pocket and set it on the table. "Why, this is Mr. Whiskers, my familiar."

Mr. Whiskers was a small albino rabbit, aptly named since he had the longest and most mobile whiskers any of them had ever seen. The rabbit hopped to each of them in turn, stood on his hind legs, and stared into their eyes for a few seconds, his whiskers twitching wildly all the time. When Mr. Whiskers had finished his scrutiny of the group, he hopped back to stare at Higgins.

Walter Higgins bent toward the rabbit in concentration. "Oh, do you really think so?" he questioned Mr. Whiskers softly. "Very well, if you're sure."

Higgins returned his attention to the group as Mr. Whiskers pulled down one of his ears and began grooming his pristine white fur. "For the first time in my memory, Mr. Whiskers has advised me to take all of you into my confidence and relate the background of why I came to live in the Pedestrian world and created this school. I'd like to tell you the story, but I think the telling and hearing of it would be more tolerable if accompanied by some coffee and perhaps some of that wonderful chocolate layer cake I know Ms. Thistlewaite has in the pantry. If you would be so kind," he raised his eyebrows questioningly at Edna and Heloise.

"Of course, Mr. Higgins," Heloise said, rising from her chair.

Leonard stood up. "I'll give you a hand, Heloise."

"Why don't you come along and help too, Rory?" Edna asked with a peculiar expression and tone of voice Rory didn't recognize.

Once they had reached the kitchen, Edna immediately turned on Rory. "What in bloody blue blazes is going on? Do you know what Higgins's story is about? Have you known about it all along? Just when were you going to let us in on this little secret?" She paused for breath.

Rory frowned down at Edna. "I'm not sure. Yes. Yes. Only when it became absolutely necessary," he replied to her barrage of questions. "Edna, before you build up another head of steam, let me explain. As you may recall, I am an investigator with the Department of Magical Justice. And as such, I am privy to some classified government information. Investigators who divulge classified secrets don't stay employed very long. And how would that look on my resume?"

Edna and Rory glowered at each other for another minute; then Edna flounced away to help Heloise make the coffee. Still fuming, she began banging cups and saucers onto a serving tray.

"What's all the noise about? Ooh, is that coffee I smell?" Vicky asked sleepily, emerging from Agnes's office.

Edna jumped, dropping a cup, which shattered resoundingly on the tile floor. "Oh, for heaven's sake, Vicky! Don't scare me like that!

You almost gave me a heart attack!" yelped Edna as she clutched her chest and leaned against the counter.

Vicky yawned and gave a full-body stretch, which immediately attracted the attention of the men present in the room. She sauntered over to where Edna was sweeping up shards of broken porcelain. "No offense, Edna, but do you really think you should have any more caffeine? I mean you seem to be a bit twitchy already."

Edna whirled on Vicky but was so flabbergasted, she couldn't utter a word. She rapidly cast her gaze about the kitchen. Leonard was rummaging around in the pantry for the cake that Walter Higgins had mentioned. Heloise was making coffee in the ornate chrome urn with the porcelain handles and spigots. Rory was hastily making his way to the pantry in a supposed effort to assist Leonard.

Edna gave a deep sigh, shook her head, and said, "I either need a vacation or a strong sedative." With that, she dropped the last cup on the serving tray, stormed across the kitchen to Agnes's office, and slammed the door.

Still looking slightly bleary, Vicky asked Heloise, "Was it something I said?"

"Never mind, dear," Heloise responded. "She's had a rather long and stressful day as have we all. Would you mind giving me a hand with the coffee?"

When the coffee and cake were ready, Heloise asked Rory to fetch Edna. Aware of Edna's current mood considering her lack of sleep and all the frantic excitement of the day, Rory approached the door to the office with caution. Tapping gently on the door, Rory called softly, "Edna, it's time to go. Are you all right?" Hearing no answer, Rory eased the office door open. Edna was reclined in the plush desk chair with her head tilted back, snoring softly. Rory smiled ruefully and thought, *If only she could be this peaceful all the time.*

Stretching out his hand, Rory gently shook Edna's shoulder. "No, not yet. I'm not ready," Edna moaned.

"Edna," Rory said gently, "everyone is gathering in the dining room. It's time to go."

Edna's eyes flew open as the legs of the chair slammed onto the floor. "Huh? What?" Edna mumbled as she looked around the room, obviously disoriented.

"It's time to rejoin the others," Rory repeated. "Our discussion in the dining room, remember?"

"Oh, sure. I'm ready. Let's go," Edna replied, trying to stifle a huge yawn.

When they entered the dining room, they noticed that not only were plates of cake and cups of coffee at each of their seats, but five large candles had been placed to encircle their group.

"This is cozy, and they have an interesting scent, but what's with the candles?" Edna asked as she took her seat.

Heloise nervously cleared her throat. "Please excuse Edna. She had a minor mishap with a vanishing potion when we were in school and accidentally obliterated the entire chapter "Maintaining Your Privacy and Keeping Secrets" in our *Basic Magic Techniques* textbook.

"Oh, very well," Walter Higgins responded cheerily. "In that case, let me explain. These candles are made with patchouli. The scent clouds the minds and fogs the senses of any attempting to overhear our conversation. Besides, it creates a nice atmosphere, don't you agree?" Higgins beamed at them for a moment before taking a sip of his coffee.

Rory leaned forward with an earnest expression. "Walter, don't you think you had better get on with your story?"

"Oh yes, of course." Higgins dabbed at his mouth with a napkin. "When I was a much younger man, a great many years ago I'm afraid, I was teaching alchemy at the University of Lemain in Three Rivers. At the same time, I was doing research with a small group of academicians and scientists on the theoretical origins of magic. We promoted the theory that magic, and the ability to use magic, is universal—capable of manifesting on all planes and in any dimension. This theory didn't please many of the government officials of Lemain at that time. They ascribed to a popular countertheory that the ability to use magic was exclusively restricted to the residents of Lemain.

"My small group was very outspoken, and we gave many lectures and symposiums at colleges and universities throughout Lemain. Our opposition on the Council soon brought pressure to bear on us to shut us down. Some of the group moved to other dimensions. Some went underground. And sadly, some tried to defy the Council." Higgins sighed deeply and looked sorrowfully around the table.

"Howie Putnam was one of the group who tried to defy the Council. He was once professor emeritus at the University of Lemain and held the Council Seat of Magic and Science. The last I heard, he was teaching a course in herbal remedies at a junior college in Outaway Bay. Poor old Howie." Higgins shook his head sadly and took another sip of coffee.

"As I'm sure you must realize by now," he continued, "I chose to move to Pedestria. I discovered a confluence of extremely strong ley lines at this location, so I made it my base of operation. Through judicious use of alchemy and the natural resources of the area, I was able to amass enough wealth to build this facility and continue my research."

Higgins gazed intently at each of them. "Now I use this school to search out talented and gifted children to determine if they possess magical ability and train them in its use. I hope to one day have indisputable proof of our theory to take back to the Lemain Council."

Everyone at the table, except Rory and Vicky who already knew the story, looked stunned. After a few moments during which the only sound was of Walter Higgins slurping his coffee, Heloise broached the silence with a question.

"Have you had any success finding children with magical aptitude?"

"I believe that most of the students currently enrolled at Sunny Acres have inherent magical ability, but I haven't yet determined a method of verification. There is also the problem of maintaining absolute secrecy." He lowered his voice conspiratorially. "A great many of these Pedestrians believe that all magic is evil, and if they discovered that magic users were teaching at this school, well"—he shuddered—"it would be a disaster of monumental proportions."

"Would it help if you had a person who could sense magic in others?" Edna asked. "Ow!" She rubbed her shin where Heloise had just kicked her under the table.

"That would be great help, indeed! Do you know of such a person?"

"Uh . . . no, not really," Edna replied, still glaring at Heloise. "I just wondered if someone with that ability would be helpful."

Vicky suddenly emitted a large unladylike yawn. "Sorry, folks, but I've got an 8:00 a.m. Tae Kwon Do class, and the candles are burning out. What do you say we wrap this up for tonight?"

Walter Higgins agreed. "Mr. Van der Haven, I'm afraid we can't have a suitable room ready for you until tomorrow, but I'm sure

Ms. Sanderson can find you an e[...]
tonight."

"Thank you, but that won't be [...]
offered to let me stay at his house."

Higgins stood and stretched slig[...]
with me tonight. Anytime you have [...]
think I could help you solve, don't [...]
I'll just walk with you to the door a[...]

At the front doors, they waited u[...]
nights and then waited until he had [...]
back to their homes for a well-des[...]

Chapter 21

Over the next several weeks, life at Sunny Acres School returned to almost boringly normal. There were a few notable exceptions. When not in class, Leonard Marshall could usually be found in the school library with Heloise—not necessarily engaged in research. Edna's usually high-strung demeanor was exacerbated by Rory's proximity and trying to think up menus for the dining hall since she couldn't match Agnes's skills, and she hadn't seen the recipe box since Halloween night. Not to mention, the kitchen was rapidly running out of peanut butter.

Agnes's enforced bed rest for her broken foot caused her to be querulous to the point that Edna snuck into her room one night and disconnected her telephone so she couldn't use the intercom to bug them every five minutes. Unfortunately, that didn't stop Agnes from sending messages via Coco or Valerie. Fortunately for all of them, Agnes was well enough to resume her duties in the kitchen in time for the Thanksgiving banquet.

Rory spent his time exploring the massive white stone building of the school and all of its outbuildings. He wasn't sure exactly what he was looking for, except that it was supposed to be an item with extremely potent magical properties. After intensive questioning, he was convinced that Heloise, Edna, and Agnes had no knowledge of any magical artifact they might have inadvertently brought to

Pedestria, although his interview with Agnes wasn't exactly what he had hoped for as she was still under the influence of painkillers.

Rory seriously dreaded his next meeting with Hattie Homborg. He didn't have any evidence of the three witches transferring a magic artifact, which would be just cause under Lemain law for their banishment to be made permanent. He also didn't have any evidence that would exonerate them.

I can't believe I'm doing this, Rory thought as he roamed the fourth floor halls of the school. *Come to think of it, if I hadn't befriended Edna during her banishment trial, I probably wouldn't be in this position. Phagnabit! What was it about that woman that made me want to do anything possible to defend her?*

Rory had been on the fast track to success in the Department of Magical Justice. Then an attractive auburn-haired wisp of a woman appeared in front of his desk pleading for help. What was he supposed to do? Offering his aid to Edna and her friends hadn't destroyed his desired career in magical law enforcement, but it had seriously slowed its progress.

He did have other career options. He could accept his father's offer to join his accounting firm or, with a couple more science courses, enter the University of Lemain's Physician's College, which would please his mother, a nurse, immensely. He had always felt bad about disappointing his parents when he insisted on entering law enforcement. He was relieved when he discovered that his brother, Justin, wanted to be an accountant like their father and his sister, Wisteria, wanted to be a physician. He hoped their desired career paths would relieve some of the disappointment he had caused by not following his parents' designs for his future.

Right at the moment, he was feeling like a total failure regardless of career choice. He hadn't been able to keep Edna, Heloise, or Agnes from being banished from Lemain. He hadn't been able to solve the mysterious disappearances of important people from Lemain. And now when he finally managed to attract the attention of someone in the Lemain Council of Magic, it was Hattie Homborg.

Vicky entered the fourth-floor hallway in her usual silent method. She immediately noticed Rory investigating the contents of a closet halfway down the corridor. Moving stealthily toward him, Vicky bent her head toward Rory's and whispered in his ear, "Freeze, you're busted!"

Without any reaction, Rory replied, "Nice try, Vic. I heard you the minute you stepped on this floor. I may have other things on my mind, but I haven't completely forgotten all my academy training."

"Yeah, well, you can't blame a girl for trying. You do know there is an office pool with a pretty large payoff for the one who can catch you off guard?"

"What kind of odds are they giving?"

"Not good enough. Everyone knows how strictly you follow company regulations. I keep hoping I'll catch you during an emotional moment and get to collect. You don't let anything or anyone rattle that calm, professional exterior you've built around yourself, do you?"

Rory stared meaningfully at Vicky for a moment before responding. "You of all people should understand why I choose to keep my feelings to myself."

"Oh, for cripes sake, Van der Haven, do you plan on growing up anytime in this millennium? Okay, so your career choice may not meet your parents' expectations. And guess what, your choice of a life partner may not meet their approval either. Who has to live this life, you or them?"

"C'mon, Vic, you know how difficult it is to live a life where your life partner and your family don't get along."

Vicky's eyes flashed dangerously. "Excuse me, partner, but I believe we were discussing your life, not mine."

Rory slowly closed the cabinet door and slid to a sitting position on the floor of the hallway. "Sorry, Vic, I'm feeling a bit overwhelmed right now."

Vicky sighed and sat down beside Rory. "Talk to me, and don't try to con me. I'm better at it than you are."

"Look, it isn't easy to open up and spill my guts when I've been trained in concealment all my life. Give me a minute here." His breath gusted out; then he continued. "As far as a life partner goes, even if I had the perfect woman standing right in front of me, I'm not ready to make a commitment. There are too many things I still want to accomplish, and I don't want anything distracting me or holding me back if it can be avoided."

"Ya know, pard, from my point of view, it sounds like you're in the middle of a big pity party. One of these days, you're going to look around and wish you had this time back and these choices to make again."

"Back off, Vic, you don't know what you're talking about!" Rory snapped.

Vicky swung around, and before Rory could react, she caught him with a strong right hook. His head snapped back and hit the wall. He shook his head and groaned, then looked blearily up at Vicky who was looming dangerously over him, cheeks red and eyes flashing angrily.

"Don't you even think of saying anything," she hissed. "You of all people should realize that I know exactly what I'm talking about!" She watched as Rory opened and closed his mouth several times, either unsure what to say or checking to see if his jaw still worked. "Think about that, buddy boy, when you're sitting around feeling sorry for yourself!"

Vicky spun around and stalked down the hallway. Storming out of the school, she slammed the door so hard, it bounced back open; and she had to slam it again. Breaking into a ground-eating jog, she started back to the cottage. She sped up, and her breath puffed out in white plumes in the crisp air. She burst through the cottage door, startling Heloise, who was reading in the comfortable chair by the window. Heloise leapt to her feet.

"What on earth is the matter?"

Vicky scowled. "Nothing is the matter! Everything is just wonderful."

Heloise put her book down and stood. "Let's go into the kitchen. I'll fix us a nice—"

"Don't suggest another cup of tea. I've had enough tea to float a boat since I've been here!" Vicky growled, stomping toward her room. When she returned, she had a bottle in one hand and two glasses in the other. "Here, this should be quite a change for you." She sloshed an inch of dark amber liquid into the glasses and thrust one at Heloise before gulping hers down.

Heloise sipped cautiously and watched as Vicky poured another glass and drank again. "Does this have anything to do with Edna?"

"No, she's in the clear this time." Vicky took a deep breath and sank onto the ottoman, gesturing the other woman to the chair. "Where is she?"

"She's still up at the school, catching up on paperwork." Heloise sipped again then asked, "I know we're not close friends or anything, Vicky. But if you need to talk, I'd be glad to listen."

Vicky stared into her glass then nodded. "It's just that idiot Van der Haven. He brought up some memories that I usually try not to think about."

"We all have unpleasant memories, Vicky. I'm sure he didn't mean to upset you."

"In a pig's eye!" Vicky snapped, not noticing Heloise's shudder. "He knows all about Steve. How dare he suggest that I don't know what it's like to regret the choices I've made!"

Vicky rose and began pacing. Heloise debated offering comforting words before deciding that it might stop the other woman's confidences. Instead, she asked, "Who is Steve?"

"My fiancé . . . He was lost in the Goblin Wars," Vicky dropped back down onto the ottoman. "I've always wished that we had ignored my father and gotten married before he left."

Before Heloise could think of what to say, Vicky again jumped up, saying, "Look, I think I need some time alone." She retreated to her room but now had enough control to close the door quietly.

The petite woman with mousy brown hair and cat's eye glasses stepped out of the interdimensional portal into the main corridor of Capital City Laboratories. She glanced apprehensively around to make sure no one had witnessed her arrival. Nervously, she tugged her cardigan more tightly about her shoulders as she hurried toward the double mahogany doors at the end of the stark white corridor.

Given the late hour, it was not surprising that there was no one to observe her movements. The woman found it equally unremarkable that a faint gleam of light showed beneath the doors she was rapidly approaching.

When she reached the mahogany doors, the woman squared her shoulders and took a deep breath in anticipation of what she was certain would not be a pleasant encounter. Before she had nerved herself enough to knock, the doors swung silently open.

On trembling legs, the woman advanced toward the massive marble desk and the empty large black chair behind the desk. The desk was intricately carved with elaborate scenes of torture, dismemberment, and death involving multitudes of magical and nonmagical creatures, including humans.

Her fascination with the desk's carving was quickly replaced by revulsion at the graphic horrors depicted there. When she raised her head, she found herself looking directly into the cold gray eyes of the most dangerous witch in Lemain, Lucretia DuMaurier. Lucretia was a handsome woman with a regal bearing but as cold and cruel as the icy northern wastelands. She came from a long line of sorcerers and scientists and had inherited the Capital City Laboratories from her father, whose primary area of study was vivisection.

"Well, it certainly took you long enough to get here, girl. What have you to report?" Lucretia demanded.

The woman licked her parched lips before replying. "The banished three don't know anything for certain yet, but with each attack, they become more suspicious. Also, two new people have arrived, Victoria Lake and Rory Van der Haven. I understand that Mr. Van der Haven is working for Hattie Homborg, but it is unknown where Ms. Lake's loyalties lie."

Lucretia leapt from her chair and began pacing behind the desk. "Blast Hattie!" she muttered vehemently. "If my granddaughter doesn't stop her infernal meddling, she'll ruin everything! Have you found the artifact yet?"

Blanching, the woman answered hesitantly, "It has been difficult to search without knowing the size or shape of the artifact."

Lucretia abruptly stopped pacing and glowered. "Pay close attention, dolt. I will explain this once and once only. The artifact is a lacquered wooden box approximately six inches by four inches by five inches deep. The lid of the box is set with uncut polished stones."

"What item of great value does this box contain?"

"The contents of the box are unimportant. The box itself is an item of unimaginable power. My gift of this artifact will prove to the master that I am his most devoted and trustworthy servant. It will ensure my place at his side when he regains his throne."

Lucretia glared fiercely at the frightened woman. "Now go back to that miserable world and find the artifact for me. Rest assured your life won't be worth pond scum if you report failure to me again."

Chapter 22

Pedestrian weather in the Laurel Mountains just prior to Thanksgiving tended to be cold, wet, and gloomy. The bright lights in the Sunny Acres dining room dispelled the gloom and provided an ambiance of warmth on this cold November afternoon.

"Hey, Jason," Jeremy Wilkins whispered to his twin at the lunch table.

Jason stopped chewing long enough to thickly mumble, "What?" before swallowing.

"That package came," Jeremy continued quietly after making sure no one else was listening.

"Which one?" Jason asked, perking up.

"That crystal-growing kit we ordered," Jeremy hissed impatiently. "You remember, the one where you just add water."

"Oh yeah," Jason sighed. "It takes a month for them to grow, doesn't it? That's a long time to wait. I was hoping it was the electronics kit."

"You know we didn't have enough money for the electronics kit. We'll have to wait for our Christmas money to get that. These crystals grow in about twenty-one days, but I was thinking about it. We could go to the chemistry lab tonight. No one will be there. I'll bet we can find something to make them grow faster."

Jason began to look more interested. "What do you think would make them grow faster?"

"I'm not sure yet. Hurry up and finish eating. We can check in the library while Ms. Amburgy is still eating."

In the dim, quiet library, Jeremy rooted through the shelves while Jason flipped through a heavy tome. Jason scribbled information into the dog-eared notebook with a pencil stub, both of which he always carried in his pocket. He jumped and glared when his brother thumped two more thick books onto the table.

"If you're done with that one," Jeremy said, "here's one with a section on chemical reactions. I'm going to look through this book about precipitants. Maybe we can add something to it that will speed up the crystallization and shorten the time we have to wait."

"Okay, that sounds like a good idea. Just remember that we need to clean up and put these books away before Ms. Amburgy gets back," Jason cautioned.

Jeremy nodded agreement and started to peruse his book. The library was silent except for the soft rustle of pages and the scratching of pencils.

"Here it is!" Jeremy exclaimed. "I can't believe it could be this simple. We can find the things we need in the chemistry lab. Now we had better get out of here before we get caught."

"Okay," Jason said and started gathering up the books.

Together they carefully replaced the books, trying to ensure that no one would realize what they had been researching. They were just about to slip out of the door when Heloise entered.

"Oh, hello, boys," she said. "Was there something I could help you find?"

"No, thanks, Ms. Amburgy. We already found it," Jason told her.

"I promise we didn't leave a mess," Jeremy added.

"I appreciate that." Heloise smiled. "You better go to class before you're late."

"Yes, ma'am," they answered in unison.

As they took their seats in history class, Jason whispered, "We need to go over all this stuff before we check the chem lab."

"Yeah, we'll do it in study hall. Then we can sneak into the lab when everyone is at dinner."

"We'll get to eat later, though, won't we?" Jason asked anxiously.

"Of course," Jeremy scoffed. "I don't want to go hungry either. We can always get something from Ms. Thistlewaite."

"Okay then, we'll do it tonight."

The two boys crept down the hallway. With everyone at dinner, this was the best time to search the chemistry lab. The only problem was that with everyone at dinner, the classrooms were closed, and the hallways were dark.

"Jeremy, can you see where you're going?"

"Yeah, that's why we brought the flashlight," Jeremy answered scornfully.

"That's fine for you," Jason grumbled. "You've got the light. All I can see is your back."

"Stop whining. If you keep making this much noise, we're going to get caught."

They moved along the hallway as quickly as they could while still remaining quiet. The dim light from the flashlight was of minimal help. Both boys sighed in relief upon reaching the dark chemistry lab.

"It's locked," Jeremy moaned in disgust.

"Move over then, and let me try it," Jason suggested, nudging Jeremy over slightly. After a minute of working, he stepped back and grandly waved his brother toward the door.

With a gentle twist, the handle turned, and Jeremy swung the door open. "Cool," he said in admiration. "You'll have to teach me how to do that,"

"Not when I finally know how to do something you don't." Jason grinned.

The boys entered the cavernous room. Jeremy swept the flashlight quickly around the room. "Come on, Jason. I'll bet we can find something over on the supply shelves." He hurried over to the far end of the room, leaving his brother to follow.

Jason crossed the room more carefully, wishing that Jeremy would shine the flashlight in his direction. As he drew near, his wish was granted.

"Hey, Jase, look what I found," Jeremy said, spinning about to face his brother. He shined the light directly into Jason's eyes.

Jason flinched away from the sudden brightness and stumbled against the shelves. One of the bottles on the top shelf teetered and then crashed onto the adjacent countertop, breaking a jar sitting near the sink. They watched as the liquids mingled and began to produce billowing clouds of white smoke.

Jeremy leaned closer to check the labels on the broken bottles. In spite of the attempt he made to cover his nose, he began to cough. "Come on, let's get out of here."

They paused to catch their breath in the hallway. "What was that?" Jason asked.

"It was hydrochloric acid, and the one by the sink was ammonia. That's what happens when you mix them."

"Is it poisonous?" Jason asked uneasily.

"No, it's not. The smoke just makes you cough. But we had better get out of here before we get caught. We'll be in real trouble for making that mess."

"So what do we do now, Jere?" Jason asked as they quickly negotiated the dark hallway in the opposite direction from the drifting white smoke.

"How about stopping in the kitchen for a snack?" Jeremy suggested. "That's a good excuse for being out this late. Besides, I'm hungry."

They made their way downstairs to the kitchen. Everyone in the school knew that Agnes always left crackers, cheese, and fresh fruit out for students having after-hour hunger pangs.

On the way back up to their dorm room, the boys passed by the infirmary. They were surprised at the activity in the room. Pamela Sanderson was speaking angrily to her assistant.

"Why on earth would you call Ms. Fitzsimons for something like this? She has nothing to do with it! Besides, she's probably gone for the day. You had better go find Mr. Higgins."

The boys ducked out of sight until the assistant left the infirmary in search of Walter Higgins. When the coast was clear, they entered the room.

"Excuse me, Nurse Sanderson, what's going on?" Jason asked.

Pamela looked up from the student she was tending. "I don't have time to chat right now, boys," she said sharply. "This is the third student brought in during the last twenty minutes."

"What's wrong with them?" Jason persisted.

"Asthma," Pamela informed him. "I don't know why all of them are reacting at the same time, but there you are."

"Possibly something got into the ventilation system," Walter Higgins suggested as he entered the room. "Is it going to cause a severe medical problem?"

"No, it's not serious," Pamela admitted grudgingly. "But I certainly hope it doesn't happen again."

Higgins gave a small smile. "I'm sure we can avoid a repeat occurrence," he assured her, looking meaningfully at the boys. "Now why don't we let Ms. Sanderson tend to her patients? It's past time for you to be in your rooms."

"Yes, sir," Jason and Jeremy agreed in unison before starting back to the dormitory.

Agnes woke early and, after throwing on a battered and baggy set of sweats, hobbled down to the kitchen. She started the coffeepot and leaned drowsily against the counter as she waited for it to perk. Once she had consumed her first cup, she felt human enough to begin breakfast preparations.

As with any holiday, the Thanksgiving breakfast menu was plain and simple. She set out a selection of cold cereal and fruit. The cart holding several toasters and loaves of bread came next, and she quickly wheeled it out.

Returning to the kitchen, she poured another cup of coffee. Agnes sipped gratefully and then began to crack eggs into a large bowl. Once the eggs were scrambled, they were returned to the cooler until it was time to cook them. Sighing with relief, she sat down to enjoy her coffee and a chocolate chip cookie.

Edna stretched and yawned widely before shuffling down the hall toward the kitchen. If asked, she would readily admit that one of the things she liked most about holidays was being able to sleep in. She was still yawning and absently scratching the smiley face boldly emblazoned on the posterior of her nightshirt as she entered the kitchen to find Heloise already awake. Heloise was sitting at the table reading a magazine with her ever-present cup of tea at her side.

"Coffee?"

"It's waiting for you on the counter. And good morning to you too, Edna."

As Edna was pouring her coffee, Suzy entered through the pet flap they had installed in the kitchen door. Suzy meowed politely in greeting and continued down the hall toward Vicky's room. Edna carried her cup to the table and sipped the steaming brew as she kept watch on the pet flap. She didn't have long to wait. In a few minutes, Rap emerged from the kitchen door. His weary gaze met hers momentarily; then he staggered over to his cushy pet bed and collapsed.

"Rough night, Rap?"

Rap turned his bleary eyes on Edna. "That would have to be one of the largest understatements I have ever known you to utter."

Edna felt a smile beginning to tug at the corner of her lips. "Oh, really? What were you doing? Tell me all about it."

"Very well. If you must know, I took Suzy to the lake in an attempt to teach her how to catch fish. She was quite enthusiastic about the process while I was demonstrating, and she didn't hesitate to share in eating the fish I caught, but her attitude changed rather dramatically when it came for her turn to catch the fish. She would emit an ear-piercing screech whenever her paw touched the water, and she positively refused to insert her face under the surface of the lake to look for the fish. She kept complaining that the water was 'wet.'" Rap's brow furrowed. "I fail to comprehend how any creature who is so terribly fond of eating fish could be so horribly inept at catching them." He sighed, rolled into a ball, and fell sound asleep.

Edna's eyes met Heloise's, and they spent the next several moments with their hands over their mouths to stifle the giggles that threatened to escape. When they had finally regained their composure, Heloise scooted her chair closer to Edna.

"Look at this article in *Magic Moments*." Heloise pointed to a boldface-typed headline in the weekly newsmagazine from Lemain. Edna read,

SPIRITUAL VISITATIONS: FACT OR FICTION?

Magic Moments reporter, Will Etheridge, has been investigating the flood of recent reports by Lemain residents of ghostly visitations by missing family members. Visitations have been reported from all over the world; and they share the unique fact that the visitors are all people who have disappeared suddenly, and mysteriously, over the past several years but were never declared dead due to lack of evidence. One such visitation occurred to Mr. Merle Osborn of Wyatt's Corner.

"I was getting ready for work, and suddenly, my wife Lucy just appeared in the bathroom mirror. I was so surprised, I almost sliced my chin clean off. She was wearing some sort of yellow-and-red uniform and a funny paper hat that looked like a boat turned upside down. She looked straight at me and said she didn't know where she was or how she got there, but she wanted to come home. Then she just faded away."

Lucy Osborn failed to return home fifteen years ago after leading a demonstration to protest government-sanctioned experiments on animals by a prominent laboratory in Capital City. Family members of several other Lemainians who have disappeared in recent years have also reported ghostly visitations over the past three weeks. Justice Department officials declined to comment on these visitations or on their lack of progress investigating the rash of disappearances that have plagued Lemain for years.

"Wow, that's weird." Edna shivered. "Kind of gives me the creeps just thinking about someone I know popping up in the bathroom mirror. Are you done with the magazine? I want to check my horoscope."

Heloise stared at Edna, dumbstruck. "Edna, don't you think it significant that these sightings were of people whose disappearances have gone unsolved or that they began right after Halloween and at least one of them has some sort of connection to the Capital City Laboratory?"

Edna thought for a moment. "Naw, probably just coincidence. Can I have the magazine now?"

Heloise gave up. She relinquished *Magic Moments* and sipped her rapidly cooling tea as Edna read her horoscope for the week. *Edna may be correct, and it may just be coincidence. But when you get too many coincidences, they start to form a pattern. I just wish I could figure out this pattern and what it may mean.*

Agnes was chopping celery and onions for the turkey stuffing when the kitchen helpers straggled in. She had the two older girls finish the breakfast preparations and serve the meal. When Valerie arrived, Agnes had her help by bringing supplies and saving Agnes extra steps.

Agnes had been in Pedestria long enough to know how to put on a traditional holiday meal. In addition to the turkey and stuffing, she prepared fluffy mashed potatoes, gravy, yams with marshmallows on top, green bean casserole, cranberry sauce, brussels sprouts, broccoli cheese casserole, corn, and fresh baked dinner rolls. She and her helpers also made pumpkin pies, apple pies, mince pies, cherry cheesecake, chocolate brownies both with and without nuts, and crispy rice and marshmallow bars.

When everyone had gathered in the dining hall for Thanksgiving dinner, they filled their plates at the buffet line. Agnes watched with deep satisfaction, feeling that she had done her ancestors proud. Seeing that everyone had been served, she released her assistants so they could eat with their friends. She joined Heloise and Edna, taking the seat they had saved for her.

"Is that all you're going to eat?" Edna asked.

Agnes looked up from the broccoli she was poking with her fork. "I guess I'm not really hungry," she said. "I'll probably eat more later this evening."

"A nice turkey sandwich in front of the television?" Heloise guessed.

"Well, that *is* the best part of the holiday," Agnes admitted.

After everyone had helped themselves to dessert, Walter Higgins stood and cleared his throat. "I would like to say a word of appreciation to Ms. Thistlewaite and her assistants. Thank you for all your efforts that brought us this wonderful meal. You have outdone yourselves, and we are grateful."

Agnes smiled and nodded shyly, wishing she had changed her clothes before dinner. She would remember that at Christmas.

Chapter 23

Almost immediately after the Thanksgiving festivities, the weather took a drastic turn for the worse. As the temperature plummeted, dark gray clouds obscured the sky, and snow flurries became a daily occurrence. Even though they had been in Pedestria for five years, not all of the witches had adjusted to the severe cold and snow that was the norm for winters at the Sunny Acres School.

Heloise ignored the slam of the cottage door while she sat quietly reading and sipping hot cocoa in the living room. She calmly turned a page as Edna rushed into the room, flinging off her sodden scarf, cloak, and shoes on the way to the roaring fire in the fieldstone hearth. For the next couple of minutes, the only sound in the cottage was the crackling and popping of the fire and the chattering of Edna's teeth as she vigorously rubbed her frozen hands together over the flames.

Using her finger as a bookmark, Heloise studiously regarded her frozen, miserable friend. "Edna, when you have finished imitating a Hyteran greeting ritual, we need to talk."

Edna turned from the fire and gave Heloise a scathing look. "W-well, i-it m-m-might h-help i-if y-you w-would s-s-share s-some of t-that h-h-hot c-chocolate," she chattered.

Without a word, Heloise left the room to return in a few moments with a steaming cup of the enervating beverage. Edna gratefully accepted the cup of hot cocoa, and Heloise resumed her seat on the overstuffed sofa.

After a few minutes in front of the fire, drinking hot cocoa, Edna moved to the rust-colored plaid armchair across from the sofa and sank gratefully into its plush embrace. "Okay, what do you want to talk about?"

Heloise closed the book in her lap and smiled sympathetically at Edna. "Edna dear, I understand that you've resisted the obstacles of Pedestria ever since we arrived here. And I understand why, but you've got to be sensible. As long as we're stranded here without access to our magic, we have to adopt some of the Pedestrian methods, especially in the matter of weather protection."

Edna glowered sullenly at the dregs of cocoa in her cup but didn't say a word as Heloise continued.

"You must have noticed over the past five years that this particular part of Pedestria has long periods of inclement weather. You know—rain, snow, ice, wind, and whatnot. I'm afraid that your cloak, scarf, and shoes simply aren't sufficient protection without being able to use your individual protection spells."

Edna looked despondently at the sodden apparel she had haphazardly cast about the room. She could swear she saw steam rising from them as they dried. Heaving a sigh that seemed to originate somewhere in the region of her navel, Edna answered, "Okay, you're right. What do you suggest I do?"

With a rare grin, Heloise set her book on the end table and sprang to her feet. "We're going shopping!"

For all of Heloise's good intentions, the proposed shopping trip took a while to arrange. First, they slogged through the chilling rain to see Agnes. Agnes was up to her elbows in flour and frantic to perfect a new recipe before dinner. Next they checked in with Vicky, whose protective surveillance was becoming more and more relaxed as time went on. Vicky had arranged a special training session of her more promising martial arts students and couldn't join them. Not wanting Edna and Heloise to be completely unprotected, Vicky gave each of them an iridescent ring that appeared to change to all the colors of the spectrum as they watched.

"What is this, a mood ring?" Edna asked skeptically.

Vicky looked momentarily perplexed; then she grinned. "Not exactly."

"Well, what *exactly* is it?"

Vicky gave Edna a slightly crooked grin. "It's top secret. I'd be happy to tell you, but then I'd have to kill you."

"Oh, very well," Edna huffed. "Keep you precious secret then. Can you at least tell me how it works, or is that top secret too?"

Serious once again, Vicky explained the manner in which the ring was to be used.

"I have a master ring, which is linked to the ones I've given you and Heloise. As long as your rings remain a solid green color, I'll know that you are all right. If the ring turns blue, it means you're entering a risky and potentially dangerous situation. If it turns red, I'll know that you're in imminent peril."

Edna stared at the ring thoughtfully for a few moments. "What if the ring turns black?"

"Oh, for pity's sake, Edna," Vicky began; then she encountered Heloise's piercing stare. Vicky lowered her head and muttered into her chest, "Don't worry about it."

"What?" Edna pressed.

Vicky raised her head defiantly. "Okay, if you insist. If your ring should happen to turn black, it means you don't have to worry about what to wear to the office tomorrow or ever again. Is that enough information for you? Does that scare you enough that you'll be careful and take precautions?"

The crease in Edna's brow slowly disappeared as a smile grew on her face. "Then all we have to do is make sure the ring doesn't turn black. Thanks, Vicky." With that comment, Edna turned and left the martial arts training room.

Heloise and Vicky watched Edna walk away. Heloise turned to Vicky and shrugged. "What can I say? Sometimes Edna is completely fearless."

Vicky frowned and shook her head. "No, she's more than fearless. She's reckless, and that scares me. Being the more sensible of the pair, I'm counting on you to keep an eye on her. Just remember, if anything serious happens to her, you're going to have to help me explain it to Rory."

Heloise nodded and set off after Edna.

Edna was waiting by the front door when Heloise finally caught up with her. "Okay, Heloise, you convinced me that I needed to go on this shopping trip. And now I'm actually kind of excited about the idea, but have you figured out just how we're going to get to town

DORMI MECKEL & DENISE CHARTIER BOBOLA

and back, especially when I plan to be loaded down with a quezillion shopping bags full of goodies?"

Heloise smiled enigmatically. "Oh, I think I've made arrangements that will provide adequate transportation for your wildest shopping spree. Look."

Just as Edna turned to look out the window next to the front door, Carl pulled to a stop in front with the school van. "Heloise, did you set me up?" Edna asked suspiciously.

Heloise chuckled. "No, dear, I just happen to know that this is the day that Carl goes in to town to pick up incidental supplies. As long as one is willing to leave the school and return to the school on Carl's timetable, he's happy to give anyone a lift. Shall we go?"

After a speedy, bumpy, hair-raising ride down the mountain to the town of Laurelwood, Carl brought the van to a screeching halt in the center of town. "You all better be back here by five o'clock, or you're going to have a long walk home!" Carl called as he dropped the van into gear and sped away.

"I've got to learn how to drive," Edna murmured as she stared at the receding van.

The shopping spree was on!

Meanwhile, Rory was continuing his unproductive search for the mysterious, unidentified magical artifact. He had dutifully, if somewhat reluctantly, been searching unsuccessfully for several weeks and was almost ready to give up the search as a lost cause; but as long as an area remained unsearched, he felt duty-bound to continue.

As he was inspecting an apparently unused and forgotten storage room on the fifth floor of the main school building, a glowing oval appeared before him. As he watched, the face of Willis, Hattie Homborg's secretary, appeared.

"Investigator Van der Haven, you are ordered to report to Secretary Homborg's office within one hour."

Immediately after Willis uttered the last word of his message, the oval blinked out. Although not unusual, Rory found it rather disconcerting that he wasn't offered the opportunity to at least try to come up with an excuse for avoiding this particular confrontation.

"Oh, dragon droppings," Rory muttered as he pulled a small black device from his jacket pocket. The flat square box resembled the electronic objects popular among the youth of Pedestria. It was approximately the size of a deck of cards, with a small view screen and alphanumeric buttons underneath. Rory quickly hit a button, which lit up the screen. From the screen, he selected an item and pressed another button then waited. In a few moments, Vicky's miniature image appeared.

"What's up? I'm in the middle of a session," Vicky's voice hissed over the little screen.

"Get somewhere private. We need to talk," Rory answered in an equally hushed tone.

In a few moments, Vicky returned to the screen. "Okay, Van der Haven, this had better be important. You know how dangerous it is for us to communicate this way."

"Yeah, it is. I just got a call from that smarmy little toad that works for Homborg. I've got to return to Lemain and report in less than an hour."

"Ouch, tough luck, pard. Do you have anything to report?"

"No. Unfortunately, I haven't found the blasted thing yet."

"What are you going to do?"

"I'm going to report to Secretary Homborg that I haven't been able to complete her assignment. What else can I do?"

"What do you want me to do?"

"Just watch those three while I'm gone. Something's not right. I've been giving this situation careful consideration, and I've come to a couple of conclusions. First, if they did bring a magical artifact to Pedestria with them when they were banished, they weren't aware of its magical properties. This means, of course, that the artifact could be any seemingly innocent object. It could be a suitcase or an umbrella or a shoelace for all we know. I absolutely do not believe that they deliberately brought it into exile with them to use against the Lemain government. I also believe that there is something hinky going on with Homborg. She has been acting extremely weird lately."

"Shoot, everyone in Lemain government seems weird these days. Don't worry, I'm keeping an eye out for our girls. In fact, I gave Heloise and Edna emergency sensor rings when they left for their shopping trip today."

Rory chewed his lip thoughtfully as he considered this bit of information. He didn't like being called away while Edna and Heloise were off school property where he could count on Higgins to keep at least half an eye on them, but he really didn't have a choice.

"Okay, just make sure you keep a close eye on your monitor ring while I'm gone. I'll be back as soon as I can, but you know how Homborg will take it when I don't give her the information she wants. I could be assigned as inspector for Guerrnian imports by tomorrow."

"Good luck, pard."

"Thanks, same to you."

Rory returned the communication device to his pocket and prepared himself before opening the portal to Lemain. Suddenly, he heard a small clinking noise in the farthest corner of the room. Moving as quietly as a cat stalking a mouse, he checked the perimeter of the abandoned storeroom, finding nothing.

Man, I must be having a bad case of nerves. Now I'm hearing things. I'd better get myself under control before I face Hattie.

With a determined air, Rory opened a portal that would let him enter Lemain at the edge of the Main Square Courtyard, immediately in front of the building housing the administrative offices of the Lemain Magic Council. Stepping from the portal into the courtyard, Rory was immediately taken with nostalgia at seeing the traditional holiday decorations.

He stared in awe at the many colored fairy lights surrounding the courtyard and flitting about the administrative building. *Wow,* he thought, *the contract to the fairy kingdom for all these lights must have cost the Council a fortune.* Inside the courtyard, many varied holiday exhibitions were taking place. All groups of different beliefs were granted space in the courtyard to exhibit their holiday rituals at this time of year. It made for a rather spectacular show. One exhibit contained vibrant colored woven items and intricately carved idols, another centered about a barnyard scene including humans and animals, yet another focused on a vast variety of candles with indecipherable glyphs, which were considered to be sacred. When Rory arrived in the courtyard, the center stage was taken over by a reenactment of the battle between the Oak King and the Holly King fighting for control of the sun.

Rory watched the reenactment for a few moments. *I wonder if I should tell Edna about seeing this. She once told me that her favorite holiday excursion, after being enrolled at Aunt Mildred's School for Wayward and Orphaned Witches, was coming here to see the two kings battle over the sun. No, that would probably just make her even more homesick than she is already.* Casting a regretful smile toward the stage, Rory turned and climbed the steps of the administration building.

Rory checked in at the registration desk and immediately proceeded toward Hattie Homborg's office. He noticed a definite lack of people in the corridors. *Probably enjoying the holiday celebrations,* he thought as he easily made his way to the bank of elevators.

Getting off the elevator at the fifth floor, Rory realized that there were no civilians or guards anywhere to be seen. His footsteps echoed eerily in the deserted hallway as he cautiously approached Hattie Homborg's office. By the time he reached the office door, his nerves were wound so tight, they practically sang with anticipated danger.

Receiving no response after knocking several times, Rory carefully turned the handle and eased the door open a few inches. Unlike his previous visits to her office, this time, Hattie did not have a multitude of guards and flunkies in attendance. She was completely alone with her back to the door, talking to someone on the crystal screen behind her desk. The screen showed orange flames flickering around an almost-skeletal face. Unable to hear what was being said, Rory took another step into the office, causing a floorboard to squeak.

Almost simultaneously, the screen went blank, and Hattie Homborg whirled to face Rory.

"How dare you? What are you doing here?" she screeched.

"Uh . . .Excuse me, Secretary Homborg, but didn't you summon me?"

"Humph. Yes, of course, I want you to give me the artifact immediately."

"I haven't been able to find it yet," Rory answered uneasily.

"What? After all this time, you still haven't accomplished the simple task of finding one magical artifact in a basically nonmagical world? What have you been doing with your time? I chose you for this assignment because I was told you are the best investigator in Lemain. If you are considered the best officer in the Lemain Investigators Squad, perhaps I should have President Thurgood reevaluate the qualifications of the entire squad."

Hattie leaned forward with her fists braced on the desk. "Do you have any progress, whatsoever, to report before I have you demoted to investigating lost love charms?"

Rory hastened forward nervously, fearing impending doom for his career.

"Wait, please, Madam Secretary, could you give me some idea of what form this artifact is so I know what to be looking for?"

Hattie glowered at him. "No, I can't!"

"Can I use a *detect magic* spell to help locate it?"

Her anger seemed to slip away as she sighed and reseated herself before answering. "No, that wouldn't help. Higgins has transported so many magical doodads to that accursed world, you'd get too many false readings." She focused a piercing glare on Rory. "Okay, I'll give you one more chance, Van der Haven. What I can tell you is that you must concentrate on the three banished witches. The artifact will be some item of whatever size or form in their possession. Now get out of here, and don't come back until you've made some progress. And let me warn you, if you don't show some progress soon, you'll be lucky if the only thing I do is have you drummed off the force."

"Yes, Madam Secretary. Of course, Madam Secretary. I'll do my best, Madam Secretary." Rory rapidly retreated from Hattie's office before she could change her mind.

When Rory returned to Pedestria, he immediately headed for the Marshalls' house. He heaved a deep sigh before sprawling in an armchair. Leonard looked up from his book with a questioning expression. Rory sighed again.

"You sound more like the big bad wolf than I do," Leonard said with a grin. "Why don't you tell me what's bothering you before you blow the house down?"

Rory looked up at Leonard and started to sigh again but stopped himself with a grimace. "I wish it were just one thing. At this point, I could probably talk all night."

"That wouldn't be a problem. It's not like we have anywhere we need to be."

"True," Rory acknowledged. "I just don't understand why I can't find the magical artifact. I've searched every inch of the school and haven't found as much as an enchanted hairpin."

"Why are you so certain the artifact is here?" Leonard asked.

"Hattie is the one insisting it's here," Rory grumbled. "And believe me, she has ways of knowing things."

"I'm certainly glad you have to deal with her and not me. She sounds like a real witch."

Rory grimaced. "Very funny, Leonard. Heloise was right about your sense of humor."

"That reminds me, where is Heloise?"

Chapter 24

In every store they entered, Edna found at least one interesting item she felt she just had to have. In Kreesge's, she found monogrammed, lace-edged handkerchiefs in individual boxes, so she bought one for every female staff member at the school. "They'll make wonderful Christmas presents," she informed Heloise. Heloise hadn't the heart to tell her that modern Pedestrian women didn't use handkerchiefs.

In Hill's Department Store, Edna was fascinated with a remote control stirring device she found in the cookware department. It was an oblong silvery object that, when placed in a saucepan and activated by a battery-operated remote control, spun around the saucepan until it was turned off or the batteries died.

"Agnes will love this!" Edna exclaimed, scooping the item into her shopping basket.

When Edna stopped at the jewelry counter and began serious contemplation of men's jewel-studded cuff links, Heloise redirected her attention to the display of women's winter coats at the front of the store. Although there was a large variety of styles, many of which Heloise thought looked warm and comfy, none of them appealed to Edna.

Next, Heloise steered Edna into Betty's Boutique where they found different styles of coats. All of the coats on display were very feminine, but not many of them seemed suited to the harsh winters they had so far experienced living in this dimension.

Heloise had felt sure that Edna would select one of these coats, but after picking out a violet satin nightshirt, Edna was ready to leave.

As they were walking down the sidewalk, Edna suddenly stopped and said, "Now that's more like it!" Heloise looked up to the sign over the door of the shop. It read ARMY / NAVY SURPLUS.

Somewhat bewildered, Heloise asked, "Edna, whatever are you talking about?"

"Look," Edna insisted, pointing at the shopwindow. Edna was pointing to a faceless mannequin modeling an olive drab arctic parka. "Now that looks warm."

"But, Edna, the coats in this store are meant for the Pedestrian military, not ordinary people."

"It's okay, Heloise. See the sign. This is the stuff they have left over after all the military already have their coats. Then they sell the extras to anybody." Without another word, Edna marched into the store as a chill wind blew down the street. Heloise followed reluctantly.

Once inside the store, the women discovered that the parka Edna had her eye on came in both olive drab and blazing white. Selecting an olive drab coat, Edna pirouetted for Heloise. "Well, what do you think?" she asked.

Heloise hesitated before answering, "It's not very flattering. Are you sure this is what you want?"

"Are you kidding? This is perfect. This coat will blend in with the trees when I go into the woods to check on my friends, and it certainly is warm. Besides, it's got all sorts of nifty storage pockets, loops, and straps." Edna narrowed her eyes. "You did say you wanted me to stay warm this winter, didn't you?"

Heloise sighed. "Edna, when you're right, you're right. If this is the coat you want, then this is the coat you shall have. Now what are you going to do about boots?"

Edna looked toward the store's display of boots and wrinkled her nose. "I don't really care for any of the boots here. Let's keep looking."

Once back on the sidewalk, they looked up and down the street. "Dear, there don't seem to be many options left for us," Heloise said.

"There's a store we haven't tried," Edna said, pointing to a two-story stone building with a sign hanging over the sidewalk reading FARM SUPPLY & HARDWARE.

"Oh, I don't think . . . ," Heloise began, but Edna was already dashing across the street, between cars in the direction of the store.

"Isn't this adorable?" Edna gushed when Heloise joined her on the sidewalk in front of the store. The grimy front window offered a view of an old milk can, a metal washboard, a kerosene lantern, and assorted tools. "Doesn't this look familiar? Doesn't it just feel right?"

Heloise looked at the aged wood and stone storefront and had to admit that it did seem familiar though she wasn't sure exactly how or why. "Okay, Edna, we can go in. But I'm not sure you'll find any suitable winter boots in here."

"Woohoo, let's go!" Edna exclaimed as she charged through the door.

Once inside the shop, Edna acted like a kid in a toy store. She oohed and aaahed over every tool and appliance. She attacked the mild middle-aged man behind the counter with a barrage of questions. After several minutes, the clerk scratched his head in bewilderment and led them to a display of boots that would be suitable for a wide variety of outdoor activities.

While Edna tried on pair after pair of boots, Heloise examined her surroundings. No matter how she tried, she couldn't shake the uneasy feeling that she was familiar with this store although she'd never been here before.

"Edna, does this store remind you of the little alchemist's shop on Tadpole Lane in Capital City?"

Edna looked up from examining a pair of surprisingly stylish boots. She thoughtfully gazed about the shop, taking in the dusty, disused appearance of the cluttered shelves, the warped dark wood floors, and the way the air appeared to grow dimmer, and actually somewhat foggy, the farther you looked toward the rear of the store.

Intrigued, Edna began moving toward the back of the store where the air seemed thickest. The back wall of the store seemed to fade in the middle, opening onto a view of a completely different store. There was a gnomelike clerk in the other store, sitting on a stool, hunched over a large dusty tome. "You know, Heloise, it does look familiar. In fact, doesn't that look like . . . ?" Edna reached out, gasping softly as her hand breached the energy barrier between dimensions.

Heloise grabbed Edna by the arm and yanked her back—hard.

"Oow!" Edna exclaimed, rubbing her bruised arm. "What did you do that for?"

"I did it because you were about to rush headfirst into a place that doesn't belong here. And before you ask, yes, I also recognized Gershwin. But he doesn't belong here either. There is something extremely strange going on here, and I want some answers before you go shooting your mouth off where all the locals can hear."

The small area at the back of the store suddenly became more crowded as Vicky appeared out of nowhere.

"What is it?" she hissed, taking in their unscathed appearance. "What were you doing?"

"I wasn't doing anything," Edna groused. "Why does everyone always assume that whatever goes wrong is my fault. And what went wrong, anyway?"

Vicky glowered at both of them, then snorted as she looked into the room beyond the hardware store wall. "I can only guess what you were up to. How could you be so stupid? Never mind. Don't even answer that. I think we'd better get out of here before we talk about it. What I have to say to you shouldn't be said in public."

Heloise kept a firm grip on Edna's arm as she pulled her toward the front of the hardware store.

"Uh, Heloise, aren't you forgetting something?"

Heloise stopped abruptly just before they reached the door of the store and glared at Vicky. "Now what?"

"Judging from the expression of the clerk, I don't think Pedestrians take kindly to people walking out of their stores with unpaid merchandise on their feet." Vicky pointed to Edna's feet, which were clad in textured, waterproof burgundy boots with sheep wool lining.

"Oh yes, of course," Heloise muttered as she fumbled in her purse for Pedestrian currency to pay for Edna's boots.

Once out on the sidewalk, Vicky pulled Heloise and Edna to one side. "Now tell me what exactly the two of you were doing to make your ring turn from green straight to red without a pause in between?"

"Our rings!" Heloise gasped. "Did it really set off the alarm?"

"No, I just came to town for an afternoon stroll. Think, woman, I used an unauthorized transitor and came rushing here because I thought one of you was in imminent danger. Would I do that just for fun?" Vicky snarled.

"Of course not. But I don't understand what caused the ring to react."

Vicky stared thoughtfully into space for a few moments. "One of you didn't by chance reach out to the gnome we saw, did you?"

Edna tossed her head defiantly. "So what if I did?"

Vicky snorted, "I knew you would be the one to rush in where wigens fear to tread."

"What do you mean?" Edna questioned. "Why would that make the ring react?"

"Think about it, Edna, you were banished from Lemain, right?" She waited until Edna nodded. "Well, think about what they would do if you showed up without proper authorization?"

Edna considered. "I suppose that I'd be in trouble."

Heloise looked at her gravely. "Edna, it would be much worse than that. I wouldn't put it past Hattie to—"

"Finally, at least one of you has a brain. If you were caught in Lemain, you would be in imminent peril, which is why your ring alerted me."

"I'm sorry that we caused you any trouble," Heloise said rather stiffly. "We didn't know what we were looking at, and it was just instinct to reach out."

Vicky made a disgusted sound before muttering, "Only if you have the survival instincts of a schluphmump."

"Well, what's done is over," Edna said in a decisive voice, oblivious to the disbelieving look Vicky shot her way. "Right now, there's something else I want to know. Heloise, I understand that you were surprised to see Gershwin and the alchemist shop back there. So was I, but why are you so freaked out?"

Heloise glanced around furtively to make sure no one could overhear their conversation before speaking. "I'm 'freaked out' as you say because if we could see a shop and a person who are located in Lemain, then it's entirely possible that the Pedestrians can see them also. Lemainians have known of Pedestria's existence for centuries, but as a matter of national security, we have kept Lemain's existence secret from them. Now do you understand?"

"I guess so, but why would the Pedestrians knowing about Lemain be so bad?'

Heloise shook her head in exasperation. "Edna, use your head. Remember how confused and out of place we felt when we arrived in Pedestria and had to learn to function without magic? Well, just imagine how Pedestrians would react if they suddenly stumbled into a world where magic is more than a theatrical show filled with illusions. It's real and used every day by everyone. It would be catastrophic for both worlds!"

"You're right. I hadn't thought about it that way. What are we going to do?"

"At the earliest opportunity, I'm going to talk to Walter Higgins. If anyone can think of a solution, he can."

Chapter 25

The closer time came to Christmas, the more enthusiastically everyone at Sunny Acres School prepared for the anticipated holiday season. Garlands of fresh evergreens with large red bows festooned the halls, permeating the school with an invigorating pine scent. Multicolored lights sparkled at every window, and carols played over the PA system all day long. Carl had even set up inflatable Christmas trees, Santas, and snowmen on the front lawn in honor of the holidays.

"I can't wait until Christmas!" Jeremy exclaimed, joining his twin at the study hall table. "We'll have a whole week off school."

"Yeah," Jason agreed. "And when we get our Christmas money, we can finally order that electronics kit."

"Would you stop worrying about the electronics kit!" his brother said.

"We've been waiting for it for so long," Jason whined.

"I know we have," Jeremy answered. "It's just that we have more to worry about than that. You know what's going to happen on Christmas, don't you?"

Jason looked at him blankly.

"On Christmas, Ms. Thistlewaite is going to make Christmas dinner," he said in exasperation.

"She makes dinner every night," Jason said. "What's the big deal about Christmas dinner?"

"I asked her this morning. She said we're having turkey," Jeremy complained.

"Not turkey again," Jason groaned. "Why does it have to be turkey? We just finished the leftover turkey soup and turkey sandwiches at lunch today."

"Not to mention turkey potpie for dinner yesterday and turkey tetrazzini the night before. That's what I told her. I asked if we couldn't have ham instead."

"What did she say?" Jason asked.

"It was really weird," Jeremy said, frowning. "She got really pale and said, 'Ham? Oh no, I couldn't make ham. It comes from pigs.' Then she kind of shuddered all over."

"That is weird," Jason said thoughtfully. "I wonder why she doesn't like pigs."

"I don't know, but it means we're having turkey again."

"I don't mind the dinner the first time," Jason commented. "It's mostly the leftovers that I really don't want."

"Yeah, me too," Jeremy said. "I wonder if we could do something about that."

Jason started to grin. "What did you have in mind?"

"I wonder if we could find something that would spoil the turkeys," Jeremy suggested.

"But wouldn't that mean that everyone would go without dinner? I wouldn't like that, and neither would anyone else," Jason objected.

"You're right. We'll have to think of something else."

"How many turkeys is she making?" Jason asked.

"Two, I think. There won't be as many people this time because so many kids are going home for Christmas," he explained.

"Okay, so if we manage to get rid of one turkey, there will still be enough for dinner, right?"

Jeremy nodded.

"That's it! What do you say if we sneak into the chemistry lab and—"

"No way, Jase! I'm not doing that again," Jeremy yelped, drawing curious looks from around the room. Lowering his voice, he hissed, "After what Higgins said to us last time, we can't go against him. He's scary when he's angry."

"All right then, but we don't have much time to figure this out."

"I read something in a magazine that just might work," Jeremy offered. "I was reading that if you fill a sealed container with a substance that expands when heated, the container will also expand."

"So maybe if we fill the turkey with something like that, the turkey might expand, and if it expands far enough . . . ," Jason continued with a mischievous grin. Then he frowned thoughtfully. "But what substance can we use to expand the turkey?"

"I have an idea about that. We could check in the library to be sure. We'll need to check the kitchen too to see what we could use," Jeremy mused.

"Right, let's go to the kitchen first. There's no point in doing all that research if we don't have the supplies."

They darted out of the study hall. They were so preoccupied that they never noticed Leonard watching them unobtrusively from the corner.

Later that evening, everyone was gathered around the kitchen table at the cottage. Even Agnes had managed to slip away from her kitchen to join them. They were all sipping a new tea that Heloise had blended.

"This is an herbal blend," Heloise explained. "It has a mixture of herbs that sooth overwrought senses, including an overworked digestive tract."

"In simple terms, it settles an upset stomach," Edna translated.

"I believe that is what I said," Heloise told her.

"It's really good," Rory said. "The 'soothing the senses' part should come in handy with everything that goes on around here."

"Speaking of things going on around here, I think that Jason and Jeremy are plotting something again," Leonard commented casually.

"When are they *not* planning something?" Edna asked grumpily.

"You might be right," Agnes said. "Earlier, they came down to the kitchen. They said they were looking for a snack, but they refused everything I offered. They just kept opening cupboard doors until I shooed them out."

"I wonder," Heloise said thoughtfully. "They were in the library too."

"What were they looking at in the library?" Edna asked warily.

"I'm not really sure. They were mostly in the science section, but they reshelved their own books, so I didn't see what they were researching."

"I'm sure we'll find out soon enough," Leonard predicted.

"We need to keep an eye on them. I don't want any surprises from those two," Edna said darkly.

"I should be able to figure out what they're up to," Rory boasted. "After all, I am a professional. I've gone up against worse than two fourteen-year-old boys."

"You don't know these fourteen-year-old boys," Leonard warned.

"Just watch and see what I can do," Rory dared. "I'll catch them red-handed."

Heloise just smiled and refilled all the teacups.

Jason and Jeremy got up early Christmas morning. They knew it would take perfect timing to sneak into Agnes's kitchen and sabotage the dinner. They hid outside the kitchen door until Agnes and Valerie wheeled the breakfast carts into the dining hall. Jeremy kept watch for Jason as he rummaged in the cabinet.

"Come over here and help," Jason called. "We'll get done faster if we both do it."

Jeremy went over and started scooping stuffing out of the turkey Agnes had placed in the roaster on the counter. Working as quickly as possible, they mixed the material Jason had found into the stuffing and then packed it tightly back in the turkey. They wiped the counter and scrambled to leave the kitchen, but Agnes returned before they could get out.

"What are you two doing here?" she snapped at them.

"We just wanted to get something to eat," Jeremy said.

"Then go out into the dining hall," she told them sternly. "I don't have any time this morning for your games."

"Yes, Ms. Thistlewaite," they chorused before hurrying out the door.

Once outside, they began to snicker. "She'll be surprised when that turkey starts cooking," Jeremy predicted.

They started in to breakfast. They missed seeing Rory come around the corner with a speculative gleam in his eye.

Agnes planned Christmas dinner for about one o'clock. She didn't understand why the Pedestrians expected their holiday meals so early, but after arriving here, she had discovered that was their custom. She would put out a light buffet in the evening for anyone feeling hungry.

The turkeys were browning nicely, and the cranberry mold was chilling; Agnes's only regret was that Edna wouldn't return her recipe box. She remembered seeing a recipe for tree moss soup that would have been fun to try. Instead, she mixed up a dish of the mushroom casserole Leonard was so fond of.

"Valerie, everything is right on schedule. I'm going to pop up to my room for a little bit. If you need anything, just let me know."

"All right, Ms. Thistlewaite," Valerie said.

Agnes sighed as she trudged up the stairs. She wished her room was closer to the kitchen. Sometimes she had to get creative to sneak off to her room at this time of the day. It was a guilty secret that when she had been bedridden, she had become addicted to a soap opera. The story was fun to follow although she was still waiting to see them using soap.

She waited until after the credits finished before turning off the television. A frantic pounding on her door startled her. Agnes hurried over to open the door. Valerie was leaning against the doorjamb, panting from her run up the stairs.

"Ms. Thistlewaite," Valerie gasped. "You need to come down to the kitchen right away."

"What's wrong, dear?" Agnes asked.

"I heard a strange noise coming from the oven. I didn't remember the turkeys making noise at Thanksgiving, so I peeked," Valerie puffed.

"What kind of noise?" Agnes asked as she closed her door and started down the hallway.

"It was a funny popping sound. Anyway, I peeked in, and one of the turkeys was kind of puffing up," Valerie explained as they stepped up their pace.

"Puffing up?" Agnes was confused.

Valerie had no time to answer as they burst through the kitchen doors. Agnes dashed straight over to the double oven and yanked the top oven door open.

"My turkey!" she wailed.

Heloise and Edna entered. "Agnes dear, we saw you running through the hall. Is everything all right?"

"Oh, Heloise, just look at my turkey." Agnes turned to face them. Instead of the expected tears, they saw a red face and flashing eyes. "I'm going to kill them!"

Edna and Heloise moved over to look into the ovens. It was a dismal sight. One of the turkeys looked like a magazine advertisement. The other did not. It had burst apart, and the stuffing had exploded in sticky clumps on the oven walls.

"Is that popcorn in the stuffing?" Heloise asked in a shaky voice.

"Now I know what they wanted so badly the other night," Agnes fumed. "When I get my hands on them . . ."

"Here's your chance," Rory offered, stepping through the door from the dining hall. Each of his hands was clamped on an identical shoulder. "I found them watching through a crack in the doorway. They were having the time of their lives until I showed up."

Agnes glared at the offenders. "Well?"

"We're sorry, Ms. Thistlewaite," Jeremy whispered.

"Sorry you were caught, most likely. Why on earth would you do something like this?" Edna asked.

"We just finished the turkey from Thanksgiving," Jason grumbled. "We didn't want any more leftovers."

"Well, you two are going to have a job tonight," Agnes told them sternly. "That mess is going to bake on until the other turkey is done. After dinner, you will report directly in here. You will not leave the kitchen until the oven and roasters are sparkling clean."

"But," Jason began to complain but stopped when his twin dug an elbow into his side.

"Yes, Ms. Thistlewaite," Jeremy said.

"Go on then," she said. "And don't you dare forget."

They all watched the boys leave the room. Rory and Heloise maintained their composure until the boys left before they both collapsed in fits of laughter.

"What's so funny?" Agnes demanded.

"Oh, Agnes, I'm so sorry, dear," Heloise said through her giggles. "You have to admit it's rather amusing."

"I have to do no such thing," Agnes told her indignantly.

"Come on," Rory said through another snort of laughter. "They're just kids. Boys will be boys and all that."

"I think you went way too easy on them," Edna complained.

"Not really," Agnes smirked wickedly. "That dressing is going to bake on to the consistency of cement. The roasters are in such bad shape that I was going to throw them out after this. Those two are going to be scrubbing for a very long time."

"There is going to be enough for dinner, isn't there?" Leonard asked, his stomach grumbling.

"I made a mushroom casserole just for you, Leonard. But we're going to have just enough turkey for dinner," Agnes said sadly. "I was looking forward to trying a new recipe for turkey paprikash."

"Maybe it's better this way," Rory said with a slight grimace. "The Wilkins boys probably aren't the only ones tired of turkey leftovers. What do you think of making ham for New Years?"

Edna, Heloise, and Agnes all looked at him, aghast, and spoke in perfect unison, "Ham? Oh no, not ham. It comes from pigs." All three women shuddered.

Dinner went well that afternoon. Everyone was in a festive mood, and laughter filled the dining hall. Walter Higgins insisted that Agnes join them at the table, so after she had the food arranged on the serving tables, she removed her apron and sat with her friends. As she had predicted, there were only a few scraps left from the turkey and very few other leftovers. She watched Leonard scrape the crusty edges of the mushroom casserole onto his plate with a satisfied smile.

"This is excellent, Agnes," he told her. "You've really outdone yourself."

"Indeed she has," Higgins agreed. "Let's give her a hearty round of applause!"

"Thank you," Agnes said with a shy smile. The pink in her cheeks matched the color of her fuzzy sweater perfectly. "I'll just go and bring out the desserts."

"Nonsense," Higgins said. "You worked hard enough today, and you take precious little time for yourself. I'm sure someone else can handle it for you." He looked down the tables with a sly grin. "Jason, Jeremy, I'm sure you wouldn't mind assisting Ms. Thistlewaite. Be good, boys. And wheel out the dessert cart, won't you?"

The twins were absolutely still for a moment, their eyes reminiscent of a deer caught in the headlights. "Yes, sir," they murmured. The boys got up and hurried toward the kitchen.

"Don't forget to bring out one of those chocolate cakes in the pantry!" Higgins called out with an anticipatory gleam in his eyes.

When the desserts were brought in, those still interested in food went over to serve themselves. Rory and Leonard helped themselves to a variety of different sweets. Vicky chose a dish of chocolate mousse. Heloise and Edna both decided on the cheesecake and added cherry topping while Agnes topped hers with strawberries and added several chocolate-dipped strawberries on the side. Higgins didn't even look at the other treats; he simply cut himself an extralarge slice of chocolate cake.

After scraping the last bit of chocolate from his plate, Higgins leaned back in his chair with a satisfied sigh. "That was superb," he said with a smile. Looking back at the Wilkins boys, he was pleased to see they were finished eating. "Jason and Jeremy, you did such an excellent job delivering the desserts that I have another job for you. I would like you to clear the tables and take care of the washing up. I'm sure you agree with my feelings that Ms. Thistlewaite deserves a break after an exceedingly stressful morning."

Both boys had the grace to look ashamed. "No, Mr. Higgins—I mean yes—Mr. Higgins." They stopped in confusion.

"Exactly," Higgins chuckled. "Therefore, you will assist by cleaning up the kitchen, under her supervision, of course. You can start clearing away now, and she will be along shortly."

"Why are you having them clean up?" Agnes asked in confusion.

"I agree that they deserve a more severe chastisement than you assigned," Higgins said with a knowing look.

Agnes, Edna, and Heloise all stared at him in open-mouthed astonishment.

"But how did you know?" Edna blurted out.

"I have my ways," Higgins informed her. "And now I believe an afternoon stroll is in order to help settle this wonderful meal." They all watched as he walked out of the room, pausing to wish a pleasant holiday to everyone he passed.

"But how did he know?" Edna persisted to her friends.

"Knowing who he is, why are you even asking?" Rory grinned at her.

Agnes stood up regretfully. "Well, this has been a lot of fun. I don't often get to eat with you, but I'd better keep an eye on those boys before I don't have any dishes left."

"They aren't that bad," Rory protested mildly.

"That's what you keep telling me, but I still don't trust them in my kitchen," she retorted before leaving.

"Higgins's idea sounds pretty good," Rory said, standing up and stretching. "How about taking a little walk? We could take the girls back home."

"Girls?" Vicky said in a dangerous voice.

"Meant in the nicest possible way," he answered quickly. "And while we're there, maybe Heloise could brew up some of that special tea from the other night," he suggested.

"Why? Would you need something to settle your tummy?" Vicky taunted.

Heloise quickly stepped in, saying, "I think that's an excellent idea, Rory. A nice cup of tea would probably be good for all of us."

They made a stop in the entryway to put on their outdoor clothing then left the school building. They walked along the snowy path to the cottage, enjoying the quiet of the woods. Suddenly, Vicky darted ahead and off the path. Seconds later, a round white missile came flying out of the trees and splatted against the side of Rory's head.

"Bang, you're dead, Van der Haven," Vicky crowed.

"I'll get you for that, Vic," he threatened.

"Catch me if you can," she called through her laughter.

Rory bent to scoop up a handful of snow. He yelped indignantly when another snowball connected with his backside. He swung around and fired his snowball with a tricky sidearm move but was disappointed when Vicky ducked it easily. Unfortunately, for her, Vicky was not paying attention to Edna. She found herself with a face full of perfectly packed snow.

"That's for splattering my new coat with snow," Edna told her.

"Two against one, huh?" Vicky asked speculatively. "Well, that should just about even the odds when it's you two against me."

With that challenging remark, the fight became fast and furious. All three of them were scooping, packing, and firing as fast as they could. Edna squawked when Rory caught her in the forehead with a poorly aimed shot.

"Hey! I thought we were on the same side!"

"In a snowball fight, it's everyone for themselves," he retorted. He then canceled his words by diving in front of her to take a hit from Vicky.

"You always were a sucker, Van der Haven," Vicky called out, prompting another volley from the other two.

Leonard drew Heloise away from the skirmish. "Did you want to join the battle?" he asked in afterthought.

"I enjoy a good snowball fight," she admitted. "But they look like they're taking this way too seriously. I'd rather not get soaked right now."

"Good. It looks like fun, but I'm not sure I'm up to it today," Leonard said, leaning back against a tree.

"Are you still recovering from the full moon?" she asked sympathetically.

"I'm doing better than usual, thanks to your tea," he told her gratefully. "It's my curiosity that's bothering me right now."

She asked, "What is it that you're curious about?"

"Earlier today, when we were all in the kitchen, we were talking about the turkey being ruined."

"Yes, I remember," she agreed.

"Well, Rory mentioned that he would enjoy ham at New Year's. All three of you acted like he had said something disgusting, and I was just wondering why."

Heloise shuddered slightly. "It's just that ham comes from pigs," she said in a hushed voice. When Leonard looked at her quizzically, she continued, "I told you about the inauguration banquet, didn't I? The one where we got into so much trouble that it caused us to be banished."

"Yes, you said that there was an exploding cake that caused all the problems," he answered.

"Well, yes, the cake was the final straw," she continued. "But before that, it was pigs."

"What about pigs?" Leonard asked, thoroughly confused.

"President Thurgood had requested us to produce holographic flying pigs on his signal. Agnes usually handled that type of effect. Unfortunately, she was a little miffed because the committee had been taking such advantage of us. Instead, she produced *real* pigs that went crazy around all that food. They attacked the guests," she finished with a little whimper.

"That must have been awful."

"It was. The cake exploding would have been bad enough, but President Thurgood was already furious with us over the pigs. Anyway, that's why none of us like to think about pigs," she finished her story.

"Well, I guess that would explain it," Leonard said.

Vicky ran up to them, cheeks flushed and eyes sparkling. "The winner and still champion!" she boasted.

Edna and Rory followed her out of the foliage. All three of them were snow covered and wet.

"You must all be freezing. We need to get you home and dried out before you catch pneumonia," Heloise chided.

They continued down the path, laughing and chatting. Once inside the cottage, they hung their coats to dry. Vicky took out her wand and, with a quick wave, had a roaring fire in the fireplace. Rory levitated a few extra chairs close to the warming flames.

"That is so wonderful," Edna signed happily. "I've missed being able to do magic."

Rory and Vicky exchanged a long look before moving closer to the fire. Within a few minutes, Leonard and Heloise came out of the kitchen with two pots of tea and a tray of cups.

"Here we go," Heloise said brightly. "I made a pot of soothing tea for us and an energizing tea for Leonard to help him recover from the full moon."

"It seems to be helping. Usually, you look terrible after the moon," Edna said bluntly.

Heloise frowned at her. Leonard smiled self-deprecatingly. Rory just shook his head and rolled his eyes.

"That's our Edna." Vicky grinned. "She's the soul of discretion."

"What?" Edna asked.

"Never mind, dear," Heloise told her.

After finishing their tea, Rory and Leonard decided to go home. They bid the women good-bye and started back to the school to collect Leonard's car.

Chapter 26

Heloise nibbled gently on the end of her pencil as she studied the book order form she'd been staring at for the past half hour. *This shouldn't be taking this long. What's wrong with me? I can't concentrate on anything these days. Blast it! All I can think about is that hardware store in Laurelwood. Actually, it's the alchemist shop that's not supposed to be in the hardware store that's bothering me.*

In an unusual fit of pique, she angrily snapped the pencil in two and flung the pieces across the room.

"Did the pencil do something to offend you?" rumbled a low voice from the office doorway.

Startled, Heloise looked into the amused countenance of Walter Higgins.

"Oh, Mr. Higgins, I'm so sorry. Please come in and sit down. I'm afraid I'm a bit out of sorts today."

Higgins entered the office and, bypassing the nicely upholstered leather chair, went to sit in the old battered green armchair that Edna favored.

"Ms. Lovejoy informed me that you have been badgering her to get an appointment to see me. Does that have any bearing on your current state of temper?"

Heloise hurried over to the door and quickly shut it after making certain no one was lurking in the hallway. When she returned to her seat behind the desk, she clasped her hands and turned to Higgins with a serious expression.

"Yes, well, you see, Mr. Higgins," she began.

"Tut-tut, Heloise. Surely with the lateness of the hour and the lack of people around, we can dispense with formality. Please call me Walter."

"Oh, of course, Walter," Heloise began again. "I wanted to ask you about something very disturbing that Edna and I saw in Laurelwood when we went shopping right after Thanksgiving."

"Oh, ho, cashing in on the Christmas sales, were you?" Higgins chuckled.

Heloise regarded him in bewilderment. "Yes—well, no—well, actually Edna needed . . . It really doesn't matter why we were shopping. Please just let me tell you what we saw."

"Very well, sorry about that, please continue."

"As I was saying, while we were shopping in Laurelwood, we entered an extremely old hardware store at the end of Main Street. It was poorly lighted and very dim inside the store, but it seemed actually foggy toward the rear of the store. When we went nearer to the foggy area, we saw . . . Are you familiar with Zarathustra's Alchemy Shop in Capital City?"

"The one on Tadpole Lane?"

"Yes, that's the one!" Heloise exclaimed excitedly. "When we got to the foggy area at the back of the hardware store in Laurelwood, we were looking into the alchemy shop! We even saw Gershwin, Zarathustra's clerk! How can that have been?"

Walter stared thoughtfully into space as he tapped his steepled fingers against his pursed lips for several minutes.

"Tell me, were you and Edna very tired by the time you saw this apparition? Maybe a little dazed with all your shopping? Or perhaps you ate something unusual for lunch that didn't agree with you?"

Heloise's eyes narrowed. "No, we were not disoriented, delusional, or having hallucinations. Come on, Walter, you know something about this. I can tell."

"Ahem. Yes, well, as a matter of fact, I am largely responsible for what you saw. As you may be aware, I and several of my friends were not on the best of terms with the Lemain government when we were at the university. We were never arrested, but because of our controversial views, we were frequently wanted for questioning for one incident or another. Since we often were present at protest rallies in those days, even organized quite a few of them, we decided it was in our best interests to absent ourselves from Lemain for brief periods of time when the local constabulary arrived to disperse the protestors."

"But why didn't you just create an interdimensional portal and step through?"

"At first, we did, which is how we discovered that the Department of Justice has a means of detecting the brief flare of magical energy used to create such portals and thence tracking the people who use them. However, with the abundance of ambient magical energy in Lemain, they cannot discern stationary interdimensional gateways from the surrounding general magic. We found it much more convenient to slip away from the rallies during the hubbub, make our way to Zarathustra's shop, and enter Pedestria through the gateway we established."

Heloise sagged back in her chair, flabbergasted. "Surely you're not still attending protest rallies and trying to elude the Justice Department. Why haven't you eliminated the gateway?"

"No, no more rallies." Walter smiled with fond remembrance. "They were quite entertaining in my youth, but they didn't accomplish a blasted thing. The only parts of government that have changed are the individuals running it. I'm afraid that governments are beasts too bloody big to be changed by the outcries of a few passionate citizens. As far as the gateway is concerned, I'm rather pleased with it. It took my friends and me a great deal of effort to create it, and you never know when it might come in handy."

"But, Walter," Heloise insisted, "what if the Pedestrians find it?"

Higgins chuckled. "Don't worry about the Pedestrians. It's highly unlikely that any of them would notice it, and if they did, they wouldn't believe what they were seeing anyway. Now, my dear, it's quite late. And I feel in the need of some refreshment. Would you care to accompany me to the staff lounge for a cup of tea or perhaps some mulled wine?"

Edna let the pen drop from her cramped fingers. She yawned deeply, then clasped her hands behind her neck, and stretched her weary muscles. It was well past dinner, and the administrative offices of Sunny Acres School had been silent for hours. A bitter wind howled, and fragile ice tracings formed a lacey silhouette on the office windows this dark night in late January.

It seemed to her as though she'd been agonizing over disciplinary reports for ages. As usual, the Wilkins twins topped the list of most prolific student offenders. Edna sighed as she looked at the five overstuffed file folders currently designated for the twins' offenses. *Pretty soon, I'll have to allocate an entire file cabinet just for those two boys,* she thought ruefully.

She had to admit that their antics were usually clever and often amusing when they weren't directed at her. What she really found hard to understand was how two obviously intelligent teenagers could continue to get caught pulling pranks. Edna's eyes widened as a thought occurred to her. Perhaps they were so smart that the pranks at which they were caught was only the tip of the iceberg, and they were allowing their relatively minor pranks to be discovered to divert attention away from more devious machinations.

She resolutely pushed her chair back from her desk and stood. *No,* she thought, *I can't continue down this avenue of thought or filling out these fardling reports without some caffeine.* She stared dismally into the murky dregs at the bottom of her coffee cup. Where could she find coffee at this time of night?

After rinsing her cup as best she could in the lavatory sink, she began her priority mission—the search for coffee. The school kitchen was out of the question. After the Christmas dinner debacle, Agnes had locks installed on all the cabinets, and everything was locked up tight at night. The only other possibility was the staff lounge that had a coffeemaker going constantly.

As she made her way up the spiral staircase to the top of the southwest tower, she wondered why the staff lounge had been located in such a remote portion of the building. *It would have been so much more convenient if the lounge was on the third or even the fifth floor. Or perhaps,* Edna mused, *Walter Higgins placed the staff lounge at the top of this remote tower to ensure that people working late would have to stretch their legs and get some much-needed exercise.* There had been an article in the staff newsletter this month about physical fitness and exercise.

As she neared the top of the stairs and the last door separating her from her ultimate goal of a suitably strong shot of caffeine, she was surprised to hear several voices. More to her surprise, she recognized the voices.

With her hand on the doorknob, she hesitated momentarily, wondering why her friends hadn't mentioned this impromptu party they were apparently having in the staff lounge. Silently she turned the knob and eased the door open. Directly across the room, there was a moderate fire in the large stone fireplace. Immediately to the left of the granite hearth, Rory and Vicky were seated at either end of a plush sofa. To the right of the hearth, Leonard was sitting in an overstuffed burgundy brocade wing-backed chair. Walter Higgins occupied the matching chair next to Leonard, and Heloise was sitting on a stool by Leonard's right hand, holding a curious object over the fire.

The five of them continued to chat convivially, unaware of Edna's presence while Heloise gently shook the strange object over the flames. It appeared to be a small flat pan covered in silvery foil, with a long loop of wire that served as a handle. As Edna watched, there was a sharp popping noise, and the foil covering the pan expanded slightly. She stood transfixed as the popping noises increased in tempo and volume, and the foil expanded until it formed a silver balloon shape over the pan.

As Heloise removed the pan from the flames, there was one last enormous pop, but not from the pan. With the sound, a huge cloud of sparks shot from the fireplace; but instead of falling to the floor, the sparkling cloud rose to the ceiling, swirled around the room, and headed straight for Edna.

Edna shrieked in terror as the sparks whirled around her. Caught in her own personal fiery maelstrom, Edna flailed her arms as the sparks burnt her clothing, skin, and hair. Higgins was the first to recover from the initial immobilizing shock. He jumped to his feet and grabbed what looked like an extremely large pen from his breast pocket. With a flick of his wrist, the "pen" telescoped out to be revealed as an eighteen-inch highly polished ebony wand. He pointed his wand at the swarm and shouted, "Continere!" The sparks coalesced into a glowing orb of yellowish orange light, which shrank to the size of a tennis ball then imploded.

By this time, all the others were rushing toward Edna, whose hair and clothing were still smoldering even though the attack of the sparks had ceased. Thinking quickly, Leonard grabbed the large vase from the sideboard and threw its contents, flowers and all, at Edna. The dousing with cold water had the combined effect of extinguishing the embers and stopping Edna's screams.

While Edna stood there, dripping water and sputtering, Vicky moved to within a few inches of her, held her palms toward her, and mumbled a few words no one could catch. Instantly, the vicious red blisters that had arisen on Edna's skin where the sparks attacked her disappeared. Edna hiccupped one last wet sob and fell into Vicky's arms.

"Oh, thank you, thank you, thank you," Edna gushed as she hugged Vicky tightly.

"Hey, it wasn't anything, really." Vicky blushed, embarrassed as she tried to pry Edna's arms away from her neck. "Do you mind? You're still a bit damp."

"Oh, of course, sorry about that." Edna hastily stepped back from Vicky. It was only then that she noticed an odor stronger than the odor of wet wool from her drenched clothing. It was the unmistakable smell of burnt hair.

Her hands darted to her head. "What about my hair?" she wailed.

"That's easily fixed," Vicky reached for her wand.

"No, sorry," Rory interjected. "The use of magic for personal grooming is strictly forbidden outside of Lemain!"

Five pairs of eyes stared at Rory, dumbfounded.

"Van der Haven, you heartless baboon, what's the matter with you?" Vicky began striding toward him with her finger pointed at his chest.

"Come on, Vic, it would mean our jobs if anyone found out. Besides, it's just singed hair. It will grow back."

Heloise hurried over and put her arm across Edna's shoulders. "It will be all right, dear. Let's go home and get you into some dry clothes. Then we'll see what we can do about giving you a nice new hairstyle. I always thought you'd look cute with short hair." Heloise steered a forlorn Edna toward the stairs.

While Vicky and Rory continued their argument in front of the coffeemaker, which Edna had failed to reach, Leonard sidled over to where Higgins stared thoughtfully at the floor while he absentmindedly compressed his wand and returned it to his pocket. "What was that? What just happened here?"

Walter Higgins turned to Leonard with a slightly worried expression. "That, my dear man, was a swarm of fireflies."

"Fireflies? I caught fireflies as a child, and they didn't burn like these! Be honest with me. What were they really?"

Higgins pierced him with a penetrating gaze. "Oh, believe me, these were 'fireflies,' just a particular species of firefly that you weren't aware of as a child. These particular insects are indigenous to the dragonlands in the southwestern area of Lemain. Fortunately, they are seldom seen in the 'civilized' areas of our home world. But when they are, the destruction is usually devastating."

Leonard swiped his hand through his hair in frustration. "So what are they doing in Pedestria now?"

"Only the goddess knows for sure, but I do think we can assume it wasn't accidental since the swarm focused solely on Ms. Fitzsimmons. Also the spell I cast was only meant to contain the swarm so I could discover who sent it. The fact that they all disappeared indicates that they were not only sent here, but they had a recall enchantment placed on them in case they were stopped before achieving their goal. The fact that they managed to penetrate the school's protection spells worries me a great deal. I'm afraid we're up against something much more sinister than we originally thought."

Walter Higgins heaved a sigh and straightened his jacket. "Well, Mr. Marshall, I believe the circumstances call for a stiff nightcap. Would you care to join me?"

Still concerned about what he'd just learned, Leonard could only nod his head and follow Higgins from the lounge with the sound of Vicky and Rory's bickering following them down the staircase.

Chapter 27

A few weeks later, people were beginning to fidget as the monthly staff meeting drew to a close. Walter Higgins glanced at his notes. "Well, that brings us to the last thing I wanted to discuss." He glanced at the staff members. "I just wanted to remind you that we will be holding our annual Sadie Hawkins dance on Valentine's Day. It will begin at 7:00 p.m. and end at 9:00 p.m. We will, of course, be needing you to chaperone the students during the dance. I have added a little change this year. There will be a staff party after the students have retired. For those of you to whom it applies, you are encouraged to bring your spouse or date. It's always so pleasant to meet and converse with those important people in each other's lives."

Leonard caught Heloise's attention and cocked his head slightly to one side. She gave him a small smile and nodded her head.

Edna watched the byplay between them and sighed. It was no surprise that Heloise and Leonard would go to the party together. She would have been astounded if they didn't. Her eyes closed briefly as she visualized walking into the party beside Rory. She opened her eyes and looked at him across the room. Well, it was a Sadie Hawkins dance, she decided. Even though the Sadie Hawkins dance was for the kids, it didn't mean that she couldn't get into the spirit of the thing.

Edna stood in the cafeteria line trying to decide between a grilled cheese sandwich with tomato soup or a chicken caesar salad for her lunch. Neither choice was particularly appealing to her, and she regretted not bringing her usual lunch of a peanut butter sandwich and an apple.

As Edna debated her luncheon choice, Ed Bigelow sidled up next to her.

"Hi, Edna. Take the salad. The grilled cheese is only good straight off the grill. It doesn't fare too well on a steam table."

Edna smiled at the music teacher. "Thanks, Ed, you're probably right," she replied, taking a plate of the recommended salad.

"Uh, Edna"—Ed Bigelow cleared his throat—"do you have a date for the Valentine party?"

Edna moved down the line and started pouring a glass of iced tea. "Actually, I'm not sure if I'm going to the party. But yes, I will have a date if I do decide to attend." She smiled apologetically.

Ed followed her to a table and sat without being invited. "I only ask because everyone is encouraged to bring a date, and anyone without a date is basically ostracized."

"Oh, I'm sure that's not true. I can't imagine anyone at the school being that rude."

"I'm sure no one means to be rude. It's just that in social settings, couples are more comfortable interacting with other couples than with the odd individual."

"Come on, Ed, you're not that odd," Edna protested around a mouthful of salad.

Ed stared at her in bewilderment for several seconds before he spoke again, "I imagine it's hard to believe, but I don't get out much."

"Surely you must know some women from town."

"There is Mrs. Higgenbottom, my landlady. She's approximately eighty-seven years old, deaf as a post, and uses a walker. I actually considered asking her until I discovered she prefers older men, like Mr. Mercer from next door—he's ninety-three. I suppose I could ask the cashier from the supermarket. Unfortunately, she's about six inches shorter than I am and twice as wide. Somehow, I don't think she's my type."

Edna had remained silent and thoughtful during Ed's musing. Just then, she noticed Agnes bustling out from the kitchen to grab a tray of dirty dishes and was inspired.

"Ed, don't ask anyone else to the party. I think I know someone who would suit you perfectly."

Ed lifted his head to look at Edna with hope and anticipation. "Who is it? Where is she? How do I contact her?"

Edna's lips twitched in a secretive smile. "You don't contact her. All you have to do is go to the Valentine party and hook up with her there."

"But how will I know who she is?"

"Don't worry, I'll introduce you. Oh, and don't be surprised if it turns out to be someone you know but didn't know you knew," Edna replied, putting down her fork and rising from the table.

Ed's only response was a feeble "Huh?" as he watched Edna's departure with a slightly stupefied expression.

Edna stopped in the library on the way back to her office. She found Heloise, Leonard, and Vicky sharing a platter of raw vegetables and ranch dip in Heloise's office. She swirled in to the room with a flourish, perched on the corner of the desk, and popped a cool, crisp cucumber slice into her mouth.

"Edna, I had no idea you would be joining us for lunch today. Let us get you a chair," Heloise said, motioning to Leonard.

"Leonard, sit!" Edna barked. Leonard immediately dropped back into his chair. "Don't bother with a chair. I'm not staying. I just dropped by to let you know we have a new project."

Having captured their complete attention, Edna prolonged the suspense while she twirled a broccoli floret in the dip and slowly savored the morsel.

"Gee, Edna, this is great theater. We're all on the edge of our seats with anticipation, but if it wouldn't inconvenience you too much, what in the bloody blue blazes are you talking about?" Vicky insisted.

"Well, I've arranged a date for Agnes to the Valentine party with Ed Bigelow."

"Oh, is that all? I thought it was something important," Vicky sniffed.

Edna and Heloise frowned at Vicky while Leonard sat quietly wearing a little smile on his face.

"That's wonderful," Heloise exclaimed. "How does Agnes feel about it?"

"Well, she doesn't exactly know about it yet, which is why I need your help. Somehow, we've got to get her all gussied up and to the party where we can introduce her to Ed, and he can monopolize her company for the evening."

"This certainly sounds like a worthwhile endeavor," Vicky said, rising from the overstuffed green armchair. "I'll leave you to it, then."

"Just a minute, Vicky," Heloise began. "It seems to me that if we're going to turn Agnes into an image of feminine beauty, irresistible to Ed Bigelow, we could use the help of someone with a flair for style and knowledge of the most effective use of cosmetics. In other words, you."

Vicky stared aghast at a smiling Heloise and a smirking Edna. "You can't possibly mean you want me to help turn the school cook, who makes such preposterous dishes as tent caterpillar cereal into a femme fatale capable of capturing men's hearts and ensnaring their minds."

Heloise took a sip of her tea and smiled slyly up at Vicky's perturbed expression. "Well, the thought did occur to me that if Agnes had a beau, she'd be more amiable and less likely to cause any problems."

The following day, Edna kept an eye on Rory in hopes of catching him alone.

Every time she saw him, he was with either Leonard or Vicky. He even sat in on Vicky's classes to help her demonstrate some new martial arts moves. It wasn't until midafternoon when Edna stopped by the dining hall for a glass of iced tea and an apple that she finally found Rory alone.

"Hello, Rory," she said cheerfully. "Mind if I join you?"

Rory looked up. "Oh, hi, Edna. Sure, sit down." He went back to staring bemusedly at his ice-filled glass.

"Is something wrong?" she asked.

"No, it's okay. I just needed a break after Vic's last class. I thought I'd try some of this"—he peered at the label on the bottle next to him—"root beer. Who would make beer out of roots?" he asked, shaking his head in bemusement. Edna watched as he took a drink. "What the . . . ?" he sputtered. "It's sweet! It doesn't taste anything like beer!" He wiped his mouth in disgust.

Edna pushed her glass of iced tea toward him. "Here, drink this," she offered. "It's one of the few cold drinks that aren't sweet in Pedestria." After a moment's thought, she added, "Although most people do add sugar."

Rory sipped cautiously at the tea. "It's not bad," he said. "Thanks."

Edna went to pour herself another glass of tea. When she rejoined Rory, she asked, "So are you going to the staff party?"

"I hadn't thought about it," he told her. "I'm not really staff."

"You know that wouldn't matter. You can go as a guest. It would be really nice if you would come," Edna said hopefully.

"I suppose you're right. Yes, I will be there," Rory decided. He finished the glass of tea and stood. "I'll see you later, Edna."

"Okay, Rory," Edna answered happily as he walked away. *There now, that wasn't so hard,* she told herself. *If I'd known, I would have asked him out long ago.* She too finished her tea and started back to work.

Chapter 28

"Remind me again, why did I agree to this?" Vicky grumbled. They were going through the ladies' section of the small department store. Vicky was getting more irritable by the minute. Edna kept wandering off in search of Goddess only knew what while Heloise seemed intent on meticulously examining each dress in the small area.

"We want to make sure Agnes is at her most attractive when Ed first sees her at the staff party," Heloise said, shuddering and quickly putting aside a lime green dress. "He usually sees her after she's been working in the kitchen all day with a spotted apron and frizzy hair."

"It will take something pretty special to overcome a first impression like that. Do you think Agnes is up to it?" Vicky asked doubtfully.

"Agnes is really very pretty," Heloise said firmly. "Her biggest problem is a lack of self-confidence." Heloise's voice trailed off as she held up a dress of a rich royal blue. It had a heart-shaped off-the-shoulder neckline, filmy sleeves, and a diaphanous skirt. "This is perfect."

Vicky eyed the dress thoughtfully. "I've never seen her wear anything that feminine."

"Of course you haven't. You've only seen her when she's been working or relaxing. She doesn't really have much occasion to dress up, you know," Heloise chided.

"I suppose you're right. If that's the one you've decided on, we can get out of here." Vicky said restlessly.

"In a few minutes, dear," Heloise reproved. "I'll just pay for this. Then we need to find some nice shoes."

"We also have to find Edna, wherever she's wandered," Vicky complained.

"That won't be a problem," Heloise said as the cashier totaled their purchase. "I'm sure we'll find her looking at the shoes."

They did indeed find Edna in the shoe department with several discarded pairs of shoes scattered around her chair. She currently had two mismatched shoes on her feet and tottered over to them on the different-sized heels.

"Which one do you like best?" she asked Heloise while striking a modeling pose.

"They are both nice," Heloise told her while Vicky gaped in disbelief. "However, you need to remember that we're shopping for Agnes."

"Oh, I know that. I've already found the perfect shoes for her," Edna said proudly. She led them over to a display shelf and pointed. Vicky began to smirk, and Heloise winced painfully.

"I don't think those would match the dress we bought," Heloise said tactfully. The shoe Edna had chosen was a strappy sandal with a four inch spike heel in a bright magenta color.

"If you don't like this color, they also come in persimmon and eggplant, and the heel would make her look taller," Edna offered hopefully.

"I think not," Heloise demurred.

Vicky just snorted derisively. "She would probably fall over and break her other foot."

Heloise looked at her reproachfully. "Here are some shoes I believe Agnes would like." Heloise looked over several pair before deciding on a plain pump with a two inch heel.

"Do you know her size?" Vicky asked.

"Only in Lemain measurements," Edna answered sullenly.

"I checked her closet before we left the school," Heloise reassured them. "Both the shoes and the dress should fit perfectly." Heloise paid for the shoes, and they left the store.

Outside, Vicky paused for a moment and glanced around the street. "Are you sure we have everything? I'm not coming back to town again for any reason."

"Yes, we have the dress and shoes we came for," Heloise mused. "You said you have cosmetics and hairstyling tools."

Vicky nodded and then eyed the bag Edna was holding. "What do you have in there?"

"If you must know, I bought a pair of shoes," Edna said.

"Not more shoes," Heloise groaned.

"Yes," Edna said defiantly. "I bought a pair like the ones I showed you for Agnes but in persimmon. They will go perfectly with *my* dress."

"Do you mean to tell me you have a date?" Vicky asked.

"Of course I have a date," Edna huffed. "How silly do you think I am?"

"Do you really want me to answer that?" Vicky smirked.

"I'll have you know I'm not silly at all, Vicky, and I'm not stupid either."

"You could have fooled me," Vicky taunted her. "As a matter of fact, you did."

Edna met Vicky's amused expression. "I wouldn't buy new shoes and plan to get all dressed up if I didn't have a date, Vicky. You just wait and see."

"I'll wait. The question is, for how long?"

"Don't make me separate you," Heloise threatened.

"Fine!" Edna snapped.

They walked silently back to the hardware store to meet Carl for the ride back to the school.

At last, the evening of the Valentine party arrived. Heloise was pinning the last few curls in Agnes's hair while Vicky put the finishing touches on her makeup. Edna flitted back and forth excitedly.

When she was finally allowed to stand up and look at the mirror, Agnes breathed out slowly and then began to smile. "Oh my."

"You were right," Vicky told Heloise. "She cleans up real good."

Heloise winced. "Grammar, please, Vicky."

Vicky just grinned unrepentantly and then glanced over at her other two companions. Edna was indeed wearing the shoes she bought on their shopping trip. Vicky had to admit she looked good in a black dress with a print of scattered flowers, which matched the persimmon shoes perfectly. Her short hair curled riotously over her head. Heloise wore a rose-colored dress with the full skirts she favored. Vicky was sure Beowulf was secreted in one of her deep hidden pockets. Heloise's hair was done up in a sleek french twist.

"Okay, if we're all ready, we had better go down," Edna advised. "Agnes's date is going to meet us outside the gymatorium." Before exiting the room, she quickly squirted Agnes with a light floral fragrance.

"Mmmm, nice." Agnes smiled. "It smells just like the sparrow lilies in Aunt Mildred's garden."

Edna nodded. "I brought it with me when we were banished, but I haven't used it until now."

Vicky's eyes narrowed, and she quickly reached out to snatch the bottle from
Edna's hand.

"What are you doing?" Edna asked indignantly. "If you wanted some, you just needed to ask."

"I don't want the perfume," Vicky said, holding the bottle close to her eyes.

Everyone looked on in amazement as she yanked her necklace off, and the pendant lengthened to reveal her wand. Running it over the bottle, she watched closely for a reaction.

"What are you looking for?" Heloise asked.

"We've been looking everywhere for a magical artifact. Did you ever consider that it might be something like this?" Vicky scowled at Edna.

"No, I didn't. It's not like I had it for a long time before we were banished. I had just bought it, and it wasn't even a shop that specialized in magic—only perfume," Edna informed her.

Vicky tapped the bottle one more time before handing it back to Edna. "It's not responding to any of my scans, so I guess it's safe to call this a false alarm. I was really hoping to finally solve the mystery."

Edna carefully placed the perfume on Agnes's dresser then led the way out into the hallway. Vicky stopped when they reached the stairs.

"You go on ahead," she told them. "I need to change before I go down."

"I was wondering," Edna said, looking at Vicky in an old tee shirt, ripped jeans, and flip-flops.

"I didn't need to get dressed any sooner because I'm not a chaperone. Therefore, I don't need to be there before the staff party."

"Why don't you have to chaperone?" Edna whined.

"Rory and Higgins thought that my style of chaperoning might stifle the party atmosphere," Vicky said. "Go figure. Sometimes having a death glare works in one's favor." She went back down the hall to Agnes's room, leaving the others to take up their staff duties.

Edna was still grumbling when they reached the bottom of the stairs. "She's not the only one with a death glare. I can glare too."

"Stop complaining, Edna," Heloise said, starting toward the gymatorium. She saw Leonard standing outside the doorway talking to Ed Bigelow, who was nervously straightening his tie. Moving to join them, she drew Agnes forward. "Hello, Leonard. Ed, I'm sure you remember Agnes."

Ed's eyes widened, and his jaw dropped. "Agnes?" He said in a questioning tone. He stepped forward, extending his hand. "You look wonderful."

"Thank you," she murmured. "You look very nice too." Agnes accepted his hand and smiled shyly when he tucked her hand into the crook of his arm.

"Let's go in," he suggested. "Higgins will be looking for us." They preceeded the others into the large room.

"I believe your idea worked, Edna," Leonard said. "Ed looked smitten."

Edna grimaced at Leonard. "Leonard, you didn't really just say 'smitten,' did you?"

"Why? It's a perfectly acceptable word, isn't it?" Leonard looked mildly confused.

Edna just shook her head and craned her neck, peering around the room.

"What are you looking for?" Heloise asked.

"I was just trying to see who else was chaperoning."

"Most of the teachers are here," Leonard told her. "But a few won't be coming until the staff party."

Edna frowned. "How about Rory? Didn't he come with you?"

"Well, no, he didn't," Leonard said, confused. "After all, he's not really part of the staff."

"I suppose," Edna said reluctantly. "But he will be at the staff party, won't he?"

"Of course, he was invited after all."

Edna smiled brightly and relaxed. "I guess I'll see him later, then. We had better get to our posts. The students are coming."

Entering the large room, they found it decorated with pink, red, and white crepe paper streamers from which dangled glittering hearts and golden cupids. Small tables at the edges of the room each had a vase of flowers and were sprinkled with heart-shaped confetti. A long table at the side had a variety of cupcakes, cookies, and brownies arranged around a large bowl filled with pink strawberry punch.

The room filled quickly; and Ed Bigelow, who was acting as the disk jockey, started the music. The teachers began to circulate among the dancers. They only had sixth grade and above to chaperone; the younger students were in the dining hall, which had been turned into a game room for their entertainment. Normally, Agnes would have been supervising the younger children; but this evening, Ed requested she stay with him.

"I want some time to talk so we can get to know each other better," he told her. "Besides, it wouldn't be much of a date if we spent it in separate rooms."

Leonard had to leave the room to hide his laughter when he overheard Edna rousting a couple out of a dark corner. "If I see you two in that position again, it had better be because you're administering artificial respiration."

Heloise was just as firm, but slightly less blunt when she tapped a dancing couple on the shoulder. "You know the rules. I need to see some air between you."

Walter Higgins himself took on the daunting task of ensuring the Wilkins boys didn't cause any mayhem or destruction. Jason and Jeremy had no desire to incur his wrath and so restrained their usual exuberance.

When the clock struck nine, the staff heaved a collective sigh of relief. Agnes directed the older members of her kitchen staff in clearing the refreshment table and replacing the empty platters and punch bowl with fresh offerings for the staff gathering. She carefully abstained, however, from doing anything that would disarrange her hair or clothing. Staff members escorted the students to the dormitories before returning to their own party.

Edna took a moment to slip out and straighten her hair and reapply fresh lipstick. When she returned, she looked around expectantly for Rory. After several minutes of waiting impatiently, she sought out Leonard and Heloise, finally locating them chatting with Agnes and Ed.

"Can I speak to you for a minute?" she requested.

"Certainly," Leonard agreed. He stepped a distance away from the others.

Edna plucked at Heloise's sleeve in a request for her to join them. "I thought you said that Rory was going to be here?"

"Yes, I did," Leonard began.

Edna cut him off. "Well, is he running late?"

"No," Leonard started to say before Edna interrupted again.

"He was supposed to meet me here," she said querulously. "I asked him to the party, and he said he would see me here."

Leonard's eyes grew round, and his pupils contracted in his best deer-in-the-headlights look. "Well . . . um . . . ," he stammered. "He told me he was meeting Vicky . . ."

Edna's eyes narrowed dangerously. "Where is he?"

Heloise put a calming hand on Leonard's arm. "Breathe slowly, Leonard, or you're going to hyperventilate. Edna, I believe I saw them heading over to the refreshment table."

Edna stared intently in that direction. It took a moment before she spotted them, but when she did, her face fell. Rory was dressed in a dark suit with a sapphire blue shirt that accented his eyes. Vicky smiled as he handed her a cup filled with punch. Looking at the other woman made Edna gasp in dismay. Under the lights, Vicky was a vision dressed in glittering gold lamé. Her dress was cut low at the neckline and high at the hem, and her blond hair cascaded over her shoulders.

"Who could possibly compete with that?" she said despairingly.

"I'm sure there's a good explanation, dear," Heloise offered sympathetically.

"Of course there is," Edna said bitterly. "I don't measure up, just like always. I shouldn't have expected anything else."

"Edna, I don't think . . . ," Leonard tried again to complete a sentence and yet again failed.

"Don't say another word, Leonard, and don't you dare mention this to Rory either!" Edna hissed.

"Edna, please calm down," Heloise soothed. "This is neither the time nor the place to lose control."

"It's okay, Heloise, I won't make a scene," Edna promised. "I also will not act like a coward." Edna strode away with her shoulders back and her head held high, determined not to let Rory or, more importantly, Vicky see just how badly she was hurt.

After watching her walk away, Leonard guided Heloise onto the dance floor. "I can see why Edna is upset. Vicky looks stunning. It's a good thing she didn't come to the student dance. She would have caused a riot."

"Do you think so?" Heloise asked coolly.

"Sure, the boys couldn't help themselves," Leonard answered obliviously.

"I see."

Leonard looked at her in surprise. "Heloise, you don't have a thing to worry about. I would choose you over Vicky or anyone else in a heartbeat."

The cold look faded, and Heloise smiled up at him. Leonard took a relieved breath and continued dancing.

Edna did an admirable job of hiding her chagrin. She circulated among the rest of the staff, making friendly conversation; she even danced with Carl a couple of times as he was also there alone. In spite of her carefree appearance, Edna did manage, as Heloise alone noticed, to carefully remain on the opposite side of the room from Vicky and Rory.

At eleven, Walter Higgins called for everyone's attention. "Excuse me, if I may have your attention. I would like to thank everyone for your attendance and support of this event. It could not have succeeded without all of you. A special thanks goes out to those of you who acted as chaperones, and as always, thank you to Ms. Thistlewaite and her assistants for their excellent refreshments."

There were a few moments of confusion as everyone called out their good nights and moved toward the doorway. Edna waited as the crowd thinned out enough for her to spot Heloise and Leonard standing with Agnes. She scanned the room again to confirm that Vicky and Rory were gone before crossing to join them. As she got closer, she noticed that Heloise looked different.

"What happened to your hair?" she asked.

Heloise flushed and ran her fingers through the hair that now fell loosely over her shoulders. "The pins fell out while we were dancing."

"That's weird." Edna frowned. "It's too bad that we couldn't bring any of those enchanted hairpins from Lemain."

"We're already in enough trouble over the missing magical item," Agnes told her. "We don't need to add any more problems."

Ed joined them and casually placed his arm around Agnes's waist. "Okay, I've got all the music put away. Have I missed anything?"

Agnes smiled up at him. "Not really, we were just saying good night." She looked over at the refreshment table. "I need to clean up this mess, so I'll talk to you later."

"I'll help," Edna said quickly. "Leonard, you'll walk Heloise back to the cottage, won't you?"

"Of course," Leonard nodded.

"Well then, let's get started, Agnes, so we'll get finished faster."

"All right, Edna. Good night everyone," Agnes said. "Good night, Ed, I had a wonderful time," she added shyly.

"Could I stay and help you clean up?" Ed offered.

"Thank you, but I think we can handle it. Edna is already familiar with the kitchen setup from when she helped out before. Thanks for offering, though."

"Okay, then, I'll talk to you tomorrow." He smiled at Agnes then looked over at Edna. "Thank you, Edna, I really appreciate your help."

"Do you want us to wait and walk back with you?" Heloise offered.

"No, don't bother. This may take a while, and anyway, I have a lot to think about on the way home. Don't wait up for me, Heloise," she suggested.

Saying a final good night, they all separated for the night.

The following morning, Edna awoke even more reluctantly than usual. Rap watched her stretching and yawning.

"Good morning, mistress," he greeted her. "You came in late last night."

"Yes, I did," Edna yawned again. "And then I couldn't turn my brain off and go to sleep."

She dragged herself out of bed and pulled her robe on before wandering out to the kitchen. Unsurprisingly, Heloise was already up and fully dressed.

"Good morning, Edna," she said cheerily. "Would you like a cup of tea before we go up to the school?"

"Is it one of your special teas?"

"It's special only in that I blended a few different flavors together. It's not my energizing tea if that's what you're asking. You know I don't like to use that too often," Heloise said while pouring her a cup of steaming tea. She watched as Edna sipped at the fragrant brew. "What time did you get in last night?"

"I think it was close to one," Edna said. "Agnes wouldn't go to bed until everything was washed and put away. I didn't wake you when I came in, did I?"

"I never heard a thing."

"Good. Anyway, when I finally got home, I couldn't go to sleep because I was thinking about Rory," Edna continued. "I think I've finally figured it out."

Heloise sat across from her and poured a cup of tea for herself. "What have you figured out?"

"It's never going to work out between Rory and me. We're just too different. I've tried so hard to be someone he could like, but I don't think he ever will. He's too worried about background, breeding, and beauty. No matter how hard I try, I'll never be able to rise above that," Edna said dejectedly.

"I think you might be right, Edna. Are you going to be all right?" Heloise asked.

"It may take a while, but I'll get over him," Edna said. "After all, I want someone who will care about me for me not because I'm pretending to be someone I'm not."

Heloise nodded her understanding. "You'll be happier that way. Just for the record, one of these days, Rory will grow up and realize what he threw away."

Edna gave a muffled sniffle. "Thanks, Heloise." She thought for a moment. "By the way, where did Rory and Vicky go after the dance?"

"As far as I know, Rory went to Leonard's house, and Vicky came back to the cottage and went to bed," Heloise said.

"Yeah right," Edna said skeptically.

"Oh, for heaven's sake, Edna! Rory and Vicky work together. Besides, I got the impression that Vicky's affections are already taken."

"Just remember that old saying, 'If you can't be with the one you love, love the one you're with,'" Edna replied.

"Edna, just go and get dressed. It's time to go to the school."

Throughout the next few days, some changes occurred in the school. Ed quite frequently was found sitting with Agnes. He told Leonard that they would be spending Saturday in Laurelwood. The changes in Edna's normal behavior were not as obvious to the untrained eye. In the close quarters of the cottage, she was polite if distant with Vicky. At the school, however, she avoided private conversation with both Vicky and Rory while still remaining her usual blunt, but friendly self with everyone else.

Heloise watched as Edna settled into her new routine. Things were quiet for now, but she had a hunch they wouldn't remain that way for long.

Chapter 29

It was a typical mid-March in the Laurel Mountains. The weather had been cold and rainy with blustering winds for two weeks. "Janet, what's wrong with this stupid machine?" Edna shouted as she pounded her hand against the Print button of the Megatron Super Copier.

"Step aside, and let me look at the control display," Janet answered. After studying the copy machine's display for a few moments, she asked, "Everything looks fine. What are you trying to copy?"

"I'm trying to copy the annual fiscal report, which will be forwarded to the stockholders and the accreditation committee. It's kind of important, like Higgins wants it Now, and this stupid machine isn't cooperating."

"Okay, just go get a cup of coffee, and let me run the copies for you."

Edna shrugged her shoulders and sighed as she turned toward the coffeemaker in the corner. The only trace of coffee left was a thin brown smear on the bottom of the pot. As Edna filled the coffeemaker with water and placed a new filter with fresh ground coffee in the receptacle, she reflected back over the odd occurrences of the past school season.

The first odd item was the attack by quatos in the woods. Then there was the episode with the semigoblins entering the school as students. I still don't understand why Higgins had allowed those students to attend classes at his school. Certainly, the battle with the goblins on All Hallows Eve in the theater in the woods had to be considered odd. The turkeys exploding at Yuletide was odd, but everyone knew the Wilkins twins were the culprits.

She ran her hands over the short curls covering her head. *Of course, there was also the firefly incident in the staff lounge. It seems pretty darn obvious that these were more than just coincidences. Fortunately, there had been no serious injuries, except to Rap. But who was behind these attacks?*

The coffeemaker gave a final gurgle, and Edna poured a cup of the rich fragrant black liquid. As Edna breathed in the arousing aroma, she wondered at how the people of Lemain could possibly have neglected to bring back this wonderful beverage to the populace of her home world.

"All done," Janet called, carrying the large stack of neatly collated reports to Edna's desk. "What's next?"

Edna grimaced. "Now I have to punch holes in them and put them in individual binders."

"Why the ugly face?"

"It's just that the entire report won't fit in the three-hole punch, and I can't ever get all the pages to line up evenly."

Janet frowned in confusion. "I don't see why they wouldn't line up. You make sure the edges are flush with the metal guide tab, don't you?" She looked up and noticed that Edna's eyes were round as saucers and that her mouth was hanging open.

"There's a metal guide tab on the three-hole punch?" Edna whispered.

Janet gazed at Edna in amazement for several seconds before speaking. "Here, I'll show you how to use the three-hole punch. Then I've got to get back to those phone calls. That is, if I can ever manage to get an outside line."

"What's wrong with the phone system?" Edna asked.

"I'm not sure, but every time I try to make a call outside of the school, I wind up connected to the kitchen. Ms. Thistlewaite seemed pretty ticked off the last time she answered. She called me a schluphmump, whatever that is."

Edna nearly choked on a mouthful of coffee as she tried not to laugh. She wished she could take Janet into her confidence and explain that schluphmumps were furry little creatures, approximately the size of unhusked walnuts, that lived along most of the riverbanks in Lemain. When threatened, their defense mechanism was to run in tight little circles until they became dizzy and fell over. Needless to say, they were classified as an endangered species.

Suddenly, Priscilla Lovejoy burst into the office. "Why aren't you in the conference room?" she demanded. "The department meeting was supposed to start twenty minutes ago! Everyone is waiting!"

"What meeting?" Edna asked.

Priscilla's face took on an even more sour expression than usual. "The admissions review meeting to decide on applicants for the summer term, of course. Didn't you get the memo I sent last week?"

Edna glanced at Janet, who shook her head and shrugged. "Sorry, guess I must have missed that one. Please tell them I'm on my way."

Priscilla aimed one last armor-piercing frown at Edna before turning on her heel and stomping angrily from the room.

Janet tried to apologize as Edna pawed through her desk looking for a pen and notepad. "I swear we never got a memo from Ms. Prissy last week, honestly."

"Never mind," Edna said in consolation as she snatched up her pen and pad and hurried for the door. "It's not the first time she's been mad at me, and I'm quite sure it won't be the last. I just wonder what else can go wrong today."

When Edna returned to the cottage much later that evening, she found Heloise and Vicky before a cheery fire in the living room. Vicky was in an armchair polishing her wand with rosewood oil, and Heloise was at one end of the sofa reading a book with the ever-present cup of tea on the table by her side.

Edna dropped heavily onto the other end of the sofa, leaned her head back, and closed her eyes.

Vicky cocked an eyebrow. "Tough day, Edna?"

"It was horrible," Edna groaned. "Anything that could possible go wrong went wrong. Janet said it was all the fault of a law created by some guy named Murray or something." She proceeded to relay the details of the mishaps that happened during the day.

"What did you expect on today of all days?" Vicky snorted.

"What do you mean? What's so special about today?"

Vicky threw a disgusted look at Heloise. "Did she pay attention in any of your classes at Aunt Mildred's?"

"A few," Heloise answered quietly with a slight smile.

"Look, I've had a thoroughly rotten day. And I'm not in the mood for any of your nasty, sarcastic comments. Are you going to tell me what's special about today or not?"

"Very well, let me spell it out for you. First, Mercury is retrograde right now, which fouls up communications and anything technological. You would have known this if you had paid attention in astrology class."

Edna looked slightly chagrined but still angry.

"The second fact to consider is the date. It's March 15. Does the Ides of March ring any bells?"

"I know very well how unlucky the Ides of March is in Lemain," Edna retorted. "But we're in Pedestria!"

"Well, duh, Edna, the Ides of March is the same no matter where you are. Honestly, sometimes I just can't believe how dense you are!"

Vicky was saved from Edna's scathing reply by Rory hurtling in at that moment.

"You won't believe the call I just intercepted on my portable screen!" Rory practically shouted.

"Whoa, calm down, pard," Vicky said as she moved a blanket from the other armchair so Rory could sit.

Vicky helped Rory get comfortable in the armchair while Heloise fetched tea from the kitchen; and Edna looked on with a mixture of curiosity, longing, and hostility battling for control of her features.

Once everyone was settled with fresh cups of steaming tea and the fire had been built up, Rory continued, "I had given up the search for today and was on my way to Leonard's house when my portable screen beeped. When I activated the screen, it was as though I was eavesdropping on a conversation between Hattie Homborg and Lucretia DuMaurier! They were discussing the rewards of successfully returning their 'evil lord' to power in Lemain and the consequences of failure." Rory paused for a sip of tea.

"I knew Hattie was evil!" Edna said vehemently.

"Actually, Lucretia was doing most of the talking, and Hattie looked pretty frightened," Rory offered.

"Don't you dare start defending Hattie Homborg to me, Rory Van der Haven," Edna began.

"Edna, hush," Heloise said sternly. "What do you think it means, Rory?"

Rory stared thoughtfully at his cup for several moments. "I think it means we're running out of time. We need to find the magical artifact they want so desperately if for no other reason than to keep it out of their hands. I also think we should consult the one friendly person we know who has connections with high-ranking government officials—Walter Higgins."

Chapter 30

Agnes was putting the finishing touches to the moist chocolate cake she was frosting for Walter Higgins. She smiled, pleased with the appearance of the swirls on the top.

"Ms. Thistlewaite," Valerie said quietly. "Easter is coming up soon. Are we doing a special menu?"

"Yes, of course we are," Agnes asnwered absently. "I was thinking of a nice leg of lamb and probably a prime rib roast. For side dishes, I believe we'll make corn pudding, creamed vegetables, and fresh greens. Add some fresh dinner rolls and trifle for dessert."

"That sounds really good," Valerie told her. "I love fixing special holiday meals. It reminds me of my mom."

"So do I," agreed Agnes. Her smile was warm for the little girl, but her mind was not on Easter dinner.

Agnes left the kitchen and started up to her room. Her shoulders were stiff, and her mouth was tight. *The holiday is coming,* she thought angrily. *The vernal equinox will be here, and Edna still has my recipe box. I can't remember all the family recipes. I did all right when I thought the box was in Lemain. Now that I know it's here in Pedestria, I want to have an old-fashioned holiday dinner like Mother used to make. It won't be the same without Mother's special holiday foods. Drat Edna.*

Once in her room, Agnes settled in front of her little television to watch her favorite soap opera. It was difficult to follow the story when her mind was still focused on her own concerns. Edna had no right to confiscate a family heirloom. There had to be some way to get the recipe box back. Finally, she turned off the television. Not only had Edna stolen her recipe box, she had spoiled her favorite story. Agnes decided that was the final straw. She was going to confront Edna and demand the return of her property.

Edna, Heloise, and Vicky met in the entrance hall to go in to dinner. Edna, to her surprise, found Agnes waiting for her in ambush.

"Edna, I need to speak to you privately," Agnes said in a stiff voice.

"Why privately?" Edna asked. "Certainly, there isn't anything you can't say in front of Heloise and Vicky."

"Fine, then. I was just trying to spare you the embarrassment of admitting in front of them that you were wrong," Agnes told her indignantly.

Edna's eyes narrowed. "Wrong about what?" she snapped.

"You had no right to confiscate my recipe box. It's my personal property, a family heirloom. And I demand that you return it immediately, or I won't be responsible for the consequences."

"Agnes, I can't believe you are still under the delusion that I stole your recipe box." Edna swiped the back of her hand across her brow. She paused for a moment, looking into Agnes's slightly watery blue eyes.

"Don't you remember bringing your recipe box to the cottage on All Hallows Eve?" Edna stared forcefully at Agnes, hands on hips.

Agnes looked perplexed. "What if I did? You still kept it from me all these months!"

"Well, duh! Between the goblin hybrids, the fireflies, Rory going wonky, and hooking you up with Ed Bigelow, returning your recipe box sank pretty low on my list of priorities."

Agnes's eyes narrowed and turned the dark blue of an impending thunderstorm.

"Look, Agnes," Edna continued. "I put your precious recipe box in a really safe place inside the cottage. I just can't remember where. Right now, I'm tired, I'm hungry, and I'm going in to dinner. If you insist, I'll even help you search for your box but not before I've eaten. Okay?"

With that final pronouncement, Edna turned on her heel and proceeded toward the dining room. Heloise and Vicky were following at a slight distance.

Agnes muttered, "I'm going to get that box back. Just see if I don't."

She returned briefly to the kitchen. The kitchen staff had everything well under control. Agnes felt that she could safely leave them in charge without guilt. She did take a moment to inform them that she would be leaving and would return as quickly as possible. She slipped out the kitchen door and quickly circled around to the path leading to the cottage. She hurried, wanting as much time as possible for her search.

Sneaking in the front door, Agnes took a moment to glance around. "Now let's see. If I were Edna, where would I hide my recipe box?" She decided on Edna's room as the most logical place to begin.

Heloise, Edna, and Vicky strolled back home after dinner. They had all enjoyed an especially delicious meal and were in no hurry to exercise it off.

"Edna," Heloise began hesitantly, "would it be so bad if we returned Agnes's recipe box? She's so unhappy over losing it, and I'm sure she won't make any of those ancient dishes again. This entire debacle has surely taught her a lesson."

"What makes you think she's learned anything? Have you forgotten that it's practically all her fault we were banished?"

"You know that wasn't intentional," Heloise protested. "She just didn't think."

"Exactly," Edna said triumphantly. "She didn't think before producing those pigs. She didn't think before making those recipes. She never thinks, and I doubt she ever will," she finished bitterly.

Heloise nodded reluctant agreement. "You're probably right, but maybe we could do something so we don't have to listen to her complaining. What if we go through the recipes and remove all the really strange ones? Then we'll give her the box."

"Do you truly believe that will solve anything?" Edna scoffed. "She'll just start complaining about her missing recipes."

"I suppose you're right."

"At any rate," Edna continued, "I already thought of that. Unfortunately, I don't remember moving the stupid thing or where I might have put it."

"You've lost it?"

Vicky chortled, "Really, you two are priceless. It's better than watching a comedy team."

"Well, thank you for finding us so entertaining," Edna sneered.

"Completely my pleasure," Vicky said. "However, let's continue this inside where we can be comfortable."

Vicky reached to open the cottage door. To her consternation, it swung easily open at her touch. "Edna, you left it unlocked again," she said in annoyance. "I can't put up with worrying whether someone is invading my living space. Do I have to tie a string around your neck to help you remember something so simple as locking a door?"

"For your information, I did lock the door," Edna said defensively. "Although I don't know what the big deal is. Who would want to break into our cottage?"

"That's not the point," Vicky told her sternly, stepping inside. She came to a dead stop in the doorway, causing Edna to crash into her back.

"What's the matter?" Edna squawked.

"Someone has been in here," Vicky said in a soft but dangerous tone.

"Stop being so overdramatic," Edna said. "And move out of the way."

Vicky stepped aside, allowing Edna and Heloise to enter. Heloise gave a soft gasp. To say that the cozy living room was a mess would not be an exaggeration. Pillows and sofa cushions were tossed around the room. Books were pulled off shelves and tossed aside. Drawers had been pulled out and dumped, the contents rifled. Even the pictures on the walls hung crookedly.

"We had better look around," Vicky said, drawing her wand. "Check your rooms first, and yell if you see anything. Then we'll all check the kitchen."

Using hand signals, Vicky directed the two women to their closed doorways.

When they were all in place, she motioned them to move in. All three of them swung the doors open and stepped inside simultaneously.

Vicky swore violently as she surveyed the wreckage that used to be her room.

"Oh my," Heloise moaned. "Who would do this?"

Edna looked around her room. Her closet was ajar, and clothes were scattered all over the floor. Two blouses were hanging from the overhead light fixture. Drawers were pulled out and emptied, and the mattress was pulled partway onto the floor. She looked back at Heloise and Vicky who were peering over her shoulder.

"Everything looks fine to me," she told them.

"Dear goddess, it looks like a tornado went through," Vicky said, stunned.

"More like Hurricane Edna," Heloise said reprovingly. "Really, Edna, how can you tell if anyone was here or not?"

Edna shrugged. "I guess I never thought about it."

Vicky rolled her eyes and shook her head. "You are impossible. Come on, we still have the kitchen to check." She moved with catlike stealth toward the final room in the small cottage, Heloise and Edna tiptoeing behind.

They stepped into the kitchen. For a moment, they were all shocked into silence as they gazed around uncomprehendingly. Unfortunately, due to the nature of a kitchen, the mess was much worse. Flour, sugar, coffee grounds, and other dry ingredients covered every surface. Emptied cereal boxes littered the floor. Their eyes scanned further, and they spotted Agnes standing on the stovetop, her head and shoulders buried in the cabinet.

"What in Hestia's name do you think you're doing?" Edna shrieked.

Agnes pulled out of the cabinet, holding the black lacquered box. "I'm retrieving my property," she hissed.

"You had no right to destroy our home!" Edna said in fury.

"*I* had no right?" Agnes answered with indignation. "You're the one that kept something that didn't belong to you. I'm simply reclaiming what's mine, and you can't stop me!"

"That's what you think," Edna contradicted.

She pushed past Heloise, who was still numb with shock. Vicky, on the other hand, seemed amused. Agnes scrambled down from the stove to meet Edna on even ground.

Edna reached out to grab the box from Agnes. Not willing to relinquish her treasure, Agnes clung on tenaciously. The resulting tug-of-war caused Heloise to intervene.

"Stop it right now!" she exclaimed, moving closer. "You are both acting like children."

"I . . . Don't . . . Care!" Edna grunted, pulling harder.

Agnes's grip loosened, and she lost hold of the box. In an equal but opposite reaction, Edna flew backward. She collided with Heloise, and they fell in a tangle of limbs. The box crashed into the table and fell to the floor in two separate pieces.

"My recipe box!" Agnes wailed.

"You almost killed us, and you're worried about that stupid box!" growled Edna.

Heloise grimaced in pain as she pushed Edna to one side. "Get off, Edna, and stop being so mean. That's what started the entire problem."

Edna looked over to see Agnes sobbing disconsolately, holding the pieces of her family heirloom. "Agnes, I'm sorry," she said penitently.

Agnes's only response was a loud sniffle.

"Let me see it, Agnes. It looks similar to one my grandmother had when I was a kid. I think I could repair it," Vicky offered, reaching toward Agnes.

"No," whimpered Agnes, clutching the box more tightly.

"Agnes, be sensible," Heloise suggested in an understanding voice. "If Vicky is able to mend it, you should let her try."

Agnes sniffled again then hesitantly proffered the box to Vicky.

"Let me see," Vicky murmured. She carefully removed the recipes and placed them on the table. Turning the box over, she examined it, looking for loose corners. "This *is* like my grandmother's trinket box." She inserted her thumbnail into a thin crack in the base of the box near the right rear corner and popped a quarter-inch square of the base out at an angle.

"What are you doing?" Agnes protested in alarm.

"Ha," Vicky crowed. "Just as I thought. Look, it has a false bottom."

Agnes, Heloise, and Edna crowded around her as she gently pried the bottom loose. Yellowed sheets of folded paper fell out onto the tabletop. Agnes grabbed at a sheet, and it crumbled to dust at her touch.

"Watch out," Vicky said sharply. "This paper is old and very fragile. If we try to open them like this, they'll be destroyed."

"Could you put a preservation enchantment on them?" Heloise suggested.

Vicky nodded then ran her finger lightly over the remaining sheets. "The rest will be fine now. Agnes, since the box is yours, why don't you open it?"

Agnes reached out and picked up the paper. Opening it, she quickly scanned the crabbed writing.

"It's signed by Elijah Witherspoon," she whispered.

"Who is Elijah Witherspoon?" Vicky questioned impatiently.

"My many times great-grandfather," Agnes said distractedly. "This seems to be about the box."

"Well, read it," Edna demanded.

To the Guardian of the Box:

These stones have been gathered at great personal sacrifice from the farthest reaches of our world. They possess great power and must not be used without great need.

Used wisely, these stones can benefit you and the ones you love. But beware. Use the stones for frivolous reasons or for personal gain—they will lose their power. Use them for evil or malice, and the spell will rebound on the invoker tenfold.

The most powerful stone is the clear quartz stone set in the center of the lid. This stone is known as the Revealing Stone. It will reveal the true nature of any person, beast, or object upon which it is focused after it is invoked. Use this incantation:

Fakers take care.
Deceivers beware.
Of this you cannot be aloof.
Revealing stone, reveal the truth.

Only a true descendant of mine will be able to invoke the power of the stones. May your days be long and prosperous.

Elijah Witherspoon

Edna looked at Heloise in surprise. "That's the incantation?" she asked incredulously.

"Shush, Edna." Heloise frowned. "An incantation doesn't have to be great poetry. It just has to rhyme."

"There's more," Agnes continued. "Listen to this."

Stone Descriptions

Red – Compulsion

> **Uninvoked** – *Compels person who touches it to acts not normally in their nature. Person in its influence will exhibit odd behavior. Effect lasts until the compulsive act is completed or a knowledgeable magician intervenes.*
> **Invoked** – *Person wielding the stone can compel anyone the stone is pointed at to do anything they desire. Effect lasts until the subject is deliberately released.*

Blue – Serenity

> **Uninvoked** – *Causes the person touching it to feel at peace. Minor irritations seem unimportant. Effect lasts until contact with the stone ceases.*
> **Invoked** – *Can ease the most troubled spirit of person or beast. Effect lasts for one cycle of the moon.*

Green – Healing

> **Uninvoked** – *Causes person touching it to feel better physically. Eliminates minor aches and pains. Effect lasts one cycle of the earth.*
> **Invoked** – *Can completely heal any injury or illness short of death. Effect is permanent but cannot prevent future illness or injury.*

Yellow – Memory

> **Uninvoked** – *Causes person touching it to remember simple things such as appointments and where they left their gloves. Effect lasts for one hour.*
> **Invoked** – *Can completely reverse the effect of the most severe amnesia. Effect is permanent but cannot prevent future memory lapses caused by injury or*

"That's the end!" Agnes gasped. "It stops in the middle of the sentence."

"The rest was on the sheet that was destroyed," Heloise reminded her. "We'll just have to find out about the other stones on our own."

Vicky used her pocket screen to contact Rory. "Hey, pard, we're at the cottage. And we've found something you need to see."

"What is it?" Rory replied dispiritedly. After so many long months of searching, he had pretty much given up on finding anything useful, let alone the magical artifact Hattie Homborg wanted.

"Just get your butt over here, now!" Vicky snapped the pocket screen shut.

"Wow, Agnes, this is so cool," Edna said admiringly.

"Agnes, how long has this box been in your family?" Heloise asked.

"I'm not sure exactly, but it's been hundreds of years." Agnes looked thunderstruck while she stood holding the box in one hand and the letter in the other.

Just then, an interdimensional portal opened, and Rory stepped into the kitchen. "What in holy hekzebah happened in here?"

The witches quickly explained Agnes's search of the cottage and finding the recipe box. As Rory read Elijah Witherspoon's letter, they stared at him expectantly.

"Well, ladies, unless I'm seriously mistaken, this must be the magical artifact Secretary Homborg is so anxious to get her hands on."

"But why would she want it? She can't use the power of the stones. She's not a descendant of Elijah Witherspoon," Heloise mused.

Vicky looked pointedly at Agnes. "Any chance you could be related to Hattie?"

Agnes thought silently for a moment. "Not that I'm aware of."

"Then why would she want it so badly if she can't use it?" Vicky wondered aloud.

"Okay, we have way too many questions and no answers. I've been trying to see Walter Higgins for weeks now and keep getting put off by Priscilla Lovejoy. This time, she's not going to stall me!" Rory said vehemently.

As the group made their way toward the school, first Rap and Suzy, then Leonard came bounding onto the path. Leonard quickly matched step with Heloise on the path.

"Sorry it took me so long," Leonard panted. "I can't run as fast in this form."

Vicky quirked an eyebrow. "Speaking of which, how did you get here so fast, pard?"

"Well, you said it was urgent." Rory shrugged. "It would have taken too long to run here as Leonard just proved. It was faster to open a portal to Lemain and then another to the cottage."

"Leonard, what are you doing here? This doesn't concern you," Heloise looked at Leonard with dismay.

"Oh, my dear, if it concerns you, it concerns me. Even if you don't realize that by now, Rap does, which is why he fetched me. I assume something important is happening."

Heloise favored Leonard with a beatific smile. "Of course, Leonard, I'm glad you showed up. We're on our way to talk with Walter Higgins. We've found the magical artifact Rory's been searching for, and you'll never guess what it is."

Leonard raised his eyebrows questioningly. "Really? What is it?"

"Agnes's recipe box!"

"I know Agnes has some rather unique recipes, but I didn't imagine any of them were magical." Leonard frowned.

"Not the recipes, the box itself is magical. At least the stones on the lid are," Heloise insisted.

By this time, they had reached the massive front doors of the school. Rory waited until they were all gathered around before he addressed the group.

"Walter should have finished dinner and be in his apartment by now, so we'll go straight there. Don't talk to anyone on the way, and if we run into Priscilla Lovejoy, let me do the talking. Edna, I'm warning you, not a single word." Rory frowned so hard at Edna, she closed her mouth with a sharp snap.

Fortunately, the only people they saw in the halls were a few students talking and laughing among themselves as they returned to their rooms. When they approached Higgins's apartment, Priscilla Lovejoy was leaving and shut the door behind her before turning to face them with a stern expression.

"If you're here to see Mr. Higgins, I'm afraid he's on a conference call and can't be disturbed," she declared haughtily as she tugged on her dull gray cardigan.

Rory drew himself up to his full stature and spoke in his most authoritarian voice. "Trust me, Ms. Lovejoy, Mr. Higgins will want to

see us immediately. We have important information for him, and he
will be extremely displeased if anything delays us."

Higgins's secretary seemed to shrink slightly under Rory's
withering glare. "Well, I'll just see if Mr. Higgins . . ." She reached
behind her for the doorknob.

Rory reached past her and pushed the door open. He then
grasped her firmly by the arms and moved her to one side of the
door. As the others filed past into the apartment, Rory bent over until
his nose and Priscilla's nose were practically touching.

"Don't worry, Ms. Lovejoy," he hissed. "We'll be careful not to
disturb him."

Rory rapidly joined the rest in the tiny, and now crowded, foyer
of Higgins's apartment.

"Well, that's one pest out of the way." Rory smiled sardonically.
"Let's go." Rory opened the door, entering Walter Higgins's living
room.

Walter Higgins's living room was furnished and decorated pretty
much as one would expect of a Victorian English drawing room. The
curtains were thick burgundy damask with a stylized floral print.
The high-backed sofa and wing-backed armchairs were upholstered
in a heavy dark blue brocade. An ornate, brightly colored Oriental
carpet covered most of the hardwood floor. The few tables in the
room were highly polished dark mahogany and seemed to be quite
sturdy despite the fragile appearance of the delicately carved legs.
The only incongruity to the décor were the pictures on the walls.
Large framed prints of paintings by Jackson Pollock, Salvador Dalí,
and M. C. Escher adorned every wall in the room.

Higgins looked up from the book he was reading as they entered
the room.

Conference call, my left foot, Rory thought.

"Well well, my good friends." Higgins grinned broadly as he closed
and placed the book on the table next to Mr. Whiskers. "I've been
wondering where you've been keeping yourselves. To what do I owe
the honor of this visit?"

Before anyone, expecially Edna, could protest that they hadn't
been allowed access to him thanks to his overly protective secretary,
Rory spoke, "We have news and many questions. We need your
help."

Higgins's smile vanished, and he held up one hand to forestall Rory's explanation. He snapped his fingers; and candles on the fireplace mantle, the bookcase, and each of the tables flared to life.

"Now we can talk privately. Leonard, would you mind locking the door? Heloise and Edna, if you step into the next room, I believe you'll find a coffee service that should accommodate all of us. Okay, Rory, please tell me what has developed."

Edna and Heloise served coffee as Rory explained discovering the magical properties of Agnes's recipe box and related the conversation he had overheard between Lucretia and Hattie.

"If you add all the facts, including the disappearances from Lemain and the attacks on the witches, I can't help but believe Hattie and Lucretia are behind all of it," Rory asserted emphatically.

"But why would they want my recipe box?" Agnes asked with a perplexed frown. "According to the letter from Elijah Witherspoon, they wouldn't be able to use the magic stones."

"My dear Agnes," began Higgins, "perhaps their idea was not to use the stones but to keep the stones from being used against them." He stood and stared out the window at the starlit sky while absentmindedly stroking Mr. Whiskers.

After several minutes in which the group held its collective breath, Higgins turned and addressed them once again.

"My friends, I believe it is time we took direct action against our adversaries. If you will continue to trust me a little longer, I need to consult some acquaintances of mine and make some arrangements. In the meantime, Agnes, you must keep that box with you at all times. But do not attempt to use any of the stones. I also think it would be advisable if you were to stay at the cottage where Vicky can provide security. Now if you will excuse me, I have much to do. Good night, all."

There was no sign of Priscilla Lovejoy as they said their good-byes and left Walter Higgins's apartment.

As they made their way down the path to Hazelnut cottage, listening to Edna grumble about the prospect of sharing a room with Agnes, Vicky quickened her steps to walk beside Rory as he led the way.

"Well, pard, what do you think? Can we trust Higgins?"

Rory sighed. "I don't think we have any choice at this point. I guess we'll just have to wait and see," Rory replied grimly.

Chapter 31

The six cloaked and hooded figures crept stealthily down the stone corridor. They kept close to the wall shrouded in shadow. Since it was almost midnight and the building was practically empty, their precautions didn't seem necessary.

Bringing up the rear of the group, Vicky moved up next to Walter Higgins. "Hissst, yo, Walter, just how did you score these robes? Honest to goddess, they look just like official Magic Council robes. And what's with the staff?"

Walter replied in equally hushed tones, "In my various forays into Lemain since my self-imposed exile, I have occasionally come across these obviously abandoned robes and simply taken them under my care, my dear. As for my staff, you never know when my lumbago might act up."

"Abandoned Magic Council robes and lumbago? Yeah right, Walter." Vicky smiled and dropped back a few paces. She knew perfectly well that Magic Council robes were assigned to specific members and once no longer in use were destroyed by law. She also had reason to be suspicious of the beautiful intricately carved mahogany staff topped with a perfectly round transparent crystal sphere.

Over the past few months, Vicky had become more curious about Walter Higgins, but despite her vast resources of information, she was unable to discover many details of Higgins's past.

The clandestine procession was led by Rory, closely followed by Heloise, Agnes, and Edna. After bumping into Agnes for the second time when she came to a complete halt in the corridor holding her family's heirloom recipe box in trembling hands, Edna snapped.

"Agnes, will you please keep moving?" Edna hissed angrily.

"I'm not sure if this is such a good idea," came Agnes's quavering reply from the shadows. "I mean, do we really need to do this right now? We only have another forty-five years until our banishment is over. We could do it then."

Edna gripped Agnes's arm tightly and forced her forward. "Look, we've already spent way too many years in banishment for something that wasn't our fault. We need to clear ourselves and get back to our lives in Lemain. Now move!"

"But if we get caught sneaking around the Magic Council building in the dead of night, they'll make our banishment permanent," Agnes croaked fearfully.

In the lead position, Rory stopped, turned, and, with a finger to his lips, uttered, "Shush." As he resumed the group's progression, he couldn't help but think he'd committed professional suicide by agreeing to be part of this plan. If this wild escapade didn't work, his name would be mud in Lemain—if he didn't wind up in the dungeons. Except for the fact that it seemed like the only way to get justice done, he couldn't imagine what had made him agree to be part of this incredibly stupid plan.

If they got caught, he was certain that his father would forgive him in time, but his mother would disown him. She had never approved of his decision to join the Lemain Department of Justice, but if he lost his position and wound up in the city dungeons, she'd never forgive his disgracing the family name. Of course, it would raise him in his grandmother Zin's eye as a rebel of the first order. Just the thought of Grandma Zin's reaction to his being thrown into the dungeons and declared an enemy of Lemain brought a smile to his face.

"Hello, Lemain to Rory, come in, Rory. Anybody there?" Vicky whispered harshly. Rory started. "If you want to daydream, there will be plenty of time for that in the dungeons after we're caught—which we will be if you don't keep this frackin' line moving!" Even in the dim corridor light, Rory could detect Vicky's steely cold glare.

"Yeah, okay, sorry," Rory replied in a sullen whisper.

Vicky moved closer to Rory. "Look, pard, you're scaring me. This is a really serious situation we're in. If you can't stay focused, I'll relieve you on point, and you can cover our rear. What do you say?"

Rory rubbed his hand roughly over his face before answering. "No, look, I'm sorry. It was just a momentary lapse. I'll be okay."

Vicky searched his face intensely for a few moments. "Okay, Van der Haven, don't let me down. I've got your back."

As Vicky made her way back to the end of their line of would-be criminals, Rory took a deep breath and assessed his condition. Rory thought he was fine, except for the fact that he was sweating like a hog in a smokehouse.

Fortunately, Rory regained his composure just in time. Just then, he heard the tramp of heavily booted feet, the kind of boots normally worn by the Magic Council guards. Abruptly, two massive figures appeared from a side hallway approximately thirty feet ahead. Rory signaled everyone to flatten themselves against the wall; then he held his breath.

"C'mon, Eldrick, it's not my fault you're having problems with Charlisse," one of the guards grumbled.

"Oh, really, Wilt?" responded the second guard. "Who said, 'Take her candy, Eldrick,' 'Send her flowers, Eldrick,' 'Get her some jewelry, Eldrick'?"

"You can't blame me for that," the first guard replied indignantly. "I thought you'd get her a pin or some earrings or a ring. I never told you to buy Charlisse a betrothal necklace!"

"How was I supposed to know it was a betrothal necklace? It's not like they put warning labels on them. You know, like 'Beware, giving this necklace to your girlfriend could cause you to become married.' Right now, Charlisse is sitting with her mother poring over a catalog planning our wedding invitations, thanks to you!"

The guards' voices and footsteps faded as they continued down the hall, embroiled in their quarrel and fortunately unaware of anyone else in the corridor.

Rory heaved a silent sigh of relief then wiped his brow with the back of his hand as he noticed a bead of sweat trickle into his left eye. Fifteen more minutes of cautious creeping down the darkened, dismal corridor brought the group to an unimpressive wooden door in the granite-block wall.

Rory stood before the door and waited for the others to join him. When they were all gathered around him, he asked once again, "Are you still determined to go through with this?"

Each of them silently looked from one to the other. Then Heloise stepped forward. "We must see this through, Rory. It's not just for ourselves. If there is evil thriving in Lemain, it's up to us to try and stop it here before it gains even more power."

Rory hitched his shoulders a bit higher and looked at Walter Higgins. "You're sure everything is ready?"

"Uh, um, what?" Walter Higgins responded absentmindedly, being preoccupied with picking bits of lint from his robes.

"What is that annoying noise?" Edna hissed in an exasperated stage whisper. She glared accusingly at Agnes. "It's you making that noise, isn't it?"

Agnes turned toward Edna with her heirloom recipe box clutched in a death grip, a look of abject terror on her face and her teeth noticeably chattering. "I-I-I'm, s-s-sorry. I c-c-can't h-h-help it. I'm s-s-so s-s-scared. I-I'm a-a-afraid I m-might h-have an a-a-accident. Of a p-p-personal n-nature, I m-mean." Even in the gloom of the corridor, Agnes's blush was evident to all.

"Oh, for heaven's sake, Agnes! Didn't you go before we left?" Edna exclaimed.

"Well, I . . . , " Agnes began to reply.

Vicky grabbed Agnes's shoulders in a firm grip. "Listen, you can do this! Remember, you are not only a witch—you're a *woman*! When the job calls for strength and destruction, you ask a man. But when intelligence, confrontation, and sheer nerve are needed, it requires a woman to get the job done. Now take a deep breath, and ready yourself for the task at hand."

Walter Higgins raised his hand and opened his mouth, about to object, but stopped when Rory frowned and motioned to him.

Agnes took a breath so deep, it must have lasted for at least half a minute. By the time she relinquished that breath, her back was straighter, her hands were no longer shaking, and there was a glimmer of fire in her eyes.

"You're right. Let's do this." Agnes marched to the door and looked at Rory. "Just like we rehearsed it, right?"

Caught off guard by Agnes's sudden change in demeanor, Rory leapt for the door to Hattie's office.

"Oh yeah, Agnes, just like we practiced." Taking a deep breath, but much shorter than Agnes's, Rory slowly opened the rear door to Hattie Homborg's office.

Upon entering Hattie Homborg's office, they immediately noticed the crystal screen wall behind Hattie's desk. One screen showed the Magic Council's private chamber, and another showed the interior of President Thurgood's office. There were even screens depicting the main entrance of Sunny Acres School, the school's dining room, and the reception room leading to Walter Higgin's office.

"Now that's what I call surveillance!" Vicky whispered.

Due to carelessness, or perhaps arrogance, there were no guards in the office. Only Hattie and her grandmother Lucretia were at the far end of the room and presently engrossed in a heated argument; so heated an argument that they didn't immediately notice the intruders.

"But you can't do it. You'll never get away with it," Hattie insisted.

"Don't be silly, child. Who would dare try to stop me?" Lucretia sneered.

"That would be me." Agnes cleared her throat as she led the group across the room toward Lucretia and Hattie. Agnes held the recipe box tightly in front of her with both thumbs pressed against the clear quartz stone in the center of the lid.

"What are you doing here?" Hattie gasped, obviously surprised by their presence. "I'll call the guards! You'll be banished permanently! And you"—she pointed at Rory—"this is treason! You'll be executed!"

"Now now, Hattie, don't be so rude to your little friends," Lucretia said quietly. "They took great risk to come here. Tsk, tsk, and after I went to such pains to ruin Thurgood's banquet and ensure they would be banished so they'd be out of the way." She had noticed the recipe box and was staring at it avariciously. "Look, they've delivered a great prize to us. The master will be pleased. Of course, if the idiots on the Council had checked the women's personal effects for magical items before they were banished as I warned them, the master would have had his prize long ago."

"This is not a prize for your master. This is the instrument of your destruction!" Agnes shouted.

"Oh, so have you discovered how to use the artifact?" Lucretia chuckled. "What a clever little witch you must think yourself. But before you become too smug, let me inform you that the properties of that which you hold were ancient and well-known to those of my order long before your puny ancestor discovered it. Give the box to me, girl. With that artifact, I can perform magical feats of which you have never dreamed. I can change the world, and my master will once again rule the universe!"

Agnes hesitated for only a moment, then taking a firmer grasp on the box, pointed the clear quartz stone toward Lucretia and Hattie and began to speak.

"Fakers take care, deceivers beware, from this you cannot be aloof, Revealing Stone, reveal the truth!"

As they watched dumbfounded, Lucretia's image changed dramatically. Before, she had appeared to be a tall handsome woman of indiscriminate age with a regal bearing. Before their eyes, she transformed into a shriveled, ancient hag surrounded by an aura as black as a night of thunderclouds. As the group, and Hattie, shrank back from the horror Lucretia DuMaurier had become, Walter Higgins whispered into his glowing opal lapel pin.

Within seconds, a dozen Council guards burst into the office with wands pointed and surrounded Lucretia. They were immediately followed by President Thurgood, Chief Magistrate Wilfred Blankenship, and the entire Legislative Magical Council of Lemain. The guards lost no time in immobilizing Lucretia with a containment spell.

"What do you think you are doing bursting in here?" screeched Lucretia while Hattie crumpled, weeping, into the large leather chair behind her desk.

"Lucretia DuMaurier, you are hereby placed under arrest for crimes against the state and sovereign government of Lemain," Chief Magistrate Blankenship declared. He gave Walter Higgins a surreptitious wink and said softly, "That eye spy you mounted on your staff worked great. We caught everything."

Lucretia swept them with the wild eyes of one who is completely insane. "You'll rue this day, all of you! I still have power and influence in Lemain! My order will continue with our plan, and the Odious Overlord will rescue his most devoted follower when he has regained his power!" With these final remarks, the guards forcibly removed Lucretia from Hattie's office.

With Lucretia no longer present, they turned their attention to Hattie, who was now staring vacantly into space and mumbling to herself.

"Mad, mad, they're all mad. It must be a family curse. Father is an imbecile, Mother is a nitwit, and Grandmother is stark raving bonkers."

President Thurgood turned to Blankenship in exasperation, "What do we do with her?"

Blankenship rubbed his jaw thoughtfully for a moment before replying, "Well, Oswald, I believe you're going to need a new treasurer. At least until Ms. Homborg has had some R & R at Brunhilde's Bed and Board for the Baffled and Befuddled."

President Thurgood clearly wasn't happy with Blankenship's answer, but he didn't voice any complaints just then. Instead, he gestured to two guards standing just inside the door. "You two, take Ms. Homborg to this bed and board place that the chief magistrate mentioned. And be sure to inform them that Ms. Homborg is not to be released until I notify them. When you've finished that chore, find that little weasel of a secretary of hers, Willis, I believe. We'll want to question him about his part in all this skulduggery."

"Oswald, do you really think it necessary to wake poor Willis and his entire family at this time of night?" Blankenship remonstrated. He immediately switched to a more conciliatory tone when he noticed the president's complexion changing to a dark magenta. "Question the man, by all means, but I think you'll find he was only an innocent flunky of Ms. Homborg's and completely unaware of her darker dealings. Probably the best thing to do with the unfortunate man would be to send him back to the General Aide Pool."

Thurgood scowled and turned toward Agnes, Edna, and Heloise. "Okay, Chief Magistrate, do you have any suggestions about how to handle these three witches?"

"Come, come, Oswald, you were right beside me when Ms. DuMaurier claimed responsibility for the peccadillo at your inaugural banquet. At the very least, I should think their banishment would be revoked and a full pardon issued."

"That's all well and good, but their banishment was imposed by an executive decree, and it must be lifted by an executive decree. For that, I'll need a full Council meeting. And until the banishment is revoked, they are here illegally!"

"Then for goddess's sake, call your meeting! In the meantime, they will be in my custody. We'll await your decree at Maude's Tavern on the Green. I'm parched."

Blankenship turned and addressed the group with a twinkle in his eye. "All you dastardly criminals are now in my custody. Follow me."

As they left Hattie Homborg's former office, President Thurgood could clearly hear Walter Higgins. "Maude's on the Green, eh, Binky? Sounds like old times."

Chapter 32

Later in the tavern, over drinks and snacks, Edna, Agnes, and Heloise discussed their possible future. Edna was the most excited of the three witches.

"This is great! We're going to be exonerated. We'll be free of the banishment! I know, we'll start up the catering business again, but we'll make our headquarters on that nice little property just southwest of Central City. After we get established, we can start a chain of packaged meals that we can sell to area grocers. We'll be the hottest thing in Lemain since flying skates!"

Heloise and Agnes exchanged looks. With an air of resignation, Heloise spoke, "Edna dear, I'm afraid that will be quite impossible. I'm not returning to Lemain. I'll be staying in Pedestria."

Agnes chimed in, "Uh, I'm going to stay in Pedestria too. Sorry, Edna."

"What are you talking about? We made this plan of running our own catering business way back in Aunt Mildred's Home for Wayward and Orphaned Witches. We almost had it made before the inauguaral banquet. What's changed?"

"Well, Edna, as you may have noticed, I'm rather taken with Leonard. And since he can't possibly return to Lemain while he's suffering with his current affliction, I feel I should remain in Pedestria with him."

Visibly fuming, Edna turned to Agnes. "Okay, and what's your excuse?"

"Oh, Edna, please don't be this way," Agnes pleaded. "You know I love you, and I loved our catering business, but that was before I met Valerie. I know Valerie not only has a lot of magic, but I'm sure she has abilities that haven't been seen anywhere for hundreds of years. I've just got to stay and help her develop her magic. I'd also like to see if anything develops with Ed Bigelow." She blushed shyly. "I hope you understand."

"What I understand is that you two are deserting me! We've been together since we were girls. I thought we would be together forever. Now you're splitting us up. No, I guess I don't understand after all." Edna folded her arms over her chest and assumed a facial expression that would have given second thoughts to the Odious Overlord himself.

Just then, Rory and Vicky arrived. They were a bit taken aback by the expressions of Agnes, Edna, and Heloise. Agnes looked sad and worried and sat wringing her hands while casting timid glances toward Edna. Heloise, on the other hand, appeared pensive and was staring intently at her glass of mead. Edna's expression was easy for Rory to read. Judging from her body language and furrowed brow, she had just been told something she really didn't want to hear, and she was trying to figure out how to turn things around so that the ending would be to her liking.

Vicky looked a question at Rory, who returned a shrug of his shoulders.

"Hey, kids, we've got good news," Vicky announced as she slipped gracefully into a vacant seat. She handed an official-looking scroll to Chief Magistrate Blankenship. "Somebody hand me a glass, and pass the pitcher."

Rory took a seat opposite Edna and took her hands in his while Binky perused the document.

"Excellent!" Binky exclaimed. "I must say, this is one of the few times in my fifty-seven years on the Council that the fatheads have actually arrived at the correct conclusion and in record time too. Ladies, your banishment has been lifted, and you have been awarded retroactive monetary damages that amount to"—here, he adjusted his reading glasses and frowned—"thirty tnups per person per year."

Everyone sat in stunned silence for a few moments. Finally, Edna spoke, "Uh, sir, are you sure you read that amount correctly? I mean, the lowliest servant in Lemain makes at least three hundred tnups per year. Surely there must be some mistake."

Chief Magistrate Blankenship slowly lowered the scroll and removed his reading glasses. "I'm sorry, my dear, but I'm afraid there's no mistake. And unfortunately, I don't have enough influence to change it."

Edna rested her head in her hands, mentally calculating the cost of food, clothing, and shelter in Lemain, wondering what the chances were of winning the Pedestria Multistate Lottery and just what the exchange rate was between Lemain and Pedestria.

Heloise broached a question. "Excuse me, Walter, Chief Magistrate, would you answer a question for me?"

"Of course, my dear, but you must call me Binky," Blankenship responded jovially. "Everyone calls me Binky. Don't they, Wally?" Then he elbowed Higgins in the ribs, causing him to choke on the mouthful of beer he had just taken.

"Oh . . . erm . . . unhn . . . of course, Binky," Higgins sputtered, trying to catch his breath.

Heloise cleared her throat nervously and began again. "Okay, well then, Walter, Binky, before the guards took her away, Lucretia DuMaurier mentioned the Odious Overlord. Do you have any idea to whom she was referring? Is this someone we should be concerned about?"

Chief Magistrate Wilfred Blankenship and Walter Higgins were silent for several minutes; both their brows furrowed in concentration. Heloise, Edna, Agnes, Rory, and Vicky studied the two men intently as they deliberated.

Higgins responded, "Well, there was a situation once a long time ago, but it couldn't possibly have any bearing on Lucretia DuMaurier's rantings. After all, he was executed with all the proper authorizations. A circle comprised of thirteen sorcerers and thirteen sorceresses simultaneously cast the annihilation spell on him. A tremendous cloud of smoke obliterated the scene, and when the smoke cleared, there was nothing left of him but his robes and an iridescent ring carved with indecipherable symbols. So it couldn't possibly have been the same person as the last Odious Overlord to be seen in Lemain who was executed over eighty years ago. There's no way there could be another Odious Overlord, is there Binky?"

The two elder wizards exchanged worried looks and rapidly looked for something wooden to rap upon.

Suddenly suspicious, Heloise asked, "What happened to the robes and ring?"

"They've been kept under lock, key, and spell in the fifth-level vault under the Council of Magic Chambers," answered Binky.

"Uh-huh," Heloise replied, "and when was the last time anyone checked to see if they were still there?"

Index